About the author

Elin Hilderbrand has lived on Nantucket for twenty years. She runs every morning, delivers her children to their sporting events, and frequents the front row at the Chicken Box. You can visit Elin's website at www.elinhilderbrand.net, follow her on Twitter @elinhilderbrand or find out more on her Facebook page www.facebook.com/ElinHilderbrand.

The Matchmaker

Elin Hilderbrand

HODDER

First published in the USA in 2014 by Reagan Arthur Books
An imprint of Little, Brown and Company
A division of Hachette Book Group, Inc.
First published in Great Britain in 2014 by Hodder & Stoughton
An Hachette UK company

First published in paperback in 2015

1

A CIP catalogue record for this title is available from the British Library

Paperback ISBN 978 1 444 72405 9
Ebook ISBN 978 1 444 72406 6

Printed and bound by Clays Ltd, St Ives plc

Hodder & Stoughton policy is to use papers that are natural, renewable
and recyclable products and made from wood grown in sustainable forests.
The logging and manufacturing processes are expected to conform to
the environmental regulations of the country of origin.

Hodder & Stoughton Ltd
Carmelite House
50 Victoria Embankment
London EC4Y 0DZ

www.hodder.co.uk

To my North, my South, my East, and my West:
Rebecca Bartlett
Deborah Briggs
Wendy Hudson
Wendy Rouillard

And ever the needle on the compass:
Elizabeth Almodobar

PART 1

DABNEY

Dabney couldn't believe it. She blinked twice, thinking she no longer had the eyes of a girl or even a young woman, thinking she hadn't been feeling well lately, and was this a *trick of her mind?* Twenty-seven years later? Subject line: *Hello.*

Dabney Kimball Beech, who had served as the director of the Nantucket Island Chamber of Commerce for twenty-two years, was in her second-floor office, overlooking historic, cobblestoned Main Street. It was late April, the Friday morning of Daffodil Weekend, Dabney's second-most-important weekend of the year, and the forecast was a springtime fantasy. It was sixty degrees and sunny today and would be sixty-four and sunny on Saturday and Sunday.

Dabney had just checked the weather for the fifth time that day, the five thousandth time that week (the year before, Daffodil Weekend had been ruined by a late-season snowstorm), when the e-mail from Clendenin Hughes appeared in her in-box.

Subject line: *Hello.*

"Oh my God," Dabney said.

Dabney never swore, and rarely took the Lord's name in vain

(thanks to cayenne pepper administered to her ten-year-old tongue by her devoutly Catholic grandmother for saying the word *jeez*). That she did so now was enough to get the attention of Nina Mobley, Dabney's assistant for eighteen of the past twenty-two years.

"What?" Nina said. "What's wrong?"

"Nothing," Dabney said quickly. Nina Mobley was Dabney's closest friend, but Dabney could never tell her that an e-mail from Clendenin Hughes had just popped onto her screen.

Dabney gnawed on one of her pearls, as was her habit when she was deeply concentrating, and now she nearly bit clear through it. She was aware that millions of people across the world were receiving e-mails at that moment, a good percentage of them probably upsetting, a smaller but still substantial percentage probably shocking. But she wondered if anyone anywhere on the planet was receiving an e-mail as upsetting and shocking as this one.

She stared at the screen, blinked, clenched the pearl between her teeth. It was grainy, which was how one judged authenticity. *Hello. Hello?* Not a word for twenty-seven years—and then this. An e-mail at work. *Hello.* When Clen had left for Thailand, e-mail hadn't existed. How had he gotten her address? Dabney laughed. He was a Pulitzer Prize–winning journalist; finding her e-mail address wouldn't have presented much of a challenge.

Hello.

Dabney's finger tapped the mouse lightly, a tease. Would she open the e-mail? What would it say? What could it *possibly* say after twenty-seven years of silence?

Hello.

Dabney could not open the e-mail. She, who never smoked and rarely drank hard liquor, wanted a cigarette and a shot of bourbon. The only thing that would have stunned her more than this was an e-mail from her mother.

Her mother was dead.

Hello.

Dabney felt like she was being electrocuted right down to her bone marrow.

Nina was at her own computer, sucking on her gold cross, a bad habit that had traveled by osmosis across the four feet between their desks.

Nina said, "Dabney, really, what is it?"

Dabney let her pearls fall from her mouth; they thumped against her chest like they were made of lead. She had not been feeling right for weeks, maybe as long as a month, and now her body was really going haywire. The e-mail from Clendenin Hughes.

Dabney forced a smile at Nina. "The weather this weekend is going to be perfect!" she said. "We are going to have *guaranteed sun*."

"After last year," Nina said, "we deserve it."

Dabney said, "I'm going to run to the pharmacy for a frappe. Do you want anything?"

Nina furrowed her brow. "Frappe?" She glanced at the wall calendar, theirs each year courtesy of Nantucket Auto Body. "Is it that time of the month again already?"

Dabney wished she weren't so predictable, but of course predictability was her trademark. She got a frappe only once a month, the day before her period was due, which was still ten days off.

"I just feel like it today for some reason," Dabney said. "Do you want anything?"

"No, thank you," Nina said. She gave Dabney an extra beat of her attention. "You okay?"

Dabney swallowed. "I'm fine," she said.

Outside, the atmosphere was festive. After four cold, punishing months, spring had arrived on Nantucket. Main Street was teeming with people wearing yellow. Dabney spied the Levinsons (Couple #28), whom she had introduced ten years earlier. Larry had been a widower with twins at Yale and Stanford, Marguerite a never-married headmistress at a prestigious girls' boarding school. Larry wore a yellow cashmere sweater and a pair of kelly-green corduroy pants, and Marguerite was in a yellow poplin blazer; she held the leash of their golden retriever, Uncle Frank. Dabney adored all dogs, and especially Uncle Frank, and Larry and Marguerite were one of "her couples," married only because she had introduced them. Dabney knew she should stop and talk; she should rub Uncle Frank under the muzzle until he sang for her. But she couldn't fake it right now. She crossed the street to Nantucket Pharmacy, but did not go inside. She headed down Main Street, through the A&P parking lot, to the Straight Wharf. At the end of the Straight Wharf, she gazed at the harbor. There was Jack Copper, working on his charter fishing boat; in another few weeks, summer would arrive in all its crazy glory. Jack waved, and Dabney, of course, waved back. She knew everyone on this island, but there was no one in the world she could tell about this e-mail. It was Dabney's to grapple with alone.

Hello.

Dabney could see the Steamship, low in the water, rounding Brant Point. In the next hour, the Chamber office would be inundated with visitors, and Dabney had left Nina all alone. Furthermore, she had left the office without "signing out" on the "log," which was the one thing Vaughan Oglethorpe, president of the board of directors of the Chamber, absolutely required. Dabney needed to turn around right this second and go back to the office and do the job that she had been doing perfectly for the past two decades.

Subject line: *Hello.*

*   *   *

Three hours later, she opened it. She hadn't planned on opening it at all, but the urge to do so mounted until it was physically painful. Dabney's back and lower abdomen ached; knowledge of this e-mail was tearing her up inside.

Dear Dabney,

I wanted to let you know that I am on my way back to Nantucket for an indefinite period of time. I suffered a pretty serious loss about six months ago, and I've been slow recovering from it. Furthermore, it's monsoon season, and my enthusiasm for writing about this part of the world has dwindled. I've given the Times my notice. I never did get assigned to the Singapore desk. I was close several years ago, but—as ever—I pissed off the wrong person simply by speaking my mind. Singapore will remain a dream deferred. (Big sigh.) I've decided that the best thing is for me to come home.

I have respected your long-ago mandate to "never contact [you] again." More than a quarter century has passed, Cupe. I hope that "never" has an expiration date and that you will forgive me this e-mail. I didn't want to show up on the island without giving you advance warning, and I didn't want you to hear the news from anyone else. I will be caretaking the house of Trevor and Anna Jones, 436 Polpis Road, living in their guest cottage.

I am afraid of both saying too much and not saying enough. First and foremost, I want you to know how sorry I am for the way things ended. They didn't have to be that way, but I categorized it a long time ago as an IMPOSSIBLE SITUATION: I could not stay, and you could not go. Not a day has gone

7

by—honestly, Cupe, not an hour—when I have not thought of you. When I left, I took a part of you with me, and I have treasured that part these many years.

I am not the same person you knew—not physically, not mentally, not emotionally. But, of course, I am ever the same.

I would very much like to see you, although I realize this is almost too much to hope for.

I am writing this from my layover at LAX. If all goes well, I should be back on Nantucket tomorrow morning.

436 Polpis Road, cottage in the back.
Ever yours, Clen

Dabney read the e-mail again, to make sure her addled brain had understood.

Tomorrow morning.

Couple #1: Phil and Ginger (née O'Brien) Bruschelli, married twenty-nine years

Ginger: It would have been presumptuous of me to call myself Dabney's best friend, because even in 1981, freshman year, Dabney was the most popular girl in the school. When I say "popular," you might be thinking she was blond, or a cheerleader, or that she lived in a big house on Centre Street. No, no, no—she had straight thick brown hair cut into a bob, and she always, always wore a headband. She had big brown eyes, a few freckles, and a smile like the sun coming out. She was about five-three and she had a cute little body, but she never showed it off. She wore either cable-knit sweaters and kilts or a beat-up pair of Levi's and an oversize men's oxford shirt. She had the shirt in four colors: white, blue, pink, and peach.

She always wore penny loafers, and she always wore a strand of pearls and pearl earrings. That was Dabney.

Dabney Kimball was the most popular girl in the school because she was genuinely kind to everyone. She was kind to Jeffrey Jackson, who had a port-wine stain on his face; she was kind to Henry Granger, who started wearing wingtips and carrying a briefcase in second grade. She included everyone in planning events like Homecoming floats and December Delight. She had grown up an only child raised by her father, Lieutenant Kimball, who was a police officer. Her mother was . . . well, no one knew exactly what had happened to her mother. A couple of different stories had circulated, as gossip does, but all we knew for sure was that Dabney no longer had a mother, which made us love her even more.

Dabney was also smarter than everyone else at Nantucket High School, except for Clendenin Hughes, who was what our English teacher, Mr. Kane, called a "hundred-year genius." Dabney was probably a ninety-nine-year genius.

Freshman year, Dabney and I were fledglings on the yearbook committee. The committee was mostly upperclassmen—it was, actually, all upperclassmen, except for the two of us. Dabney felt that, despite our lowly status, freshmen should be represented just like the other three classes, and that no one was going to look out for us if we didn't look out for ourselves. So that winter, Dabney and I hung out a lot. We would go to yearbook meetings every Tuesday and Thursday after school, and when we were finished, we would watch the boys' varsity basketball team.

I had a huge, horrible crush on Phil Bruschelli. Phil was a sophomore, and in the varsity games he mostly sat on the bench. If the team was ahead by more than twenty points, Phil would go in for a few minutes. One such time when this happened, I grabbed Dabney's arm in excitement.

I'll never forget the look on her face. It was what I'll now call amused recognition. She said, "You like him. You like Phil."

"No, I don't," I said. Because even though Dabney and I were practically best friends, my crush on Phil wasn't a secret I was willing to share.

"Yes," she said. "You do. I can see it. You're all . . . pink."

"Of course I'm pink," I said. "It's a hundred degrees in here and I'm Irish."

"Not your face, silly," Dabney said. "Your, I don't know, your aura is rosy."

"My aura?" I said. "Rosy?"

After the game, Dabney insisted that I wait with her in the hallway outside the boys' locker room. Her father was coming to pick her up, she said.

"Why aren't you walking?" I asked. Dabney lived right across the street from the school.

"Just wait with me," Dabney said. And then she pushed my hair back off my shoulders and flipped up the collar of my IZOD shirt. She was so close to me I could have counted her freckles.

I said, "How come you don't have a boyfriend? You're so pretty and everyone likes you."

She said, "I do have a boyfriend. He just doesn't know it yet."

I wanted to ask her whom she meant, but at that instant Phil Bruschelli walked out of the locker room, all six foot three of him. His dark hair was still damp from the shower and he was wearing a dark-brown shearling jacket. I nearly fainted away, he was so cute.

Dabney stepped into his path. "Hey there, Phil."

Phil stopped. "Hey, Dabney."

Dabney said, "Nice that you got a little playing time today. Varsity game, you must be psyched."

He shrugged. "Yeah, whatever. Coach says I have to pay my dues. Wait until next year."

Dabney pulled me close to her side. "You know Ginger, right, Phil? Ginger O'Brien? We're doing yearbook together."

Phil smiled at me. My vision blurred. I teetered. *Smile!* I thought. *Smile back!* But it felt like I was going to cry instead.

Phil said, "You serve at church, right? You're an altar girl?"

I felt flames of embarrassment licking my cheeks. Rosy indeed. I nodded, and then made a chirping noise like a sparrow. Who wanted to be recognized as an altar girl? And yet, I was an altar girl, and I had been since I was ten years old. It wasn't exactly a secret.

Phil said, "My mother makes me go to Mass once a month, and I see you there whenever I go."

"I'm not surprised you noticed Ginger," Dabney said. "She's gorgeous." With that, Dabney hooked her arm around my neck and kissed my scorching-hot cheek. "See ya, gotta go! My dad is here!"

She bounded out the door to the back parking lot, but her father wasn't waiting. Lieutenant Kimball drove a squad car, which I would have noticed. There were no cars waiting. Dabney was walking home, abandoning me at a time when I needed her to prop me up. I decided I would never forgive her.

But then Phil asked if I liked basketball and I said yes, and he asked if I wanted to come watch him play for the JV team the following afternoon, and I said sure. He said he would have a lot more playing time in that game, and I said, *Okay, great*. And he said, *Well, I'll see you tomorrow, don't forget me!* And I felt like a flock of birds had startled in my chest.

Phil and I have been married for twenty-nine years and we have four beautiful sons, the youngest of whom plays power forward for Villanova University.

Rosy indeed.

Dabney left the Chamber office at four-thirty as usual. All preparations for Daffodil Weekend were in place; Dabney could have organized it in her sleep—thank goodness—because her afternoon had been consumed with rereading Clen's e-mail and then obsessing about it.

I suffered a pretty serious loss about six months ago, and I've been slow recovering from it.

What kind of loss? Dabney wondered. Had he lost a good friend, a lover? Dabney had lost her father from a heart attack a decade earlier, and her beloved chocolate Lab, Henry, had died at the age of seventeen, just before Christmas. But neither of these losses compared with the loss of Clendenin.

Not a day has gone by—honestly, Cupe, not an hour—when I have not thought of you.

She would be lying if she said that she had not thought of him, too. The love of her life, her perfect match, her Meant to Be. The father of her child. How it had pained her to break off contact. But years and years later, Dabney was stunned by the wisdom and maturity of her decision.

The only way I am going to survive is with a clean break. Please respect my wishes and let me, and this child, go. Please, Clendenin Tabor Hughes, do me the favor of never contacting me again.

He had been so, so angry. He had called Dabney in the middle of the night, and over the staticky, time-delayed phone line, they had screamed at each other for the first time in their relationship, often stepping on each other's words until Clen ended the call by saying, *We all make choices,* and slamming down the phone. But he had let her do things her way. He had not contacted her.

IMPOSSIBLE SITUATION: I could not stay, and you could not go.

That was about the size of it.

Despite this, Dabney had thought Clendenin might appear at the hospital when she gave birth. She had thought he might materialize in the back of the church on the afternoon she married Box and, just like in the movies, interrupt the priest at the critical moment. She had thought he might attend Agnes's first piano recital, or show up at Dabney's fortieth birthday party, at the Whaling Museum. She had thought he might come back to the island when his mother, Helen, died—but Helen Hughes had been cremated and there was no service.

Dabney had always thought he might come back.

If all goes well, I should be back on Nantucket tomorrow morning.

Dabney walked home from work, wishing it were a weekday so that she would have the house to herself, time and space to think. Dabney's husband, John Boxmiller Beech—Box, to his familiars—held an endowed chair in economics at Harvard and spent four nights a week in Cambridge, teaching. Box was fourteen years older than Dabney, sixty-two now, his hair gone completely white. He was a brilliant scholar, he was witty at dinner parties, he had nurtured Dabney's intellect and saved her in a million ways. Not least of all, he had saved her from the memories of Clendenin Hughes decades earlier. Box had adopted Agnes when Agnes was only three years old. He had been awkward with her at first—he had never wanted children of his own—but as Agnes grew, Box enjoyed teaching her how to play chess and quizzing her about European capital cities. He groomed her to go to Harvard and was disappointed when she chose Dartmouth instead, but he was the one who had driven back and forth to Hanover—sometimes through ferocious snow-storms—because Dabney wouldn't leave the island unless her life depended on it.

Tomorrow morning. It was Friday, which meant that Box was at their house on Charter Street. He would be Dabney's escort all through the festivities of Daffodil Weekend, although he was slower now after his knee replacement, and he had a hard time with the name of anyone he hadn't known for twenty years. Box would be working, and therefore distracted, but if Dabney knocked on the door of his study, he would set down his pen and turn down the Mozart and he would listen as Dabney spoke the words he had surely been dreading for more than twenty years.

I've had an e-mail from Clendenin Hughes. He's coming back to Nantucket for an indefinite period of time. He's arriving tomorrow morning.

What would Box say? Dabney couldn't imagine. She had been honest with Box since the day she'd met him, but she decided, while walking home, that she wouldn't tell him about Clen. She re-vised history so that she had deleted the e-mail without reading it, and then she deleted it from her deleted file, which meant it was gone, so gone that it was as if it had never existed in the first place.

Couple #8: Albert Maku and Corrine Dubois, married twenty-two years

Albert: Dabney Kimball was the first person I met at Harvard. She was sitting on the side steps of Grays Hall, crying her eyes out. All the other freshmen were carrying their trunks and boxes across Harvard Yard with their good-looking, well-dressed parents and their rambunctious brothers and sisters in tow. I watched people hug and scream—happy reunion!—they had gone to Camp Wyonegonic together, they had been bitter lacrosse rivals, one at Gilman, one at Calvert Hall, they had sailed together from Newport to Bermuda, they had skied in Gstaad—it just got more and more absurd, and I could not listen a second longer without feeling woefully displaced. I was from Plettenberg Bay, South Africa—my father a truck driver, my mother the head of housekeeping at a tourist hotel, my tuition at Harvard paid by a scholarship through the United Church of Christ. I did not belong in Grays Hall, at Harvard, in Cambridge, in America. I slipped out the side door with the intention of escape—back to the T-station, back to Logan Airport, back to Cape Town.

But then I saw Dabney crying, and I thought, *Now, look, Albert, there is someone else at Harvard who seems as miserable as you.* I sat down on the hot step and offered her a handkerchief. My mother had sent me half a world away, to the planet's most prestigious university, armed with little more than a dozen white pressed handkerchiefs.

The first white handkerchief won me my first friend. Dabney accepted it, and unceremoniously blew her nose. She did not seem surprised by my presence, despite the fact that I was six foot six and weighed 165 pounds and had skin the same purple-black color as the plums sold by the fruit vendor in Harvard Square.

When she finished blowing her nose, she folded the handkerchief into a neat, damp square and laid it on her dungaree-covered knee.

"I'll launder this before I give it back," she said. "I'm Dabney Kimball."

"Albert," I said. "Albert Maku, from Plettenberg Bay, South Africa." And then, as a flourish, I said, *"Ngiyajabula ukukwazi,"* which means, "It's nice to meet you," in Zulu.

She burst into tears again. I thought maybe the Zulu had frightened her and I made a mental note not to use this tactic ever again when introducing myself to someone in America.

"What's the matter?" I said. "Are you lonely? Are you scared?"

She looked at me and nodded.

I said, "Yes, me too."

Later, we walked to Mr. Bartley's Burger Cottage. This was a famous burger place mentioned in the freshman handbook. We ordered burgers with onions and chili sauce and cheese and pickles and fried eggs, and we ordered fries with gravy, and as I ate I thought happily that this was American food, and I loved it.

Dabney Kimball had been born and raised on Nantucket Island, which was sixty miles away on land and another thirty over the sea. She told me she was the fifth generation of her family to be born on the island, and I understood that for an American, this was an accomplishment. Her great-great-great-grandfather had traveled to Nantucket when he was only newly graduated from Harvard himself.

Dabney didn't like to leave the island, because of something that had happened when she was a child, she said.

"Oh, really?" I said. "What?"

I thought maybe she had been mugged or had been in a highway accident, but she pressed her lips together and I realized I had probably overstepped the bounds of our brand-new friendship by asking.

"There is no university on Nantucket," she said. "Otherwise, I would have matriculated there." She picked at the last remaining fries, swimming in gravy. "It's a phobia. I leave the island and I panic. I only feel safe when I'm on that island. It's my home."

I told her my home was Plettenberg Bay, and that I had not, until two days earlier, ever been out of South Africa. But Plettenberg

Bay wasn't an island, and I had traveled around the country quite a bit with the choir of my church youth group—to Cape Town, Knysna, Stellenbosch, and Franschhoek, to Jo-burg and Pretoria, the capital, and to the fine beaches of Durban. Compared to Dabney, I felt worldly.

"Also," she said, "I'm in love with a boy named Clendenin Hughes. He goes to Yale, and I'm afraid I'm going to lose him."

Ah, she had me there. At that time, I knew nothing about love.

Dabney and I remained friends for all four years at Harvard. She went home to Nantucket each weekend and over the span of each school vacation, and every time she left for home, she invited me to come with her. I had an idea of Nantucket as a white place, an expensive place, an elitist place, and despite the fact that someone as fine as Dabney lived there, I felt that a painfully lean, dirt-poor African boy with purple-black skin on a church scholarship would not be welcomed, and I always said no.

But then finally, during spring break of senior year, when I had been accepted at medical school at Columbia Physicians and Surgeons, and I had a pocket full of money from working as a bellman at the Charles Hotel, and my self-confidence was plumped not only by my future as a doctor and ample pocket cash but by the realization that I had become sort of American (I enjoyed movies with the actor Mickey Rourke, I drank the occasional beer at the Rathskeller), I said that yes, I would go.

Dabney drove, at that time, a 1972 Chevy Nova, which I folded myself into for the ride to Hyannis, where we would catch the ferry to Nantucket.

Dabney said, "And guess what? My friend Corinne Dubois is coming, too."

I didn't want Dabney to sense my disappointment. I craved Dabney's attention; I didn't like the idea of being rendered mute while Dabney gabbed with her girlfriend, this Corinne Dubois.

"She's great, wonderful, beautiful, smart, you'll love her," Dabney said. "She's about to graduate from MIT with a degree in astrophysics."

We picked up Corinne Dubois outside the Museum of Science on Edward Land Boulevard. She had curly, copper-colored hair. She wore long silver earrings and a long peasant skirt and dark round sunglasses. I noted these things in an instant and I was not particularly overcome except by thinking that Corinne Dubois did not look like a person about to graduate from MIT with a degree in astrophysics. But when she climbed into the car, I smelled her perfume, and something stirred in me. She slammed the door and pushed her sunglasses on top of her head and I introduced myself.

"Albert Maku," I said, offering my hand.

She shook it mightily. "Corinne Dubois," she said. "Lovely to meet you, Albert."

Her eyes were green, and they were smiling at me. And although I had not known what love was, I felt it then.

Dabney noticed. She looked at me and said, "Albert, you're rosy."

And I thought, *How does a man with the blue-black skin of a plum look rosy?*

But I knew she was right.

Dabney Kimball Beech was descended from a long line of strong women, with one exception.

Dabney had been named after her great-great-great-grandmother, Dabney Margaret Wright, married to Warren Wright, who had served as captain of the whaling ship *Lexington* and had died during his second trip at sea. Dabney had three sons, the youngest of whom, David Warren Wright, married Alice Booker. Alice was a Quaker; her parents had been abolitionists in Pennsylvania and had helped fugitive slaves. Alice gave birth to two girls, and the elder girl, Winford Dabney Wright, married Nantucket's only attorney, Richard Kimball. Winford was a suffragette. Winford gave birth to one son, Richard Kimball, Jr., called Skip, who dropped out of Harvard and scandalously married an Irish chambermaid named Agnes Bernadette Shea. Agnes Bernadette Shea was Dabney's beloved grandmother. Agnes gave birth to David Wright Kimball, Dabney's father, who fought in the Americans' first efforts in Vietnam, then came home and served as one of Nantucket's four policemen. He married a Nantucket summer girl named Patricia Beale Benson.

Patty Benson, Dabney's mother, represented the weak link in the genealogy. She left Nantucket when Dabney was eight years old and never returned.

When Dabney discovered she was pregnant (and really, if one wanted to talk about scandal, there was no greater scandal in the year 1988 than Dabney Kimball's becoming pregnant out of wedlock), she had wished for a son. To have a daughter after growing up without a mother seemed a challenge beyond Dabney's capabilities. But when a baby girl was set in Dabney's arms, the love specific to all new mothers overtook her. She named the baby Agnes Bernadette after her grammie and decided that the only way to ameliorate the pain of her mother's abandonment was to do right herself. She would be a mother first, a mother forever.

As Dabney approached her house on Charter Street, she saw Agnes's Prius in the driveway.

Agnes! Dabney's spirits soared. Agnes had come home for Daffodil Weekend! Agnes had surprised her, which meant, Dabney assumed, that all was forgiven.

Dabney didn't want to think about the misunderstanding at Christmas. It had been the worst misunderstanding since, well… since the only other real conflict Dabney and her daughter had ever had, back when Agnes was sixteen and Dabney had explained who her real father was. Compared to that hurricane, the blowup at Christmas had been minor.

Dabney stepped in through the mudroom door.

"Agnes?" she cried out.

Agnes was in the kitchen, eating a sandwich at the counter. She looked skinny to Dabney. Her jeans were hanging off her hips. And—even more shocking—she had cut her hair!

"Eeeek!" Dabney said. She reached out and touched Agnes's shorn head. All that beautiful, straight dark hair, the hair that had reached down to Agnes's nearly missing behind, had been chopped off. She looked like a boy.

"I know, right?" Agnes said. "It's so different, I feel like someone else. Yesterday morning in the mirror, I didn't even recognize myself."

Dabney pressed her lips closed against the fifty annoying mom questions that threatened to escape: *When did you cut it? Why did you cut it? Oh, honey, why?*

Agnes took a bite of chicken salad sandwich and Dabney thought, *Yes, eat, eat!* She thought this was her punishment for never going to visit her daughter in New York, despite at least two hundred invitations to do so. Her daughter had come home looking like a cross between Twiggy in the 1966 *Rolling Stone* shoot and a teenage boy newly released from juvie.

Agnes swallowed and said, "CJ convinced me to do it."

CJ, of course.

Dabney hugged her daughter. "How is CJ?" she asked.

"Great!" Agnes said. "He's here. He came with me."

"Did he?" Dabney sounded excited and happy, even to her own ears. "Where is he?"

"He went for a run," Agnes said.

"Oh, good!" Dabney said. To her, the "oh, good" sounded okay. It sounded like, *Oh, good for CJ, out enjoying this glorious spring weather!* What she meant was, *Oh, good, she didn't have to deal with CJ right this second.*

Dabney took a cleansing breath and renewed her vow not to be critical of CJ. Charles Jacob Pippin was forty-four years old to Agnes's twenty-six; he was only four years younger than Dabney. But, as Box had pointed out, Dabney had no room to complain about the age difference because Box was fourteen years older than Dabney and it had rarely, if ever, been an issue. CJ was divorced from a woman named Annabelle, who—he was eager to mention—now lived in Boca Raton, heedlessly spending the million dollars a year CJ paid her in alimony. CJ was a sports agent in New York; his client list included nine New York Giants and four prominent Yankees, as well as some top-ranked tennis players and golfers. CJ had met Agnes the preceding September at the annual benefit for the Morningside Heights Boys & Girls Club, where Agnes was the executive director. CJ had written a large check to the club, and then he had danced with Agnes in the Waldorf ballroom all night long. The following Monday, a box containing two dozen brand-new basketballs had arrived at the club, followed on Tuesday by a slew of new art supplies. On Wednesday, Giants running back Victor Cruz called the club to see if he could come in to sign autographs for the kids; at first, Agnes had thought it was a prank call. On Thursday, a huge bouquet of flowers arrived for Agnes, along with an invitation for her to have dinner with CJ at Nougatine on Friday.

It was a wooing straight out of the movies, and Dabney couldn't blame Agnes for succumbing. What twenty-six-year-old could resist? CJ was smart, successful, and sophisticated—he could talk about everything from Frank Lloyd Wright to the World Wrestling Federation. Since they had started dating, CJ had taken Agnes on trips to Nashville, Las Vegas, and Italy, where they drove down the Amalfi coast in a rented Ferrari.

Box, who was impressed by no one, thought CJ was the greatest thing since sliced bread. CJ golfed, he understood economic theory, he was a Republican. In Box's mind, it was a two-for-one deal: a beau for Agnes, a friend for him.

The fight at Christmas had started when Agnes asked her mother if she and CJ were a perfect match.

Dabney's heart had seized. She was "Cupe" for Cupid; she was Nantucket's matchmaker, with forty-two couples to her credit, all of them still together. Dabney could tell if a couple was a perfect match just by looking at them. She saw either a rosy glow or an olive-green haze. However, Dabney didn't like to offer her opinion on couples she didn't fix up herself. It was pointless. People were going to make their own decisions regardless of Dabney's predictions. Hot, passionate love—and even worse, lust—were the enemies of reason and good sense.

Dabney said, "Oh, honey, I have no idea."

Agnes said, "Mom, please. Please tell me."

Dabney thought about Agnes and CJ. For Christmas, CJ had given Agnes a pair of Christian Louboutin heels, a new iPad, and a gold Cartier love bracelet, which he dramatically locked onto her wrist. This final gift, especially, underscored CJ's controlling nature. He liked Agnes to watch what she ate, and he liked her to exercise at least once a day, preferably twice. He disapproved of

Agnes's girlfriends; he thought they were "a danger to the relationship" because they met for cocktails and went to clubs in the Meatpacking District on the weekends. Now, Dabney suspected, most of the friends had fallen away. When CJ and Agnes walked together, CJ pulled her along like she was a recalcitrant child.

CJ was always charming with Dabney, but charming in a way that verged on ingratiating. He liked to reference that fact that he and Dabney were practically the same age. They had both grown up in the eighties, the era of the J. Geils Band and *Ghostbusters*; they were both in high school when the Union Carbide disaster killed half a million people in India. Dabney didn't like that CJ had changed his name after his divorce; his first wife, Annabelle, and everyone else in his life at that time, had called him Charlie. Dabney was alarmed when CJ said he didn't like dogs ("too dirty,") and that he never wanted to have children. Agnes loved children; that was why she worked at the Boys & Girls Club. Now, Agnes had started saying that she didn't care if she had children or not. Dabney wasn't sure how to explain it reasonably, but she sensed something rotten, possibly even sinister, under CJ's charismatic facade.

When Dabney looked at Agnes and CJ, she saw a haze that was the gray-green of clouds before a thunderstorm. Normally, when Dabney saw a miasma that bad, the couple split right away.

Dabney saw no choice but to tell Agnes the truth. A mother first, a mother forever.

"No," she'd said. "You are not a perfect match."

Agnes had packed her suitcase and left that very afternoon, a day and a half early, ignoring their usual day-after-Christmas tradition of prime-rib sandwiches and board games. She had left without taking any of her gifts; Dabney had been forced to pack them up and mail them to New York.

Box had been confused when he emerged from his study. "Wait a minute," he said. "What happened? Why did they leave?" Agnes had left without saying goodbye to Box, and Dabney knew she had done so because she didn't want Box to have the chance to try to persuade her to stay.

Dabney had sighed. "I told Agnes something she didn't want to hear."

Box lifted his square, black-framed glasses so that they rested in his snowy-white hair. He was a gifted and esteemed man, but there were times when Dabney wished she would be spared the lecture. Box thought her matchmaking was frivolous and silly on a good day, and abominably meddlesome in the private affairs of others the rest of the time. "What?" he asked. "What did you tell her?"

"I'd like to keep that between her and me," Dabney said.

"Dabney." His eyes were a piercing blue, clear and cold, exacting.

"She asked if I thought she and CJ were a perfect match."

Box raised his chin a fraction of an inch. "Certainly you didn't offer your opinion?"

Dabney didn't answer. Her feet were together and her hands were clasped in front of her kilt. She was the errant student facing the headmaster. Box was her *husband*, she reminded herself. They were equals.

Box's visage turned a florid pink. "Certainly you *did* offer your opinion. Otherwise she wouldn't have run off."

"Run off," Dabney said. It was a bad habit of hers to repeat the phrases Box used that she found asinine. Like "run off." That was Professor Beech trying to sound not only Harvard-like but British. Heroines in Edwardian literature "ran off." Agnes had climbed into her Prius and absconded without noise or toxic emissions.

"Rude of them not to say goodbye," Box said. "I would have

expected more from CJ. You just don't stay in a man's house, and then up and leave without a word."

"You were working, darling," Dabney said. "The closed door is very intimidating, as I've told you hundreds of times. I'm sure they didn't want to disrupt you."

"They wouldn't have been *disrupting* me," Box said. "I was only reading. And there is nothing intimidating about a closed door. All they had to do was knock."

"It's my fault," Dabney said. The day after Christmas and the day after the day after Christmas were now ruined.

Box breathed audibly. He wanted to say something punishing, perhaps, but like the perfect gentleman he was, he refrained. He knew that Agnes's departure was punishment enough.

The weather for Daffodil Weekend would be perfect, but that was it; everything else about Dabney's life was disheveled and topsy-turvy. Her daughter had come home—that was good—but she had brought CJ with her, and that was bad. And Clendenin Hughes would be arriving on Nantucket the next morning. Dabney did *not* feel well—her abdomen was tender, her back was sore, she was fatigued. On top of everything else, she probably had Lyme disease!

Dabney dealt with her mixed bag of circumstances the way she had dealt with everything else in her forty-eight years: she used forbearance. She began by calling Ted Field's office and scheduling an appointment for Monday morning. Ted Field, the doctor of choice on the island, was wildly popular and always overbooked. But Dabney knew she would get an appointment because decades earlier, at her own wedding, Dabney had introduced Ted Field's receptionist, Genevieve Lefebvre, to her husband, Brian (Couple #17). They had been married twenty-one years and had five daughters.

"What's the matter?" Genevieve asked. "You sick?"

"Not quite right," Dabney said. "Maybe Lyme. I don't know. Maybe old age."

"Oh, hush. You look the same as you did when you were seventeen," Genevieve said. "The doc can see you at nine."

That accomplished, Dabney felt marginally better. Maybe Lyme. Maybe just stress.

She was able to grit her teeth and make it through the rest of the day. She greeted CJ warmly, then sent him and Agnes out to pick up the blanket of daffodils and the daffodil wreath that would festoon the Impala in the Antique Car Parade the next day. She called Nina and apologized for being distracted in the office and for needlessly snapping at her.

(When Dabney had returned to the Chamber of Commerce without a strawberry frappe from the pharmacy, Nina had squinted at her in confusion. "So where did you go, then?"

And Dabney said, "You need glasses, Nina."

Nina had recoiled as though Dabney had smacked her across the nose with a newspaper, and Dabney felt like a terrible, cranky friend.)

Now, Dabney said, "I really don't feel well. I'm coming down with something, I think."

"Get rest tonight, sister," Nina said. "Tomorrow is showtime."

Dabney put the finishing touches on the tailgate picnic for the next day, although she had prepared most of it in advance. Dabney made the same picnic every year because, just like Thanksgiving and Christmas, Daffodil Weekend was all about tradition. The ribbon sandwiches were the highlight of her picnic—crustless Pepperidge Farm white bread with a layer of egg salad (yellow), a layer of scallion cream cheese (green), and a layer of maraschino cherry cream cheese (pink). Agnes and Box teased her both for making the ribbon sand-wiches and for enjoying them. It was WASP cuisine at its very essence, they said. Why not serve Velveeta on Triscuits while she was at it? Or a dish of pickled cauliflower? Dabney ignored the taunts; their aversion simply left more ribbon sandwiches for her, and for Peter Genevra, superintendent of the water company, who stopped at her picnic every year to wolf down half a dozen.

Dabney also made a bourbon-glazed spiral-cut ham, a loaf of braided honey-curry bread, poached asparagus with hollandaise sauce, and a tortellini salad with herbed mayonnaise. She served lemon tarts from the Nantucket Bake Shop. She bought a bottle of Taittinger champagne for herself and Agnes, good white Bordeaux for Box, and a twelve-pack of Stella Artois to offer those who stopped to visit.

As Dabney was cutting the crusts from the Pepperidge Farm loaf, Box entered the kitchen. He had arrived that morning while she was at work; she hadn't seen him since Monday at 7:00 a.m., when she'd dropped him at the airport as she did every Monday morning.

"Hello, dear," he said, and he kissed her chastely on the cheek. His greeting alone summed up the way things were between them. Pleasant, civilized, sexless. He called her "darling," or occasionally "dear." When they were dating and first married, Dabney used to long for Thursday afternoons because back then, Box would leave Harvard when his last class was over at three, and he would often make it to the island by five. Dabney would meet his plane or his boat and they would head straight home to make love. Now, Box stayed in his faculty apartment on Thursday nights. He worked until seven or eight and then went out to dinner with colleagues. He tried to convince Dabney to come to Cambridge on Thursday evenings. There were so many new restaurants, they could attend the reading series at the Coop or go to the Symphony. But Dabney always declined. Box knew that asking Dabney to come to Cambridge was like asking her to scuba dive without an oxygen tank in Marianas Trench. She believed, in her own mind, that she simply would not survive.

Box grew weary at her refusal to travel, and Dabney grew aggravated at him for trying to prod her into it. *I never pretended to be anyone else!* she had shouted at him a few years back. The shouting had been startling to them both—theirs was not a marriage where emotions ran hot—and the discussion died there. Box stayed in Cambridge on Thursday nights, and Dabney stayed on Nantucket.

Now, as usual, Dabney said, "How was your week?"

"Good," Box said. "My Turkish editor called. They're picking up the new edition."

"Oh, wonderful," Dabney said. In addition to holding an endowed chair, Box had authored the macroeconomics textbook used by more than four hundred universities across the country. It had been translated into twenty-four languages. Box wrote an updated edition every three years; the amount of income this generated was nauseating. Box made somewhere between three and four million dollars a year off the textbook; his salary from Harvard was a mere three hundred thousand. The money meant little to Box and even less to Dabney, other than that they never had to worry about it. Their house on Charter Street was historically preserved in its every element, and they had slowly and carefully filled it with antiques and art. It would pass to Agnes. Dabney was the proud owner of a 1966 tomato-red Chevy Impala with a white vinyl top, which was something of a money pit, but she treasured it. Box drove a battered Jeep Wrangler on Nantucket and an Audi RS 4 on the mainland. They never took vacations, because of Dabney, although Box went to London for two weeks every June to teach at the School of Economics, and he attended a conference in November that switched locations—San Diego, Amsterdam, Honolulu. They anonymously donated a hundred thousand dollars each year to the Morningside Heights Boys & Girls Club, where Agnes worked, and a hundred thousand to the Nantucket Cottage Hospital. And that was the extent of their spending.

Dabney wondered if Clendenin Hughes knew she had married a celebrated and esteemed economist. She presumed he did. One could find out anything on the Internet now. Was Clen jealous? Of course, Clen had won a Pulitzer; Dabney had discovered this by reading the alumni notes in her high school newsletter. She had felt a surge of pride for him, followed by annoyance. She had thought, *For what he gave up, he'd better have won a Pulitzer!*

She wanted to stop thinking about Clendenin Hughes.

"How was *your* week?" Box asked. "I take it you're all aflutter for the weekend? Can you give me the rundown again?"

"Dinner tonight at the Club Car," Dabney said. "I made the reservation for two, but we'll have to bump it to four, since Agnes and CJ are here." She paused, thinking about how Box and CJ would fight for the check. That was another thing about CJ: he always had to pay for everything, otherwise he became downright sullen. "Parade at noon tomorrow, and picnic at one."

"Collapse in exhausted heap by five," Box said.

Dabney said, "I have an appointment with Ted Field at nine o'clock Monday morning."

"Really?" Box said. "Are you not well?"

Dabney stared at the perfect squares of white bread on the cutting board. Those squares were her life—or like her life had been until the e-mail arrived that morning. "Not well," she confirmed. "I'm thinking maybe Lyme."

Box said, "Have you been bitten by a tick?"

"Not that I know of," Dabney said. The last time Dabney had walked in the moors was the preceding fall, with their dog, Henry. Just thinking of Henry made Dabney weepy.

"It's not like you to get sick," Box said. "I can't even remember the last time you had a cold."

"I know," Dabney said. Her voice was filled with impending tears. It was also not like Dabney to get dramatic or emotional. She knew that doing so now was making Box uncomfortable.

"I would offer to stay on Monday," Box said. "But..."

"You can't," Dabney said. Mondays at one, Box taught a seminar on Tobin to twelve handpicked seniors; it was his favorite class.

"I suppose I could ask Miranda to cover it," Box said.

Ah, yes, Miranda. Thirty-five-year-old Australian economics prodigy Miranda Gilbert, with the naughty-librarian glasses and the enchanting accent. She had been Box's teaching and research assistant for the past four years. Dabney had always been a little jealous of Miranda. But Box would never keep a secret from Dabney as she was now doing. She should just tell him: Clendenin Hughes would be arriving on Nantucket tomorrow. So what? To *not* tell him turned it into a bigger deal than it was. To not tell him made it seem like Dabney was affected by it.

Dabney was affected by it.

"How *is* Miranda?" Dabney asked.

"Miranda?" Box plucked a maraschino cherry from the jar and ate it, then grimaced. "She's fine. Dr. Bartelby is getting ready to propose, I guess."

Dr. Bartelby, Miranda's boyfriend, was an internist at Mass General. Dr. Bartelby (whose Christian name was Christian) and Miranda had come to visit the Beeches on Nantucket the past three summers. "He *told* her he's getting ready to propose? That takes all the fun out of it."

"I'm not sure how it works these days," Box said. "But I do believe Miranda is about to join the married ranks."

A wave of dizziness overcame Dabney and she steadied herself against the counter.

"Are you all right?" Box asked. He put a hand on her lower back, but even that light touch hurt.

She had to make the ribbon sandwiches before the bread dried out. And the asparagus needed to be trimmed and roasted. Agnes and CJ would be home soon with the daffodils for the car. Decorating the Impala on Friday evening was one of Dabney's favorite parts of the weekend. But all Dabney could do was stagger through the kitchen and into the library, where she collapsed on the sofa. Box covered her with an afghan crocheted by her beloved grammie, the first Agnes Bernadette. Dabney felt like she was going to die.

Forbearance: her ancestors had endured much worse, Dabney knew. Her great-great-great-grandmother, Dabney Margaret Wright, had come to Nantucket from Beacon Hill, leaving behind home, furnishings, and society. She and their three sons had moved into a house on Lily Street while Warren sailed off to hunt whales. He had been gone for eighteen months on his first trip, then home for six months—and he never returned from his second trip. Dabney Wright had made the best of a tragic situation: she joined the congregation of the Summer Street Church, and befriended other women who had been widowed by the sea. She had not complained, at least not in Dabney's imagination. She had kept a stiff upper lip.

And Dabney, too, would persevere. After Dabney recovered from her spell, she assembled the ribbon sandwiches and wrapped them in wax paper. She roasted the asparagus. Agnes and CJ took charge of bedecking the Impala: a daffodil wreath on the grille and a blanket of daffodils laid across the wide trunk. Dabney showered and put on her navy and yellow Diane von Furstenberg wrap dress. It was one of the dresses Patty Benson had left hanging in her closet when she abandoned her husband and daughter. Dabney didn't attach sentimental value to things, or at least she didn't in this case. She wore her mother's dresses all the time because she liked them, and they fit.

Dabney tried to make a reasonable effort at dinner at the Club Car, despite the fact that she wished she were in bed with a bowl of soup and a Jane Austen novel. Instead, she ordered the lamb chops, as she always did, and Box selected an excellent Australian Shiraz to go with them. One sip of the wine set Dabney's head spinning.

She said, "You know, Box was teaching at Harvard when I was a student there, but I never took one of his classes."

Agnes stared at her mother. She had ordered the crab cake, but she hadn't taken a single bite. "Yes, Mommy, we know."

CJ smiled at Dabney. He was wearing a navy blazer and a sumptuously patterned Robert Graham shirt. Before they left the house, Box had admired CJ's chocolate suede Gucci loafers and then said to Dabney, "You should get me a pair like that!" Dabney had to admit, CJ presented well, he smelled good, and he had a nice head of wavy salt-and-pepper hair and straight white teeth. Too white, like maybe he treated them. But that wasn't a reason to dislike the man. CJ had ordered the lamb chops, medium rare, just like Dabney had, and this reminded Dabney of a time the autumn before when he had ordered exactly the same thing as she had. It was as if he was copying her in an attempt to be found agreeable.

CJ said, "If I remember correctly, you were an art history major? You wrote your thesis on Matisse?"

"We named our dog, Henry, after him," Agnes said softly.

CJ, who did not care for dogs ("too dirty"), didn't respond to this. He said to Dabney, "You should go see the Matisse chapel in Nice."

It wasn't likely that Dabney would ever make it to France, but she gave him credit for trying.

"My favorite painting is *La Danse,*" Dabney said. "It's at MOMA, but I've never seen it."

CJ said, "The director at MOMA is a friend of mine. So if you ever decide to come to New York, I'll set something up."

Dabney drank her wine. She didn't touch her lamb chops. She had absolutely no appetite.

She imagined Clendenin Hughes walking into the dining room of the Club Car, throwing Dabney over his shoulder, and carrying her out. Then she indulged in a moment of deep self-pity. She had lived a calm and peaceful existence, a happy and productive existence—until this morning.

She drank her wine.

Between dinner and dessert, champagne arrived at the table, and not just champagne but a bottle of Cristal. Dabney blinked. Both she and Agnes were fond of champagne, but it gave Box a headache, and, as wealthy as he was, he would never have spent three hundred dollars on a bottle of Cristal.

They all sat silently as the server uncorked the bottle and filled four flutes. Dabney was confused. She gave their server—a severe-looking woman in a white dinner jacket—a beseeching look, but the woman's face was as implacable as a guard at Buckingham Palace.

Suddenly, CJ cleared his throat and stood up, raising his glass. "Agnes and I have an announcement to make."

Oh no, Dabney thought. *Nononononononono.*

Agnes smiled shyly and raised her left hand so that Dabney could see the diamond—Tiffany cut, platinum setting, bright and sparkling perfection. Dabney urged happy excitement onto her face.

"Agnes has agreed to be my wife," CJ said.

Dabney uttered a cry of horror, which they all mistook for delight. She alone was able to see the green fog emanating from Agnes and CJ like toxic radiation.

"How wonderful!" Dabney said.

Box stood to embrace Agnes and then CJ, and Dabney, realizing that this was an appropriate response, followed suit. She held Agnes's hand—the same hand Agnes had pressed into clay as a kindergartner, the same hand Dabney had high-fived when Agnes had scored a 1400 on her SATs—and admired the ring.

"What a *beautiful* ring!" Dabney said. This, at least, was true. CJ had nailed the ring—simple, classic, timeless. The stone was enormous. Dabney guessed three carats, or nearly.

But the ghoul-green haze enveloping Agnes could only signify some future catastrophe—CJ would cheat on Agnes with one of the Giants cheerleaders, or an intern in his office. Or he would do something worse. Dabney wouldn't wait to find out. She would, somehow, figure out a way to save her daughter.

On Saturday morning, Dabney felt even worse than usual, thanks to too much Shiraz, the cataclysmic news of "the engagement," and Clen's looming arrival. Despite this, she donned her usual Daffodil Parade clothes—yellow oxford shirt, jeans, navy blazer, penny loafers, and her beautiful straw Peter Beaton hat with the navy grosgrain ribbon. She had her clipboard, which listed the 120 entries for the Antique Car Parade. The sun was shining, the air was actually balmy; Dabney felt warm in her blazer and considered removing it, but she knew she would be chilly once she was riding out to Sconset in the Impala with the top down.

Main Street was a swarm of festive humanity. Everyone wore yellow and green to celebrate the three million daffodils blooming on Nantucket. There were children with daffodils painted on their faces and daffodils wound around the handlebars of their bikes. There were dogs with daffodil collars. Every single person seemed to want Dabney's attention. In years past, she had handled this situation with grace and aplomb. She used to love knowing everyone and having everyone know her. She used to trade inside jokes with the town administrator and the garbage collector, the bookstore owner, the woman who owned the lingerie store, Andrea Kapenash, wife of the police chief, Mr. Berber, the fifth-grade teacher who had been Agnes's favorite, a certain summer resident who sat on the board of the New York Stock Exchange, and a different summer resident who anchored the six o'clock news in Boston. This was a cross section of humanity who had one thing in common...they all loved Nantucket Island. But in this contest, Dabney was the undisputed frontrunner. She loved Nantucket more than anyone else had ever loved Nantucket. She knew her devotion was unusual, possibly even unhealthy, but on a day like today, it didn't matter. Today she was among like-minded people.

Dabney chatted with everyone who crossed her path, but she felt like she was speaking in an automated voice, like the voice that played on the Chamber of Commerce voice mail when one called after business hours. Yes, it was magnificent about the weather, no, she couldn't remember a nicer day, no, she couldn't believe another year had passed, yes, she was ready for summer, she was always ready for summer. Good to see you, she said, but her words clinked like counterfeit coins. Could everyone tell? Dabney yearned to grab someone by the arm—even the channel 5 news anchor—and spill her guts. *I don't feel well at all, there's something wrong with me, Clendenin Hughes is coming back to Nantucket today, he might even be here as we speak, and my husband doesn't know. My daughter announced last night that she is engaged to a man who seems like the Second Coming, but whom I alone know to be unsuitable. And there is nothing I can do or say. Here I am, Nantucket's matchmaker, ostensibly a romance expert, and yet my life is unraveling. Nothing is as it should be.*

Can you help? Can you help me?

Dabney bumped into Vaughan Oglethorpe, the Chamber board president, her *boss,* who stood out like a sore thumb in his black shirt, black tie, and black suit. Vaughan was the island's only undertaker, and he could cast a pall over the sunniest of days. His hair was whiter than when Dabney had last seen him, and his nose more beaky; he was starting to resemble the national bird. He was as tall and lanky as ever, but more hunched in the shoulders; he looked like Lurch from *The Addams Family,* or like some other benevolent monster. Perfect for an undertaker.

"Dabney," he said. The lugubrious voice, too, suited his profession. Vaughan had known Dabney her entire life—he had been an old beau of Dabney's mother, Patty Benson—and he liked to take credit for all of Dabney's successes on the job.

"Hello, Vaughan," she said. "How do you like this weather?"

Vaughan stroked his bony chin, his expression dour. He smelled like embalming fluid; often when Dabney stood this close to him, she held her breath. She looked down at her loafers.

"What a turnout!" he boomed suddenly. "You've done it again, Dabney! Good work!"

"Thank you, sir," Dabney said.

"No!" he shouted. "Great work!"

*　　*　　*

As usual, Box drove the Impala in the parade while Dabney rode shotgun. This smarted a little, as it did every year. The Impala was *Dabney's* car; Box drove it exactly once a year, in this parade. Why didn't Dabney drive and Box ride shotgun? This, after all, was Dabney's festival. But Agnes and Nina Mobley and even Box himself thought it *looked* better if he drove. Dabney should be free to wave at the crowds like she was passing royalty.

Fine, Dabney said. Fine, whatever.

Agnes and CJ sat in the back, exuding the smugness of the newly engaged. Dabney wanted to scowl, but she couldn't. All eyes were on her. She had to smile. She had to *beam*. She put a hand on top of her straw hat to keep it from blowing away.

Once they had parked in Sconset, under giant elms showing off their new spring leaves, Dabney poured herself and Agnes a glass of champagne. Dabney wasn't one to seek solace in alcohol, but circumstances were piling up against her so rapidly that she saw no alternative. She took a nice, long sip of champagne, which sparkled against her tongue. Any second now, she would relax.

She set out the picnic on a card table covered with her yellow linen tablecloth, used only this one day a year.

She realized that she had forgotten to pick up the lemon tarts from the Nantucket Bake Shop.

"Oh my gosh!" she said. "I forgot the tarts!"

Box was uncorking the white Bordeaux. He shrugged. "It doesn't matter," he said. "No one ever eats them anyway."

Dabney stared at her husband. *Forbearance,* she thought. But emotion overcame Dabney's sturdy genes: her eyes filled with hot tears. She turned away from Box, and from Agnes and CJ, who now seemed like some hideous two-headed monster, and all the others who were starting to mill on the street. She couldn't let anyone see her crying about the forgotten tarts. She felt like Clarissa Dalloway, who decided that she would get the flowers for the dinner party herself. This picnic, with the ham, and the asparagus, and the ribbon sandwiches that everyone felt comfortable *ridiculing,* was Dabney's picnic. It was an expression of her very self, and yet here was John Boxmiller Beech, the brilliant and celebrated economist, telling her it didn't matter. Which was the equivalent of saying that she, Dabney, didn't matter.

She stumbled down the street, wishing she were alone, wishing she were anonymous, wishing—for the first time in her forty-eight years—that she were not stuck on this island where every last person thought he knew her, but where in reality no one knew her.

Oh, something was wrong.

Dabney's vision was blurred by tears, and by drinking champagne on an empty stomach. She knew she should return to the car and eat a ribbon sandwich. There was a big crowd around the 1948 woodie wagon, which had won Best Car three times in the past decade; this year they had done a *Wizard of Oz* theme. The police chief, Ed Kapenash, was dressed as the Scarecrow.

Dabney didn't stop, didn't turn around, she just kept going. Clarissa Dalloway had survived, but someone at her dinner party had committed suicide. Was that right? And then of course Virginia Woolf had done herself in. She'd walked into the River Ouse with rocks in her pockets.

Dabney felt unsteady on her feet. Her hand was shaking so badly that champagne spilled onto the cuff of her yellow oxford.

She saw him waiting at the corner of Main and Chapel Streets. He was straddling a ten-speed bicycle, the same one he had ridden everywhere as a teenager because there had been no money to buy him a car. He used to ride that bike whenever he met Dabney to be alone. They used to meet in the Quaker Cemetery, they would meet at the old, abandoned NHA property called Greater Light, and they would meet at the high school football field. Their song growing up had been Van Morrison's "Brown Eyed Girl," not only because Dabney had brown eyes but because of the line about making love in the green grass behind the stadium. That line had been written for her and Clen.

She knew it was him even though he in no way resembled the twenty-two-year-old she had last seen at Steamship Wharf in 1987. He was bigger—seventy or eighty pounds heavier at least—and he had a mustache and a beard. He was a grown-up, a man.

He was wearing a red T-shirt, jeans, and a pair of black Chuck Taylors. Twenty-seven years later and he still wore Chuck Taylors? In high school they had been the only thing he would spend money on. He had owned five pairs.

Something else was different about him, something off balance. It took Dabney another second to realize that Clen had only one arm. She blinked, thinking it was a trick of the light, or the champagne. But what she saw was real: his left arm was a stump. There was the sleeve of his red T-shirt, and nothing below it.

I suffered a pretty serious loss about six months ago, and I've been slowly recovering from it.

He had lost his arm.

Dabney's vision grew dark at the edges, but there was still color—the red of Clen's T-shirt and the green glen and weak tea of his Scottish hazel eyes. *I could not stay, and you could not go.* She couldn't speak. Nina Mobley would be looking for her, as it was time to judge the picnics. *It doesn't matter, nobody ever eats them anyway.* Clen! She wanted, at least, to say his name, just his name, but even that was beyond her. She was in the power of some other force; something had her by the back of the neck and was pushing her down. *I hope that "never" has an expiration date.* She wanted to ride away on his handlebars. Any second now, she would relax. He was there. It was him.

She did not stop for him. She walked on. Even if she could have spoken, what would she have said? She was unprepared. She wasn't feeling well. Around the corner, hidden by hedges, she tried to breathe, but found she could not breathe. She heard the sound of breaking glass and realized the champagne flute had dropped to the road and shattered. There was wind in her ears. Her knees gave way.

Blackness.

Silence.

Couple #30: Dr. Gary Donegal and Lance Farley, partners ten years

Dr. Donegal: I started seeing Dabney in 1978, my first year on Nantucket. Dabney was, in fact, my first patient. She was twelve years old; her mother had left the family four years earlier, and Dabney's father, who was a policeman, was worried about Dabney's emotional well-being as she entered adolescence. Dabney refused to leave the island; she was convinced that if she left Nantucket, she would die. Or something worse.

"Something worse?" I said.

Officer Kimball then explained to me that the last time Dabney had been off Nantucket was in December 1974, when her mother, Patty Benson, took Dabney to Boston to see *The Nutcracker*. They had orchestra seats for the evening performance of the ballet and a suite at the Park Plaza afterward. Patty, Officer Kimball said, had come from money and was used to doing things this way. She was also spoiled, selfish, and entitled, he said. A summer person, he said—as if this were the explanation for her unpleasant qualities. He then went on to tell me that Patty Benson had left the Park Plaza Hotel in the middle of the night and had never returned.

"Never returned?" I said.

"Never returned," he said. He knew Patty hadn't met with foul play because she had given the hotel's concierge Officer Kimball's phone number and a twenty-dollar tip to call and tell him to come to Boston to collect their daughter.

When Dabney awoke in the suite in the Park Plaza, Patty was gone. The concierge sent up one of the chambermaids to stay with Dabney until her father arrived.

Dabney never saw or heard from her mother again. Eventually, Officer Kimball hired a detective and discovered that Patty Benson was living in Texas, working as a flight attendant on the private jet of some oil millionaire.

I realized I had my work cut out for me with Dabney. The refusal to leave Nantucket was a natural response to having lost her mother, to being left behind in a hotel room like an empty shopping bag, or a half-eaten club sandwich.

Dabney was happy enough to talk about her mother. Her mother had grown up spending summers in a big old house on Hoicks Hollow Road. The Benson family had belonged to the Sankaty Beach Club; her mother used to say that tan skin was healthy skin. Her mother liked black-and-white movies with singing and dancing, liked lobster tails on Christmas Eve, and did not care for her husband's Wharf Rat tattoo. Her mother read to Dabney every night before bed and some nights fell asleep in Dabney's bed; she promised that Dabney could get her ears pierced on her twelfth birthday, but that the only acceptable earrings were pearls.

Dabney wouldn't talk about *The Nutcracker* trip or waking up in the hotel alone or the fact that her mother had not contacted her in two, then three, then four years.

I had seen my share of obsessive-compulsive disorder and agoraphobia and paranoia, but I had never seen a combination of the three the way they presented in Dabney. I am, perhaps, making things sound worse for her than they were. She was an exceptional child, and as she grew into a teenager, she only became more exceptional. She was lovely to look at, intelligent, clear-eyed, perceptive, kind, poised, articulate, and funny. But when it came to leaving Nantucket, she had a blind spot. She wouldn't leave the island unless her life depended on it, she said.

I met with her twice a month. We tried antianxiety medications, none of which proved very effective, but we finally made enough progress that when she was accepted to Harvard, she said she would go.

Even I was surprised by this.

She said, "I told you that I wouldn't leave the island unless my life depended on it, and now my life depends on it. Am I supposed to stay here and wait tables? Work as a nanny? I have to go to college, Dr. Donegal. I'm smart."

I agreed with her wholeheartedly: she was smart. I was sure that when she got to Harvard, she would realize there was nothing to fear. No one else would disappear.

This didn't end up being quite true. Her boyfriend, Clendenin Hughes, went to Yale and became engrossed in his studies and his life there. Dabney traveled once to New Haven to see him, and it ended badly. Officer Kimball was working double shifts that weekend, and hence I was dispatched to go get her.

It was on the ride from New Haven back to the Cape, eight years after our therapy started, that I finally got Dabney to talk. She started with things I knew: she was fatally in love with Clendenin Hughes—"fatally" meaning she was pretty sure the love would kill her, or the fact that he didn't love her the way she loved him would kill her. He wanted to go places and see things, and she couldn't, and he didn't understand, and she couldn't explain. New Haven had changed Clen, she said. I told her that going new places did sometimes change a person, new experiences shaped us, and Dabney said that she liked who she was and was determined to stay that way. She had not been changed by Cambridge, and I suggested that was because she hadn't truly let Cambridge into her heart. She didn't respond to this, and the next time she spoke, she told me that the night her mother left, she told Dabney that she was woefully unhappy with her life. She was no longer in love with Dabney's father; she had been blinded, she said, by the romantic notion of a war hero. She used to love Nantucket as a summer haven, but living there year-round had spoiled it for her. She hated it now with every cell of her body. She felt like a coyote in a trap, she said. She would chew off her own leg to escape.

Dabney said, "When I looked at my mother, she was sitting in a cloud of green smoke. I knew she was leaving, and the thing was, I also knew it was for the best. My father and I were Nantucketers to the core, and my mother hated us for it."

I was just about to reassure Dabney that her mother did not hate her, but that she, Dabney, was in some sense the coyote's leg. She was that which her mother had sacrificed in the name of freedom.

But before I could articulate this, Dabney asked me a surprising question.

She said, "Dr. Donegal, have you ever been in love?"

I stopped seeing Dabney as a patient after she graduated from college, although she never truly left my sights. I heard about Clendenin's exodus to Southeast Asia and Dabney's pregnancy, and a few years later I heard about her marriage to the Harvard economist, and when I bumped into Dabney and her daughter and said economist one morning having breakfast at the Jared Coffin House, I told her how happy I was for her. Then, a few months later, Dabney called me. At first I suspected marital trouble, or grief counseling because her father had just died of a heart attack, but what Dabney said was, "There's someone I want you to meet. When can you come for dinner?"

The person she wanted me to meet was a man named Lance Farley, who had recently bought an antiques store in town and who had just joined the Chamber of Commerce. It was clear from the moment I shook hands with Lance Farley what Dabney was up to. I, of course, knew about Dabney's reputation as a matchmaker, about her supposed "supernatural intuition" when it came to romance. I had heard about her many successes and how she saw either a rosy aura or a green fog. I remembered the story about her mother on the night that she left. But still, I put as much stock in Dabney's matchmaking as I did in the answers on a Ouija board.

But as we drank gin and tonics in the Beeches' secluded, grassy backyard and then dined on grilled swordfish and Bartlett Farm tomatoes and homemade peach pie, and as Lance and I discovered a shared love for Bach and the early novels of Philip Roth, and the northern coast of Morocco, I admitted to myself that maybe even after eight years of spelunking in the hidden recesses of someone's brain, there were still things to be discovered. Maybe Dabney did have a supernatural intuition about romantic matters.

Who was I to say she didn't?

BOX

Dabney fainted on Main Street in Sconset. Box hadn't even noticed that she was missing; he had been too busy pouring a glass of Montrachet and fixing a ham sandwich. Nina Mobley had come looking for Dabney; the judging of the tailgate picnics was about to begin, and they couldn't start without Dabney. Box had waved a casual hand at the mayhem around him. "I'm sure she's here somewhere." Dabney was the most popular woman on the island. She knew everyone and everyone knew her. She was probably off talking to Mr. So-and-So about the window boxes of his house on Fair Street, or she'd bumped into Peter Genevra from the water company and was feeding him marshmallow-and-Easter-egg sandwiches.

But fifteen minutes later, Dabney still hadn't turned up. Nina was antsy. Should she start the judging without her?

"Judge without Dabney?" Box said. "Is that even an option?"

"Not really," Nina admitted. "I need her."

Box nodded. Dabney and Nina were best friends, but Dabney was the dominant one of the pair. She was Mary Tyler Moore to Nina's Rhoda, the Lucy to her Ethel.

An instant later, the son of the fire chief—Box recognized the youth but couldn't recall his name—approached to tell Box that Dabney had fainted in the street, and the paramedics were tending to her now.

It was as Box threaded his way through the crowd on Main Street that he saw the man on the bicycle.

Box took a stutter step; his right knee had been replaced the year before and still wasn't 100 percent reliable. Box hated himself for looking again, but something about the man struck Box. Big guy, bearded like a lumberjack, one arm.

The man raised his good arm, not in greeting, Box thought, but as an acknowledgment. *I'm here.*

Clendenin Hughes? Was that possible? Box was terrible with names but far better with faces. He had looked up Hughes several times on the Internet and had even read a few of his pieces, including the series on Myanmar, which had won him the Pulitzer. Furthermore, the man looked just like Agnes; it was uncanny. That was him, Box was almost certain.

Had Dabney seen Hughes, then? Was that why she'd fainted? Her old lover. Agnes's father. It had been more than twenty-five years since Hughes had left Nantucket. He lived overseas, in Southeast Asia somewhere. As Box understood it, Clendenin Hughes was a man who needed political unrest and foreign women and espionage plots to keep his gears turning.

As Box understood it, Hughes no longer had any connection to the island.

And yet, there he was.

Clendenin turned the bike around—skillfully, considering he had only one arm—and pedaled away.

One arm?

Box hurried to the rotary. He was sixty-two years old, way past the point in his life where he should feel threatened or jealous. But something gnawed at him. He quickened his step, to tend to Dabney.

Box took Dabney home and put her to bed with three aspirin and a glass of water. Daffodil Weekend had gotten the best of her this year. She had allowed herself to stress out over a pagan celebration.

As her eyes fluttered closed, he thought to ask her about Clendenin Hughes. But he didn't want to upset her—or himself—any further.

Box had met Dabney twenty-four years earlier at the Sankaty Head Golf Club during a Harvard alumni event. Box was attending at the request of the development office; they liked certain faculty members to show up at such events and glad-hand. Box had been to Nantucket once before, in the late seventies, when he and a few buddies from Harvard had hiked out the slender, sandy arm of Coatue and slept on the beach in tents. He had hardly been to the beach since then.

The event at Sankaty consisted mostly of captains of industry with golfing tans and their Nantucket Lightship basket–toting wives drinking scotch and eating pigs in a blanket, but suddenly Box found himself talking to a girl who had graduated from Radcliffe only four years earlier, a girl born and raised on Nantucket named Dabney Kimball. She had studied art history, but her roommate had taken Econ 10, so Dabney knew who Box was. Soon she was offering to take him on a tour of the island the following day.

"Oh, you don't have to do that," he said. She was wearing a madras headband in her brown hair and her face had a fresh-scrubbed look. Box would never have called himself an insightful person even back then, but he had been able to tell that underneath Dabney's simple, pretty package lay hidden treasure.

She said, "Oh, please? It would be such an honor. I love showing the island off. I'm an ambassador of sorts."

"But surely you have other plans?" he said. She was young enough to spend her Sundays playing boccie on the beach, or sailing around the harbor while lying across the front of her boyfriend's sloop.

"I have a two-year-old daughter," she said. "But my grand-mother watches her on Sundays, so I'm free all day."

A two-year-old? Box thought. If she had graduated four years earlier, she would have been twenty-six. If she had a two-year-old, she would have gotten pregnant at twenty-three. Very few Rad-cliffe women had children right out of college. They all went to law school now, business school, medical school—or, in the case of art-history majors, they spent years doing graduate studies in Florence or Vienna. Box checked Dabney's hand for a ring, but her fingers were bare. She wore no jewelry except for a strand of pearls and matching pearl earrings.

"Okay," Box said. He was agreeing to the tour without even wanting one. "Thank you. I'd like that."

Agnes stayed home with Dabney on Sunday morning while Box and CJ golfed at Miacomet. When Box got home, Agnes said, "I'm worried about her, Daddy. What if I called in to work this week and stayed here with her?"

"You know your mother won't let you do that," Box said. "She's not going to stay home from work, and she wouldn't want you to either. Think about the kids."

Agnes was the executive director of the Boys & Girls Club in Morningside Heights, a job that paid next to nothing but that gave her enormous satisfaction. It was a job that, quite frankly, scared Box and Dabney. Their daughter sometimes stayed at the club un-til eight or nine at night with a handful of kids who had no one at home to feed them or put them to bed. Box wrote Agnes a sizable check each month to pay for her rent on the Upper West Side and a car service home whenever she left the club after dark. He sus-pected, however, that Agnes was too modest to use the car service regularly. He suspected that Agnes took the subway.

While they were golfing, CJ had admitted that Agnes's job unnerved him as well, and said that after they were married he was going to encourage her to work for a different nonprofit, preferably one in midtown. Box had agreed that this was a good idea.

"The kids aren't more important to me than my own mother," Agnes said.

"Your mother will be fine," Box said.

"Are you sure?"

"I'm sure," Box said. "She has an appointment with Dr. Field in the morning. It's probably just Lyme disease. Three weeks of antibiotics, she'll be as good as new."

"Okay," Agnes said. "CJ has a client negotiation in the morning, so we'll leave tonight."

"I'll take care of your mother," Box said. "I promise."

On their tour of the island nearly a quarter of century earlier, Dabney had driven Box to Quaise and Quidnet, to Madaket and Madequecham, to Shimmo and Shawkemo in her battered 1972 Chevy Nova. It wasn't the car he'd expected a young lady like her to drive; she seemed like someone who would be more comfortable in a Saab convertible or a Volkswagen Jetta, but then she explained that she had been raised by her father—a Vietnam vet and a Nantucket policeman—and he had turned her into a motorhead. This term, coming out of Dabney's wholesome mouth, made Box throw back his head and laugh. But Dabney was dead serious. She had purchased the Nova with her own money, and she wanted to trade it in for a Camaro. Her dream was to someday own a Corvette Stingray split-window with matching numbers in Bermuda blue. She was a devoted Chevy girl, she said.

She was sorry that the Nova didn't have four-wheel drive only because that meant she couldn't take him up the beach to her favorite spot, Great Point.

"That's okay," Box had said. He didn't tell her that the tour had already run so far over his time limit that he'd missed the ferry he had booked back to the mainland.

She said, "I'll take you to my second-favorite spot. And we can eat. I made lunch."

Her second-favorite spot was Polpis Harbor, where she parked overlooking the sparkling water and the scattering of sails. Dabney pulled a wicker basket out of the Nova's trunk. She had made fried chicken, macaroni salad, and strawberry pie. She handed Box an icy cold root beer, which was the most delicious thing he could remember tasting in his forty years.

Up until that point, Box had been a confirmed bachelor. He had dated dozens of women—most of them very smart, some of them very pretty, and one or two who were both. But Box had always imagined love as a musical note, and so far nobody had struck the right one. But the note resonated loud and clear that afternoon at Polpis Harbor with Dabney. It was a sweet, thrumming sound that nearly knocked him off his feet. He, who had never really given a thought to anyone's feelings but his own, wanted to know her. She seemed ripe for the picking; he loved her pert, freckled nose. But he also knew he should proceed cautiously.

"Tell me about your daughter," he said.

By Tuesday afternoon, Box had a phone call from Ted Field.

He said, "The tick panel was clean. It's not Lyme, not babesiosis, not tularemia, thank God. Her symptoms are pretty wide-ranging and not inconsistent with a tick-borne disease, so I put her on a course of antibiotics anyway, just to be safe."

"Okay," Box said. "Thank you."

"Her white blood cell count was high," the doctor said. "She might want to go to Boston to get that checked out."

"You know my wife," Box said. "What are the chances she'll go to Boston?"

"Slim to none. I know because I suggested it to her. I just don't want to miss anything more serious."

"Do you think it's something more serious?" Box asked.

"Possibly?" Ted Field said. "Or it may be as simple as a wheat allergy. Gluten is the new bogeyman."

Box hung up the phone and stared at it for a moment. Something more serious? Dabney never got sick. In his heart, Box believed that Dabney was suffering from stress. Anyone watching her work would have thought she was in charge of running a ten-billion-dollar multinational company: she took her job that seriously. And then there was the specter of the man on the bicycle. Clendenin Hughes—or maybe not. Maybe Box had been mistaken.

He picked up the phone to call Dabney at the Chamber. It had been so long since he'd called her at work that he had forgotten the number. Oh—3543, of course. There had been years and years when he had phoned Dabney at work every single day—to check in, to ask about the weather, to find out the score of Agnes's field hockey game, to tell her he loved her. But possibly just as many years had passed since he'd grown too busy to call every day. He had classes, students, office hours, graduate assistants and department meetings to manage, his textbook to write and revise, articles to critique and publish, associate professors to advise, the crumbling markets in Europe to analyze and comment on (he appeared as a guest on CNBC two or three times a year). He'd also been receiving phone calls from the Department of the Treasury, which, although flattering, required intricate, time-consuming problem solving. He routinely complained that he needed four extra hours in each day. He started secretly to resent having to travel to Nantucket every weekend, and so he'd recently asked Dabney how she would feel if he spent one weekend a month immersed in work in Cambridge.

She had said, "Oh. That would be fine. I guess."

She had said this with equanimity, but Box—although not gifted when it came to reading minds—figured out that it would *not* be fine. Or maybe it *would* be fine? Dabney was as self-sufficient and independent a woman as Box had ever known, and over the years, their union had settled into a comfortable arrangement. They were like a Venn diagram. She lived her life and he didn't interfere—and vice versa. The space where they overlapped had grown more and more slender over the years. He assumed that this was normal, as was his waning sex drive. His nonexistent sex drive. He had considered going to a doctor and getting a pill, but that struck him as embarrassing, and beneath him. Dabney wasn't complaining, anyway. Box figured that he and his wife had simply settled into the well-feathered nest of middle age.

Nina Mobley answered on the first ring. "Nantucket Chamber of Commerce."

"Hello, Nina, it's Box," he said. "Is my wife there?"

"I'm sorry," Nina said. "*Who* is this?"

"Box," he said, feeling mildly annoyed. Though it *had* been aeons since he'd called. "John Boxmiller Beech. Dabney's husband."

"*Box?*" she said. "Is everything all *right?*"

"Nina," Box said. "Is my wife there, please?"

Dabney came on the phone. "Is everything okay?"

"Yes, yes," Box said. " I just had a call from Ted Field, who told me you passed the tick test but that he put you on antibiotics anyway."

"He did. But I'm not taking them. I feel much better."

"If he prescribed them," Box said, "then you'd better take them."

"I feel much better," Dabney repeated. "Why did he call *you* anyway? I'm the patient. You're not my father. He shouldn't have called you."

Box was tempted to agree with her, patient confidentiality and whatnot. But he and Ted Field had rowed together at Harvard a million years earlier; they were friends. Box wondered if Ted had called because there really might be something more serious going on.

"He said your white blood count was high, and that you should probably go to Boston to get it checked out."

"Not going to happen," Dabney said.

"Or it might be a wheat allergy. Perhaps you should stop eating bread?"

"Box," Dabney said. "I feel much better."

He had been married to the woman for twenty-four years; he realized that no one told her what to do—but he did not like being dismissed.

"You'll never guess who I saw at the Daffodil Parade when I was headed to find you. Can you guess?"

"Who?" Dabney said.

"I saw Clendenin Hughes!" The mock joy in his voice was grating even to his ears. "He was riding a bicycle!"

Dabney laughed without sounding at all amused. Maybe she thought he was kidding around, or maybe she thought he was being cruel.

"I have to go, darling," she said. "I have work to do."

Box had spent a year courting Dabney before they slept together. She had been keen about giving him the tour of the island and making the picnic—but as soon as he'd kissed her, after taking his first bite of her strawberry pie, she'd inched backward.

He'd said, "I'm sorry, is this not what you want?"

She had welled up with tears and that had made her even more fetching—her big brown eyes shining. "I want to want it," she said.

At the time, he had not understood what that meant. He was an economist: he dealt in absolutes. But her inscrutable answer doubled his ardor. He decided he would do whatever it took to capture Dabney Kimball's heart.

What he eventually learned was that Dabney Kimball's heart was missing. It had been pillaged by Clendenin Hughes, a boy she had loved since she was a teenager. Hughes was Agnes's father, although by the time Hughes found out that a child existed, he had already embarked on a new life overseas. Hughes had wanted Dabney to move to Thailand, but she couldn't, because of the confines of her psyche. Instead, she decided to raise Agnes without one word or dollar from Hughes. Dabney convinced herself that she would be better off if she never heard from Clendenin Hughes again. And she hadn't. But the fact of the matter was that Hughes had taken the tender, beating center of Dabney with him.

For most of that year, Box spent his weekends on Nantucket at the Brass Lantern Inn. He paid a month at a time for a room with a queen canopied bed and a chintz armchair, where he graded student papers. He grew accustomed to the smells of cinnamon-scented candles and the cheddar scones served at breakfast. The proprietor of the inn, Mrs. Annapale, discovered that Box was on the island in pursuit of Dabney Kimball. Mrs. Annapale had known Dabney since she was born and believed her to be a lost cause—not because of Clendenin Hughes but because the girl's mother had abandoned her in a fancy hotel room when she was only eight years old.

"And you know," Mrs. Annapale said, "people are never quite right after something like that happens."

Box had triumphed solely because of his persistence. He showed up in the bitter cold of January and in the windy gray of March. He brought peonies and potted orchids for Dabney and stuffed animals and storybooks for Agnes. He read to Agnes, despite having no experience with children. He brought bottles of single-malt scotch for Officer Kimball and cannoli from the North End of Boston for Dabney's grandmother, who soon allowed him to call her Grammie instead of "Mrs. Kimball." He had won over the daughter, the father, and the grandmother, but Dabney remained just out of reach.

Then, in June, Box left to teach for the first time at the London School of Economics, and he missed three consecutive weekends on Nantucket. When he finally returned to the Brass Lantern, he found Dabney waiting for him in his room, sitting on his queen canopied bed.

She said, "I was afraid you'd never come back."

They made love for the first time that night. Box knew it had been a long while since Dabney had been with a man, and he knew the only man she had ever been with was Clendenin Hughes. Clendenin Hughes *was* sex to Dabney, and as much as Box wanted to set out to change her mind in a swift, masterful conquering, he proceeded slowly and gently. And she didn't shy away. She cried out in pleasure, and then she asked him to do it all again the next morning.

He proposed over cheddar scones.

That had been twenty-five years earlier. John Boxmiller Beech was an economist, his area of expertise was guns and butter, supply and demand. He was the first to admit, he knew nothing about the mysteries of the human heart.

Nina Mobley, married seven years, divorced seven years

I am negative proof. I am the one Dabney tried to warn. But did I listen?

I had been working at the Chamber of Commerce as Dabney's assistant for two years when I started dating George Mobley. I had lived on Nantucket my entire life and I had known George forever. He was five years ahead of me in school, but his sister was only a year ahead of me, and his father was a scalloper who also ran the island's most popular fish market, where my mother was a faithful patron. (Like all good, old-school Catholics, we ate baked scrod every Friday.) I knew the Mobleys, everyone knew the Mobleys, but I never gave George a thought. I knew he had gone to Plymouth State, and studied statistics, but then he headed down to Islamorada to work on a fishing charter. He had ended up a fisherman like his father, but a far more glamorous kind—sailfish, marlin, fish you hang on the wall.

Then George's father died in spectacularly tragic fashion—he was thrown off the bow of his boat during a storm, his leg caught in the ropes, and he drowned. George came back to the island for the funeral, which I attended with my mother, and at the reception afterward I started talking to George. It was the deep freeze of January, but George was a golden tan color from his year of fishing on blue water. He had a kind of celebrity, being the bereaved. I was honored that George would talk to me.

I never asked for Dabney's opinion of George Mobley, and she didn't offer it. George would stop by the office on Friday afternoons to take me to the Anglers' Club for appetizers. He had moved back to Nantucket to take care of his mother and sister. Dabney was always her friendly self, saying, "Don't you two look cute! Have fun now!"

But when George proposed, Dabney chewed on her pearls for a long time, instead of jumping up to congratulate me. And I thought, *Oh boy, I know what that means.*

Dabney spent the next six months hinting that I should cancel the wedding. But I was in love. I told Dabney that I didn't care about the green fog. I would not be talked out of marrying George.

At the Methodist church, as Dabney, who was serving as my maid of honor, arranged the hem of my dress, she said, "Nina, my darling, I'm going to tell you this now while I still can. I don't think George is the man for you. I think you should run out the back door. In fact, I'll go with you. We can go to Murray's for a bottle of rum and get drunk instead. We can go dancing at the Chicken Box."

I looked down at Dabney and laughed nervously. I knew Dabney was right—and not because Dabney had been blessed with a sixth sense, but because I felt it inside myself.

"Well," I said. "It's too late now."

George and I bought a house on Hooper Farm Road. In a span of seven years, I had five children: two sons, then a daughter, then twin sons. George's mother and unmarried sister lived down the street, so I was able to continue working at the Chamber. I had to work—we needed the money and I needed the time out of the house for my sanity. Things were crazy but I was happy enough, and I was tickled to prove Dabney wrong. The green haze had been an illusion, caused by Dabney's own prejudice.

But then things went south with our finances. After doing a little digging, I discovered that George was a regular at Mohegan Sun and Foxwoods, he had a bookie in Vegas, he had gambled away all our savings, and the kids' college funds. He had taken out a line of credit on our house and after three missed payments, the bank repossessed it. George and I and the kids were forced to move in with George's mother and sister. I lasted for fourteen months, then I found a year-round rental and left George.

"You were right," I said to Dabney. "I never should have married him."

"You have the kids," Dabney said.

I hid my face in my hands.

It was amazing to me that I could know someone my whole life, I could live with him for nine years, sleep next to him in bed every night, give birth to five of his progeny, hold his hand during the Lord's Prayer at Mass, high-five him when our eldest son got his first base hit, believe every word that came out of his mouth—including the made-up reasons for his trips off-island every Sunday—and still not know him at all. The only thing being married to George Mobley had taught me was that other people are a mystery. And the people who lie and keep secrets are always the people you'd least expect.

DABNEY

She lasted three days without giving in.

Box returned to Harvard for the end of his semester: he had exams, graduation, then the class reunions, including his own fortieth.

Dabney lied to Ted Field, and to Box, and to Nina, telling them she felt better. She did not feel better. She felt worse. She was exhausted, she had no appetite, and she had pains all through her middle—shooting pains as well as a general ache. But this wasn't something antibiotics could cure. She had been infected by Clen's return.

Dabney couldn't stop thinking about him: Clen wearing Chuck Taylors like a teenager, Clen riding his bike like a teenager, Clen with one arm. *I have suffered a pretty serious loss...*

Dabney had loved Clendenin Hughes since she was fourteen years old, when he told their English teacher, Mr. Kane, that Flannery O'Connor wrote like an angry, lonely woman. Dabney could picture Clen in his jeans and his flannel shirt and his ratty Chuck Taylors, his hair too long, the inflamed pimples on his temple, his knee constantly jogging up and down because his body held energy that could not be contained. He had been on the island for only a couple of weeks at the time of his parry with Mr. Kane. Mr. Kane had said to Clen, *And how do you know what an angry, lonely woman sounds like?* And Clen had said, *I live with one.* The rest of the class laughed, but his answer had struck Dabney as painfully honest. Then and there, she decided she was his.

Dabney had been matchmaking since the ninth grade, but what nobody knew was that the first couple she had set up was herself, with Clen. On the day he spoke out in Mr. Kane's English class, Dabney's field of vision had turned pink. She had thought there was something wrong with her, possibly a migraine, but as days passed, she realized that the pink appeared only when she was in Clen's presence—and so it became clear that the pink meant she had fallen madly and forever in love. The second time she saw this pink it was surrounding Ginger O'Brien as Ginger watched Phil Bruschelli play basketball in the high school gym. Ginger and Phil had been married for twenty-nine years. All the couples Dabney had set up had been bathed in luscious pink and all were still together—perfect matches, forty-two of them.

How had she been wrong about Clen?

Did the magic of it not apply to her own self, perhaps?

It had started out well. Dabney had pursued Clen's friendship; she initiated conversations, first about books and then later about more personal things. In December of that year, a surprise early snowfall came to Nantucket, and Dabney invited Clen to go tobogganing. He had kissed her at the top of the hill at Dead Horse Valley, and that was that. They had been together for nine years before Clen left for Thailand—all through high school, through four years of long-distance while Dabney was at Harvard and Clen at Yale, and then back together on Nantucket for a year, both of them living with their respective parents, Dabney managing a T-shirt shop in town, Clen writing for the *Nantucket Standard*.

That final year had been difficult. Dabney finally felt safe and content, home and at peace on her island, but Clen had been restless and angry, still the boy whose energy could not be contained.

Had Dabney thought their relationship would last? She hadn't been able to imagine the alternative.

But it had not lasted, no, not at all. Clen had left for Thailand, and there had followed twenty-seven years of silence. And yet something *had* lasted because Dabney couldn't stop thinking about the man. It was absurd! Dabney was furious with herself. No one else could control her. She would not go to Clen today, or tomorrow. She would not go to him, ever. But certainly he knew where she lived? Everyone on Nantucket knew that Dabney Kimball Beech lived in the fish lots, on Charter Street. He could look her up in the phone book; she was plainly listed. Furthermore, he could come walking into the Chamber whenever he pleased.

It was for this reason, or so she told herself, that Dabney left work on the third afternoon and drove out the Polpis Road. She would see Clen, say hello and goodbye, and leave. If she bumped into him on the street, it would be awkward, but at least the initial contact would be out of the way.

However, as she approached the mailbox marked 432, she hit the gas rather than the brake, and sped right past. She kept going—past Sesachacha Pond, past Sankaty Head Golf Course, through the village of Sconset, until she was back on the Milestone Road heading west. The top was down on the Impala and she howled into the open sky. She felt like she had won some kind of game or contest. Clendenin Hughes wanted to see her! But she would not go!

She tossed and turned that night with the knowledge that Clendenin Hughes was on the island, in his bed. She knew he was thinking of her.

She got up several times to peer out the window to see if he was standing in the street in front of her house. He had never seen her Impala. When he'd left, three cars ago, she was still driving the Nova.

So many years had passed. She knew from reading about him when he won the Pulitzer that he had never married or had other children.

She thought about taking a sleeping pill. Box had some in the medicine cabinet left over from his knee replacement, but instead Dabney lay wide-eyed in bed. She was too antsy to read—even Jane Austen wouldn't soothe her—and she had no appetite. She felt the velvet dark of four o'clock change into the birdsong hour of five o'clock, which slid into the first pearly light of six o'clock. She went downstairs and made coffee. She put on clothes for her power walk—her gray yoga pants and a crimson T-shirt emblazoned with a white *H*. (Box kept her outfitted like a faculty wife, though she had been to campus only twice since she'd graduated.) She slipped on her headband, drank her coffee standing up, and tied her sneakers. She set out onto the streets of Nantucket an hour earlier than normal, which wasn't like her, but that stood to reason as she was not feeling at all herself.

She arrived back at the house at quarter past seven, energized. She ate a piece of whole grain toast with blueberry jam and half a banana. Tomorrow, she would eat the other half of the banana over her shredded wheat. Everything was fine, normal.

It was only in the shower that she started to cry. The weight of the sleepless night and the enormous burden of the situation poured over her. She got out of the shower, threw on her yoga pants and a T-shirt, and, with her hair still wet, she climbed into her car.

He was sitting on the porch of the cottage in a granny rocker, smoking a cigarette, with a gun across his lap like a character in a John Wayne Western. His beard made him look like a hermit, or a serial killer.

When Dabney stepped out of the car, he didn't seem at all surprised. He dropped the cigarette into a jar of water at his feet and it hissed upon extinguishing.

"Hey, Cupe," he said.

Hey, Cupe.

His voice. She had not accounted for how hearing his voice would affect her. She feared she might cry, then she realized that crying was far too mild a reaction. She would do something else. She would melt, or turn into a pillar of salt, or spontaneously combust. What happened to a person placed in a situation like this?

Box might try to turn this into a formula: if one started with the amount Dabney had loved Clen, then took its derivative and divided it by twenty-seven years, one would certainly end with only a small decimal of 1 percent. Dabney should feel nothing, or practically nothing. She should be able to say, *Hey, Beast*—because in their long-ago life, that had been their private nomenclature, Cupe and Beast—and shake Clen's hand or give him a gentle hug because of his arm, and say, *So, how have you* been?

Dabney briefly closed her eyes: pink. Pink was normally a cause for celebration. But not today.

Clen descended the porch steps and stood before her, and she was funneled into the green glen and weak tea of his Scottish hazel eyes. He was older, and bigger, and lopsided, but the sound of his voice and the beauty of his eyes threatened to bring Dabney to her knees. Their love had been a castle, the castle had been reduced to rubble, and Dabney had cleared the rubble away teaspoon by teaspoon for more than a quarter century until she was sure there was nothing left but a barren clearing inside her.

Why then this rush of feeling, a molten stream of pure silver desire, and a golden glinting of what she feared was love. It had been so many years since she'd felt love like this—love she had known only with Clendenin, love she had forsaken but that she had secretly hoped and prayed would return—that she barely recognized it.

Love.

She couldn't speak. It was just as it had been when she saw him in Sconset on his bicycle. She could not get air. Was she going to faint again? She did *not* feel well. The return of Clendenin Hughes was killing her.

"You came," he said.

His voice.

She broke. Sobbing, tears, she felt raw, exposed, and human. Before the e-mail had arrived in her in-box (subject line: *Hello*), it had been months since Dabney had cried. The death of their dog, Henry. And before that it had been years—tears of joy, Agnes's graduation from high school, again from college.

"You are still so beautiful," Clen said. "Exactly as I pictured you. You look just as you did when you stood on the wharf as my ferry pulled away."

"Stop it!" Dabney screamed. She was shocked at the volume and pitch of her voice, shocked that her voice worked at all. But really, how *dare* he start out by conjuring the worst day of her life! He had been standing at the railing of the Steamship on a blindingly blue September day. He had waved at Dabney, shouting out, *I love you, Cupe! I love you!* Dabney had been unable to shout or wave back. She had stood still as a post, mute with sorrow and fear and regret—and anger at herself for the weakness and failings of her psyche. *She could not go with him.* She felt as perhaps the first Dabney—Dabney Margaret Wright—had felt when she stood in nearly the same spot and watched her husband, Warren, set sail on the whaling ship *Lexington*.

Dabney Margaret Wright would never see her husband again.

Dabney Kimball had seen pink with Clendenin for so many years that she had been convinced they would end up together. But watching him disappear toward the horizon shook her confidence. She thought, *I will never see Clendenin Hughes again.*

Yet, here he was.

He moved to embrace her. She batted at him, pummeled his chest—still being careful of his missing arm; weird how Dabney could be afraid of something that wasn't there—but Clen pulled her in with his one strong arm, brought her close. She could smell him, he smelled the same, and he was still the same relentless bastard. He *would not quit* until the world saw things his way.

"Let go of me!" Dabney said.

"No," he said. "I will not let go. I waited far too long for this moment. I have wanted nothing more in this life than to hold you again."

"Stop!" Dabney said.

"Just relax," Clen said. "You can walk away and never come back, but please just give me a moment to hold you and give you one kiss."

Dabney succumbed. She hugged him fiercely around the middle and inhaled his scent and felt a rush of desire so strong it made her dizzy, and she wobbled. She felt Clen's mouth in the part of her hair, and the warmth of this was unbearable. She raised her face to him and then they were kissing. It was insane, reckless kissing, kissing like Dabney had never known—but that wasn't quite true. It was kissing like Dabney had known only with Clendenin when they were teenagers, when the wonder of kissing had first entered their lives. Their mouths, lips, tongues were searching, hungry, aching. It was that kind of kissing, so old it was new again, and with the kissing came desire so intense it hurt. He was instantly hard against her leg. She remembered sex with him, how desperate and mind-altering it had been, how it had felt like the earth was tilting, how she had howled with the first shuddering orgasms of her young body, and how he had placed the side of his hand into her mouth for her to bite so that her cries would be stifled. He would later show her the teeth marks and they would climb onto their bikes and ride to the pharmacy for strawberry frappes, Clen grinning like a fool, Dabney sweetly sore and tender against her bicycle seat.

So many things she had not allowed herself to remember.

She pulled away and there was a sucking sound, like a vacuum seal being broken. The sun went behind the clouds.

"I can't," she said.

"You can," he said. He was short of breath. "You just did."

"That was…I don't know what that was."

He growled a laugh. *Beast.* She had called him Beast because of his size, and his unruly dark hair, and his noises, and the ferocity that surfaced in him when he got riled. When she was first getting to know him, he reminded her of a character from a fairy tale—not an animal per se, but not quite human, either. He had arrived on Nantucket wounded from his life before, in Attleboro. His alcoholic father had drunk himself to death at the kitchen table. Clen had been wild and strange, and the smartest person Dabney had ever known.

"I'm married," she said.

"I don't care," he said.

No, of course he wouldn't care. He had bucked against convention and authority and *the rules* the entire time Dabney had known him. She assumed this was still true. He had graduated as valedictorian of their high school class, but had barely escaped being expelled for losing his temper with their history teacher, Mr. Druby, over the philosophical stands of Malcolm X. Clen had used profanity in his outrage, and he had called Mr. Druby an ignoramus (which Dabney had thought sounded like some kind of dinosaur), and it was only the ensuing wrath of Clen's mother, Helen Hughes (for everyone, including the principal, was afraid of Helen Hughes), that had saved Clen.

"I don't care if you don't care," Dabney said. "I care. Box is a good man."

"The economist," Clen said with derision.

"Yes."

He was studying her. She couldn't meet his eyes; it was too dangerous. Green glen and weak tea, Scottish hazel, the most mesmerizing eyes she had ever seen. Dabney knew this because they were also Agnes's eyes.

Oh, God, Agnes.

Dabney said, "I have to go."

"Come inside," he said. "See my place."

"No," she said.

"Just come look," he said. "Then you can leave. It's a step up from the shack behind the Lobster Trap."

The shack where Clen used to live with his mother, who waited tables at the restaurant. Dabney had lost her virginity in that shack, at Christmastime of her junior year in high school, while Helen Hughes had been off-island, shopping.

She didn't exactly agree, but she found herself following Clen up the steps to the porch of the cottage.

"What's with the gun?" she said.

"BB gun," he said. "I've been shooting one-handed at the crows."

Inside, the cottage was like a very large five-star hotel room, done up in a rustic beach theme. King bed with Frette linens, honey onyx marble in the bathroom. There was a well-appointed galley kitchen and a long pine table where a computer hummed. Legal pads and pens and newspapers were strewn about, anchored down by half-a-dozen dirty coffee cups. There was also a highball glass containing a scant inch of what Dabney knew was bourbon.

He told her that the cottage and the main house belonged to a wealthy Washington family who came to Nantucket only the first three weeks of August, and then again for a week at Thanksgiving, when Joe Biden was a regular guest at dinner. The main house had six bedrooms, Clen said, a gourmet kitchen, and a swimming pool. The family was allowing Clen to live rent-free because he had won a Pulitzer and because he had agreed to do the simple caretaking duties he could physically handle during the eleven months the big house lay fallow. This basically meant that Clen was to make sure the house didn't burn to the ground or get robbed. He was to make sure the thermostat stayed at sixty-five degrees so that the pipes didn't freeze.

"I want you to come back tomorrow," he said. "I'll make you lunch."

She said, "I can't come back."

"Yes, you can."

"I'm *married,* Clen."

"I saw your husband, the professor, on the street in Sconset, you know. He was hurrying after you, I supposed."

"Yes," Dabney said. "I fainted."

"Fainted?" Clen said. "Because of me?"

"Well, seeing you didn't help."

"But you came here today, to see me. And if you came today, you can come tomorrow."

"No, I can't."

"Why not?"

"Because!" she said.

"Because why?"

"Will you stop?" she said.

"No. I will not stop. I returned to Nantucket for you. Because I haven't stopped loving you for one second."

It was her turn to growl, but her growl sounded like the final bleat of a lamb about to be slaughtered. "I don't believe you."

"I dated one other woman," Clen said. "Her name was Mi Linh, Vietnamese woman, beautiful."

Dabney flinched.

"Our relationship lasted five years," he said. "We lived together in Hanoi. At the Chinese New Year, I bought her a strand of pearls. She wore the pearls to dinner at the Hotel Metropole. They looked fine on her, but I asked her to take them off. I asked her never to wear them again." He coughed, and even his coughing was familiar. He had started smoking the day he got to New Haven. Dabney hated herself for holding on to all these details. "She threw them in Hoan Kiem Lake. An offering for the turtle."

"Lovely," Dabney said.

"I was glad to see the pearls disappear," he said. "Pearls were you. Mi Linh wasn't you, and never would be. We broke up a few weeks later."

Dabney let the last words of that story float away on the air.

"Why now?' she said.

Coughing. Deep breath. "My arm."

She nodded. "What happened?"

"If you come back tomorrow," Clen said, "I'll tell you."

She opened her mouth to say, *I'm not coming back tomorrow,* but she saw little point in continuing the verbal tug-of-war with him. She turned to go.

"I'm going to make you take your words back," he said.

"What words?" she said.

A beat of silence. She made the mistake of meeting his eyes. Weak legs. But no. *Forbearance.*

"You know what words," he said.

And then, suddenly, she did know.

"Goodbye, Clen," she said.

Dabney called Nina at home and asked her to come into the office right away, even though it was barely eight thirty. Across the street, the newspaper van was unloading at the Hub, but aside from that, Main Street was quiet.

Nina climbed the stairs heavily, then perched on the edge of her desk, her expression that of a person about to jump off a building. "Am I being fired?" she asked.

"What?" Dabney said. "No. Gosh, no. Why would you ever think that?"

"In eighteen years, you have never asked me to come in early," Nina said.

This was true. If there had been a need to come to work early, Dabney had been the one to do it.

"I'm not firing you, Nina," Dabney said. "I would never fire you." Nina accepted the cup of coffee that Dabney had gotten her from the pharmacy. She took the white plastic top off the cup and blew. Normally, Dabney brought Nina a cup of ice, too, but today she was so nervous that it had slipped her mind. It hadn't occurred to Dabney that Nina might be nervous, too.

"What is it, then?" Nina said. She squinted at Dabney as if maybe the answer were written in small print on Dabney's forehead.

Dabney began to pace the small office. She knew every inch of it by heart: the wall of brochures of each of the Chamber members, the towering stacks of Chamber guides, the photographs of Ram Pasture at sunset and Great Point Lighthouse, taken by Abigail Pease, the frayed oriental rug that Dabney had rescued from her father's house on Prospect Street, the two desks that had been salvaged from the old police station. She and Nina referred to them as their *Dragnet* desks. Dabney worked at her father's old desk; she remembered sitting at it as a girl as her father processed paperwork for a DUI, or joked with Shannon, the pretty, blond dispatcher. The Chamber office was her home, but it offered her zero comfort right now.

Dabney said, "We've worked together for so long that you probably think you know everything about me."

"Almost everything," Nina said.

"Almost everything," Dabney said. "However, I'm pretty sure

what I say next will shock you." Dabney sipped her coffee. Diana at the pharmacy made Dabney's coffee perfectly—cream, six sugars, two dashes of cinnamon—every single morning. But today, this also offered zero comfort.

"What?" Nina asked. "What will shock me?"

Was Dabney really going to say it? She had been taught the lyrics to "American Pie" by an Irish chambermaid named May at the Park Plaza Hotel decades earlier. Singing it always calmed Dabney's nerves. *Bye bye, Miss American Pie.*

"Clendenin Hughes has come back to the island," Dabney said.

Nina spilled coffee down the front of her blouse. This, Dabney had predicted. She handed Nina a wad of napkins.

"It gets worse," Dabney said. "I went to see him this morning. As in, a little while ago."

"Oh my gosh golly, golly gosh," Nina said. There were long seconds of processing this; Dabney watched Nina work through her shock. "Well." Pause. "Really." Pause. "Of course you went to see him." Pause. "How could you not?"

Dabney and Nina had not been friends when Dabney and Clen split, but you didn't work across from someone for eighteen years and not tell her all the secrets of your heart.

Nina said, "And did you…"

Drove my Chevy to the levee but the levee was dry. "I kissed him," Dabney whispered.

"You did?" Nina said. She did some deep Lamaze-type breathing, which she usually saved for phone conversations with her ex-husband, George. "Wow. Wowowowow. This is big. This is huge. Do you remember five or six years ago when I asked you…"

"Of course I remember," Dabney said.

If Clendenin Hughes ever came back to Nantucket, Nina had asked, *what would you do?*

And Dabney had said, *I will stand on my head and spit in my shoe.*

"So now what?" Nina asked.

"He asked me to go over there tomorrow," Dabney said. "He said he would make me lunch."

"More likely he wants to eat you for lunch," Nina said.

"Nina!"

"I think you should go," Nina said. "It's not like we're talking about some cute waiter from the Boarding House. We're talking about Clendenin Hughes. Your first true love."

My only true love, Dabney thought. Then she hated herself.

"I can't do it," Dabney said. "I won't do it."

"I hate to break this to you, Dabney," Nina said. "But you're not the first person in the history of the world to think about having a love affair. I almost did it myself."

"You did not!" Dabney said.

"With Jack Copper," Nina said. "I was at the Anglers' Club one night when George was off-island, gambling, although I didn't know that at the time. Jack and I were talking and drinking, and drinking and talking—and then I said I had to leave and he said he'd walk me to my car. He kissed me good night in the parking lot and...it could have gone further. He wanted it to, and so did I. But I stopped it."

Dabney exhaled. "Because you are a good and faithful person."

"I've always regretted it," Nina said.

"Have you?" Dabney said.

"I have," Nina said. "Sometimes you regret the things you do, but they're over and done. Regretting the things you didn't do is tougher, because they're still out there...haunting you. The what-ifs."

Dabney considered this for a second. It was true: Clendenin

Hughes had haunted her all these years. Not going to Bangkok haunted her. The what-may-have-been haunted her.

Nina said, "I have to say, I'm relieved."

"Relieved?"

"I really thought you were going to fire me. Or tell me something awful, like you were dying."

My only true love. Dabney felt like she was dying. Her insides were in an agonizing knot. She reached for her pearls and started gnawing. Then the office phone rang and Dabney and Nina both sat down at their desks for business as usual.

Before she answered the phone, Dabney said, "You won't say a word about this, right?"

Nina said, "I'm insulted that you had to ask."

The following day at eleven thirty, an e-mail popped up in Dabney's in-box from Clendenin Hughes. Subject line: *Are you coming to lunch?*

Dabney clicked on the e-mail, but there was nothing else to read. She deleted the e-mail, then deleted it from her deleted file.

The following Monday, she saw Clendenin's bicycle on Main Street. It was leaning up against a tree right in Dabney's line of vision. If Clen knew how her desk was positioned in the office, he would have realized that she couldn't look out her window without seeing the bicycle.

Dabney stood up and stretched.

She said to Nina, "Do you mind if I open the window?"

"Be my guest," Nina said.

Dabney threw up the sash and peered out to get a closer look. Was it Clen's bicycle? Silver ten-speed with the ratty tape unraveling from the curved handlebars. A relic. Definitely Clen's bicycle.

"It's balmy," Nina said.

"Huh?" Dabney said.

He had left it there on purpose, she decided. To taunt her.

She sat back down at her desk. She had packed herself a lovely BLT on toasted Portuguese bread for lunch, using the first hothouse tomatoes from Bartlett Farm. But she couldn't eat a thing. She still felt awful. In the morning, she decided, she would start the course of antibiotics that Dr. Field had prescribed.

She said, "I'm going to run some errands."

"Errands?" Nina said.

"I'm going to light a candle at church," Dabney said.

Nina squinted at her. "What?"

"For my father's birthday."

"Your father's birthday was last week," Nina said.

"I know," Dabney said. "And I forgot to light a candle. And I need some thread from the sewing center."

"Thread?" Nina said.

"My Bermuda bag is missing a button," Dabney said.

"You don't know how to sew a button," Nina said. "Bring it to me. I'll do it."

Dabney signed out on the log, writing "errands." "I'll be right back," she said.

When Dabney got down to the street, she headed straight for Clen's bicycle. He hadn't even bothered to lock it up; he was still living in Nantucket 1987. Anyone might steal it. Dabney considered climbing on it herself and pedaling away.

Then she realized how difficult it would be to lock up a bike with only one arm, and she felt awful.

She looked around. Where was he? He had parked in front of

the pharmacy. Was he at the lunch counter, having a strawberry frappe? She poked her head in.

Diana, a stunning West Indian with her head wrapped in a hot-pink bandanna, saw Dabney and waved. "Hey, lady!"

The hot pink caught Dabney's eye. Pink pink pink. But Clen wasn't at the counter. Dabney felt a stab of disappointment.

Dabney waved and said, "Hello, lovey, goodbye, lovey, I have to dash!"

"Busy lady!" Diana said.

Dabney hurried down the street to the Hub. Clen and his newspapers; of course, *of course* he was at the Hub. Dabney straightened her headband. The day *was* balmy, and she feared she was perspiring. Just the walk down the street had left her winded and a little dizzy. Tomorrow, the antibiotics.

Dabney stepped into the Hub, one of her favorite spots in town, with its smell of newsprint and penny candy. Greeting cards, magazines, fake Nantucket Lightship baskets, buckets of seashells and starfish, Christmas ornaments, saltwater taffy.

No Clen.

She left the Hub and stood on the corner. Where was he? She had been so strong, she had deleted his e-mail, she had not driven back out the Polpis Road, she had not given in to temptation, but it had taken nothing more than seeing the bicycle to start her chasing him.

And what would she do when she found him? What would she say?

She would say: *I want you to leave. There's no reason for you to be here. You said you came back for me, but your mere presence on this island is making me . . . ill. Ill, Clen. I can't handle it. I'm sorry, I do realize it's a free country, but you have to go.*

She gazed down Federal Street.

Post office? Was he mailing a letter back to Vietnam, to beautiful Mi Linh?

Dabney was jealous of Mi Linh, a woman who had thrown a perfectly good strand of pearls into a lake for a turtle. Surely that had been a joke?

Dabney headed to Saint Mary's to light a candle for her father. Her father had never really liked Clendenin; her father had found him smug. Her father used to say, *That boy is too smart for his own good.*

Dabney walked up the ramp of the church, holding on to the hand railing. She was sweating. One place she was certain *not* to see Clendenin Hughes was the Catholic church.

Cool, dim, quiet, peaceful: the inside of the church was a salve. Dabney inserted two dollar bills into the collection box and said a prayer for her father. Then, something she had never, ever done before: she fed the box two more dollars and said a prayer for her mother.

Bye bye, Miss American Pie.

She emerged from the church feeling calm, light, and virtuous.

When she headed back up Main Street, she couldn't believe her eyes.

Clen's bicycle was gone.

Exasperating!

That night, she couldn't sleep.

The following night, no sleep.

The third night, at two o'clock in the morning, she called Box. He answered the phone on the eleventh ring. Anyone in her right mind would have realized the poor man was asleep and hung up.

"Professor Beech," he said. He must have thought the call was a drunk student who had mustered the courage to complain about a grade.

"Do you love me?" Dabney asked.

"What?" Box said. "Dabney? What is it? What's wrong?"

"Do you *love* me?" she said.

"Yes. Of course I love you."

"Don't 'of course' me," Dabney said. "Tell me something real. Tell me how you really feel."

"What on earth is wrong with you? Did you have a dream?"

"We aren't close anymore," Dabney said. "You're always *working!* We never have sex anymore."

"Sex?" Box said, as though he'd never heard the word before. "You do realize that I have to administer final exams to three hundred students in the morning, right?"

"I don't give a hoot about your three hundred students!" Dabney said. "I want to know if you love me. If you desire me."

There was a pause. Then a sigh. "Yes, darling, I love you. You are my heart's desire."

"Am I?" Dabney said.

"Yes, Dabney. You are."

"Okay," Dabney said, but she was not placated.

"Good night," Box said.

Dabney hung up.

She woke up in the morning exhausted and anxious, which was not good, because it was the day that she and Nina were interviewing job candidates. They had enough money in their budget to hire two information assistants and pay them twenty dollars an hour to answer the phones, which would start ringing nonstop the Thursday before Memorial Day.

One of the assistants would be Celerie Truman, who had worked at the Chamber the summer before. Celerie—pronounced like the underappreciated vegetable—was the most enthusiastic information assistant Dabney had hired in twenty-two years. Celerie had been a cheerleader at the University of Minnesota and had discovered Nantucket through her college roommate. She was the kind of peppy individual who could shout cheers in a stadium of sixty thousand people while wearing shorts and a halter top in minus-thirty-degree weather. And she had turned out to be a magnificent ambassador for Nantucket. Certain visitors had stopped by the Chamber office just to meet Celerie because she had been so helpful on the phone.

Dabney was relieved to have someone as knowledgeable and on the ball as Celerie back in the office. No training necessary. Celerie was a disciple of the Dabney Way of Doing Things. By the end of last summer, she had even started coming to work wearing a strand of pearls.

They had to hire only one other person. Nina had placed a classified ad, and this had garnered the usual hundred applicants. Nina, through years of experience, had winnowed the list of potential candidates down to three of the most promising for herself and Dabney to interview.

"The first guy is twenty-six years old, between years of dental school at Penn. He started coming to Nantucket when he was ten. His parents own a house in Pocomo, so he'll live with them."

"Dental school," Dabney said, yawning. The lack of sleep had left ugly black circles under her eyes, and she thought her skin was turning a funny color. "That's a first." She checked with Nina for confirmation. "Right? We've never had a dental student?"

"Law school, medical school, Rhodes scholar, the guy writing his doctoral dissertation on the Betty Ford Clinic after having been there three times, the wacky woman who was writing the Broadway musical..."

"Ruthie," Dabney said. "She brought the worst-smelling lunches."

Nina held up her hand. "Let's not talk about it."

"A dental student sounds good," Dabney said. "Clean, hygienic. Not like the guy from Denmark who never bathed."

"Franzie," Nina said. "Let's not talk about him, either."

"What's this kid's name?" Dabney asked.

"Riley Alsopp," Nina said.

Dabney had been hiring information assistants for twenty-two years and her instincts were spot-on; despite smelly lunches and body odor, Dabney had never actually had to fire anyone. As soon as she met Riley Alsopp and noted his excellent handshake and heard his pleasant speaking voice and took in his brilliant smile, and his needlepoint belt featuring hammerhead sharks ("My mother made it for me") and the copy of *One Flew Over the Cuckoo's Nest* under his arm ("I've decided to go back and read the classics this summer"), Dabney's mood instantly improved. She knew there would be no reason to interview any other candidates. When they were finished with Riley, she could go home and take a nap.

She sat Riley Alsopp down, brought him a cold bottle of water, admired his thick brown hair and his tapered fingers and his battered boat shoes, and asked the standard first question.

"Why do you want to work at the Chamber of Commerce, Riley?"

She closed her eyes for a second and thought: *Please do not say, "Because I want to work in town." Please do not say, "Because it seems easy." Please do not say, "Because I worked as a waiter at the Languedoc last summer and I got caught stealing from the till." Please, please,* please *do not say, "Because Celerie Truman is my girlfriend and we thought it would be fun to work together."*

He took a breath and laughed a little. "I guess there's only one reason. Because I love Nantucket."

Dabney beamed at Nina and Nina squinted back at Dabney

and gave a nearly imperceptible nod. Dabney knew what Nina was thinking: *We have interviewed scores of candidates together and only a handful have ever given us this simple, perfect answer.*

Dabney said, "You're hired!"

"Really?" Riley said. "Just like that? I memorized all these facts and statistics about the island. Don't you want to hear them?"

"Nope," Dabney said. "I trust you. But I do have two questions: when can you start and when do you have to leave?"

"I can start tomorrow," Riley said. "And I go back to dental school on September fifteenth, so I can work until the twelfth or so."

"Wonderful!" Dabney said. What a bonus! Most information assistants said they could work until Labor Day, but then their grandmother would die sometime around the twentieth of August, and either Dabney or Nina got stuck answering the phone for the remainder of the summer.

They all agreed that Riley would start work the following Monday, he would bring two forms of ID for his W-2, and he would meet Celerie.

As Riley Alsopp was walking toward the door, he stopped at Dabney's desk and picked up a framed photograph of Agnes.

"Is this your *daughter?*" he asked. "Or, wait…your sister?"

Dabney tried not to let any gloating show on her face. People always mistook her and Agnes for sisters.

"My daughter, Agnes."

Riley Alsopp stared at the photograph. It was an artsy black-and-white shot of Agnes standing at the top of Main Street in the snow. She wore a white knit hat and gloves, and her long, dark hair cascaded over her white ski parka. "She's beautiful," Riley said. "Like, *really beautiful.*"

Dabney studied Riley for a moment, and something inside her

unfolded. "Thank you," she said. She, of course, thought Agnes was the loveliest creature ever to grace the earth, but Dabney was always surprised when other people called Agnes beautiful. Dabney sometimes felt almost jealous, believing Agnes was hers alone to appreciate. But Dabney was pleased by Riley Alsopp's compliment. She could tell that it was genuine.

"Do you have a girlfriend?" Dabney asked. As soon as she asked, she realized the question was inappropriate and absolutely none of her business.

"I'm free as a bird," Riley said. "The only two females in my life are my mother and my chocolate Lab, Sadie."

His mother and his chocolate Lab, Sadie? What a doll! It took everything Dabney had not to swoon.

BOX

He stood at the lectern and read aloud the standard exam procedure while Miranda Gilbert passed out blue books to the squirming, anxious Econ 10 students. Box was dreadfully old-fashioned, he knew; nearly everyone else at Harvard administered exams via the Internet, but Box refused. Next year, he would have to capitulate. Next year, he supposed, the company that made blue books would be out of business.

He yawned, more loudly than he meant to, into the microphone. One of the students in the back row called out, "Late night, Professor Beech?"

A muted chuckle rippled through the room. Miranda turned to offer him a sympathetic smile, and Box said, "You all fail," which roused genuine laughter.

He had not been able to fall back asleep after the phone call from Dabney.

Tell me something real, she had said. *Tell me how you really feel.*

He had really felt annoyed, and unamused. Two o'clock in the morning! Had she been drinking? he wondered. The call was entirely out of character. Dabney had never, ever, not once in twenty-four years of marriage, done anything like that.

We're not close anymore. We don't have sex anymore. I want to know if you love me. If you desire me.

Normally, after the Econ 10 exam, Box took Miranda to lunch; it was the only time during the semester that he did so. He liked to keep their relationship professional; this was really the best way, especially since they spent so much time together. It was always Miranda who tried to forge something like a friendship. She occasionally coaxed Box out to see a movie, which he agreed to only when the solitude was getting to him. They dined together with colleagues, but never alone, except for this one lunch. Box didn't want people to talk, although he assumed people talked anyway. Miranda was a very beautiful woman, smart as a wizard, and she'd worked for him for four years, demonstrating her loyalty, patience, and steadfastness. Box could recognize all her enticing qualities without feeling anything romantic. His only mistress was his work, his reputation, his career. But it was helpful to have boundaries.

The phone call from Dabney was bothering him so much that he decided it was best, all the way around, if he passed on lunch with Miranda.

"I'm afraid the chap in row thirty-five was correct," Box said. "I didn't sleep well last night. I have to forego our usual lunch, I'm afraid. I'm sorry."

"No apology necessary," Miranda said, though her rich, plummy voice was clipped. He had hurt her feelings, he supposed. It seemed that where the women in his life were concerned, he could do nothing right.

DABNEY

Thursday morning, there was an e-mail in her in-box from Clendenin Hughes. Subject line: *?*

Dabney clicked on it, thinking, *?!???!!*

It said: Meet me tonight at 9:00, Quaker Cemetery.

"Oh my God!" Dabney said, then she clapped her hand over her mouth. Again, the Lord's name in vain! All the virtue she felt after lighting the candles on Monday evaporated.

"What?" Nina said. She squinted at Dabney and lowered her voice to a whisper. "Is it Clen?"

Dabney nodded. It was a relief to have someone to tell. Keeping it bottled up inside wasn't healthy. "He wants me to meet him at the Quaker Cemetery tonight," she said.

"That's spooky," Nina said. "Will you go?"

"No," Dabney said. "No way."

On Thursday nights Dabney always stayed home for Sandwich and a Movie, and this Thursday, she decided, would be no different. She picked up a Cubano from Foood For Here & There, arranged it on a plate with some potato chips, fixed herself a glass of ice water with lemon, and switched on the TV in the den. She noticed that *Love Story* was playing on TMC, starting five minutes hence. *Love Story* was Dabney's favorite movie of all time; that had been true even before she went to Harvard. One year, Dabney had dressed up as Jennifer Cavalleri for Halloween, which basically meant she wore what she usually wore—a red turtleneck, headband, and pearls—and carried a copy of *Love Story,* the novel, as a clue to her identity.

Dabney could have recited the script line-for-line: there was Jenny calling Oliver "Preppie," there were Oliver and Jenny in Widener Library, there they were driving up to Ipswich to meet the coldhearted father, there were the hockey games and the scene where Jenny is beautifully tanned on the sailboat. Jenny wants to go to Paris, but there will be no Paris. The reason she can't get pregnant is that she's sick, she has leukemia, she is going to die.

Dabney sneaked into the kitchen during a commercial to put her plate into the dishwasher and get a bar of dark chocolate. She glanced at the clock. It was 8:45.

Dabney returned to the den to watch the end of the movie, but she couldn't get comfortable. She had been taking antibiotics for three days, but she still felt lousy. And she was distracted. It was 8:48, then 8:50.

He would be there. She knew he would be there. They used to meet at the Quaker Cemetery all the time in high school. *That's spooky,* Nina had said. What was spooky was that Agnes had been conceived in the Quaker Cemetery, Dabney was sure of it.

She put on her spring coat and left the house. She decided to take Box's Wagoneer rather than the Impala. The Impala was the most recognizable car on the island.

She drove by the Quaker Cemetery at a few minutes after nine. She slowed down, her eyes scanning the southeast corner for the gravestone of Alice Booker Wright, Dabney's great-great-grandmother, which had been their usual meeting place.

She saw the outline of him—a hulking, dark figure sitting on Alice's grave.

He waved at her with his right arm.

She hit the gas.

She drove back through the streets of town thinking, *Go back, go see him, kiss him again.* Oh how she longed to kiss him again. She remembered the smell of the cut grass in that cemetery and the squish of mud under their feet and the rough-hewn edge of Alice's headstone rubbing against Dabney's back, the taste of Clen's neck, his voice, his eyes, his knee bouncing up and down, his feet shod in Chuck Taylors, how he loved them, he was stubborn, he wouldn't stop wearing them no matter how old he got. Desire presented in Dabney like mercury in her veins. *Go back to him!*

But no, she wouldn't. She pulled into her driveway and hurried back into the house, short of breath. She had left the TV on, and the final scene of the movie was playing: Oliver sitting alone in the snow.

The phone rang, startling her. Would Clen be brazen enough to call the house? Then she realized that the phone call was from Agnes. Agnes called every Thursday night at nine thirty because she knew her mother would be home for Sandwich and a Movie. Thank God that Dabney had come back! If Dabney hadn't answered, Agnes might have grown worried and called Box, and then there would have been some explaining to do.

"Darling!" Dabney said.

"Mommy?"

Dabney said, "Honey, are you okay?" Did she dare hope there was trouble in paradise, Agnes's engagement to CJ on the rocks? Oh how Dabney would inwardly rejoice!

"It's my job," Agnes said. "I found out yesterday that we didn't get funding from National for the summer. The club is shutting down until the school year starts back up." With these words, she started to cry.

"Oh, honey," Dabney said. "I'm so sorry."

"I knew it was iffy," Agnes said. "I should have mentally prepared myself."

"So what will you do all summer?" Dabney asked. She had a dreary picture in her head of Agnes working as a temp in CJ's office, fetching coffee, answering the phone.

"I'm coming home," Agnes said.

"What?" Dabney said. "To Nantucket?"

"Yes, Nantucket. I don't hate it as much as you think, Mom."

"I didn't think you hated it," Dabney said. However, Agnes didn't love Nantucket the way Dabney did. She hadn't been home for the summer since her freshman year in college. Agnes had inherited Clendenin's taste for globetrotting. There had been trips to France and Italy in high school, then a summer in Ireland, then a summer working at a camp for disadvantaged children in the Bronx, which had eventually led her to her current job. "I just thought you might want to stay in the city with CJ."

"He wants me to stay," she said. "But Manhattan stinks in the summer. I'd much rather be at the beach. I can work as a counselor at Island Adventures; I already talked to Dave Patterson. I can plan the wedding. And I can hang out with you and Dad."

Agnes was coming home for the summer! Dabney felt lightheaded.

"CJ is really busy," Agnes said. "He has to negotiate contracts before training camp starts for his football players, and one of his clients for the Yankees, I can't tell you who, is in the process of being traded to San Diego. But I'm trying to get him to come up on weekends when he can."

"Weekends," Dabney repeated. She would spend a summer's worth of weekends with CJ? When Dabney closed her eyes, she saw a thick, olive-green fog. Agnes's coming home was the best surprise Dabney could have hoped for. Dabney could save Agnes. And Agnes, quite possibly, could save Dabney.

CLENDENIN

He couldn't cut a steak, he couldn't tie his shoes, and he couldn't button the cuffs of his shirt. A grocery cart was okay, but not a grocery basket. Childproof pill bottle, forget about it. Chopping a tomato was difficult but not impossible; he hadn't yet tried to shuck corn. Typing was a slow and arduous process, so he wrote everything longhand now, then read it into a special program on his computer. He had a hard time folding his laundry, and uncorking a bottle of wine.

He could shave, but he had always hated shaving anyway, so he'd let his beard grow in for four months, two weeks, three days—the amount of time that had passed since he'd lost his arm.

Transactions like paying the pizza guy from his wallet and then accepting the hot box was a complicated dance that frustrated Clen and embarrassed the deliveryman. It was his left arm that was gone, so shaking hands was still okay.

He probably shouldn't hold a baby, but there were no babies in his life.

He could crack an egg, flip an omelet, ride his bicycle, and swim. And he could smoke, thanks to the invention of the Bic. Lighting a match was a trick from his past.

Usually when dusk descended, which happened later and later as June approached, Clen stood on his porch and took aim at the crows with his BB gun—he was getting pretty good—and then he smoked a cigarette and dropped the butt into the mayonnaise jar half filled with water at his feet. It was a nasty habit he'd picked up overseas; it had been impossible to live in Bangkok, and later Hanoi, and later still Siem Reap, and not smoke. He had thought he would give it up when he returned, but he had given up so much already that he couldn't quit the cigarettes.

He either made himself something to eat (an omelet, fried rice) or he called something in, hence the awkward relationship with the pizza-delivery guy, although Benny knew him now.

And then, when it was fully dark, Clen climbed into the car left at his disposal—he had gotten a special driver's license, valid as long as he wore his prosthetic, which he never did—and he drove into town, past the house on Charter Street where Dabney lived.

If he had told anyone he did this, they would have thought him a stalker, a creep, a man hopelessly mired in the past. He didn't feel like any of those things. He drove past Dabney's house because he liked to see the lights on and think of her inside—tossing a salad or sticking fresh flowers in a vase of water, or reading Jane Austen in bed.

He knew she was married. He knew there was next to no chance that she would leave the economist just because Clen had decided to come back. But he loved her in a way that could not be ignored, and so he was determined to try. The kiss in front of his cottage had been the kiss of a lifetime. If he got nothing else, he would be happy with that.

In every dream he'd had since being back on Nantucket, he had both his arms. It was because of Dabney. She returned him to his whole self.

Clen had found out about the baby in a letter from Dabney, the sort penned on a thin, light-blue airmail envelope—from the out-side, identical in appearance to the three letters Dabney had sent that had preceded Clen's arrival in Bangkok, those saying how much she loved and missed him. The letter about her pregnancy had reached Clen after he returned to Bangkok from a grueling three-week assignment in Pattaya, which was a more disturbing, derelict, and soulless place than Clen could have imagined existed. He had been overseas for slightly less than two months, enough time for him to have gotten a hang of the way things worked, but also to have become disenchanted.

I don't know how to say this, Dabney had written. *So I'll just say it: I'm pregnant.*

And then later in the letter: *I want nothing from you. I considered terminating but I can't bring myself to do it. I am due in May.*

May, he thought. Meaning that Dabney had gotten pregnant in August, a few weeks before he left. They had had frequent, clinging, urgent sex in those final days, and Clen had not always used a condom. One night in the Quaker Cemetery came to mind.

Their parting had gone more smoothly than he'd imagined. When the job offer came from the Southeast Asia desk of the *New York Times,* he had thought Dabney would...flip out, cry, scream, beg him not to go, threaten suicide or murder. But she had been resigned, even happy for him. She had smiled, and said, *I'm so proud of you. You have to accept, Clen. This is the opportunity of a lifetime.* She had been so even-keeled about it that he'd thought, momentarily, that she had decided to go with him.

No, she said. *I'm staying here.*

So what you're saying is we're breaking up?

She said, *We are a perfect match. No matter what happens, we're going to end up together.*

And you really believe that? he said.

Let's wait, she said. *And see what happens.*

It was the mature thing to say, but he couldn't help feeling injured by it. This was stranger still because it was *him* leaving. The two of them with their Ivy League degrees had spent the past year on Nantucket working jobs that were beneath them. Clen had been itching to go someplace bigger, more important, someplace where news was actually happening. He had been thinking of New York. A relationship with Dabney would have been plausible from New York—back every weekend or every other. But Bangkok?

He had waved goodbye to her from the Steamship, yelling her name and telling her he loved her until she was out of sight. Then, he had retched over the side of the boat.

Upon receiving Dabney's letter, Clen borrowed a thousand dollars against his future salary and bought her a plane ticket. He called her from a sweltering Western Union office, believing that now that Dabney was pregnant, she would have to come. He was far more excited about the prospect of seeing Dabney than about having a baby. What did that even mean, *having a baby*? He wasn't sure, but he had *not* expected Dabney to say what she said, which was, *I will not come there. I'm going to have this baby alone.*

What? he said.

The only way I will survive this, she said.

He didn't understand. *What?* He was shouting, despite the queue of Australian backpackers behind him, listening to his every word.

Is if you promise never to contact me again. Cold turkey. Never contact me again. Please respect my wishes. Please.

We can make it work here, he said. *I'll rent a bigger place, and hire a woman to help you with the baby!*

Clen, she said. *Please.*

Please what? He was ready to pull his hair out in frustration. *Just come, Cupe. I bought you a plane ticket.*

I can't! she said. *I'm not sure you get it, or that you've ever gotten it. I can't do it, I'm too afraid, and afraid isn't even the right word.* Clen could hear her breathing; he could tell she was trying not to cry. *I'm sorry, Clen. I just can't.*

Okay, he said. *Fine. You win. You win, Dabney! I'll quit my job. I'll come home.*

No, she said. *Absolutely not.*

What? he said.

Do you think I want you to end up like my mother? If you come back to live here on Nantucket, you will have a small life, a lot smaller than the life you're going to have overseas anyway. And you'll hate me, and you'll resent our child, and you'll take off in the middle of the night and I'll never see you again. She paused. *No,* she said. *No way. I don't want you to come home.*

I won't do that. You know I won't do that.

What I know, Dabney said, *is that you won't be happy here, writing for the* Nantucket Standard. *You're too talented. You're the hundred-year genius, just like Mr. Kane used to say. You need to face the facts.*

What facts? You're pregnant with my child.

It isn't going to work either way. It isn't going to work!

I thought you said we were a perfect match, destined to end up together!

Well, I was wrong, Dabney said. *I was terribly, horribly, awfully wrong. I have been right about everyone else, but wrong about us. There is only one solution, one way I'm going to survive, and that is if you let me go. Just please let me go.*

I can't let you go, he said. *I love you!*

Silence.

What? he said. *I leave, and suddenly you don't love me?*

She said something too softly for him to hear. He imagined her words like raindrops falling somewhere into the South Pacific.

I didn't catch that, he said.

Not suddenly, she said.

There was suggestive coughing from one of the Australians in line and Clen waved a desperate hand over his head, as if to say, *I'm drowning here, buddy. Please let me try to save myself.* This was the conversation of his life, he realized that. He also knew it might end up costing as much as the plane ticket he had just purchased.

Tell me you don't love me, he said.

I don't love you.

You're lying, he said. *You know it and I know it. You're lying, Cupe.*

You will find someone else, she said. *And so will I.*

As anyone who has ever been in love would know, those words blew him to bits, as though he had stepped on a land mine, or a booby trap set by guerrilla forces. It was the worst pain he had ever sustained. Worse than being hit by his drunk father, worse than waking up and finding his father dead at the kitchen table and then having to knock on his mother's bedroom door and tell her the news.

Okay, he said. *Fine. Cold turkey. Not another word. You understand that, Cupe? Not. Another. Word.*

He was calling her bluff, or so he'd thought.

The only way I'm going to survive is with a clean break, she said. *Please respect my wishes and let me, and this child, go. Please, please, do me the favor of never contacting me again.*

Dabney.

Silence.

Dabney!

He would have thought she'd hung up but he could still hear her breathing.

Fine, he said.

Silence.

If that's what you want, he said.

Silence.

We all make choices, he said.

He had always been smarter than everyone else, and he'd thought that might help him, but in this case it didn't matter. Possibly, it made things worse. What he imagined as the finely calibrated gears of his mind were thrown practically into reverse, so that anything he tried to do—track down a source in Surat Thani, or kick-start his motorbike, or cook rice—ended up a disaster.

In May, he learned that Dabney had given birth to a baby girl and named her Agnes Bernadette, after her grandmother. He couldn't count the number of times—when he was riding in the stinking hot third-class berth of a train, or slogging through rice paddies, or meandering through the markets looking for ripe mangoes but being offered teenaged girls—when the name had popped into his head like a chiming bell.

Agnes Bernadette.

He had heard from Agnes herself only once, shortly after her sixteenth birthday. Dabney had finally told Agnes about her true paternity and Agnes, unbeknownst to Dabney, had sent a letter to Clen in care of the *New York Times.* The letter had been forwarded to Clen, who at that time was living in Hanoi, in a good flat in the French Quarter. He had just won the Pulitzer and he had an offer for a book deal; for the one and only time in his life, he had been flush with cash, and there had finally been talk of transferring him to the Singapore desk, which had become his sole professional aspiration. Clen and his girlfriend, Mi Linh, drank a lot of champagne and ate dinner twice a week at the Hotel Metropole. They spent weekends at a resort in the cool hills of Sapa; Clen rented a junk and they sailed the emerald waters of Halong Bay.

Agnes's letter had been straightforward: she now knew that Clendenin was her real father and she wanted to meet him; her mother, however, could never find out. Agnes was spending the summer in France. Could Clendenin meet her in France?

Clen had chewed on his answer for as long as he dared. The worst thing, he realized, would be not to respond at all. He wanted very much to buy a ticket to Paris and meet Agnes there. The whole idea of it was cinematic. He understood from the tone of her letter that Agnes didn't need him to be a father; she had the economist for that. She did, however, require a connection. She was sixteen years old, on the verge of becoming a woman, trying to accrue self-awareness, and she wanted to fill in the missing link. Which was him.

What Clen couldn't swallow was this meeting taking place without Dabney's knowledge. He assumed that, seventeen years later, Dabney had made some sort of peace with his absence. She had married, she ran the Chamber of Commerce, and she had, he could only assume, a happy life. If he went behind her back and met Agnes in Paris and she found out about it—well, that wasn't something Clendenin could risk.

Clen had written back to Agnes and tried to explain all this. The letter he'd sent had been ten pages long. It was an atonement of sorts, because that many years later he had come to understand that Dabney's telling him she didn't love him was the ultimate act of love. She hadn't wanted him even to consider coming home because she knew he would be unhappy, unfulfilled. *Not returning to your mother, and by circumstance, you, is the great shame of my life. I offer no excuse other than I was young and selfish, and I believed myself to be destined for great things. In the years since I've left Nantucket, I have seen sights both sublime and horrific, and I have tried to uncover truths and bring light and sense to this often misunderstood part of the world. But although I have never met you, I have always been aware that my greatest accomplishment is that I fathered a child. You.*

Clen had both anticipated and dreaded a response. If he and Agnes started a secret correspondence, Dabney would be devastated as well. There was no good way for a relationship between them to proceed, and yet he wanted it to. He wanted it to.

But it was a moot point. Agnes never wrote back.

He couldn't reel in a fish, or dig a grave, or change a tire. He couldn't shuffle a deck of cards or deal a hand of poker. He would never be able to help Dabney fasten her pearls. This last thing bothered Clen more than he thought it might.

But he wasn't disheartened, yet. He had the kiss, which redoubled his determination. He was going to keep trying. He was going to make Dabney take those words back, and admit that she had never meant them in the first place.

Couple #40: Tammy Block and Flynn Sheehan, married three years

Tammy: *I am the match Dabney doesn't like to talk about.*

We'd all like our lives to be nice and neat. High school, college, marriage, kids, job, church, community, two-week vacations in Aruba or Tuscany—and then watch your kids, and then their kids, follow suit. Some people have lives like that, and some don't.

I dropped out of Fairleigh Dickinson University (we all called it "Fairly Ridiculous")—or, rather, I failed out—after three semesters. I just couldn't handle the reading, it put me to sleep, plus I was drinking every night and smoking a lot of dope. I married a guy I met at a biker bar, a guy I barely knew. We drove to Atlantic

City and got hitched, then we moved up to Rhode Island because my new husband was going to work as a fry cook for a buddy opening a fish restaurant. I got pregnant, had a son, then a year later, another son. My new husband left me for one of the waitresses at the fish restaurant and then those two ran off and I never saw a single support check.

I needed a way to make a living while being a full-time mom—at that point, I was qualified to be either a prostitute or work the register at the CITGO—and seeing that these were piss-poor options, I went for my real estate license.

I had a talent for selling houses, and my secret weapon was that which had served me well my whole life—apathy. You want the house? Great. You don't want the house? Someone else will.

I landed on Nantucket ten years ago the way many people land here, I suppose—I came for a vacation and decided I never wanted to leave. I sold my Victorian on Prospect Street in Providence for three times what I paid for it, banked the profit, and rented a cute three-quarter house on School Street. (Three-quarter house meant two windows to the right of the front door and one window to the left. I was crazy for architectural terminology.)

Dabney Kimball Beech lived one block over, on Charter. I used to see her out walking every morning, and I have to tell you, she didn't seem like anyone I would want to be friends with. It was the headband that put me off, I think, and the pearls. Who wore pearls at seven o'clock in the morning to go power walking? I quickly learned that Dabney was the director of the Chamber of Commerce and that she was quite beloved around the island. When I interviewed for an associate-broker position at Congdon & Coleman Real Estate and I mentioned I lived on School Street, the man interviewing me said, "Oh, you're neighbors with Dabney Kimball."

I said, "Yes."

He said, "If Nantucket elected a president, she would win by a landslide."

I decided it would be wise, as a Realtor brand-new to town, to meet Dabney Kimball, so I strategized to be out watering my front flower bed at seven in the morning when she walked past.

I thought she might ignore me, but she stopped and literally beamed at me. And that was my introduction to the magic of Dabney Kimball Beech.

She said, "Hey there! You just moved in a few weeks ago! I've been dying to meet you. I'm Dabney."

I said, "I'm Tammy Block." We shook hands.

She said, "You're the newest Realtor at Congdon & Coleman."

I had only had the job for twelve hours. How could she have known?

I said, "Yes, that's right."

She said, "And I've seen your boys waiting at the bus stop. They're so handsome."

I smiled proudly because who can resist compliments about one's children? But then I grew wary. This was probably just lip service.

Dabney said, "Today is Tuesday. I'm alone tonight. Come over for some wine, will you?"

I did go for "some wine." We finished two bottles, along with a dish of smoked almonds and some really good French cheese and savory crackers and quince paste, which I had never tasted or even heard of before, but which was delicious. Things were like that at Dabney's house—refined and lovely and eclectic, but not fussy. She made me feel completely at ease, even after I learned that her husband was some kind of famous economist who taught at Harvard, and Dabney herself had gone to Harvard. Usually when I was in the presence of educated people, I felt embarrassed about my pathetic three semesters at Fairly Ridiculous, but I did not feel that way around Dabney.

She asked me if I was married. I said, *Long divorced.*

She got a twinkle in her eye and told me she was something of a matchmaker. Forty-two couples to her credit, all of them still together.

I laughed and said, "Oh dear God, don't even try. I don't need a husband, or even a boyfriend. What I need is a plumber to fix the toilet in the boys' bathroom. It runs incessantly."

The very next day, Flynn Sheehan was standing at the top of my friendship stairs. I caught my breath. He had the most arresting blue eyes I had ever seen.

He said, "Dabney Kimball sent me?"

I thought, *She has sent me a husband.* And boy, was she spot-on. Just looking at Flynn Sheehan gave me butterflies.

He said, "Something about needing a toilet fixed?"

I laughed, then introduced myself and welcomed Flynn Sheehan inside. I was glad I had just come from work and was still wearing a dress, heels, and makeup. I led Flynn Sheehan up the stairs.

He said, "How long have you been renting the Reillys' house?"

I said, "Three weeks."

He said, "I basically grew up in this house. Kevin Reilly was my best friend. He was killed in Iraq in ninety-one."

"Oh, God," I said. "I'm so sorry."

"That's why I came on such short notice. Kevin's parents aren't exactly known for their upkeep of this place..."

"Oh," I said. "The place is fine. It's charming. I love everything about it, except the running toilet."

Flynn stopped at the top of the stairs. He was looking at marks made on the doorjamb, pencil marks and initials I hadn't even noticed.

He pointed to a mark near his waist. "This is Kevin, age five, and me age five. Kev at ten, at twelve, me at thirteen, Kev at fifteen."

I studied the marks: FS 2/10/77. KR 8/29/83.

Flynn pointed to the highest mark, at about his present height. "This was the last time we did it, right before he left. He had me by half an inch."

I looked where Flynn pointed. FS 3/30/91. KR 3/30/91.

Flynn blinked. "He was like a brother to me."

I didn't know what to say but I felt my heart doing funny things, things it hadn't done in a long time.

Then I noticed his wedding ring, and I thought: *Story of my life.*

Flynn fixed the toilet in thirty seconds, and when I tried to pay him, he waved me away. He was the most attractive man I'd seen in years and he had shown me the softest part of his heart within three minutes of meeting me. But he was married.

At the door, he handed me his card. FLYNN SHEEHAN PLUMBING. The address was a P.O. box. I found myself wanting to know where he lived. I would drive by his house and try to catch a glimpse of his pretty wife.

He said, "If you need anything, and I mean anything, even if it's not plumbing, I want you to call me."

I felt myself redden. I wondered what he meant by that.

Then he said, "The Reillys are my people. If anything goes wrong with the house, they would want me to take care of it."

I nodded. "Okay."

Flynn descended the friendship stairs and strode out to his truck, whistling.

"Goodbye!" I called after him. "Thank you!"

A day later, when I saw Dabney, she said, "So, you met Flynn?"

"Yes," I said. "Thank you for sending him."

Dabney gazed at me. She had dark brown eyes, but they seemed to send out gold sparks at times. "So what did you think?"

"He fixed the toilet in half a minute. I probably could have done it myself if I'd bothered to give it a try."

"No," she said. "I mean, what did you think about Flynn?"

"Nice guy," I said.

"You're rosy," she said. She jumped up and down like a little kid, then she snapped her fingers. "I knew it! I knew it! You're rosy!"

"Rosy?" I said.

"You liked him."

"Dabney," I said. "He's married."

Dabney's face fell and I felt like I had just toppled her ice-cream cone.

"Yeah," she said. "I know."

I learned something quickly about Nantucket. Although it was a small island, you could go months without seeing someone. I went six months without seeing Flynn Sheehan. Indeed, I went for days and weeks without thinking about him. And then he would pop into my mind—most often when I walked up the stairs and saw the hash marks on the doorjamb—and I would hope and pray that the kitchen faucet would leak, or the light would go out in the refrigerator.

Then one night I happened into American Seasons for a celebratory drink. I had just sold my first house, a fixer-upper on Pilgrim Road, listed at $1.2 million. The listing broker had to get home to his family, but my boys were at football practice until seven, so I had a couple of free hours. I didn't think anyone would be at the bar at American Seasons at five o'clock—but I was wrong. When I walked in, Flynn Sheehan was sitting there alone, with a tall beer in front of him.

I said, "Flynn, hi! Tammy Block, I'm the one who rents the..."

"Reilly house," he said. He gave me a sort of half smile, and I thought my heart would stop. "Like I could ever forget you."

I have gone on long enough, and the story from here takes a bad turn. Some people had neat and orderly lives, and some people's lives were messy and morally ambiguous. I have lived the latter. Did Flynn and I have an affair? Yes. It pains and embarrasses me to confess that. Did Amy Sheehan—who was, in anyone's objective opinion, a miserable woman—discover the affair by looking at Flynn's cell phone records and spread the news of my slutty debauchery all over the island? Yes. Was I ready to pack up my belongings, uproot the kids, and move off the island? Yes.

There were only two reasons I didn't do this. One was: I loved Flynn Sheehan with every fiber of my being. After Amy smeared our names like blood all over every street in town, he had a difficult choice to make. He could try to repair his marriage and salvage his family, or he could leave. He called me up at eleven o'clock on the night the news broke and said, "I left her, Tammy. I love you."

The other reason I didn't leave Nantucket was because of Dabney Kimball Beech. As soon as she heard the news, she knocked on my front door. I ignored her. I didn't want to hear her lecture. Surely anyone with a life as perfect as Dabney's would never understand adultery—even though, technically, she was the one who had set me up with Flynn.

When I didn't answer the front door, she knocked on the back door. When I didn't answer the back door, she started tapping on my windows. I had to hide in my powder room, where she couldn't see me. But she was relentless, and finally I gave up. I let her in the back door and waited for the beatings to begin.

She hugged me. Then she sat down at my kitchen table. She said, "I am going to hold your hand until you stop crying."

I cried for quite a while. I cried and cried. When I finally stopped to blow my nose, I said, "Why did you send him to me when you knew he was married?"

"Because," Dabney said, "you two are a perfect match. You're meant to be together."

Dabney was right. Flynn divorced Amy and married me on the beach in Madaket with only our children and Dabney and John Boxmiller Beech in attendance. There are still people on this island who won't speak to me, who won't meet my eye in the supermarket, who wouldn't give me a referral for a sale if I were the last Realtor left on Nantucket. But I have Dabney—and she is not the person she appears to be.

She is so much more.

DABNEY

She was beside herself with excitement. Agnes's Prius was due to arrive on the five o'clock ferry. It wasn't just a weekend visit; it wasn't a few days at Christmas. She was really staying the *entire* summer!

Unfortunately, Box was going to miss Agnes by a matter of hours. He had come to Nantucket for the weekend, but that morning Dabney had delivered him to the airport. He would go back to Boston tonight, and fly to London in the morning. He would be gone two weeks.

"I feel like we never see each other anymore," Dabney said.

"The lives we lead," Box said.

Dabney clung to Box tightly, which he seemed to resist, and when she raised her face, he kissed the tip of her nose like she was a child.

"Please, no more histrionics," he said. "It doesn't become you."

"Histrionics," Dabney said. "That sounds like a newfangled major at Harvard."

"I was referring to the middle-of-the-night phone call last week," he said.

"I know what you were referring to," she said. "I was trying to amuse you."

"Waking me up in the middle of the night to ask me questions you already know the answer to isn't amusing."

"I'm sorry," Dabney said, although she had already apologized three separate times over the weekend.

He patted her shoulder. "I'm off," he said.

He grabbed the handle of his carry-on and strode toward his gate.

"I love you, darling!" she called out after him, but this must have qualified as histrionics because he didn't respond. He didn't even turn around.

Dabney planned to leave the office at four thirty so she could get home before Agnes arrived, but just as she was packing up, her computer chirped. She checked the screen. E-mail from Clendenin Hughes. Subject line: *Fried rice.*

Delete it, she thought. Agnes was on her way. *Delete it!*

The lives we lead. She opened the e-mail. It said: Come to my cottage for dinner tonight. A crate arrived today with my wok in it. Please? 8:00.

She was tempted to respond: I can't. I'm having dinner with Agnes.

His daughter.

She was tempted to respond: No. No way. But she feared that any response, even a negative one, would only encourage him.

She deleted the e-mail, then deleted it from her deleted file.

Dabney was standing in the driveway when the Prius pulled in. She was aghast to see CJ behind the wheel.

Agnes climbed out of the passenger side and ran to hug her mother. "I'm here!" she said. "I can't believe all of my stuff fit in that tiny car!"

CJ greeted Dabney with his usual enthusiasm, like she was the only person in the world he wanted to see. He smelled wonderful. He said, "I didn't want your daughter to have to do the drive alone."

"Of course not," Dabney said. She swallowed. "How long can you stay?"

"I'm flying back at nine o'clock tonight with my client, *whisper whisper.*" CJ winked at Dabney. "Private plane."

Dabney hadn't heard the client's name—either she was losing her hearing on top of all her other maladies, or CJ hadn't meant for Dabney to hear. She didn't care; she was relieved that CJ wasn't staying over.

"I have chicken marinating," Dabney said.

"I took the liberty of making dinner reservations at Cru," CJ said. "You'll join us, I hope?"

Dabney faltered. Were they *really* hoping she would join them, or did they want to be alone? She felt a wave of exhaustion and weakness; the pain in her abdomen had returned with a vengeance. The antibiotics had done absolutely no good. She supposed her next step was to stop eating wheat. Goodbye to her morning cereal. Goodbye to her beloved BLTs. She might as well stop breathing.

"Please come, Mommy!" Agnes said. "You love oysters!"

Dabney adored Cru—it was chic, polished, and fun. That evening, the restaurant was offering nine kinds of oysters, and Dabney decided to order three of each.

"Great idea," CJ said. "I'll do that, too."

Dabney and CJ's oysters were presented on an iced platter roughly the circumference of a Goodyear tire. Dabney doctored her oysters the way she liked them—fresh lemon first, then horseradish, then half with a dab of cocktail and half with mignonette.

"Ah, now see," CJ said. "I'm a purist. I eat them naked."

The server had brought them a list of the oysters, which ran clockwise around her platter so that they could identify each one.

Dabney beamed. "It's like a party game!"

CJ had ordered a drink called a Dirty Goose, which came in a martini glass, and he threw it back in one gulp, then spun his finger at the waiter, indicating he wanted another. There were hot rolls on the table. Dabney's first challenge in not eating any wheat was to skip the rolls. She nudged the basket toward Agnes.

"Have a roll, darling. You're far too thin."

"I'm fine, Mom, thanks," Agnes said.

"CJ, would you like a roll?" Dabney asked.

"No, thank you," CJ said. "Agnes and I don't eat carbs."

"You don't?" Dabney said. This was news to her. Agnes looked like she could use a big plate of fettuccine Alfredo every day for the next month, but she knew not to press the matter.

Dabney ate the Belon from Maine, then the Hama Hama from Washington State, then the Kumomoto from British Columbia, which was an all-time favorite of hers.

"Would you like one, Agnes?" she asked.

Agnes studied the platter. Of course she wanted one! Dabney and Box were oyster connoisseurs; it was one of their few extravagances. Box ordered twelve dozen Blue Points and twelve dozen Kumomotos for their annual Christmas party. Dabney made a homemade mignonette with crushed fresh raspberries. Agnes had grown up with oysters the way other children had grown up with Pepperidge Farm Goldfish.

"No, thank you," Agnes said.

"Please, honey, help yourself. We can always order more. How about the Island Creek?"

CJ polished off his Dirty Goose and set the empty glass down so hard on the table that Dabney was surprised it didn't break.

"No, thanks, Mom," Agnes said.

"If Agnes wants an oyster," CJ said, "she can have one of mine." He lifted one dripping out of its shell and fed it to Agnes like she was a baby bird.

Dabney felt a combination of helplessness and anger rise in her throat. She ate a Wellfleet.

CJ said, "So, Dabney, you've succeeded in stealing my fiancée away from me this summer."

French Kiss from Nova Scotia. Dabney accidentally took a hit of horseradish up her nose, and she reached for her water. "Pardon me?"

"I hope you're happy."

"I…?" Dabney looked to Agnes for help. Agnes's eyes were

wide and imploring. Dabney realized that she had been set up as some kind of fall guy. "Well, really, I...when Agnes told me about the funding issue at the club..."

"Agnes doesn't have to work again, ever," CJ said. "At the club, or anywhere else. I'm more than able to take care of her in the manner to which she's been accustomed, and then some."

"Right," Dabney said. "I realize this..."

"But you wanted her here at home. I get it, your only daughter back in her childhood bedroom for the summer. Before she gets married and leaves you forever."

"It's not like that," Dabney said. Agnes had now bowed her head; her chin was tucked to her chest. She wasn't going to say a word in her own defense, or Dabney's. She was *afraid* of CJ. Agnes, who had been sailing and water-skiing since she was five, who had flown to Europe by herself at the age of fifteen, and who routinely took the subway home from 125th Street at night in the dark, was afraid of CJ Pippin. She clearly hadn't told him that it had been *her* idea to come home to Nantucket. It was *she* who wanted the beach and the familiar house and the comforting presence of her parents and a chance to work one last summer at her old job as an adventure counselor.

Suddenly their table was engulfed in a ghost-green miasma that was only too familiar to Dabney.

A third drink arrived for CJ, another Dirty Goose. He said, "I'm not going to tell Agnes she can't go. But I'd really like her to come back to New York every weekend. And if not every weekend, then every other weekend."

Dabney felt for a second like she and CJ were divorcing and discussing a custody arrangement.

"You can come here anytime," Dabney said. "We have plenty of room."

CJ snorted and took a healthy pull off his drink.

"I'm forty-four years old," he said. He glanced at Agnes, who now had her hands clasped at her chest like a praying mantis. "I'm past the point where I want to stay in someone's *guest room*. If I come back this summer, I'm going to want my own place with Agnes, so we have the necessary privacy. But it's a little late to start looking, and I'm unsure of which weekends I would even be free enough to travel. My clients, Dabney, are really just kids—some of them only nineteen and twenty years old. I need to be available for them twenty-four/seven. Summer is a busy time, especially for my NFL players. I assume you've heard of Bantam Killjoy?"

Dabney had not heard of Bantam Killjoy. Was he talking about a person? Or a new video game?

Dabney shook her head.

"He was the number-one draft pick, wide receiver out of Oklahoma, nominated for the Heisman. Big media favorite because both his parents were killed in the Oklahoma City bombings when he was a baby."

"It's a really sad story," Agnes said. "With a happy ending. But Bantam needs CJ's guidance, almost like an older brother, or an uncle."

"Yes, I'd imagine so," Dabney said. "I'm sorry. I don't follow college football except for the Harvard-Yale game."

"Well, signing Bantam Killjoy was a big coup for me, and my main goal this summer is to make sure he gets to training camp. That will take precedence over coming back here, unfortunately. If Agnes wants to see me, she'll have to come to New York."

Dabney sucked down an East Beach Blonde from Rhode Island. CJ had made a big deal about ordering the oysters—again, just as Dabney had—but he had yet to eat a single one. The only oyster missing from his platter was the one he'd fed to Agnes. Dabney suspected that CJ didn't even *like* oysters. He had ordered them only because Dabney had. And this, perhaps, got closer to what Dabney didn't like about CJ. He reeked of insincerity; he did things just for show.

Dabney said, "Now you're just being ridiculous."

"Ridiculous?" CJ said. "Let's talk about ridiculous. Your daughter has been asking you for four years to come to New York, and for four years, you've said no..."

Dabney speared a Yaquina from Oregon, which was a tiny oyster, about the size of a quarter, but she almost couldn't get it down. "As I'm sure Agnes has shared with you, I suffer from a bit of a phobia..."

CJ smacked his palm on the table. "You're her mother and you've never come to see her."

Agnes put her hand on CJ's arm, but he brusquely shook it off. *Did he* hit *her?* Dabney suddenly wondered.

"And another thing," he said. "Agnes told me that your crystal ball says we don't belong together."

"I don't have a crystal ball," Dabney said. "I wish I did."

"Then I'm not sure what criteria you're using to determine who's a 'perfect match.'"

"No criteria," Dabney said.

"No crystal ball, no criteria," CJ said. "I think your matchmaking is bullshit."

"Well," Dabney said, "you wouldn't be alone in that opinion." She sucked down a Wianno.

CJ pushed his platter of oysters at Agnes. "Here, honey," he said. "You have them."

Agnes gazed morosely at all the beautiful, fresh oysters, which were now swimming in slush.

"Or have a roll," Dabney suggested again.

"We don't eat carbs," CJ said. "She'll eat the oysters. Won't you, baby?"

Their waiter came back to the table. "How are we doing?" he asked.

Dabney did not say, *I hope my future son-in-law is drunk and NOT simply cruel, although I fear that's the case.* She did not say, *Please bring me a glass of champagne or good white Bordeaux because I can't make it another second without a drink.* She did not say, *He's trying to make me feel like a bad mother, but I know what a bad mother is because I had one, and I am NOT a bad mother.*

No, instead Dabney smiled at their server and thought, *I have tried all nine oysters and they were delicious—sweet, creamy, briny, sublime. There is nothing more sublime than a cold, fresh oyster.* She was slipping away, she could feel it, the green smoke was getting into her eyes and lungs.

"Everything's fine," she said. But it took effort.

As soon as the server sailed away, Dabney set her napkin on the table and said, "Excuse me, please." She wasn't feeling well, it was the green smoke, or it was the wheat allergy, perhaps, threatening to turn her insides to dust. *The lives we lead,* she thought.

"Darling?" Dabney said to Agnes. "I'm not feeling well. I think I just need air. I'll meet you at home, okay?"

"Okay," Agnes said. "Do you want us to go with you?"

"No, no," Dabney said. She waved at CJ by way of goodbye and thought, *Have a safe flight home with* whisper whisper.

She hurried from the restaurant. She was lovesick, pure and simple.

She called Box as she walked up Main Street. He could hardly object; it was only seven thirty.

"Hello?" he said.

Dabney heard Mozart playing in the background and figured he was drinking a glass of white Bordeaux before he had dinner. Would he go out or cook for himself? Would he go out alone or with colleagues, or possibly with Miranda Gilbert? Dabney had been to his faculty apartment only twice in all the time he'd lived there, and she'd never spent the night.

"Darling?" she said.

"Yes? Dabney? Everything okay? Agnes arrived safely?"

"Safely," Dabney said. "CJ drove her up."

"Good man," Box said.

"He's not staying," Dabney said. "Private plane back tonight with whisper whisper."

"I'm sorry?" Box said.

"Apparently he's developed an allergy to our house," Dabney said. "Or he's trying to punish me because I said he and Agnes aren't a match. Or he's trying to control Agnes."

"Dabney," Box said. "Are you okay?"

"Not really," Dabney said. "I'm not really okay at all." She realized she was verging on histrionics, but she couldn't help herself. What should she do? Tell Box about Clendenin?

"You need to pull yourself together, darling," Box said. "Perhaps call Dr. Donegal?"

Dr. Donegal, her therapist. Box thought she was going mad.

Well, she was going mad.

"I don't want you to go tomorrow, darling," Dabney said. "I want you to cancel London. Please. Come back to Nantucket. Agnes is here, and...I'm here."

"Cancel *London?*" Box said. "I'm sorry, darling, did you just ask me to cancel *London?*"

"Yes," Dabney said. "Please."

"You do realize this has been set up for the better part of a year,"

Box said. "They can't just find another lecturer. And Jesus, Dabney, they pay me a king's ransom."

"We don't need any more money," Dabney said. "I think we can both agree on that."

"The money is hardly the point," Box said. "It's my reputation and my word and everything else. And you are overreacting. Something is bothering you, but my coming back to Nantucket isn't the answer."

Dabney was quiet.

Box said, "I'll be back in two weeks, darling."

He wasn't going to cancel London. There was nothing Dabney could say or do. His reputation, his word, his brilliant and esteemed career in economics was on the line.

"You're right," Dabney said. "Of course, you're right."

"Get some rest," Box said. "You're overtired is my guess. And you're looking too thin. Good meals and sleep, darling. I'll be back before you know it." With that, Box hung up.

Dabney reached home but did not go inside. She was spinning. She had eaten nine oysters but she was still hungry. There was chicken marinating in the fridge; she could throw it on the grill. *Go into the house and grill the chicken,* she thought.

She checked her phone. Quarter to eight.

Please? 8:00.

The lives we lead.

She climbed into the Impala and drove out the Polpis Road.

PART 2

JUNE/JULY

AGNES

Box asked her to keep an eye on her mother while he was in London.

"She hasn't been feeling well," he said. "She's been acting strangely."

"Of course, Daddy," Agnes said.

However, Dabney was so independent and Agnes so consumed with her own problems that it took a few days for Agnes to realize that her mother *was* acting strangely. Almost like she was hiding something.

On Agnes's first day home, Dabney got up to go for her walk, as always, wearing her headband and pearls. She left the house as Agnes was fixing herself a cup of coffee with real cream. (Life's joys were in the details; CJ took only skim milk in his coffee and he insisted that Agnes do the same, but CJ was now hundreds of miles away and Agnes wanted cream, dammit!)

By the time Dabney was dressed and ready for work, Agnes was at the table, eating a plate of scrambled eggs, whole-grain toast with homemade blueberry jam, and crisp bacon. This was, for her, a decadent breakfast. CJ always ate a power shake—spinach, wheat grass, seaweed. Agnes sometimes grabbed a Vitaminwater on the way to the subway, and on the weekends she ate half a grapefruit. As Agnes crunched a piece of bacon, she thought of how horrified CJ would be if he could see her stuffing her face, still in her pajamas at a quarter to eight, and she hadn't exercised, hadn't done so much as touch her toes. CJ was out the door every morning at six a.m. to run in Central Park and then go to the gym, and he liked Agnes to join him. He told her before she left that he feared she would fall away from her routine. His biggest fear, she supposed, was that she would return to him fat and lazy.

Agnes had assured him this wouldn't happen. But as she snarfed down her delicious eggs, she realized that he had a right to be concerned. She had been home for less than twenty-four hours and was already being a slovenly pig. The thing was, it felt good.

Dabney said, "Honey, I would have made you breakfast."

"I'm a grown woman, Mom," Agnes said. "Do you want me to make you a piece of toast? I hogged everything else."

"I'm happy to see you eating," Dabney said. "You're too thin."

"*You're* too thin." Her mother's clothes were hanging off her, and her cheekbones were jutting out. "Daddy says you're not feeling well."

"Wheat allergy, I think," Dabney said.

"You and everyone else in the world," Agnes said. "So I guess no toast for you."

Dabney said, "I'm headed into the office. There's a Business After Hours tonight at the Brotherhood, so I'll be home late, after dinner. You'll fend for yourself?"

"Of course," Agnes said.

Dabney smiled, then kissed Agnes's forehead. "I love you, darling. I'm so happy you're here."

Agnes had moved right back into her childhood bedroom, which her mother had redone as a guest room. There was an all-white king bed with navy accent pillows, and luscious, buttery pine furniture. The room was filled with light, and it was situated all by itself at the east end of the house. Agnes wasn't sure what CJ found so objectionable about it.

Agnes missed CJ terribly—but at the same time, not at all. She could eat freely when she was away from him, and she could breathe freely. CJ was so perfect, so beautiful to look at, so confident in his manner, so successful in his business, and so absurdly generous, that Agnes wondered what exactly he saw in her. Agnes was young and pretty and she was a devoted do-gooder, but she had seen photographs of CJ's ex-wife, Annabelle (Agnes had googled her, and had creeped her on Facebook and Twitter). Annabelle was as gorgeous as a model, her hair and makeup always perfect. She had sat on charitable boards and chaired events; she had been an actual socialite, with socialite friends who had apartments comprised of entire floors in Park Avenue prewar buildings, whereas Agnes lived in a one-bedroom walk-up on West Eighty-Fourth Street. CJ had lived on Park Avenue as well, but he had lost his apartment in the divorce, and then Annabelle had sold it and bought a waterfront property in Boca Raton, where she served on charitable boards, chaired events, and lived off CJ's money.

Freeloader, he called her. *Good for nothing. She doesn't realize the value of money because she never had to earn it.*

Aside from this, CJ didn't say much about Annabelle or about why the marriage had failed, even though Agnes had repeatedly asked. CJ said that both he and Annabelle had signed a paper agreeing never to discuss the particulars of their split. A gag order. This had sounded reasonable at the time, but after what Agnes had heard from Manny Partida a few weeks earlier, Agnes wasn't so sure. She thought spending the summer away from CJ might be the best thing.

Manny Partida was Agnes's boss, the regional director, the head of every Boys & Girls Club in New York City. He was the one who had come in to tell Agnes that National wouldn't be funding any summer programs for her club that year. Agnes was devastated; she had more than six hundred members, and what exactly were those kids supposed to do all summer without any programming? Agnes loved the kids at her club in direct proportion to how little they had. Her favorite children, ten-year-old twins named Quincy and Dahlia, were homeless; they lived with their mother in a shelter, but not always the same shelter. They each brought a rolling suitcase to the club, which Agnes kept safe in her office so that no one would pilfer their things. Dahlia liked to make fairy houses out of twigs and grass and sometimes even old straws and McDonald's cups that she found on the perimeter of the club's crumbling asphalt basketball court. Agnes could have cried just thinking about the two of them without a safe place to go all summer.

As if this weren't upsetting enough, Manny had another bomb to drop.

He said, "A little bird told me you're engaged to Charlie Pippin?"

"CJ," Agnes said. "Yes, I am." She looked down at her left hand, though her fingers were bare. The diamond CJ had given her was too valuable to wear safely to work.

"When I knew him, which wasn't that long ago," Manny said, "he went by Charlie."

"You knew him?" Agnes said.

"He was a big donor, one of the biggest, at the Madison Square Club, ten, twelve years ago," Manny said. "He and his first wife."

Agnes nodded. On one hand, she didn't want to hear about CJ and Annabelle, and on the other hand, she craved every detail.

Manny said, "I realize people change."

Agnes smiled uncertainly. "Excuse me?"

"People change," Manny said. "He changed his name, and he switched affiliations to the Morningside Heights Club, which is good because you can certainly use the money. But I'd advise you to be careful."

"Careful?" Agnes said.

"Rumor has it he wasn't very nice to his first wife."

"Wasn't nice?" Agnes said.

Manny held up his palms. He wore a light blue T-shirt under a khaki suit and a three-inch silver cross on a chain around his neck.

"I'm not saying he hit her, because I don't know the specifics. But there were stories flying around for a while. Something happened at one of the benefits for the Madison Square Club. They had both been drinking, the wife had bid on something quite expensive without asking his permission, he lost his temper, and I heard…" Here, Manny trailed off. "This is just what I heard, Agnes, and so take it with a grain of salt. But I couldn't live with myself if I didn't tell you. I heard he got physical with her."

"What?"

"Hair pulling, arm twisting, some not-so-nice stuff." Manny stood up. "But again, that was ten, twelve years ago, and people change. Just please, Agnes, please be careful. You're one of the best directors I have, and I only want to see you happy."

Manny Partida had left the office, and Agnes had sat glued to her chair for a long while, thinking that Manny Partida was full of shit, or whomever was feeding his ear was; the people at the Madison Square Club were probably mad or jealous that CJ had moved his financial allegiance uptown, and that he had brought Victor Cruz in to sign autographs! Lorna Mapleton, who was the director at Madison Square, was in her sixties; she thought Agnes was too young to be at the helm of a club. *Physical?* Agnes couldn't imagine CJ being physical with her. It was true he had a temper, especially when he was drinking, and Agnes had heard him slice people to ribbons over the phone. But he was always gentle with Agnes, he cared about her well-being, that was why he liked her to exercise every spare moment and why he watched her diet—no carbs, no cheese, no sauces. Her body was his temple, he said. He would never hurt her.

Agnes hadn't told Dabney what Manny Partida said—God, no, that would have sent Dabney into a tailspin—but Agnes had decided on the spot that she would spend the summer at home on Nantucket.

That first afternoon, Agnes walked into town. She wasn't a town person the way Dabney was. Dabney loved town. For her, the allure of Nantucket was found on the grid of four square blocks. This was where the action was—the real estate agents, the insurance agents, the pharmacy with lunch counter, the art galleries and florists and antiques stores, the churches, the post office, the administration buildings, the clothing boutiques, the T-shirt shops. Town was where the people were. Dabney loved people, and anyone found on the streets of Nantucket, if only for an hour or two on a day trip, she thought of as "her people."

Agnes, on the other hand, preferred anonymity, which was why she liked Manhattan. This might have been a response to growing up as Dabney Kimball's daughter. She had never gotten away with anything as a teenager; if she took a drag of a cigarette on the strip off Steamship Wharf or if she held hands with a boy on the bench outside the Hub, it was reported back to Dabney within the hour. This was why Agnes preferred the quieter, more remote parts of Nantucket—the far-flung beaches, the trails through the state forest, the secret ponds.

But today she felt otherwise. Today she wanted to be recognized as Dabney Kimball's daughter. She stopped in at Mitchell's Book Corner and browsed for a moment, then she crossed the street to check out the cute party dresses at Erica Wilson. She tried on a flirty yellow number and bought it on a whim—it was bright, the color of summertime. In the city, she, like everyone else, tended to wear black.

She window-shopped, meandering like a tourist, and was shocked when nobody recognized her. Ms. Cowen, who had been Agnes's field-hockey coach, walked right past her. Of course, Agnes hadn't lived here since graduating from high school. And she had cut her hair. But still, Agnes felt weirdly displaced. This was where she was from, but she didn't quite belong here.

There was only way to rid herself of this feeling. She headed upstairs to the Chamber of Commerce office.

The Nantucket Chamber of Commerce was located above what used to be an old bowling alley, and the office always smelled vaguely of bowling shoes. To combat this, Dabney occasionally lit green-apple-scented candles. The combination of bowling shoes and green apple came to define the Chamber and, by association, Dabney herself.

When Agnes walked in, she was greeted by a shriek—happy, excited, perhaps a touch manic.

Nina Mobley.

"Agnes! Your mother told me you were here, but I didn't think I'd be lucky enough to see you on the first day!"

"Hey, Nina," Agnes said, bending down to give Nina a squeeze. Nina, like Dabney, seemed never to change—frizzy brown hair, gold cross at the neck, squinty eyes. Nina had always been a squinter, as if the world lay just out of focus.

Agnes noticed that Dabney's desk was unoccupied, and by habit she poked her head into the "back room," where the information assistants sat, answering the phones. There was a girl with a high, blond ponytail chattering away about her "favorite restaurant, American Seasons"—and at the near desk sat a guy with thick brown hair that curled up at the collar of his pale blue polo shirt. The two of them were so cute and perfect that Dabney might have picked them out of a catalog. The guy was finishing off a frappe that Agnes identified as having come from the pharmacy lunch counter across the street; he was at the slurpy-sounding end. When he looked up and saw Agnes, he jumped to his feet. She noticed that he was wearing Hawaiian-print board shorts and flip-flops, which were both in violation of Dabney's usual dress code.

"Oh, hey!" he said. "I'm so sorry. Can I help you? I'm Riley Al-sopp."

Agnes smiled. He seemed quite earnest; he must be new, maybe too new to know about the no-beachwear rule. Agnes had worked as an information assistant one summer, and she had hated it. Her mother had made her wear a knee-length khaki skirt and button-down oxford shirts. ("I look like *you*," Agnes had complained.) Her mother had insisted that when Agnes wasn't on the phone with potential visitors, she should be memorizing the Chamber guide and learning the arcane details of the island's whaling history.

Riley, however, had a copy of Salinger's *Raise High the Roof Beam, Carpenters and Seymour, An Introduction* open on his desk. Odd. He was too old for a summer reading list.

"I'm Agnes," she said. "I'm..."

"Dabney's daughter," he said. "Your mother talks about you all the time. And I've seen your picture." He smiled at her, showing off very straight white teeth.

Agnes turned around. Unlike most offices, where the bosses hid in the back, here Dabney and Nina sat in the front room. This, of course, was Dabney's idea. She wanted to be the first person some-one encountered when he or she walked into the Chamber. But Dab-ney's desk was still empty, and now Nina Mobley was on the phone.

"Where is my mother?" Agnes asked Riley Alsopp. "Do you know?"

"She went out around lunchtime," Riley said. "And she hasn't been back."

"Lunchtime?"

"Noon or so," he said. "You can check the log." Next to them, the blond ponytail yammered on about her *other* favorite restau-rant, Cru. Cru better for seafood, she said. American Seasons bet-ter for land animals.

Land animals? Agnes thought.

Riley Alsopp winked at Agnes. He said, "I'm still learning the ropes."

Agnes said, "Is this your first summer?"

"First summer working here," he said. "I've been coming to Nantucket since I was ten. I'm in dental school now, at Penn."

That explained the teeth, Agnes thought. But not the Salinger or the board shorts. Agnes was confused about her mother. Dabney had left at noon or so, and she hadn't come back? It was nearly three.

"Where did my mother go?" Agnes asked. "Did she say?"

Riley shrugged. "I'm not exactly privy to office secrets."

"Right," Agnes said. Did Dabney have a doctor's appointment, maybe, that she hadn't mentioned?

Riley said, "Are you coming to Business After Hours tonight? It's at the Brotherhood of Thieves."

"No," Agnes said. "I don't go to those anymore. I got dragged to them as a kid. By the time I was fifteen, I had sneaked more than my share of bad Chardonnay."

Riley laughed. The guy was so *cute,* her mother must have pounced on him immediately, and maybe forgiven him the board shorts.

"Well, Riley, it was nice to meet you," Agnes said. Her inflection, she realized, was eerily like her mother's at that moment. She turned, and was dismayed to find Nina still on the phone. Nina would know where her mother was.

The blond ponytail hung up her phone and announced to the room, "Those folks are *definitely* coming to Nantucket for a week in September!" She put two fists in the air in a V for victory. Then the blond ponytail noticed Agnes and nearly vaulted over her desk.

"You must be Agnes!" she said. She offered Agnes an extremely strong handshake. "I'm Celerie Truman. This is my second year as an information assistant here at the Chamber. I am a really, *really* big fan of your mother's."

Agnes suppressed the urge to laugh. Where did Dabney find people with such wholesome energy?

"Oh, hi!" Agnes said, again channeling her mother's tone. "Nice to meet you, Celerie." She paused, hoping she had pronounced the girl's name correctly. Celerie like *celery?* What had her mother thought of *that?* Dabney was very particular about names. She believed that the only suitable names were those befitting a Supreme Court justice: Thurgood Marshall, Sandra Day O'Connor. Celerie was not a Supreme Court justice name.

"I hope you're coming to Business After Hours," Celerie said. "It's at the Brotherhood, which is my other *other* favorite restaurant. My casual favorite."

"Sadly, I won't be there tonight," Agnes said. She sounded so much like her mother it was frightening, but the words were coming out that way unbidden. She heard Nina getting off the phone. "Excuse me!" She waved at Celerie Truman and Riley Alsopp.

They were so gorgeous, both separately and together, that Agnes wondered if the back room of the Chamber was a matchmaking laboratory this summer. Leave it to her mother.

Agnes presented herself at Nina's desk. "Where's Mom?"

Nina clasped her hands at her bosom. "Tell me about New York!" she said. "Is it wonderful? And you're getting married! At Saint Mary's and the Yacht Club, your mother said."

There was catching-up required. Agnes knew this. She hadn't had a chance to talk with Nina at Christmas or on Daffodil Weekend. Nina Mobley had five children to ask after; Agnes had babysat for all of them. But Agnes didn't have the presence of mind for chitchat right now.

She quickly checked the log. Dabney had signed out at five minutes to noon, listing *errands/lunch* as the reason for her absence.

"So, wait, I'm sorry," Agnes said. "Did Mom say where she was going?"

Nina took a deep breath, then emitted a nervous laugh. "She had errands."

"Errands?" Agnes said. "What kind of errands?"

Nina Mobley squinted at Agnes. "Oh, honey," she said. "I wish I could tell you."

Agnes walked home, thinking that she and her mother must have just missed each other—or that Dabney had run to the grocery store for more eggs, or to Bartlett Farm for hothouse tomatoes. But would she do that in the middle of a workday? Never! And those errands wouldn't take three hours. Dabney had been acting strange, Box said. Dabney did have a slew of peculiarities—a rare form of OCD and agoraphobia that made her incapable of leaving Nantucket—and then her mystical matchmaking power. Maybe she was seeing Dr. Donegal, her therapist. Or maybe she was having a midlife crisis and Agnes would find her in the cool dim of the Chicken Box, drinking beer and shooting pool.

Ha! Agnes was making herself laugh. Dabney would be at home.

But Dabney wasn't at home. Agnes felt irrationally upset about this, as if she were a child who had been abandoned. And, to boot, her mother's cell phone was lying on the kitchen counter, charging. Really, what good was a cell phone if you didn't take it with you when you left the house? Agnes considered calling Box in London. It was nine thirty at night over there; Box would probably be at dinner. Agnes hated to interrupt him—and besides, what would she say? *Mom left work three hours ago and I don't know where she went.* The island was only so big; Dabney had to be *somewhere.*

Agnes trudged up to her bedroom and threw herself across her bed. She was tired enough to sleep until morning.

She awoke to the strains of Alicia Keys singing "Empire State of Mind," her cell phone's ringtone, handpicked for her by one of the little girls at the Boys & Girls Club. Agnes was groggy and her limbs felt leaden, but she reached for her phone, thinking it would be her mother.

She saw when she picked up that it was five o'clock and that it was CJ calling. How had she slept for so long? What was *wrong* with her? She considered letting the call go to her voice mail; CJ would sense sleep in her voice and she didn't feel like explaining that she had eaten five thousand calories already that day and had just woken up from a two-hour nap. But CJ did *not* like getting Agnes's voice mail. When he called, he expected her to answer.

She cleared her throat. "Hello?"

"Agnes?" he said. "Are you okay?"

She stretched out like a cat. The room was catching the mellow slant of the late-afternoon sun across the wooden floor. Agnes's apartment, as lovely as it was, didn't get this kind of natural light. In the background of the phone call, Agnes heard sirens and hub-bub, the city. She didn't miss it one bit.

"Yes," she said. "I'm fine."

"You didn't call once today," CJ said. "I thought you couldn't live without me."

"Oh," Agnes said. "Well, I can't."

"Good," CJ said. "I just left the office. I'm headed to the gym and then I'm meeting Rocky for a game of squash. What are you up to?"

Agnes sat up and listened to the rest of the house for sounds of her mother. The house was silent. "Nothing."

"You and your mom have big plans tonight?" CJ asked. "Peanut butter sandwiches and Parcheesi?"

"No plans," she said.

"Is everyone on Nantucket aflutter with the news of your re-turn? Are all your old boyfriends banging down your door?"

"No," Agnes said archly.

"Hey, baby, don't get angry. If anyone should be angry, it's me. I have to live here in the big city without the woman I love."

"We'll be together in ten days," Agnes said.

"*If* I make it up there," CJ said. "I can't stay in your parents' house again. I hate to be a diva that way, but I'm just too old. I'm on the wait list for a room at the White Elephant, so we'll keep our fingers crossed for that. Otherwise, you can come home to New York."

Agnes blew her nose. She didn't *want* to go back to New York. She had just arrived on Nantucket and she wanted to stay and en-joy it. Her job as a counselor at Island Adventures camp started the next day. Agnes wanted a routine. She wanted sun and beach and ocean air. She wanted to be with her mother.

"It would be much better if you could come here," Agnes said.

"Well," CJ said. "We'll have to wait and see."

Agnes thought again about what Manny Partida had told her. Agnes didn't think CJ would ever hurt her. But she hated being spoken to like a child.

"I hear my mother downstairs," Agnes said. "I should go. I'll call you later, baby. Bye."

But downstairs was quiet and growing darker. Dabney hadn't returned. She had gone back to the office, Agnes supposed, after running her mysterious errands, and now she would be headed to the Brotherhood, for Business After Hours.

Dabney pulled the yellow dress out of the shopping bag and stared at it for a long minute.

If I make it up there.

She shucked off her shorts and T-shirt and slipped on the dress. Mascara, lip gloss, a hand through her hair, and a pair of gold sandals. She would stop in at Business After Hours, she decided, for old times' sake.

Glass of mediocre Chardonnay in hand—it was a step up from the boxed wine of her teenage memory—Agnes threaded her way through the party in search of her mother. The best part of the Brotherhood was the old part—a basement grotto with low, beamed ceilings and stone walls and scarred wooden tables. Agnes had loved to come here growing up, although, for some reason, Dabney allowed it only when it was raining. The room was lit by candles; it had the contained coziness of the hull of a ship. Agnes always used to order the Boursin cheese board. Bread, butter, cheese, mustard, pickles, candlelight, rain, sometimes an acoustic-guitar player—it was a good memory that distracted Agnes for a minute.

The place was jam-packed with familiar faces. Everyone was chatting and drinking and picking up fried jalapeños and mini Reuben sandwiches from passing trays. Agnes snagged a sandwich for herself (carbs, how she craved them!), then a jalapeño, then another sandwich—all the while scanning the room for her mother. There was Tammy Block, the Realtor whom Dabney had set up with Flynn Sheehan, creating earth shock waves of scandal a few years back; there was the travel agent, the owner of a popular gift shop, there was Barley Ivan, who made beautiful Lightship-basket furniture, there was the flamboyant gallery owner, and there was Ed Law, legendary owner of Nantucket Cotton, the T-shirt shop where Dabney and then, a generation later, Agnes had worked as teenagers.

Agnes couldn't find Dabney, yet she knew her mother must be around somewhere. Dabney had invented Business After Hours years and years ago—monthly cocktail parties where Chamber members gathered to "discuss issues in the business community," which was a grand euphemism for drinking and gossiping.

There was the guy who owned the body shop and towing business. There was Hal Allen of Allen Heating and Cooling; Agnes had dated his son, Duke, in high school.

Old boyfriends banging down the door?

Where was her mother?

There was a guitar player tucked in the back corner, playing a Jack Johnson song. Agnes exhaled and concentrated on the music for a second. Jack Johnson songs always made her think of hibiscus leis and coconut drinks. She was dying to go to Hawaii on her honeymoon, but CJ had been to Hawaii "too many times to count" with Annabelle. CJ wanted to take a cruise to Alaska. Agnes had heard that Alaska was beautiful, but it sounded cold, and who wanted a cold honeymoon? And spending her honeymoon in the cramped quarters of a cruise ship held even less appeal. But CJ had insisted she would love it.

The song ended, there was a smattering of applause, and the guitar player said into the microphone, "This next one is for Agnes, who is back on Nantucket for the summer."

There was a collective murmur. *Agnes? Is that Agnes?* Her cover was blown, although she hadn't ever had a hope of remaining incognito. Agnes craned her neck to get a look at the guitar player. He smiled—those teeth, the Hawaiian-print board shorts. It was Riley, from the office.

He launched into "Puff the Magic Dragon," a childhood favorite of Agnes's, learned at circle time in Montessori, although Riley would have had no way of knowing that. Unless Dabney had told him.

Agnes chatted away, sounding exactly like her mother—*Oh, it's so good to see you, yes, it's been a while, home for the summer, working at Island Adventure, so great to be back, there is no place like Nantucket!*—until finally Riley took a break and appeared at her elbow with a fresh glass of mediocre Chardonnay.

"Hey," she said. "Thanks for outing me. I did love the song, though."

"I can't believe you came," he said.

"You didn't tell me you were *performing,*" she said.

"I didn't want to oversell myself."

"You were great," Agnes said. How thrilled Dabney must have been when she discovered that Riley played the guitar! "I hope my mother is paying you extra."

"I'm playing for tips," he said. He showed her a plastic cup with a single five-dollar bill in it.

"Riley," Agnes said. "Is my mother here?"

"I haven't seen her."

"She's not here," Agnes said. She drank the remaining Chardonnay from the plastic cup. She knew her mother wasn't here because if Dabney were here she would have been the epicenter of the party.

Agnes studied Riley. His eyes were brown, like his hair, and he had one dark freckle on his cheek. She could tell just from looking at him that his parents were still married, that he had grown up with siblings, probably sisters, and that his life had unfolded smoothly, making it easy for him to be a surfer, and a guitar player, and an aspiring dentist.

Agnes figured he was a good egg. Her mother hired only good eggs.

"Did my mother come back to the office this afternoon?" Agnes asked.

"No," Riley said. "Nina said she was running errands."

"This is so strange. My mother is the most transparent person who ever lived. She does not disappear like this."

"I know nothing," Riley said. "I've worked at the Chamber for two and a half weeks. Your mom and Nina have all this shorthand, and secret code, and nicknames for people, and Celerie and I can't figure out what they're talking about. I'm pretty sure that's by design. I think we're only meant to see the tip of the iceberg."

"Well, you're not supposed to wear board shorts to work," Agnes said. "Did my mother give you a hard time?"

"No," Riley said. "She told me they were fabulous."

"She did?" Agnes was starting to feel like the planet was spinning the wrong way on its axis.

"She did," Riley said. "If you want to know where your mom is, maybe you should ask Nina."

"I tried, this afternoon," Agnes said. "Nina isn't giving her up."

"Well, I'm finished playing," Riley said. "Do you want to get out of here? Go somewhere else, maybe?"

"God, yes," Agnes said.

They climbed into Riley's Jeep, a forest-green Wrangler with a six-foot soft-top surfboard strapped to the roll bars. It was the quintessential Nantucket vehicle. He told her he'd owned it since he was eighteen and had driven it only on the island, back and forth between his parents' house in Pocomo and the south-shore surfing beaches.

"I'm sorry it's covered in dog hair," he said. "I have a chocolate Lab named Sadie, and she is the queen of this particular castle."

"Oh my God," Agnes said. "We had a chocolate Lab for thirteen years named Henry. My mother *loves* chocolate Labs. I think I just figured out why my mother hired you."

Riley laughed. "Believe me, I'm used to people loving me for my dog. Now, where should I take you?"

Agnes plucked at the yellow silk of her dress and arranged it around her legs. She wasn't used to anyone asking her what *she* wanted. In her life at home in New York, CJ made all the decisions. He picked the restaurants and the Broadway shows and the parties they would attend, he told her when to meet him at the gym, he picked the color of her nail polish when she got a pedicure.

What did *she* want?

"I want to find my mother," she said. "And I'm starving."

Riley held up the plastic cup with the five-dollar bill. "How about somewhere cheap?" He started the car, then looked over his shoulder as he shifted into reverse. "Food first," he said. "Then find."

They stopped at the Strip on Steamship Wharf, where Agnes got a cheeseburger with waffle fries (carbs and more carbs!), and Riley got three slices of pizza and two Cokes. They drove to Children's Beach and ate in the car overlooking the harbor.

"I used to come here as a kid," Riley said.

"Yeah, me too," Agnes said. She didn't mean to trump Riley's childhood nostalgia, but the grassy expanse of Children's Beach had been etched in her brain from her earliest memories. Her great-grandmother had pushed her on the swings and taught her how to pump her legs; Box used to sit on the green slatted benches reading *The Economist* while Agnes mastered the monkey bars. Her mother had planted her funny old red-and-white-striped umbrella, which exactly matched her red-and-white-striped bathing suit, in the sand at the shoreline while Agnes filled buckets with a slurry of sand and water.

"So what brings you home this summer?" Riley asked.

"I work at a Boys and Girls Club in Upper Manhattan, and we lost our summer funding," Agnes said.

"Lucky break?" Riley said.

"Some people might see it that way," Agnes said. "I worry about my members. This literally leaves six hundred kids without anywhere to hang out this summer."

"Whoa," Riley said.

"I'm trying not to dwell on it," Agnes said. "I tell myself they'll all go to the public library where it's air-conditioned, and they'll read."

"That's a good vision," Riley said. He folded his pizza in half; a rivulet of orange grease ran down his chin. Agnes handed him a napkin. "I love kids. That's one reason why I'm becoming a dentist. I mean, I'm interested in the medicine of it, but my dream is to build a strong family practice. I want to watch kids grow up, hear about their lacrosse games and their baton-twirling competitions, and their first dates."

"I sometimes worry that I get too attached to the kids at the club," Agnes said. She thought of Quincy and Dahlia, baking on hot squares of sidewalk. She had once told CJ that she wanted to adopt them and give them a safe home. But, as CJ had pointed out, Quincy and Dahlia already had a mother. And CJ didn't want kids at all—not biological, not adopted. "Some of them have really tough lives. It's difficult not to become overly invested in their well-being."

Riley smiled at her. "You have a good heart," he said. "Like mother, like daughter."

Suddenly, Agnes felt anxious. "Is it okay if we go? Is it okay if we go find her?"

Riley tossed his pizza crust out the window, where it was pounced on by hungry seagulls. "Of course," he said.

Nantucket was only thirteen miles long and four miles wide, but it was by no means a small or simple place. There were countless dirt roads and mysterious acres. Agnes didn't know where to start looking. But wherever Dabney was, she was driving the Impala, and thus she would be hard to miss.

"Should we go east or west?" Agnes asked.

"East?" Riley said. "Maybe she went to Sconset?"

"Sconset?" Agnes said. Dabney had always had lukewarm feelings about Sconset, in much the same way Union soldiers had lukewarm feelings about General Lee. There had been a period of time, years before Agnes was born, when Sconseters had wanted to secede. They had wanted their own town building and their own board of selectmen—and this had rubbed Dabney the wrong way. Now, as director of the Chamber, Dabney had to embrace and promote Sconset—the entire Daffodil Weekend was celebrated there—but Sconset fell prey to Dabney's rules: she would go once a year to the Chanticleer, once a year to the Summer House (but only for drinks and the piano player; she didn't trust the food), and once a year to the Sconset Casino for a movie. Every single day of the summer, she suggested that visitors bike out to Sconset, where she advised them to have lunch at Claudette's or ice cream from the Sconset Market—but she would never do these things herself. Agnes did not see her mother going to Sconset—for secret errands or otherwise. "Not Sconset. Let's head west."

Riley took a right onto Cliff Road, and Agnes began the lookout. She checked the driveways of all the grandiose homes on the right that overlooked the Sound. Maybe some friends had appeared from off-island and persuaded Dabney to play hooky from work and from Business After Hours? Her friends Albert and Corrine Maku sometimes showed up and demanded spontaneous fun. There might have been other people Agnes didn't know about—maybe one of her couples from 1989 or 2002 or 2011?

Really, what other explanation could there be?

Riley fiddled with the radio and, finding nothing satisfactory, turned it off. He said, "So, Agnes, do you have a boyfriend?"

"A fiancé," she said.

"Oh, okay. I'm sorry, I didn't know. Your mother didn't tell me you were engaged, and you're not wearing a ring."

Nope, Agnes thought guiltily. She had taken off her ring. Agnes had accidentally seen the receipt for the ring lying on CJ's mail table; it had cost him twenty-five thousand dollars. Agnes had nearly fainted. A twenty-five-thousand-dollar ring. Agnes could never, ever wear it to Morningside Heights, nor could she wear it on Nantucket as she led biking and rock-climbing excursions. The ring was in its box on her dresser. It was pretty but useless, a caged parakeet.

"My mother didn't tell you?" she said.

"No, but like I said, I'm not exactly privy to office secrets."

"It's not a secret," Agnes said. "Although maybe my mother wants to keep it that way. She doesn't approve."

"No?"

"No." Agnes sighed. "You do know, right, that my mother is a matchmaker?"

Riley threw his head back and laughed into the evening air.

"She's set up forty-two couples," Agnes said, "all of them still together. She's *famous* for it. She sees an aura—pink if it's good, green if it's bad. And my aura with CJ is green, so she can't give her blessing."

"You're kidding," Riley said.

"Not kidding."

"I told you I was only seeing the tip of the iceberg," Riley said. "She's a matchmaker! No wonder she was so excited when I told her I played Tevye in *Fiddler on the Roof*."

Agnes smiled. It was impossible to sustain a bad mood with this guy: he was too happy-go-lucky. "You'd better watch out," she said. "I think she has plans for you and Celerie."

"You think?" Riley said. "I was considering asking Celerie out, actually."

Ridiculously, Agnes experienced a pang of jealousy at this statement. Oh my God, what was *wrong* with her? "You should!" she said.

"But I think she has someone back home," Riley said. "In Minnesota."

"Minnesota is pretty far away," Agnes said.

"You're right," he said. "Okay, I'll do it. I'll ask if she wants to go up to Great Point with me on Saturday."

Another pang of jealousy: Agnes *loved* Great Point. To her, the perfect summer day was a cooler full of drinks, a couple of avocado BLTs from Something Natural, and a trip up to Great Point in a Jeep like this one—top down, radio blaring.

Agnes watched as Riley negotiated the curves of Madaket Road. He and Celerie would make a good couple. Agnes had thought that when she saw them together at the office. But earlier, at the office, she hadn't known Riley. She hadn't heard him play "Puff the Magic Dragon," she hadn't watched him eat pizza, she hadn't talked with him about her job. It was amazing how, after the past hour, she now felt like she had some sort of claim on him. The thought of him bestowing his affection on Celerie with her bouncy ponytail and her cheerleader moves and her favorite this and other-favorite that was upsetting.

No—what was really upsetting was that Agnes couldn't locate her mother. They weren't going to find her driving out to Madaket, of this much Agnes was suddenly certain.

"Would you mind taking me home?" Agnes asked.

Riley hit the brakes and the case of his guitar bumped against the back of Agnes's seat, emitting a dissonant chord. "What? Are you sure?"

"I'm sure," Agnes said. "This is silly. It's a wild-goose chase. I'll just wait for my mother at home."

"Oh," Riley said. "Okay, no problem. But just so you know, I'm happy to keep looking." He sounded wistful. Well, he had been enjoying the adventure, and now it was over. It had nothing to do with Agnes.

"I appreciate that," Agnes said. "But I'd like to go home."

Riley's cute face with his perfect, straight white teeth settled into an expression of something like hurt or regret. But that would be erased, Agnes was sure, once he asked out Celerie and Celerie said yes. It would, no doubt, be rosy auras all around.

*   *   *

It was ten thirty when Dabney finally walked in the door. Agnes was sitting at the kitchen table with an empty glass of milk in front of her. She had eaten half a dozen of her mother's oatmeal cookies and had let three of CJ's phone calls go to voice mail.

Dabney was clearly startled to see Agnes; she nearly dropped her Bermuda bag. "Oh! Darling, I'm sorry...I didn't expect...what are you doing...what?"

Agnes studied her mother. She was wearing the same navy polo shirt and madras skirt, penny loafers and pearls that she'd been wearing when she'd left that morning. Her hair was smooth in its headband. But something was different. What was it? She looked like she'd gotten sun. Had she been at the *beach?* Agnes wondered. She thought of Riley and Celerie up at Great Point, but that served only to irritate her further.

"Where have you been?" Agnes said. Her voice had a jagged edge. She could remember using such a tone with her mother only once before.

Dabney's expression was inscrutable at first. This woman, whom Agnes had believed to be so transparent, *was* hiding something. Tip of the iceberg, indeed!

"Tell me right now!" Agnes said. She was only too aware that she sounded like the parent in this scenario. "You left work at noon. You didn't answer your cell phone! You *skipped* Business After Hours! Where. Have. You. Been."

Dabney's eyes shone defiantly.

"Out," she said.

The reversal, Agnes thought, was complete.

DABNEY

She was utterly predictable; she never failed to act exactly like herself. The only surprising thing she had ever done in her life was to start this extramarital love affair.

But it was Clendenin Hughes. He had plucked her heart out of her chest when she was fourteen years old and she had never been able to reclaim it.

Love was her only excuse.

As soon as Dabney opened the door to Clen's cottage, she smelled garlic and ginger. Clen was at the stove; when he turned around, he didn't look surprised to see her, which she found maddening. She handed him a bottle of Gentleman Jack; she had stopped at Hatch's on her way to his house.

He said, "Only you would bring a hostess gift to a sexual rendezvous."

"That's not what this is," she said.

He said, "Wanna bet?" And in one fluid movement, he scooped her up with his strong right arm, threw her over his shoulder, and carried her to the bed.

There was only one thing to do: she laughed.

"Stop!" she said.

"What?"

"Turn off the burner on the stove," she said. "You don't want to burn the house down."

"Wanna bet?"

*   *   *

It was the same, it was different. She didn't have time to say what was which or which was what because there was no thinking involved. It was, in fact, like going up in flames. His mouth devoured every part of her, his skin burned against hers, his size crushed her, but as much as he gave her, she wanted more, faster, more. He sucked her nipples and she groaned, pressing herself against his thigh, leaving him wet there. How *long* had it been since she'd felt this way? When he thrust into her, she nearly broke in half; she opened her mouth and howled like an animal. She had slept with only two men in her life—Clen and Box—but Clen now was a third person. She was intoxicated by his physicality. His tongue, his lips, the way he tasted, the way he smelled, her hands in his thick hair, her cheek against his beard, skin on skin. It had been years since she'd even remembered she had a body, desire, *needs*.

When it was over, he peppered her face and neck with kisses as the sweat cooled on her body. She reached out and stroked the curve of his stump. The skin there was as soft as a baby's skin.

She closed her eyes. She saw cherry blossoms, bubble gum, and raspberries so ripe and juicy that they fell from the branches with the slightest touch.

When it was time for Dabney to head home, she started to cry.

Clen said, "Oh, Cupe, don't." Which made her cry harder.

"Come tomorrow," he said.

"I *can't!*" she said.

"Just for five minutes," he said. "Please."

The next day, Dabney signed out on the log at noon, writing *errands/lunch*.

"More errands?" Nina said slyly.

Dabney gave her a pointed look.

"I don't think you should sign out on the log when you leave," Nina said. "Just go. Vaughan hasn't checked the log in years."

Dabney appreciated Nina's leniency and her willingness to be an accomplice, but signing out on the office log had become a discipline of working at the Chamber, and Dabney couldn't bring herself to abandon it. She would conduct her love affair during business hours, but she would still sign out, thereby holding fast to one shred of her personal integrity.

The "five minutes" turned into an afternoon by the pool. Clen made watermelon margaritas and they floated on blow-up rafts. Clen was still a good swimmer, despite his missing arm; he moved through the water cleanly, with power. Dabney gazed at him with amazement and he said, "I bet you thought I'd go in circles, didn't you?" The water brought out his playful self; they splashed and dunked each other and poured more margaritas and generally acted like the teenagers they had been, so long ago.

Every time she thought to get up and leave, she found a reason to stay.

She said, "I can't believe I'm going to miss Business After Hours. I haven't missed a Business After Hours in fourteen years."

He said, "I'll order pizza and french fries and wings."

She said, "I can't have pizza. I've given up wheat."

He said, "That's the most preposterous thing I've ever heard."

He was right. Whatever was wrong with her, it wasn't a wheat allergy.

He said, "You're too thin."

She said, "I'm down to 106, which is what I weighed in eighth grade."

He said, "Jeez, Cupe."

She thought, *Lovesick*. She hadn't allowed herself to feel any guilt yet, but when the guilt kicked in, she feared, she would disappear. Box was in London. He stayed in a suite at the Connaught, and his daily life included a chauffeured Bentley that transported him back and forth between the hotel and the School of Economics, and to dinner at Gordon Ramsay and Nobu. His landscape was Big Ben, St. Paul's Cathedral, the National Gallery, Covent Garden, the London Bridge, and the Thames. Dabney could say the names of these places and things, but she had no concept of what his life there was like, just as he had no clue what her life was now like.

When he returned, she would have to tell him.

They ate dinner in bed, and Dabney drank a beer, something she hadn't done since the summer of 1987. She groaned and grunted with delight as she ate, she pulled strings of cheese from the pizza with her fingers and dangled them into her mouth. She sucked the sauce off the chicken bones, she dragged piping hot fries through ketchup, mayonnaise, and mustard, then back again. She would never have eaten like that in front of Box, but with Clen she was perfectly at ease.

It was for this reason, she supposed, that she said, "I'm worried about Agnes."

The name *Agnes,* although spoken casually, sucked all the oxygen out of the room.

Dabney immediately stiffened. "I'm sorry," she said. "I shouldn't have mentioned it."

"No, no," Clen said. "Please. Please tell me. What is it?"

"She's engaged," Dabney said.

Clen coughed. "Agnes is getting married?"

"Yes," Dabney said. Her voice was barely a whisper—the late, dark hour and the fraught topic seemed to require it. "To a man named CJ Pippin. He's a sports agent in New York."

Clen said, "And Agnes and this CJ person who is a sports agent in New York…are they a perfect match?"

"No."

"Really?" Clen seemed felt suddenly alert, intrigued. "And you're allowing it, Cupe?"

Dabney laughed. "Allowing it? That question shows just how little you know about having children."

"You're right," he said. "What I know about children I could write on my thumbnail and still have room for the Lord's Prayer."

"I have to go," Dabney said. The pain of their shared past, over a quarter century gone, was exquisite.

She stood on her tiptoes to kiss him goodbye. "It's been a long time since I've had a day like today," she said. "Thank you."

"Dabney?"

"What?"

"I want to meet her," he said.

"Who?" she said. And then, "No."

"Dabney."

"No."

She turned and walked to her car, shaking her head.

All the way home, she thought, *Agnes, Agnes, Agnes.*
And you're allowing it, Cupe?

A few days later, Dabney overheard Agnes on the phone with CJ. Dabney didn't mean to eavesdrop, but once she was within earshot, she couldn't move away.

Agnes said, "I don't see what your problem is with staying *here*…my mother *likes* you…yes, she *does*…you have to let that go, CJ…no, I am not coming to New York…it's summertime, I belong here…I don't want to, CJ…yes, baby, of *course* I love you…I could say the same to you…okay, baby, I'm sorry, I'm *sorry,* I said!" Tears. "CJ, please, *I'm sorry!*"

And you're allowing it, Cupe?

No, she was not allowing it. It was time to step in.

Dabney's first thought was Dave Patterson, who ran the Island Adventures program. He was scruffy, outdoorsy, and entrepreneurial. He had built Island Adventures up from a camp for ten kids to the sought-after program it was now, serving two hundred kids, and he had bought his own real estate and had built his own facility, including a fifty-foot rock-climbing wall. But Dave lived on Nantucket year-round—he, like Dabney, would never leave (another reason she liked him)—and as much as it pained her to say it, she didn't envision Agnes living year-round on the island.

Dabney had another idea for Agnes, and that was Riley Alsopp.

Was Dabney troubled by the fact that Riley had done the obvious and asked Celerie Truman out on a date?

Not really. Dabney had heard about the date in excruciating detail from Celerie, who had appeared at the Chamber office half an hour early just so she could talk to Dabney about it. Never mind that Dabney was Celerie's boss, never mind that Dabney was Riley's boss, never mind that Dabney, as director, might not love the idea of her two information assistants—who had to work next to each other all summer—dating. Celerie seemed eager, frantic even, to tell Dabney the whole story.

What had happened was this: Riley had planned on taking Celerie to Great Point for the afternoon, but Great Point had been closed due to nesting piping plovers, so Riley had suggested Smith's Point—same idea, a remote spit of sand, but on the other side of the island. Celerie had been game—heck yeah, she had never been to Smith's Point or Great Point. One of the failings of her first summer was not having befriended anyone with a 4WD vehicle; all of Celerie's friends drove Mini Coopers, so she had gone exclusively to Surfside. On the way from Great Point to Smith's Point, Riley's Jeep ran out of gas. The Jeep was older, the gauge unreliable. They were close to Cisco Brewers, so they decided to spend the afternoon there, drinking beer and listening to live music in the sun.

All good, right? Wrong! Celerie drank too much too quickly and didn't eat anything. It seemed the only food served at the brewery was from a hot-dog cart, and Celerie, as her name suggested, was a vegetarian. She had a Sheila's Favorite from Something Natural back in the Jeep, but by the time she thought of it, it had been sitting in the sun for hours and would be poisonous. Riley suggested calling a cab, or asking his father to pick them up—but Celerie, being drunk, insisted on one thing and one thing only and that was drinking more. She began to act like a real ass-hat (her word). She approached the lead singer of the band and suggested that he let Riley sing. The lead singer had no interest in relinquishing his microphone to Riley, but Celerie persisted in harassing him. Riley told the lead singer not to worry, he didn't want to sing. Celerie started to cry, insisting that Riley really did want to sing, and then, seconds later, she began to throw up. She was so sick that she monopolized the brewery's main bathroom for two hours. Riley waited for her just outside the door, continuously asking could he help, could he call a taxi, could he call her roommate?

When she finally did emerge, Riley had his Jeep waiting. His father had come with a gas can. Riley drove Celerie home and walked her to her door. By that point, it was dark and her roommate was out at the Chicken Box. Celerie made it inside to the living room, where she passed out facedown on the rag rug.

It was, she informed Dabney, the most embarrassing experience of her life, short of what had happened to her during sophomore year, which was too mortifying to relay, even now.

Celerie also said that Riley had called the next day to check on her, and that when Celerie launched into her serial apology, "I'm sorry, so sorry, so sorry!" he said, "Please don't worry about it, happens to the best of us, my fault for forgetting the sandwiches, maybe we can try it again sometime."

Celerie had looked imploringly at Dabney and said, "Do you think he'll ask me out again?"

Dabney realized then that she was being asked her opinion as a matchmaker. *I must be sick,* she thought. Her radar for such manipulation was failing.

She smiled at Celerie. "One never knows."

But of course Dabney did know: Riley was just being polite. He had been well raised. Riley needed someone a few years older; Celerie was scarcely twenty-two.

Riley needed Agnes.

But perhaps not as badly as Agnes needed Riley.

And while she was working on Agnes, why not Nina as well?

Dabney had tried to interfere in Nina's love life once before, when she told Nina not to marry George Mobley. Nina hadn't listened and Dabney hadn't blamed her; Dabney had waited too long to speak up and the relationship had too much momentum to stop. It had been like a boulder rolling down a hill. Nina had been left with a mountain of debt on one side of the seesaw, and five bright, talented kids on the other. In the seven years since Nina's divorce, she had not gone on a single date. She told Dabney she was too tired, too busy, and too disenchanted.

The name that kept presenting for Nina was Jack Copper. Dabney was stuck back in the conversation where she told Nina about Clen's return, and Nina had confessed to nearly hooking up with Jack. Jack Copper was single, he had always been single, and he was wiry, perpetually sunburned, craggy, salty. He had a South Boston accent that drove people like Box nuts, but that Dabney happened to adore. *Arararar, wicked pissah, I gotta stop smokin', arararar, kinda tough when you live at the bah.* Jack Copper ran a fishing charter off his forty-two-foot Whaler; he always caught fish, which attracted a lot of fancy clients. He drank beer at the Anglers' Club, he shot darts at the Chicken Box, he drove a Chevy pickup truck. He always talked to Dabney about her Impala, and he, too, dreamed of a Corvette Stingray split-window with matching numbers in Bermuda blue. Jack Copper wasn't a bad choice. Dabney might not have come up with his name on her own, but she was intrigued that Nina regretted passing him up.

Dabney dialed the number for Eleanor Sea Fishing Charters. "Eleanor Sea" was named for Eleanor C.—Jack's mother, who had once owned a boardinghouse on India Street.

Dabney had been expecting to leave a message on the machine; guys like Jack never answered their office phones, especially not during the summer. She was surprised when Jack picked up.

"Coppah heah."

"Hi, Jack," Dabney said. "It's Dabney Kimball!"

Dabney told Jack that he had won the raffle at the last Business After Hours and that the prize was a hundred-dollar gift certificate to Hatch's liquor store, and could Jack come into the office and pick it up that afternoon?

She knew Jack would not turn down free beer.

"Hell yeah!" Jack said. "I'll be theah at three o'clawk."

Dabney was delighted when Nina appeared at work wearing a sassy red tank dress that slowed off her cleavage. Nina rarely dressed like that. It was almost as if she knew.

At two thirty, Dabney said, "I'm going to take a late lunch. I should be back in an hour or so." She signed out on the log.

Nina said, "I don't know why you do that."

Dabney said, "I'm a goody-goody."

Nina said, "Well, you used to be. I'm not sure I would use that term to describe you anymore."

Dabney said, "I think Jack Copper is stopping by to pick this up." She dropped an envelope on Nina's desk.

Nina said, "What is it?"

"A gift certificate for Hatch's. He won it in the raffle at the last Business After Hours."

"No, he didn't," Nina said. "Hal Allen won the raffle." She squinted at Dabney. "You weren't even *at* the last Business After Hours."

"Make sure Jack gets that," Dabney said. "He's coming at three to pick it up."

"Dabney," Nina said, "what are you doing?"

But Dabney was halfway down the stairs, and she pretended not to hear.

When Dabney returned an hour later (after going out the Polpis Road to spend "five minutes" with Clen), the office was filled with green smoke. Dabney raced up the stairs, as panicked as if she'd set the building on fire.

The front room, where Dabney and Nina sat, was thick with

the green fog, but Nina's desk was unoccupied. Dabney poked her head into the back office. Both Celerie and Riley were on the phone, yammering cheerfully away, oblivious to the atmospheric disaster right outside the doorway. Of course, Dabney reminded herself, *they* couldn't see it. Only she could.

She waved her arms until Celerie put her call on hold.

"Yes, boss?" she said.

"Where is Nina?" Dabney said. "She's not at her desk."

Celerie shrugged. "She was here a minute ago, talking to some guy in a white visor."

Dabney zipped back out to the front office, waving away the pea-green soup, and checked the log. Nina hadn't signed out, but Nina wasn't the stickler about it that Dabney was. She might have left with Jack to get a coffee, or a drink.

Then Dabney thought she heard a noise coming from the conference room. Dabney hoped she was imagining it. She had to check. If the conference room was empty, then she would run down the street to the Anglers' Club.

She opened the door to find Jack Copper and Nina hooked together at the hips and at the mouth, leaning against the table used for board meetings. The green smoke was so thick that Dabney could barely see them, but she could tell they were seriously going at it.

"Hey, you two!" Dabney said brightly.

Immediately, they separated, and the air cleared enough for Dabney to see the stricken look on Nina's face.

"Nina, I need to talk to you for a second," Dabney said. "And, Jack, you can go. You got what you came for, right?"

Jack tugged at the bottom of his fishing shirt and adjusted his visor. "Um...yup," he said. "See you later." He beat a hasty retreat out of the conference room. Dabney waited until she heard his footsteps on the stairs before she closed the door. The air had cleared dramatically.

"God, that was embarrassing," Nina said. "I feel like I'm sixteen again and you're my mother. Why didn't you *knock?*"

"I didn't know where you were," Dabney said. "I was worried."

"Worried about what?" Nina said. "We were just kissing. That *is* why you called him up, right? That is why you paid a hundred dollars of your own money for a second gift certificate, right? That is why you told him to come at three and conveniently exited stage left at two thirty. Right?"

"Right," Dabney said. "I'm sorry."

"No, *I'm* sorry," Nina said. She looked out the window, down Main Street, at the receding figure of Jack Copper, hurrying away. "That's over, for sure. He'll never come up here again. Now if I want to see him, I'll have to hunt him down. Thanks a million."

"I actually did you a favor," Dabney said.

"A favor?" Nina said. "*You* get to go out and have fun. You've seen Clen practically every day since Box has been in London. And do I say a word about it? No! Because you are my best friend and I want you to be happy. But you don't feel the same way about me."

"I do, though," Dabney said.

"You don't!" Nina said. "You set me up just to tear me down."

"When I got to the office, I saw green smoke," Dabney said. "Just like with George! Jack Copper isn't a perfect match for you, Nina."

"I don't *care* if he's a perfect match!" Nina said, her voice louder now. "I just want a man to pay attention to me! I just want to have fun! Isn't there a third category? Where you see happy-for-now yellow? Or a peaceful blue? Or a pulsing-hot red?"

"No," Dabney said. "It doesn't work that way."

"Well, too bad," Nina said.

"I want to find you someone special," Dabney said. "Someone right. Someone for forever."

"I don't want someone for forever! I want someone for *today!* And you just chased him away!"

"You *do* want someone for forever," Dabney said. "I know you do." She welled up with tears. "And even if you don't want it, I want it for you." Tears streamed down Dabney's face. She had been so sure Jack Copper would work, but no—he was the wrong choice. Dabney's instincts were way off.

Nina plucked Dabney a tissue. "Dabney," she said, "what is wrong with you?"

But Dabney wasn't sure.

AGNES

She had a group of ten bikers heading out to Quidnet Pond. Six boys, four girls, all of them strong riders except for a child named Dalton, who hailed from New York City (Park Avenue between Sixty-Ninth and Seventieth) and who attended Collegiate. Dalton had gruesomely chapped lips and one of the reasons he was lagging behind and holding up the group was that he had to stop every three to four minutes to apply his SPF 30ChapStick. That, and his bike helmet—which Agnes noted was the most expensive bike helmet money could buy—didn't fit properly and kept slipping forward into his eyes. He had nearly had a collision with the girls in front of him thanks to said helmet.

Agnes hated to admit it, but she wasn't very fond of Dalton. She had snapped at him earlier, telling him he had to keep up or he would be demoted to the nine-year-olds' group. It wasn't a very nice thing for her to say. She wasn't really angry at Dalton—he was merely annoying—she was angry at CJ. CJ had canceled coming up for the weekend; the room at the White Elephant hadn't come through, and that apparently was a deal breaker.

"I don't see why you can't stay at the house," Agnes had said. "Box is in London and my mother is never home."

"I won't be comfortable," CJ said. "I won't be relaxed. And if I'm going to spend time with you, I'd like to be both of those things."

Uncomfortable and ill at ease because of Dabney, Agnes thought. If Dabney had been in London, CJ would have come.

He said, "I'd like you to come to New York this weekend."

"No," she said. "I can't."

"Why not?" he said.

She had tried to come up with a reason. She *could* go to New York, but she didn't want to. CJ would be on the phone all weekend anyway, negotiating the never-ending Bantam Killjoy deal. BK had been drafted by the Jaguars, but he was unhappy; he wanted to be out West. CJ was trying to get him to Kansas City or San Diego. Or at least that was what Agnes thought was happening; she had sort of lost track.

"I'm on *Nantucket,* CJ," she said. "I'd like to go to the beach. Enjoy summer."

"We can enjoy summer in the city," he said. "We can walk in Central Park and put our feet in the fountain. We can go to a Yanks game. We can get reservations at any restaurant in the city. You want me to book at Le Bernadin? Minetta Tavern?"

"Um…" she said. "Maybe next weekend?"

"It doesn't even sound like you want to see me," CJ said.

"I do," Agnes said. She had then sung out a chorus of apologies that she didn't quite mean.

*   *   *

At the turnoff for Quidnet Road, Agnes gathered her campers. There were some fun personalities here—Archie, Samantha, Bronwyn, and Jamey (boy) and Jamie (girl). But everyone was hot and thirsty, the water bottles were down to the last inches, and the kids were eager for a swim and lunch.

Agnes gave the final directions—slight left onto Quidnet Road, half a mile to the pond, lock up, head to the beach, stay together, no one in the water until Agnes blew the whistle—and they all waited for Dalton to catch up. He was forty yards back, ChapStick break.

Just then, Agnes's attention was snared by the sight of the Impala barreling up the Polpis Road. Her mother, sunglasses on, was at the wheel, singing. Agnes caught the strains of the Rolling Stones' "Hang Fire."

Agnes waved. She shouted, "Mom! Mom!" But the Impala cruised past; Dabney was too intent on where she was going to notice her only child.

Where was she going? Agnes couldn't very well follow her.

The campers were intrigued. "Was that your mom?" Samantha asked. "Like, your Mom mom?"

Agnes realized that to her campers, she probably seemed too old to have a mother.

"Was that her *car*?" Archie asked. "A 1967 Chevy Impala?"

There was a motorhead in every group. Agnes nodded. "That was my mom," she said. "My Mom mom. And yes, that's her car."

"Your mom must be *cool*," Archie said.

That night at dinner, Agnes waited until Dabney had finished her first glass of wine and poured her second before she asked. Again, it looked like her mother had gotten sun. The freckles on her cheeks were plentiful and pronounced.

"I saw you on the Polpis Road today," Agnes said. "By the Quidnet turnoff? I was with my campers. Where were you going?"

Dabney took a bite of her grilled salmon with homemade dill sauce, then made a face of ecstasy. Agnes had to agree: her mother cooked like a goddess. Agnes had gained three pounds since she'd been home.

Dabney said, "The summer between my senior year in high school and my freshman year in college, I got a flat tire on Main Street." She dabbed her lips and took a sip of wine. "In the Nova. I popped it against the granite curb right outside of Murray's Toggery. And no sooner had I gotten out of the car to look at the damage than a police car pulled up." Dabney smiled. "And it was Grampy!"

"Oh," Agnes said.

"What are the chances my own father would wander by at the exact moment my tire popped? I was very happy to see him, even though he made me change it myself. You remember what your grandfather was like."

"Mom," Agnes said. "Where were you going today?"

"I just thought of that story because of how funny it is to run into, you know, your parents, or your kids, when you're out doing other things, living your life."

"Mom."

Dabney lifted a spear of asparagus with her fingers and nibbled it. "I had lunch at Sankaty Beach Club," she said.

"Really?" Agnes said. This didn't sound right. Dabney didn't like to go to the Sankaty Beach Club, because her mother, Patty Benson, had been a member there, and thus Dabney had decided the place was cursed. "I thought you refused to eat there."

"Well," Dabney said, "I did today."

NINA MOBLEY

Dabney was out of the office when Marcus Cobb came in to register with the Chamber. Marcus Cobb was actually Dr. Marcus Cobb, an ophthalmologist, who was setting up a practice on Old South Road.

A real eye doctor! Nina thought.

He was of medium height, had a shaved head, and was dressed in a shirt and tie. Nina loved a man in a shirt and tie, probably because she had grown up on Nantucket, where nobody wore a shirt and tie except for the high school superintendent and the insurance guys across the street.

Nina said, "You know, I could use a pair of glasses. I haven't been able to see clearly in years."

This made Dr. Marcus Cobb laugh. He thought Nina was kidding.

Couple #17: Genevieve Martine and Brian Lefebvre, married twenty-one years, five daughters

Genevieve: When I first met Dabney, I was twenty-one and she was seventeen and we worked together at Nantucket Cotton, a T-shirt shop which was the most successful retail spot on the island. I was from Canada, I had just graduated from McGill with a useless degree in French language and literature, and I had come to Nantucket because I had accidentally fallen in love with my cousin's husband. I came from a large Catholic family and my mother, who was positively *verklempt* with me, told me to leave the country and pray to God for forgiveness.

I took the first job I was offered; the T-shirt shop was desperate for help. Dabney, although four years younger than me and still a teenager, was my manager. The owner, a man named Ed Law, told me I was to listen to Dabney and take all my direction from her. She was, he said, the best employee he'd ever had.

Dabney was a cute girl—she always wore jeans, loafers, opera-length pearls, a headband, and, during her shift, a pink crewneck T-shirt that said NANTUCKET NATIVE in navy letters across the front. Ed Law had had the T-shirt custom made for her, she said. And I thought, *Wow, Ed Law is a cool dude.*

Dabney was the one who told me that Nantucket Cotton was the highest-grossing retail space on the island, outearning even the galleries and the jewelry stores. Every visitor to the island wanted to leave with a souvenir, Dabney said. A T-shirt was lightweight, inexpensive, and practical. Ed Law had been the first person on the island to branch out beyond the name of the island. He created a T-shirt satirizing the first line of the famously lewd limerick. The T-shirt said: I AM THE MAN FROM NANTUCKET.

We sold thousands.

What I quickly learned about Dabney was that not only was she a good manager—she was organized and fair with our work schedule, responsible with the cash register and the "bank," and she led by example with her work ethic (she folded a T-shirt better than I'd ever seen it done, and stacked them in order of ascending size, which wasn't mandatory by Ed Law's standards, but that was how Dabney liked it done)—she was also a superstar when it came to customer service. She engaged the customers, and asked where they were from and where they were staying. She had encyclopedic knowledge of the island and would always suggest restaurants to people, or off-the-beaten-path places to bike and picnic. People loved it! Most customers ended up buying extra T-shirts because of Dabney, and then Ed Law got the idea to sell tourist maps for three dollars apiece, and Dabney would customize the maps for everyone who came in based on their individual needs and desires.

"You should work for the Chamber of Commerce," I said.

She beamed at me. "You're right!" she said. "I should!"

"But what would Ed Law do then?" I said. And we laughed.

Dabney had a boyfriend named Clendenin Hughes, who would wait for her at the end of every shift. He would sit on the bench out in front of the shop and read until Dabney was finished. Then he would take her hand and they would walk off.

I worked with Dabney for three summers, until I had an ill-fated love affair with Ed Law. I had just earned forgiveness for my cousin's husband, when I had to start all over again. After leaving Nantucket Cotton, I waitressed at the Atlantic Café, and then I decided I needed a "real job," and I was hired as a receptionist by Ted Field, who at that time was so new to the island, he made me feel like a local.

Meanwhile, I continued to get involved with married men, despite my best efforts to avoid them. It wasn't me; it was them. They lied to me. Ed Law had insisted he was separated, on the verge of divorcing—not true at all. When Dabney was graduating from Harvard, I was dating Peter the Fireman, whom I later discovered had . . . a wife and two kids in Billerica, Mass. And when I found out Dabney was pregnant, I had just broken up with Greg, a pilot from Bermuda. Married.

I could ask for forgiveness all day long, but it wasn't helping. It was like an affliction, or a disease I was carrying.

I saw Dabney at the grocery store—in the middle of February, in the middle of the night—her belly about ready to burst. I gasped at the shock of it. Hugely, roundly pregnant, Dabney Kimball, who had been so responsible with the cash register.

She was buying chocolate ice cream. She looked over and saw me, but she did not smile.

"Oh, hi, Genevieve," she said.

My heart swelled with affection. Dabney was one of the only people who pronounced my name correctly, with four syllables. Ge-ne-vie-eve.

I said, "What's this? Is the baby . . . yours and Clen's?"

She looked at me with flat eyes. "No," she said. And then she walked away.

Well, one can't work as a receptionist at a doctor's office and not hear all the gossip: yes, it was Clendenin's baby, no, it wasn't Clendenin's baby, it was someone else's, a summer kid's, then no, it wasn't the summer kid's, it was Clendenin's after all. Probably, maybe Clendenin's, nobody was sure, and Clendenin himself was gone, off to be a reporter in the Sudan.

When the baby was born, I knew her name and weight within the hour: Agnes Bernadette, seven pounds fourteen ounces, eighteen and a half inches long. But there was no announcement in the paper.

And I thought, *How did the sweetest, smartest, most together young woman I had ever met end up like this?*

For a baby gift, I special-ordered a tiny pink T-shirt that said NANTUCKET NATIVE in navy letters across the front. An inspired gift, I thought. Dabney sent a card on her monogrammed stationery: Love the T-shirt . . . so many good memories . . . thank you for thinking of us. But that was the last I saw or heard from her for a while. At that time, Ted Field was not her doctor.

Then, a few years later, I received an invitation to Dabney's wedding. She was getting married to an economics professor from Harvard! I was thrilled for her, if a little jealous. I was dying to meet someone suitable—someone single—and get married.

Dabney and Box wed at the Catholic church and held the reception in the backyard of Dabney's grandmother's house on North Liberty. It was a wedding exactly like one would expect for Dabney—there were lots of roses and champagne cocktails and tasty hors d'oeuvres and a string quartet played Vivaldi, and Dabney looked beautiful in an ivory lace dress. She was in photographs with everyone, including the caterers and the valet parkers. Agnes wore a little pink dress that matched the color of the roses and I thought, *This is a more fitting ending for someone as magnificent as Dabney.*

Just before we were to be seated for dinner, Dabney grabbed my arm.

"I'm moving you," she said.

"What?" I said. I held a place card that said Indigo Table, which Dabney snatched out of my hands.

She said, "I haven't been a very good or attentive friend the past few years, I know that. But I am going to make up for it now. Follow me. I want you at the Pink Table."

The Pink Table was up front, at the edge of the dance floor, where the orchestra would soon be playing. I felt like I was on an airplane, getting bumped to first class, or at a hotel being upgraded to an oceanfront suite. I hoped Dabney wasn't moving me solely because she felt guilty about neglecting our friendship. We had had a great time laughing in the shop about "the Man from Nantucket," but we had also bonded on serious topics—her mother leaving, her all-consuming romance with Clendenin, my unwanted role as the "other woman." I loved Dabney, I was always going to love Dabney, no matter where I was seated at her wedding.

Then I saw Brian. Blond guy with nice broad shoulders and little glasses.

"Genevieve," Dabney said. "This is Box's second cousin once removed, Brian Lefebvre. He just graduated from Harvard Law School and he's setting up a practice on the island."

Lefebvre, I thought. *He's French. Harvard Law School. Moving to Nantucket.*

I took a seat next to him and smiled. It all sounded good, but I was wary.

"Nice to meet you, Brian," I said. "I'm Genevieve Martine." We shook hands. He seemed very nervous, which I found charming.

Dabney said, "I'll let you two get acquainted. I have to go smile for the camera."

I saw Brian reach out and touch Dabney's arm. I saw him mouth the words *thank you,* and I busied myself with unfolding the pink linen swan on my plate and placing it neatly in my lap.

He said, "So, Genevieve..." Off to a good start because he pronounced my name perfectly. "What do you do on the island?"

"I'm the office manager for Dr. Ted Field's family medical practice," I said.

"Oh," he said. "And are you...single?"

"Yes," I said. "Are you?"

He nodded his head emphatically. "Yes," he said.

He wasn't wearing a ring, but as I had learned, this meant nothing.

"Really?" I said.

"Well," he said.

And I thought, *Yep, here it comes. He's separated, but divorce is pending. He's married, but his wife lives overseas. He just said he was single because he was stunned by my beauty; what he really meant was that he is married.*

"I was married," he said. "A long time ago. Five years ago. It lasted seven months, no kids. I like to think of it as taking a mulligan."

"A mulligan," I said. "Like in golf."

"Right," he said. "Where you get to start over without being penalized."

I narrowed my eyes, still skeptical. "But you are divorced, right? Legally divorced?"

"Not only divorced," he said. "Annulled." He leaned closer to me and whispered, "I'm Catholic. The annulment was very important to my mother."

I couldn't believe it. I said, "You're telling me the truth, right?"

He said, "Dabney told me to bring my divorce papers along to show you. She told me to bring my annulment signed by the bishop. But I thought she was kidding."

I laughed mightily at that. "She told you to bring your divorce papers?"

He smiled and blushed and in that moment was just about the most adorable man I had ever laid eyes on.

And then I realized what was happening. We were at the Pink Table. Pink—of course!

BOX

He received an e-mail from the Department of the Treasury: the president and the secretary needed him in Washington. He let the e-mail sit unanswered for nearly twelve hours while he decided what to do. Then, somehow, an aide tracked him down at the Connaught, and left a message with the front desk. A girl just out of university handed the message to Box with wide-eyed awe. It probably seemed to her like something from a movie, but to Box the news was merely tiresome. He threw the message away.

But when he awoke in the morning, there was a voice mail on his cell phone from the secretary himself. The president badly needed his consult; he was getting a lot of pressure from Wall Street about interest rates and trade sanctions in North Korea. Things were a mess now, but they might be looking at an even bigger mess, and "we all know how the president feels about his legacy vis-à-vis the deficit." And, "Please, Box, as a favor to me personally, as a service to your country..."

Box sat on the edge of the bed and exhaled. First-term presidents were worried about reelection; second-term presidents, their legacies.

Dabney hadn't wanted him to come to London at all. He couldn't imagine her reaction when he called and asked if he could extend his trip for a week in Washington.

But it was the President of the United States, and the Secretary of the Treasury, and, more important, it was work. As at least one of his students pointed out each semester, most economic theory had no actual bearing on people's *lives*. But this would. If Box didn't go and put his hands on it, someone else would, and he or she would muck it up.

He called Dabney.

"Darling," he said. He then launched into his careful argument: the Secretary of the Treasury, the nation's economic policy, another week away, he was sorry. But even with a side trip to Washington, he would be back on Nantucket by the Fourth of July.

Dabney surprised him by saying, "Of course, darling, by all means, if the secretary needs you—go! I'm so proud and thrilled for you. What an honor!"

Box had to agree with her: it was an honor. He was glad that Dabney was back to her supportive and agreeable self. She was far more encouraging than he'd anticipated.

"Thank you, darling," he said. "For understanding."

"Don't be silly," Dabney said.

Her voice was light, even joyful. She must be feeling much better, he thought.

Box called the secretary back.

DABNEY

Nina walked into the office wearing a chic new pair of glasses and announced that she had a date with Dr. Marcus Cobb for the following Wednesday night.

Dabney was nearly speechless. "Who is Dr. Marcus Cobb?" she asked. The name sounded familiar, but Dabney couldn't place it. It sounded like the name of one of the guys Oprah had elevated to celebrity status—Dr. Phil, Dr. Oz—but that wasn't right.

"The eye doctor," Nina said. "He joined the Chamber earlier this week."

"Right!" Dabney said. She had just processed his application yesterday. "I am *losing* it!"

"He asked me out when he came into the office," Nina said.

"Did he?" Dabney said. She was surprised that this was the first she was hearing of it. "Where is he taking you?"

"To the Galley for dinner," Nina said.

The Galley Beach was not just a good first date, it was the *best* first date. "I can't believe it," Dabney said.

"You can't believe someone would want to take me out?" Nina said.

"No!" Dabney said. "It's not that." She didn't know how to explain what she was feeling. If Nina was finally going to go on a date, Dabney had wanted to be the one to set her up. She wanted to redeem herself for the Jack Copper debacle. "When do I get to meet him?"

"I'm not sure," Nina said. Her face held an expression that Dabney couldn't decipher. "I think maybe I'd like to take this one slow...maybe keep it to myself for a while...would you understand if I didn't introduce you right away?"

"I promise not to say anything," Dabney said. "I know I messed up with Jack, Nina. I would love to meet Dr. Marcus Cobb, just get a look at him, and I swear not to say a word about auras or smoke. I swear!"

"Dabney," Nina said, "I'm asking for space with this one. Okay?"

"Oh," Dabney said. "Okay." She tried not to feel hurt. She supposed she should be glad that Nina had taken care of things on her own. Dabney was terribly busy.

* * *

She and Clen had been spending nearly every afternoon together—either at the pool or at the beach. Clen preferred the pool. It was less of a hassle and the wind didn't ruffle his newspapers and there was indoor plumbing, as well as the blender for margaritas. Dabney was becoming accustomed to frozen drinks and homemade sandwiches—one more delectable than the last—delivered to her chaise.

Dabney preferred the beach because to her, the beach *was* Nantucket, and it returned her to the summers of her youth. Once upon a time, Dabney and Clen had been the King and Queen of Madequecham Beach. Clen was in charge of bringing the keg each Sunday, and Dabney organized the firewood, the charcoal grills, the hot dogs and hamburgers and marinated chicken thighs, the chips and potato salad and brownies. They played horseshoes and touch football and they threw the Frisbee. They listened to the Who and the Boss and Van Morrison. *Making love in the green grass, behind the stadium with you, my Brown-Eyed Girl.*

They had good, long talks during those afternoons. Clen told her the story of how he'd lost his arm, which was so horrific and disturbing that Dabney couldn't bear to think about it. She would reach out periodically and stroke the skin of his stump and think of what a brave man he was, what a resilient man.

She signed out on the log nearly every day, writing, *errands*. Her errands were: Beach. Pool. Sandwiches. Talk. Love.

Love.

Clen had said to her, "Take the words back. I want to hear you take them back."

She laid her hand on his cheek and looked into the green glen and weak tea of his eyes. "I take them back."

I don't love you.

"Tell me you didn't mean them when you said them."

She said, "I didn't mean them when I said them. I have always loved you, Beast, and I always will."

It was, all of it, something like a state of bliss, but it was coming to an end. They had been granted a week's reprieve when Box called to say he was going to Washington.

"The president?" Clen had scoffed. "Are you sure he isn't exaggerating his own importance?"

Box had flaws like everyone else, but exaggerating his own importance wasn't one of them. Dabney was just grateful for an extra week of freedom.

Agnes, however, was growing more curious by the day. *Where were you going today? I saw you driving on the Polpis Road. Why were you not at work? I called the office at three o'clock and they said you'd stepped out. Again. What's going on, Mom? Is there something you want to tell me? Are you seeing Dr. Donegal again, because if you are, I think that's great. Nina says you're out doing errands. What kind of errands? Does Nina know where you're going?*

Dabney yearned to tell her daughter the truth.

Clen said, "Why don't you?"

Maybe if she'd been having an affair with Dr. Marcus Cobb, or a young waiter from the Boarding House, she would have confided in her daughter. But Clendenin Hughes was a nuclear bomb.

A week after Agnes turned sixteen, Dabney had started teaching Agnes to drive in the parking lot of Surfside Beach. They went in the evenings after dinner, just the two of them, and Dabney rode shotgun and offered tips she thought might be helpful. They drove

Dabney's Mustang, which had been an impulse buy after her Camaro died. She'd had the Mustang for only eighteen months total (buying a Ford had been a mistake), but the car would have great importance to her because in it she had told Agnes the truth.

Dabney didn't remember her exact words. What would she have said?

Honey, sweetheart, darling…Daddy—Box—isn't your biological father. Your biological father is a man named Clendenin Hughes.

It had gone something like that.

He lives in Asia now. He left the country before I discovered I was pregnant and it was impossible for him to get back. It would have been far easier for me to go over there, but I couldn't go, and so I told him to please let me raise you on my own. I'm not explaining this well, darling, it was very complicated.

Clendenin Hughes. He lives in Thailand now, I think, or Vietnam.

All Dabney could remember was Agnes's high-pitched, hysterical screaming like Dabney was stabbing her in the eye with a fork.

She had waited too long. Dr. Donegal had said thirteen. Box had wanted her to know at age ten.

But Dabney was Agnes's mother; Dabney was in charge of what her daughter knew, and when.

Dabney hadn't wanted Agnes to know at all, ever.

What did it matter? Really, *what?* Box had been a good father. He had been with Agnes since before lasting memory. Why mess up Agnes's beautiful head with information she would never, ever need?

Because it was the truth. Because it was blood. Dabney and Box had done a lot of, if not actual lying, then sidestepping of the truth. Agnes had asked why she looked nothing like Box and Box had said, "Human genetics are capricious, my pet." Agnes had asked

Dabney about the photographs of her and Clen together in the yearbook. *This was your boyfriend, Mom? Yes, I suppose it was. Whatever happened to him? Oh, he's long gone.*

Agnes had never seen her birth certificate. Clen's name wasn't on it. Dabney wouldn't allow it; she'd been too freshly wounded, too consumed with baffling emotion. Dr. Benton, who was the doctor on Nantucket before Ted Field, had done the delivery and he had every idea who the father was, but Dabney looked him dead in the eye and said she had no idea. She said she had slept with a lot of boys the preceding summer.

On the line for father, it said: *unknown.*

Dabney had decided to confess on Agnes's sixteenth birthday because of the birth certificate. Agnes needed a copy to apply to a summer study program abroad, and whereas Dabney had been able to handle the birth certificate up until that point—for school registration, Little League, etc.—now it was impossible to keep it out of Agnes's hands. Agnes could have taken five dollars to the registrar at any moment and gotten a copy herself.

The screaming. *You lied to me. You lied about my very being. How can I trust anything you say ever again? How do I know you're even my mother? I wish you weren't. I wish you weren't my mother.*

Dabney was prepared for all this. Dr. Donegal had told her to expect it. Of course, it was one thing to know it was coming and another to actually experience it. Dabney was glad she had chosen to break the news while she was still in the driver's seat of the Mustang. Agnes might have floored it—straight over the sand and into the ocean.

I wish you weren't my mother.

Other girls Agnes's age threw out lines like that all the time, Dabney knew, but Agnes never had. Dabney wouldn't lie: it hurt, and it hurt worse because Agnes had every right to be angry. Dabney had withheld pertinent information, perhaps the most pertinent. Dabney *had* lied to her about her very being. Dabney had misjudged the timing. She had wholeheartedly disagreed with Box about telling Agnes at ten. What ten-year-old was mature enough to understand paternity? Agnes had only just learned what sex was. And at thirteen, Agnes had been going through puberty—she got her period, she started shaving her legs, her face broke out—no, Dabney wasn't going to add to her worries by telling her about Clen.

At sixteen, Agnes was mature, responsible, intelligent, and calm. Dabney had thought she would take the news in stride. It explained why there were no pictures of Box with Agnes as a baby, and why they shared no physical characteristics.

But Agnes was hysterical. She was beyond angry, beyond upset. Dabney had driven from the Surfside Beach parking lot to their house on Charter Street while Agnes wailed. The windows of the Mustang were rolled up, but Dabney was still convinced that everyone on the island could hear.

When they reached the house, Agnes called Box in Cambridge. Dabney had thought that Agnes would be equally upset at Box for keeping the secret—but no. Agnes merely wanted Box's confirmation that what Dabney had said was true (as if Dabney would lie about something like that?), and finding it so, she cried and cried, allowing Box, and only Box, to console her.

To Agnes, Dabney was the liar, the slut, the enemy. Agnes didn't speak to Dabney for three weeks, and even after that, things were strained.

A mother first, a mother forever. Dabney had lived by these words, but that didn't mean she hadn't made mistakes. She had made a mistake in not telling Agnes sooner. *I'm sorry, darling!*

Box wasn't happy with Dabney, either. She had suffered through a great big dose of *I told you so*.

Dabney wondered if she should have waited until Agnes was eighteen, or twenty-one. Maybe her mistake wasn't in waiting too long but in not waiting long enough. Maybe she should have waited until Agnes had enough experience to realize that life was a complicated mess and you could count on being hurt the worst by the person you loved the most.

However, in the weeks following the revelation, she noticed that Agnes expressed curiosity about Clendenin Hughes. Dabney's yearbooks ended up on the floor of Agnes's bedroom. Agnes googled Clen on the family computer; she brought up a list of his articles and may even have read a few. And then Dabney found a letter addressed to Clen, care of the *New York Times*. It was lying on top of Agnes's math textbook, in plain sight, as if Agnes had wanted Dabney to see it. More likely, it had been left there as a form of torture.

Dabney had wanted few things in life as much as she had wanted to read that letter.

Then, as it always did, summer arrived and Agnes attended her program in France, and she came home weeks later with a penchant for silk scarves at the neck, and for calling Dabney "Maman," and a ferocious new love of macarons. She brought Dabney the foolproof baguette recipe, and mother and daughter baked bread together and ate it with sweet butter and sea salt—and once, magically, the addition of an ounce of dark chocolate—and everything pretty much went back to normal. Dabney was Mom, Box was Dad, and Clen's name wasn't mentioned again. Life went on.

*   *   *

But Dabney wasn't naive. She knew she had done some real damage and inflicted some real hurt, just as her own mother had when she disappeared for good, leaving Dabney in the care of May, the Irish chambermaid. Dabney feared that perhaps her mothering was flawed and doomed because she had received such poor mothering herself.

But no—no excuses. Dabney had never felt sorry for herself; she was her own person. She had made a decision, right or wrong. *We all make choices.*

But to tell Agnes that Dabney was now in love with Clendenin Hughes, her biological father, and having an affair with him?

We all make choices?

No.

Dabney woke up in the morning unable to get out of bed. She couldn't describe it. There was pain…everywhere.

Agnes said, "Do you want me to call Dr. Field?"

"No," Dabney said. It was not stress, or guilt. She was lovesick. "Just call Nina, please, and draw the shades." The sun was giving Dabney a headache; she wanted the bedroom dark. It was such a sin, Dabney wanted to cry, but there was no option. Her body felt invaded by pain, colonized by pain.

Agnes brought a glass of ice water and two pieces of buttered toast. The toast would never be eaten.

"I called Nina and told her you were sick," Agnes said. "Can I bring you anything else?"

"Just please don't tell Daddy," Dabney said. "I don't want him to worry."

*   *   *

The following day, Dabney woke up feeling fine. A little flannel-mouthed, maybe, but otherwise fine. So maybe not lovesick, maybe a twenty-four-hour bug.

"We're going to dinner tonight at the Boarding House," Dabney said. "Put on something pretty."

Agnes said, "You just feel sorry for me because CJ canceled. I'm going to stay home and mope. Eat Oreos from the bag, watch bad TV."

"Reservation at seven o'clock," Dabney said. "I'll meet you at the restaurant, though, because I have to run some errands."

"What errands?" Agnes said.

"Wear something pretty!" Dabney said.

AGNES

When she got to dinner at the Boarding House, Dabney was already waiting at the usual table on the patio, but there was a third chair added, and Riley Alsopp was sitting in it.

Dabney beamed as Agnes approached. "There she is!" she said.

Riley Alsopp stood up. He was wearing a shirt and tie, khaki pants, and flip-flops. He grinned when he saw her. "Hey, Agnes!"

Agnes thought, *My mother is so obvious.*

Dabney excused herself before dessert. "You two stay and enjoy," she said. "I'm going back to the house. I'm still not feeling a hundred percent." She dropped her napkin onto her empty plate. She had devoured her dinner. "The bill is all paid, Riley. My husband insists on a house account. He would eat here breakfast, lunch, and dinner seven days a week if he could. Anyway, stay and have an after-dinner drink, please, or another beer, whatever you want." Dabney was busy gathering up her Bermuda bag and her cardigan, trying to beat a quick yet organic-seeming retreat so that Agnes and Riley could be alone. Agnes had seen her mother do it again and again and again.

Agnes pitched forward in her seat. As a defense against the matchmaking, Agnes had drunk too many glasses of Shiraz. "You know she's trying to set us up, right?"

Riley exhaled in a long stream. "Right."

"She gets an idea in her head," Agnes said.

"Does she *see* something?" Riley said. "I mean, has she told you if she's seen... if we're like... pink or whatever?"

Agnes smiled at him. Pink, rosy, she and Riley Alsopp? She briefly imagined what being in a relationship with Riley would be like, and the first word that came to her mind was *easy*. Did she *want* easy? She couldn't believe she was thinking this way. She was engaged to CJ, and just because she was angry with him did not mean she could pair off with someone else, even cute, easy Riley Alsopp. She said, "How was your date with Celerie?"

"Unequivocal disaster. She got really drunk and threw up."

Agnes said, "Jeez, I might be next. I've had a lot of wine."

Riley said, "It wasn't her drinking or puking that was the problem. There was just a disconnect. Lack of chemistry. On my end, anyway. The problem is that I have to sit next to her all day long and I can tell she's just waiting for me to ask her out again."

"But you're not going to?"

"I'm not going to."

Agnes grabbed his hand. "Let's follow my mother."

"What?"

She pulled him up. "We're going to follow my mother. She's keeping a secret."

Riley trailed Agnes out of the restaurant and onto the street. "What kind of secret?"

"She goes somewhere. She's hiding something. That night, when she was supposed to be at Business After Hours...?"

"Yeah," Riley said. "Where was she?"

"She came home at ten o'clock. She wouldn't tell me where she'd been."

Agnes hurried along Federal Street, then turned up Main. She saw Dabney across the street, half a block ahead of them.

"I bet you a million bucks when she gets to our house, she climbs into the Impala and drives off."

"You think?"

"We're going to follow her," Agnes said. "In my Prius."

"You drive a Prius?" Riley asked. "How do you like it?"

Agnes rolled her eyes. Everyone asked her that. "It's fine. Great on gas."

In Agnes's Prius, they stalked Dabney up Main to Fair, and then up Fair to Charter. On Charter, Agnes held Riley back. They couldn't get too close to the house.

"I bet she gets right into the car," Agnes whispered.

Dabney did not get into the Impala. She opened the gate and entered the house through the side door. Agnes thought perhaps she'd gone to grab her keys. She waited. The light came on in Dabney's bedroom.

Agnes suddenly became aware that she and Riley were holding hands—like, really holding hands, with their fingers entwined. Riley had warm, strong, dentist's hands.

Riley stroked Agnes's thumb with his thumb.

Agnes pulled her hand away. If CJ could see them right now, Agnes thought, he would have hired a hit man. She shivered, remembering what had happened with her hair. She said, "Riley, I'm engaged. To be married."

Riley cleared his throat. "I know," he said. And then in a softer, sadder voice: "I'm sorry."

The light in Dabney's bedroom went out. Agnes held her breath, certain that her mother would emerge. But she didn't. The house and the street were quiet. The mystery remained unsolved.

Agnes got out of her car and walked toward the house. She felt deflated. No one in her life was cooperating. "Good night, Riley," she said.

CLENDENIN

The cleaning lady for the house he was caretaking, Irene Scarpilo, gave her notice. Irene's daughter was pregnant with twins; Irene was moving to Plymouth to be closer to her.

"I need a new cleaning lady," Clen said to Dabney.

"Consider it done," Dabney said.

Clen squeezed her. They were sitting side by side on the first point of Coatue. They had driven out in the economist's beat-up Wagoneer. They were eating lobster rolls that Dabney had prepared. The sandwiches were delicious and the day was sparkling, but they were both in a somber mood. The economist was returning that evening.

"What are you doing for the Fourth?" Dabney asked.

"I have a party," Clen said.

"Really?" Dabney said. She sounded surprised—and for good reason. Clen hadn't been anywhere or seen anyone but Dabney since he'd been back.

Elizabeth Jennings had invited Clen to her annual bash on the Cliff. Elizabeth and her husband, Mingus, had been in Vietnam with Clen for a half-dozen years or so before Mingus died. Mingus had been the *Washington Post* bureau chief, and Elizabeth had been the consummate ex-pat wife. She had gone along for every adventure, and had thrown parties for homesick Americans at their flat in the French Quarter of Hanoi. Clen had shared Thanksgiving with the Jenningses for a number of years. Somehow, Elizabeth had always gotten her hands on a turkey. Now, Elizabeth was back in the States, living in Georgetown, and on Nantucket in the summer.

"Whose party?" Dabney asked.

Clen thought she sounded jealous.

"Elizabeth Jennings? She lives on the Cliff?"

"Oh my God," Dabney said.

"You're going."

"We're going. Elizabeth is a board member of the Chamber, and we've gone to her party for the past three years. Box is coming home from Washington especially for it."

How Clen loathed the use of the pronoun *we* when it pertained to Dabney and the economist.

"How do you know Elizabeth?" Dabney asked.

"I knew her husband overseas." Clen paused, thinking it was probably best to tread lightly. "Mingus and I worked together in Saigon first, and then Hanoi. He was my partner in crime."

"Sounds dangerous," Dabney said.

"Did you ever know Mingus?" Clen asked.

"No. I've only known Elizabeth a few years, since she bought the house. She set out to meet everyone who was anyone on Nantucket. She's a bit of a social climber, I think."

"Oh," Clen said. He had always been fond of Elizabeth. Clen and Mi Linh and Elizabeth and Mingus had vacationed together in Hoi An, among the three-hundred-year-old Chinese buildings carved from teak, with a thousand colored paper lanterns strung across the cobblestoned streets. They used to take café au lait on the terrace at the Cargo Club, and sometimes leisurely boat rides down the river in the evenings. Hoi An was a magical place. Elizabeth would photograph the Vietnamese children and then give out pencils and candy and bubble gum. *Keeping the Vietnamese dentists in business,* Mingus used to say. It was hard for Clen to reconcile the woman he had known in Vietnam to the woman who now hosted parties at her summer house on Cliff Road. It was like she had an Eastern and a Western persona. He supposed the same was true of him.

"If you and the economist are going," Clen said, "then I should probably stay home."

"Don't be silly," Dabney said.

"I'm not being silly," Clen said. "We can't all go."

Dabney did not refute this.

But when the afternoon of the Fourth rolled around, Clen decided he would go to the party after all. He had gotten used to seeing Dabney every day, but he hadn't seen her the day before and he wouldn't see her the day after, or the day after that. Maybe Sunday, she'd said, if she could get away.

He was going to Elizabeth Jennings's house because he missed Dabney and wanted to put his eyes on her.

He wore his blue seersucker suit, which he'd had custom-tailored in Hanoi in the months after he'd won the Pulitzer. One sleeve of the jacket hung limp as an air sock on a still day. Clen didn't like parties because some drunk was always sure to ask about his arm.

Khmer Rouge, he would say. *Machete.*

The drunk's eyes would pop. *Really?*

Yeah. Boring story.

The party started in the front yard, where everyone lined up to be photographed on the front porch by Elizabeth. She no longer used the old Leica she'd had in Vietnam; now, it was something fancy and digital.

The last thing in the world he wanted was to have his picture taken. He looked to the left and the right, wondering if he could skirt Elizabeth and her camera and enter the house from the side door. He wanted to get to the bar. Elizabeth, being a Washington hostess and the wife of a prominent journalist, would have good scotch.

Clen looked up in time to see Dabney and the economist smile for Elizabeth's camera. Clen felt a wave of some nasty emotional cocktail—jealousy, anger, sorrow, longing. There they were together, a couple. Dabney was wearing a red silk halter dress that wasn't like anything he'd ever seen her in. She had on red high heels. The dress and shoes were pretty and stylish, but she didn't look like Dabney. She was, however, wearing pearls, and a navy headband with white stars, and she was carrying her Bermuda bag. The economist looked old—the white hair, the glasses, the double-breasted navy blazer as though he were the commodore of the Yacht Club (*Was he the commodore?* Clen wondered), the look of smug superiority because he had just spent the last week behind closed doors with the president and the Treasury secretary.

You're going to tell him, right? Clen had asked.

Yes, she had said. *Once he gets back. Once he gets back and set-tled in. I'm going to tell him. I have to tell him.*

After the photo was taken, the economist held the door open for Dabney, and she disappeared inside.

Clen thought to go home, but he couldn't leave her.

BOX

He was impossible to miss—big, tall, bearded fellow with only one arm. Elizabeth Jennings had been leading him around all night, showing him off, the Pulitzer Prize–winning journalist, Clendenin Hughes. They had known each other in Vietnam, Elizabeth trilled. *Can you imagine?* Then she went on to hit the Clendenin Hughes highlights: the series about the Khmer Rouge, the tyranny in Myanmar, the best coverage of the caning of Michael Fay, the Thaksin debacle in Bangkok.

Box turned away. Elizabeth Jennings had no idea that Hughes had impregnated Dabney. If she had known this, she would never have invited all three of them to this party.

Dabney was talking to the Massachusetts congressman (D) by the raw bar. The guy was a windbag, but he had worked with Dabney on keeping chain retailers off Nantucket, and she was forever indebted, and thus had to listen to him detail his woes with the Steamship Authority. Box tried to swoop in to rescue her, in the process helping himself to a few oysters. Good food and better wine here at Elizabeth's. And a glorious view across Nantucket Sound. It was a clear night, ideal for the fireworks. The secretary had tried to get Box to stay in D.C. and attend the celebration on the Mall, but Box found that he was happy to be on Nantucket.

He gave up on Dabney. He feared she might do the sorority bump-and-roll—hand Box over to the tedious congressman and disappear into the crowd.

Box fixed himself a plate of fried chicken and ribs and coleslaw and corn salad and then wandered into the living room. Cocktail parties weren't really his thing anymore; they were too much work. People who knew who he was approached him with an agenda, and people who didn't know who he was tended to bore him. Dabney thought him a terrible snob, but he was sixty-two years old and had, quite frankly, earned the right.

He had tried to get Agnes to come to the party; the evening would have been far superior with her there, besides which he had barely seen her since he'd been back. But she had been headed to Jetties Beach to watch the fireworks with some fellow who worked for Dabney at the Chamber. Box wondered aloud if this was a date—Agnes seemed to be going to a lot of trouble making a picnic—and he also wondered what had happened to CJ. Agnes said, "No, Daddy, not a date, we're just friends, and Celerie is coming, too. I'm actually kind of chaperoning. It's a long story."

Box didn't like long stories, especially not those related to scheming romance. That was Dabney's territory.

CJ, Agnes said, was spending the holiday in a luxury box at Yankee Stadium. He had wanted Agnes to come down to the city, but Agnes had work the next day, so that wasn't really practical, and Box agreed.

"Have fun," he said. And Agnes gave him an extra-long hug and said, "Mom and I are so glad you're home. We missed you so much."

Box wondered about this.

*　　*　　*

He was sipping a very nice Louis Jadot Chardonnay when Clendenin Hughes walked into the room with a full tumbler of scotch. Hughes saw Box and stopped short. He executed a half turn, as if to leave the room. Box couldn't blame him, but he didn't want to let Hughes escape. This was too rich an opportunity.

"Excuse me!" Box called out. He stood. "Mr. Hughes?"

Despite his size—he had at least six inches on Box—Hughes looked very young at that moment. Young and vulnerable, and of course he had only the one arm. Box reminded himself to proceed civilly.

"Professor," Hughes said. At least he wasn't pretending not to know who Box was.

"Call me Box," Box said. "Please." He reached out to shake hands, but Hughes was holding his drink, so Box awkwardly retracted his hand.

Hughes said, "Nice party."

"Yes, Elizabeth always does a beautiful job," Box said. "Do you know her well?"

"I do, actually. Her husband and I worked together in Asia for six years. I think I can claim to be the only man at this party who has seen Elizabeth ride an elephant."

"I'm sure you're right about that," Box said. "And you, you're back on the island permanently? Staying here?"

"Permanence is hard to commit to," Hughes said. "But this is home. I grew up here."

"Yes," Box said. "Of course, that's right."

Hughes rattled the ice in his glass. "And how do you know Elizabeth? From Washington?"

"No," Box said. "From here on island. I live here half the year, and the other half in Cambridge. I still teach a full course load at Harvard."

"I'm aware," Hughes said.

"You've done your investigative work, then," Box said. "You're a newspaperman, so I can hardly be surprised."

"I don't wield nearly the influence that you do," Hughes said. "Behind closed doors with the President of the United States? I could only dream of that."

Box stared at Hughes. "You heard I was with the president? You... spoke to Dabney, then?"

Hughes rattled his ice again. It was a tell; he was nervous. "Yes," he said. "I bumped into Dabney on Main Street and she filled me in." Somehow his drink had disappeared. "Well, anyway, I should get some food before the Glenfiddich hits bottom. Good to see you..."

"Wait," Box said. "You bumped into Dabney on Main Street? She didn't mention that to me."

"It was no big deal," Hughes said. "A casual run-in on the street."

"You and Dabney used to be quite close," Box said.

"Yes, quite," Hughes said. "I'm sorry if that bothers you. Everyone has a past."

Box didn't know what to do with the rage that was consuming him. It was *jealousy,* he realized. He was insanely, criminally jealous of this man in front of him, the man who had broken Dabney's heart and then absconded with the fragments. Box and Dabney had been married twenty-four years and those years had been good ones for both of them. They had raised a daughter, created a lovely home, and pursued fruitful careers. Dabney had given Box her genuine smile and her keen intellect and her sweet disposition and her warm body—but he had never had her heart.

Because this man had it.

Box gritted his teeth, and reminded himself to *proceed civilly*. "I understand chance meetings on the street," he said. "But I would appreciate it if, from now on, you would give my wife a wide berth. It can't be easy for her to have you back on this island."

Hughes said, "I'm sorry, I don't see that it's any of your business."

"No, *I'm* sorry," Box said. "It *is* my business. Dabney is my wife."

Hughes set his glass down on a side console that was probably an antique and should not be seeing a wet glass without a coaster. Box was considerate this way, but Mr. Hughes, of course, was not. Mr. Hughes was a boor and a philistine and didn't know the first rule for caring for fine things.

Hughes said, "I realize you are currently married to Dabney, Professor. But that doesn't give you the right to comment on my relationship with her."

"You caused her a great deal of pain," Box said.

"What do you know about it?" Hughes asked. "Were you *here* when it happened? No, you were not. You aren't qualified to speak on the subject of my shared past with her, sir."

The "sir" hit Box sideways, spoken as it was with such contempt. "I raised your daughter."

Hughes pressed his lips together but said nothing. Box took a step closer, his fists clenched.

"I drove her to ballet class, I took pictures of her before the prom, I paid for her college education."

Hughes nodded. "Yes. Yes, you did."

But Box wanted more than just an acknowledgment of the fact. He wanted a thank-you, or a grand apology, preferably both and preferably with some fucking humility. Box couldn't remember ever being this angry before. What reason would he ever have had—an irreverent student? A frustrating department meeting? "She is mine," Box said. "And Dabney is mine."

"You sound pretty sure about that," Hughes said.

Before Box knew what he was doing, he rushed Hughes and swung at him, meaning to hit him in the jaw but instead catching him under the clavicle. The punch hurt Box's fist and it threw Hughes off balance. Hughes fell into the side console, toppling a lamp and knocking his glass to the floor, where it shattered.

"Really?" Hughes said. He rubbed the spot where Box's punch had landed. "You want to fight? I will *kill* you, and I will do it with one arm."

Box took a stutter step back. He had no doubt that Hughes *could* beat him bloody and blind with only one arm. He had started something he couldn't finish—a fistfight in Elizabeth Jennings's living room.

"Please," he said, raising both his palms. "I'm sorry."

"You hit me," Hughes said. "And now you're sorry."

"Clen!" Dabney wobbled into the room, unsteady on her heels. "What are you *doing?*" Then she saw Box. "Honey?" She looked rapidly between them. "What are you two doing?" She bent over to pick up pieces of broken glass off the floor.

Box, with a similar instinct for propriety, righted the lamp. He said, "Darling, let me do that. You'll cut yourself."

Hughes said, "Your husband punched me."

"Clen," she said.

"He punched me, Cupe. He started it."

Dabney looked at Hughes with the shards of glass in her up-turned palm. "Go enjoy the party," she said. "Please. We'll get this."

"Dabney."

"We'll *get* this," she said. "Go."

"I'm going home," Hughes said.

Box was struck by the way the two of them spoke to each other. He was no expert on love or romance; he didn't claim to have any special emotional insight. But he could tell just from hearing that brief exchange that they shared an intimacy. It sounded like they talked every day.

"No," Box said. "I'll go."

AGNES

Riley had called with a favor.

Celerie had asked Riley to go with her to the fireworks at Jetties Beach. She had asked him in the office, with both Dabney and Nina listening, and thus he hadn't been able to make up an excuse to turn her down. He couldn't lie in front of Dabney and Nina.

Riley said to Agnes, "Listen, I need you to come with us. Please."

"No," Agnes said. "No way. The other night, I think you got the wrong idea..."

"I know you're engaged," Riley said. "It didn't sink in before because you don't wear a ring, and then your mother told me your fiancé canceled on the weekend..."

"My mother told you that? Of course she did."

"But let's be friends," Riley said. "Buddies, pals, okay? That's allowed, right?"

"That's allowed," Agnes said, although this wasn't true. CJ was the most jealous man alive. Agnes had noticed this on their third date. They were having dinner at Peter Luger, and Agnes had bantered with their waiter. The next thing she knew, CJ was up out of his chair, asking the maître d' to move them to another section of the restaurant.

Then there was the incident with Wilder from work. Wilder was the outreach coordinator at the Boys & Girls Club, and from time to time he and Agnes would go for a beer at the Dubliner. Once, CJ showed up at the Dubliner unannounced, with one of his clients in tow—a linebacker for the Washington Redskins—at the exact moment that Wilder was tugging on the ends of Agnes's hair, in an imitation of Vladimir, the most annoying child at the club. When Wilder explained to CJ and the linebacker—a man who was the size of a tree and covered in tattoos—why he was pulling Agnes's hair, CJ had laughed maniacally and asked him to do it again. *We want to see you do it again, don't we, Morris?* Morris had grunted. *Go ahead,* CJ said, *pull my girl's hair again.* Wilder had excused himself for the men's room, then left the bar. The next day, CJ had taken Agnes to Bumble + Bumble, and he sat and watched as Agnes donated thirteen inches of her thick brown hair to Locks of Love.

Many things about this memory disturbed Agnes. She had never asked CJ how he knew she was at the Dubliner in the first place.

Agnes thought she would most likely never have a good male friend again, so she might as well enjoy Riley's companionship this summer. Besides, she didn't have any plans for the Fourth. Her parents were going out.

Agnes packed a picnic for three, following Dabney's suggested menu and recipes: hero sandwiches, dilled potato salad, cherry tomatoes stuffed with guacamole, blueberries and raspberries with vanilla-bean custard. Beer, a bottle of champagne, cheese straws, spicy nuts.

So far this summer, Agnes had gained five pounds.

Riley brought his guitar. Celerie was in charge of blankets, trash bag, plastic cups, bottle opener, all paper products, and sparklers.

It wasn't as bad as Agnes had expected. She had been certain it would be awkward—Celerie wanted a date with Riley and Riley wanted a date with Agnes. For this reason, Agnes had worn her engagement ring. The diamond was too big to be ignored. Celerie noticed it immediately, and Agnes sensed not only her relief—Agnes wasn't a threat if she was engaged—but her enthusiasm.

"Your mother didn't tell me you were getting *married!*" Celerie said, in her most upbeat cheerleader voice. "Will you get married on Nantucket?"

"Yes," said Agnes. "At Saint Mary's. Reception at the Yacht Club."

"I want to get married on Nantucket," Celerie said. She bobbed her head.

Celerie was all decked out in red, white, and blue. She wore red denim shorts and a blue-and-white-striped T-shirt and red flip-flops, and—this Agnes found both touching and strange—she had pushed her blond hair back with a navy grosgrain headband with white stars, the exact headband Dabney wore tonight.

Celerie had bought the two headbands so that she and Dabney might match.

Riley said nothing during this exchange. He was trying to lead them through the crowd while carrying his guitar case and the cooler with the drinks.

Celerie said, "Is your fiancé a nice guy?"

Agnes thought Celerie sounded younger than twenty-two. What kind of question was that? Of course he was a nice guy, otherwise Agnes wouldn't be marrying him.

Agnes nodded, and they walked along.

But then it struck Agnes that *nice* wasn't the first word that came to mind when describing CJ, and he might not have seemed *nice* even by Celerie's midwestern standards. CJ was confident and magnetic. He knew what he wanted, he had the world on a string, he could fix any problem—or so it had seemed to Agnes. In her daily workday, which involved a lot of chaos, CJ was stability. And life with him was exciting—the restaurants, the celebrities and professional athletes, the money, the perks, the parties. The glamour of life with CJ was intoxicating. Agnes often wondered how his ex-wife, Annabelle Pippin, had walked away from all that. It must have been like detoxing from a drug.

Agnes thought about what Manny Partida had said: *I couldn't live with myself if I didn't tell you.*

CJ would never be physical with Agnes, no more physical than asking her to cut her hair, although it was true that CJ required more maintenance than a litter of shar-pei puppies. And he liked to have his way.

They found a good place in the sand on Jetties Beach and set up camp. There were couples and families all around them—everyone happy and sunburned and hungry. Agnes took great relief at plopping down on the blanket, forming a triangle with Celerie and Riley, coolers in the middle. She opened a beer for Riley and poured champagne for herself and Celerie.

Celerie said, "We should have a cheers. Toast the birth of our nation."

Agnes loved the girl's earnestness. She held up her plastic cup. "Cheers!"

They all touched glasses. Celerie smiled at Riley and said, "I'm being good tonight!"

And Riley said, "Be sure to eat!"

Agnes pulled out the cheese straws and the spicy nuts, and Riley removed his guitar from its case and began strumming. Agnes gazed up at the Cliff. Her parents were up there at a party, being proper adults. Dabney wouldn't pull any of her crazy disappearing acts now that Box was home.

Agnes fiddled with her ring. It was loose; she needed to get it sized. CJ didn't know it was loose, because when he presented it to her, Agnes kept proclaiming how perfect it was. She should have told him it was loose, and she should have told him the diamond was too big. She could never, ever wear it and feel safe in the neighborhood where she worked. But that would, inevitably, lead to CJ's telling her she shouldn't be working in that neighborhood. After they were married, he wanted her to quit.

The sun was going down. Agnes drank her champagne. Riley was playing "Good Riddance," by Green Day, and the people around them were singing.

I hope you have the time of your life.

CJ was at Yankee Stadium, watching a double header against the Angels that would end with fireworks. Agnes had been in the luxury box before, and it was fabulous. CJ would be drinking a Dirty Goose, eating sparingly off the tray of crudités (unless he was cheating, as Agnes was; she hoped he was stuffing his face with baked Brie), and schmoozing with the players' wives and members of the Steinbrenner family.

She felt a pang of longing for him and wished for a second that she were at Yankee Stadium. But then she corrected. The Bronx with CJ was fun, but it wasn't Nantucket.

Riley played "Only the Good Die Young," and even more people sang along. It was turning into a regular concert. Requests came in—"Country Road" and then "Sweet Home Alabama." Agnes closed her eyes and listened to the voices melding around her. Her feet were buried in the sand and the champagne had warmed the very center of her. She was conscious of being alive and being present: a clear night, a golden beach, good food—and now, thanks to Riley, their favorite songs, to which they knew all the words.

"'High Hopes!'" Celerie called out.

Of course, Agnes thought.

She wasn't sure when she had lost the ring, but if she had to guess, it had probably fallen off while she was serving up the picnic—cutting the hero sandwich or scooping the potato salad. All Agnes knew was that as she was walking off the beach in a stream of humanity— everyone commenting on how the fireworks this year had been better than ever—she noticed the ring was no longer on her finger. At that instant it felt like her heart thudded down between her feet. She stopped in her tracks; the people behind her were not pleased.

"Oh, God," she said.

"What?" Riley said. He was ambling alongside her while Celerie forged ahead. Dealing with crowds was a particular skill of hers, as she had spent a good part of her college years negotiating the Humphrey Metrodome.

My ring, Agnes mouthed. She literally couldn't bring herself to say the words. They were too awful. She tried to blink herself back five or six hours to the moment when she decided that wearing the ring was a good idea. No, it had *not* been a good idea. She should have left it at home, in its box on her dresser.

"Your ring?" Riley said.

"It's gone," Agnes said.

Celerie was lost to them up ahead when Agnes and Riley decided to go back to where they had been sitting to try to find the ring. It was dark, and the sand was cold and littered with trash. Agnes eyed the wide swath of Jetties Beach. Who could say for sure which six square feet they had occupied? With all the people walking past, the ring would be buried.

Agnes felt nauseated. It was gone.

She stopped walking. Even though the cooler and picnic basket were lighter now, her arms ached.

"Riley," she said, "let's just go. We're never going to find it."

He had such a despondent look on his face, Agnes would have thought the ring had been given to him by his fiancée who was a fancy New York sports agent.

"We have to look," he said. "We have to try."

Agnes agreed, though she thought it was pointless. They did have to try. The ring was expensive, and beyond that, it was invaluable. It could be replaced, she supposed, in that she could buy another three-carat Tiffany diamond in a platinum setting, but it wouldn't be the same ring, and CJ would know.

This was awful. Agnes could barely breathe. Riley stood above her, shining the light of his cell phone on the sand.

He said, "Celerie is calling. Should I see if she wants to help us?"

Agnes picked up handful after handful of sand, visualizing the ring. Celerie would bring a certain energy to the search, but right now, Agnes wasn't sure she could handle another person's well-intentioned concern.

"Can you just tell her we'll meet her later?" Agnes said. Celerie had been keen on heading to the Chicken Box to meet up with her roommate. "You can go, Riley. You do not have to stay here with me. This is my fault. I am such an *idiot!*" Agnes shouted this last word at the night sky, enormous and star-filled above them. This whole big, wide world, this beach with its infinite grains of sand, one ring—a classic diamond solitaire, the most beautiful thing she could ever have hoped to own.

"I'm not going to leave you," Riley said. He let Celerie's call go to voice mail.

Half a dozen times, Agnes thought to give up the search, but then as soon as she was ready to dust off and walk dejectedly home, she thought, *What if it's in the next handful? Or the handful after that?*

The party up on the Cliff was still raging, although Agnes presumed her parents had left by now. Box didn't like to stay out past ten.

What would they say when she told them she had lost the ring?

Riley said, "We can come back early tomorrow morning with my father's metal detector."

This was the third time he'd suggested the morning, and the metal detector. He knew the search was fruitless.

"You can leave," Agnes said, also for the third time.

"Agnes..."

"What?" she snapped. She flipped over onto her butt and regarded Riley, who was dutifully holding up the incandescent rectangle of his phone.

He plopped onto the sand next to her and put one of his strong, warm, dentist's hands on her knee. "Listen," he said. "I'm sorry about the ring."

"CJ is going to kill me," Agnes said.

"He might be upset," Riley said. "But I'll point out, it's just a *thing.* A precious, valuable thing, I know. But still only a thing."

Agnes would never be able to summon the courage to tell CJ she'd lost it, which meant that she would have to try to replace it without his knowing. How would she ever come up with the money? She made sixty-eight thousand dollars a year at her job, and she had eleven thousand dollars in savings. She could spend her savings on another ring and pay the rest off in installments, she supposed. Or she could go to her parents for the money. *Mommy, Dad, I need twenty-five thousand dollars in order to buy a new engagement ring, and yes, I do know that's as much as a semester's tuition, room and board at Dartmouth, but if I don't replace the ring to its exact specifications, CJ will break up with me.*

She could never, ever ask her parents for the money. Maybe Box alone? He liked CJ a lot.

But no.

She had to find it. She wished it had been locked onto her finger, like her Cartier love bracelet.

She searched, handful after handful of sand, inch after inch of beach. She plucked out every pebble, stone, and shell.

"We can come back in the morning," Riley said. Time number four. "With the metal detector."

"I can't leave," she said. "The tide. What if the tide washes it away?"

"The tide doesn't come up this far," Riley said.

Agnes started to cry. The ring was gone. CJ would never forgive her. She would be placed in a category with Annabelle Pippin, a woman who had needlessly wasted his money. Manny Partida had said that CJ lost his temper with Annabelle because she had bid too high on an auction item *without his permission*—these last three words being operative. It wasn't that CJ couldn't afford it. It was that *he hadn't okayed it.*

Agnes thought about finding the receipt for the ring on his mail table. It had been right out in the open when Agnes let herself into CJ's apartment and CJ was in the shower. Almost as if he had wanted Agnes to find it.

Twenty-five thousand dollars.

Agnes would apologize, but he might not forgive her, just as he still hadn't forgiven Dabney for saying that he and Agnes weren't a perfect match. What Agnes realized at that moment of sitting on the cold beach, sifting through handful after handful of sand, crying her eyes out, was that Dabney was right. CJ was not only wrong for her but, probably, bad for her.

"Here," said Riley. He handed her a gently used napkin from the picnic basket, and Agnes blotted her eyes and blew her nose.

Agnes had been dating CJ for an entire year before she told him that Box wasn't her biological father. She had wanted to keep that part of her history private, but when it looked like things were getting serious, she told him the truth. CJ had told her it was okay, she didn't need to be ashamed or embarrassed, he was glad she had finally felt comfortable telling him. He had smiled at her reassuringly and said, "It explains certain things about you."

"Certain things like what?" she asked.

But he hadn't answered, and Agnes's world had tilted a little more out of kilter.

Down the beach, some kids were setting off bottle rockets. Agnes let Riley pull her to her feet.

DABNEY

She watched Box stride across Elizabeth Jennings's front lawn toward Cliff Road, where they had parked the Impala. Dabney knew she should follow him, but she couldn't make herself go.

She wanted to be where Clen was.

The second Box walked out the door, Dabney raised her eyebrows at Clen and said, "What happened, really?"

"He hit me," Clen said. "Punched me." He pointed at his chest.

"I find that hard to believe," Dabney said. "What did you say to him?"

"I know you'd like this to be my fault," Clen said.

"That's not true."

"You need to tell him, Cupe."

"I know I do. But…"

They were interrupted at that moment by Elizabeth Jennings herself, who came rushing into the room in her usual imperious manner. Dabney knew Elizabeth because Elizabeth had sat on the Chamber of Commerce board of directors for the past eighteen months. If Dabney was very honest, she would admit that she found Elizabeth a bit self-important and her so-called elegance a bit practiced. Elizabeth was popular in Washington circles; she was a hostess along the lines of Sally Quinn and Katharine Graham. What else did Dabney know about her? Her résumé stated that she had attended Mary Washington and worked briefly as an administrative assistant at the State Department. Dabney knew she came from old Washington money; she was related somehow to President Taft. Dabney knew that Elizabeth had had two daughters, and that her husband had died. Dabney did *not* know that Elizabeth's husband, Mingus, had been friends (indeed, partners in crime!) with Clendenin Hughes. This was unfortunate indeed.

"I heard there was a brouhaha in here," Elizabeth said. Her eyes skipped about the room, narrowing in on the rug under the side console, which was askew. She bent to straighten it. When she stood, she glared at Dabney like she was an errant child. "Dare I ask what happened?"

"Oh," Dabney said. She was afraid to look at Clen. "Nothing."

"I lost my balance," Clen said. "Dropped my glass and it broke. I'm very sorry, Elizabeth."

"I hope you're all right," Elizabeth said.

"Fine," Clen said. "We got the shards picked up but you might want to vacuum in the morning."

Elizabeth beamed at Clen, as if nothing delighted her more than the thought of pulling out her Dyson or giving an extra instruction to her cleaning lady. Ever the gracious hostess, Dabney supposed.

"And John?" Elizabeth said, addressing Dabney. "Where has he gone off to?"

John? Dabney was temporarily stymied, until she realized that Elizabeth was asking about Box. Nobody called him John. That Elizabeth chose to do so only increased Dabney's ire.

"He left," Dabney said bluntly. She had other words at her disposal that would have softened the blow—*he had to scoot, he wasn't feeling well, he was tuckered out after all the excitement at the White House*—but Dabney didn't feel like granting Elizabeth the favor of a lovely excuse.

"Well, he's very naughty and didn't say goodbye," Elizabeth said. She then seemed to take stock of the situation before her—Dabney and Clen alone together in the living room where a glass had broken and an endowed chair of economics at Harvard had left a party without thanking the hostess. Elizabeth Jennings knew nothing of Dabney and Clen's past—or did she? one could never be certain—but neither was the woman naive. She probably had a good idea about what had transpired, or at least its general nature. She might be mentally sharpening the tines of her gossip fork.

Leave, Dabney thought. *Go home, and find some way to apologize to Box. Or end the shenanigans now, and just tell him the truth.*

* * *

But Dabney did not leave. She headed back onto the deck, ostensibly in search of another glass of vintage Moët & Chandon which she did not need. She was almost instantly captured by the congressman, who apparently had already bored everyone else at the party and hence had no choice but to give Dabney a second helping of his opinions.

Clendenin was at the end of the porch. Elizabeth still held his arm, rather proprietarily, Dabney thought. Jealousy started as a burn at her hairline.

Clendenin and Elizabeth?

The good thing about the congressman was that he didn't require any actual conversation from her. He talked and Dabney had only to nod along, and at the appropriate moments say, *Right, yes, I see, of course.*

Clendenin and Elizabeth had spent time together "overseas." Elizabeth wasn't afraid to travel; she was a woman who arrived in the lobby of the Oriental Hotel smoking a cigarette in a mother-of-pearl holder while some Thai boy in traditional garb dragged in her Louis Vuitton steamer trunk. But Dabney was being ridiculous. She had seen too many movies.

Dabney drained her champagne quickly and the congressman snapped at a waiter to have it refilled, a gesture born less out of rudeness, she suspected, than out of the fear that Dabney might abandon him for the bar. Another glass of champagne appeared, and a different waiter materialized with fruit tarts that were as pretty as stained glass. Dabney demurred; she couldn't eat a thing.

Clendenin and Elizabeth. Dabney would lose him to the East— or the burnished memories thereof—*again!*

Jealousy consumed her face: her lip was curling, her molars grinding.

Look my way, Dabney thought. She would be okay if Clen made eye contact.

But he was engaged in conversation; he was making a point to Elizabeth and another couple whom Dabney didn't recognize. She heard his voice but not exactly what he was saying. She had forgotten how lively he could be in public. He was handling himself brilliantly now, so well that Dabney hated him a little. The group was hanging on his every word.

This was her punishment, she supposed, for what she was doing to Box.

The fireworks began and everyone turned to watch them explode over the harbor. *Enjoy them,* she thought. But no, she couldn't, not without Clen. She had half a mind to yank Clen away from Elizabeth. Scandal would ripple through the party, but what did Dabney care? She would be able to watch the fireworks with the safe, heavy weight of Clen's arm around her.

Love was awful. She hated love.

And to make matters worse, the congressman seemed suddenly to realize that he was standing next to a living, breathing woman.

"Dabney?" he said. "Are you all right?"

Dabney raised her face to the sky just as a giant white chrysanthemum of fire burst open above them. Dabney hoped her face was illuminated in such a way that her excruciating heartache looked like rapture.

AGNES

She found her engagement ring sitting in the pool of icy water at the bottom of the drinks cooler.

Not lost. Here in her palm. Not gone.

Not gone! Not lost!

There weren't words for her relief.

But there was another emotion shadowing the relief, an emotion without a name, which felt like an escape hatch closing.

DABNEY

On July 5, she was too sick to rise from bed. She'd called in to work, leaving Nina a message on voice mail, saying that the flu had returned with a vengeance and, if she was lucky, she would be in at noon. But even by nine she knew there would be no way. She could barely make it to the bathroom. Agnes was at work and Box was downstairs in his study. She heard him early in the afternoon, banging around in the kitchen making lunch, but he didn't come up to check on her. She needed ice water and Advil. She had to wait until five thirty for Agnes. She also asked Agnes for her cell phone, and Agnes gave her a confused look. The landline was right next to Dabney's bed.

But Agnes brought the water and the medicine and Dabney's cell phone—and a piece of buttered toast, which Dabney couldn't eat.

"Thank you," Dabney whispered.

"Oh, Mommy," Agnes said.

That night, Box did not come up to bed, and Dabney supposed he was either angry or ashamed, but she couldn't predict which. She had a dream that Clendenin and Elizabeth Jennings were playing mah-jongg on a wooden raft at Steps Beach, and the raft was engulfed in a miasma of rosy pink. Clen and Elizabeth Jennings a perfect match?

She woke up and thought, *No!*

July 6, sick. Dabney heard classical music downstairs, but Box did not appear.

Her cell phone remained silent. She wanted Clen to text, but maybe he was angry with her, too, or he was ashamed, or he was besotted with Elizabeth Jennings. Maybe both Box and Clen would forsake her. They would abandon her, as her mother had.

Dabney's father had done a wonderful job in raising her, but it was fair to say that there had always been a part of Dabney that had felt unloved.

July 7, sick. Agnes stayed home from work; Dabney tried to protest but forming the sentence was too difficult. Then Agnes explained, "It's raining, Mom. Pouring rain. Camp is canceled today."

The sound of the rain against the window was comforting.

Dabney heard Agnes's voice from downstairs. "Daddy, she's really bad. Should we take her to the hospital?"

Box said, "Give her one more day."

One more day, Dabney thought.

How was he getting clean clothes? she wondered. And what were he and Agnes eating?

At midnight, a text from Clen: *Tell me when I can see you.*

On the morning of July 8, Dabney woke up feeling like a flat, empty version of herself, but she was well enough to shower and go downstairs for a bowl of shredded wheat.

Box was at the table with his black coffee and the *Wall Street Journal*. He looked at her over the top of the paper. "You feel better?"

She nodded.

He nodded. He said, "I have to go to Washington tomorrow. I'll be back on Friday."

Dabney thought, *Washington. Back Friday.*

Dabney made it to work by noon.

AGNES

Riley left a message on her voice mail that said, "Your mother signed out on the log at three o'clock and I followed her. She drove out the Polpis Road to number 436. She turned in the driveway."

Agnes listened to the message twice. Riley had *followed* Dabney? That was an audacious maneuver. He had done it for Agnes. Or because he was naturally curious, or he was intrigued that Dabney was keeping a secret.

Agnes googled 436 Polpis Road and found that it was owned by Trevor and Anna Jones, people Agnes had never heard of.

That evening, Dabney was back in the kitchen, making dinner— grilled lamb, fresh succotash, baby lettuces. Box was still in his study, but Agnes assumed he would soon be lured out by the aroma of the roasting meat, garlic, and rosemary. The last three nights, they had ordered in Thai food.

Agnes said, "Mom, do you know anyone named Trevor or Anna Jones?"

Dabney was tossing the salad. Agnes sensed the slightest hesitation with the utensils.

"No," Dabney said.

"Really?" Agnes said. "You know everyone. Trevor and Anna Jones? They live on the Polpis Road?"

"No," Dabney said. She met Agnes's gaze straight-on. "I don't know Trevor or Anna Jones."

DABNEY

The board of directors met four times a year: in January, in April, in July, and in October. Dabney loathed the board meetings. She started dreading them weeks in advance, even though they always proceeded smoothly.

The meetings were held in the conference room, which was tiny and airless; it was the same room where Dabney had unfortunately barged in on Nina and Jack Copper. The conference room held a rectangular table and ten chairs. It had one small window, which opened from the top, and one electrical outlet, where Dabney plugged in a standing oscillating fan. The fan blew everyone's papers about and made a lot of noise, but experience had taught them that holding the July meeting without the fan was next to unbearable.

All ten of the directors showed up to the July meeting because Elizabeth Jennings and Bob Browning, the only two summer residents on the board, attended that meeting. Normally, Dabney stood at the July meeting because there wasn't room for an eleventh chair, and she was not among equals. She was the employee. These were her bosses.

Dabney had the treasury report done and the grant requests from the regional tourism council, as well as a full recap of Daffodil Weekend and a plan for Christmas Stroll. She had a dozen bottles of cold water in the center of the table, and extra pens. She wasn't sure why she felt so much anxiety; nothing ever went wrong in these meetings. The directors listened to Dabney's description of how well the Chamber was doing, and they looked at how thick and detailed Dabney's grant reports were, although nobody ever read them. They all simply nodded in approval and adoration, and Vaughan basically patted Dabney on the head like a good dog, and the meeting was adjourned.

Today, as usual, the arriving board members greeted Dabney— Jeffrey Jackson kissed her cheek as he always did, and Martha asked lovingly after Dabney's new laptop as though it were a pet. Betty and Karen were more solicitous than usual. Betty actually offered Dabney her seat at the table, but Dabney declined. Forbearance. She couldn't sit while one of the directors stood.

Old Mr. Armstrong from Nantucket Auto Body said, "Dabney can just sit on my lap."

Everyone laughed at that, although weakly, because Mr. Armstrong was a dirty old man and probably would have loved to have Dabney on his lap.

Elizabeth Jennings did not say hello to Dabney or even look in her direction, which gave Dabney a queasy feeling. Dabney picked up a packet from the center of the table and handed it to Elizabeth. "Here you go, Elizabeth."

Elizabeth accepted the packet without thanking Dabney or even looking at her, then she turned immediately to Karen the Realtor, who had apparently been at the Company of the Cauldron with Elizabeth the night before. They started talking about the salmon.

A snub, then, Dabney thought. She had been snubbed. Wow. She looked around the table to see if anyone else had noticed it, but of course everyone else was minding their own business, or poring over the packets, attending to the business of keeping Nantucket the busy hive of commerce that it was.

Dabney was on autopilot through the meeting as she stood with the fan shooting air down her back. That was the only way she was going to make it without fainting. Forbearance. *She* had not acted badly at Elizabeth's party, she told herself. It was Box and Clen. Clen had tried to leave the room when he first saw Box, he said, but Box had pursued the conversation and it grew nasty quickly. They were fighting over Dabney, but there wasn't any way Elizabeth Jennings would know that. She was perhaps just angry about Box's poor showing, or about Clen's broken glass.

The budget was in order, the grant reports were meticulously completed, and the coffers were full. They were so full that Dabney had decided to do that which she rarely did and ask for a raise—not for herself, but for Nina Mobley. The room was very hot and Dabney felt like all her blood was pooling at her feet. Elizabeth Jennings's cinnamon-colored hair was perfectly straight and smooth, tucked behind one ear, and her nails were perfect, a soft coral color.

She had been holding Clen's arm so proprietarily at the party.

He's not yours, Dabney thought. *He's mine.*

Dabney cleared her throat, to make herself known. She had not warned Vaughan that this request for a raise was coming, because he always asked at the end of each meeting if there was any other business not on the agenda.

It was so hot that Dabney's vision started to splotch. Bob Browning was nodding off; Karen the Realtor was blatantly texting.

Vaughan said, "Everything appears in order. Is there any other business?"

"Yes," Dabney said.

They all turned to her. Her feet were tingling. Was it possible for one's feet to fall asleep while one was standing?

"Yes, Dabney?" Vaughan said.

"I'd like to request a raise," Dabney said.

There was a murmur through the room. Jeffrey Jackson, who could be counted on to side with Dabney in every instance, said, "You deserve one."

"Not for me," Dabney said. "Obviously. I'm very happy with my salary. I'm thinking of Nina Mobley. She has done an exceptional job, and has increased the amount of responsibility she's taken on, especially in the last few months." Dabney paused. "I'd like to see her receive a pay raise of twenty percent."

Elizabeth Jennings made a dismissive noise, air through her nose, with a little haughty laugh attached.

"Well," she said. "That's a hell of a bomb to drop at the end of a meeting."

Hell, Dabney thought. *Bomb.* Had Elizabeth said *hell of a bomb?* Dabney swayed. She could feel herself losing her feet. She reached out to hold on to the back of Martha's chair.

Old Man Armstrong shouted out, "*How* much does she want?"

"It's not her," Dabney said. "It's me. I mean, I'm the one asking…for her. She doesn't even know I'm asking. But she deserves a raise. I would like to see her get a raise. She's doing her job, and…" Dabney nearly said, *and she's doing mine.* But she realized at the last minute how bad that would sound. "And she's doing it well."

"We'd like to think *all of you* are doing your jobs well," Elizabeth said. "That's what we pay you for. To do your jobs well. You don't get *extra* money for doing your job well." Elizabeth was looking at Dabney now with piercing eyes. Elizabeth hated Dabney. But why? Dabney had never had an enemy before. There had been Jocelyn, at Yale, at the despicable tailgate. Jocelyn had been in love with Clen, or whatever the collegiate approximation of "in love" was. Now, Elizabeth was after Clen—and she knew, somehow, she *knew,* that Dabney was standing in her way. How did she know?

How did she know?

"Never mind," Dabney said. She watched her hand do a slow-motion dance in front of her face, as if wiping away the idea of a raise for Nina Mobley. "Wait, let's discuss this," Jeffrey Jackson said. Jeffrey Jackson had a port-wine stain on his neck and the lower half of his face, and in elementary school, two other boys had been cruel about it, and Dabney had defended Jeffrey. Ever since, he had been Dabney's devoted champion.

"There's nothing to discuss," Elizabeth said. "At least not right now. This room is an oven, and it's nearly six o'clock, and I don't know about the rest of you, but I have other plans for my evening. I think we should table the discussion of a raise for Ms. Mobley until the next meeting."

"Agreed," Karen the Realtor said.

Dabney blinked; sweat trickled down her back. She wanted to see how Vaughan Oglethorpe would handle this. He didn't like other board members to overrule his authority, but when Dabney looked over, Vaughan's face had turned to melting wax.

Dabney thought, *I'm going to faint.*

But thankfully, Vaughan adjourned the meeting. Martha stood to leave, and Dabney collapsed in Martha's chair.

CLENDENIN

Elizabeth Jennings invited him for dinner at the Straight Wharf.

Clen said, "I have to tell you, Elizabeth, I'm not really one for the Nantucket restaurant scene."

Elizabeth said, "Not a worry. Come to my house instead. Seven o'clock tomorrow night."

She hung up without giving him a chance to say no.

*   *   *

He brought a six-pack of Singha beer, which he had miraculously been able to find at Hatch's. This was the beer that he and Mingus and Elizabeth had drunk in Bangkok and Saigon years and years earlier.

Clendenin knocked on Elizabeth's front door, feeling like an ass. What was he *doing* here? This felt like an exercise in pointless nostalgia.

She shrieked with joy at the sight of him. She appeared to be three sheets to the wind already. She shrieked again with the presentation of the beer. "Singha?" she said. "Am I really seeing this? Did you have it flown in? And it's icy cold. Do you remember how good an icy cold Singha used to taste after running around in that godforsaken heat? You're a genius!"

Elizabeth was wearing a seafoam-green cocktail dress with tiny sequins and her feet were bare. Elizabeth was an attractive woman—the cinnamon-colored hair, the long nails, the perfume— and Clen had never been able to shake a vision of her climbing out of the swimming pool at the resort in Nha Trang. That red bikini. But there had always been a desperate edge to Elizabeth, a part of her that was trying too hard—and then, too, she wasn't Dabney.

On her deck a table was set for two, and candles burned in hurricane lamps. But first Elizabeth poured him a Glenfiddich and they gazed at the Sound below.

This was a date, Clen realized. She had asked him there on a date. He hadn't considered this before. He supposed he had thought there would be other people there or that she'd asked him out of kindness or boredom. He was an old friend from another life.

Mingus and Clen had drunk like crazy at La Caravelle in Saigon, then piled onto a motorbike, which they'd crashed in front of the Reunification Palace. Mingus and Clen had drunk like crazy at the Majestic, and at the Continental as well. What did Clen remember specifically? Rattan ceiling fans, Singapore slings, peanut shells on the floor; he and Mingus used to smoke unfiltered Luckys, lighting one from the next. The cigarettes had killed Mingus, lung cancer at fifty-two.

Mingus had returned to the States when he was diagnosed. He had died in Washington; Clen hadn't made it back for the funeral. He had, however, sent a long letter to Elizabeth, which was less sympathy than a prose poem of memories: Bangkok, Singapore, Mandalay, Rangoon, Siem Reap, Saigon, Hanoi, Hoi An—and the weeklong vacation in Nha Trang. They had stayed at a five-star resort that Elizabeth paid for. She had insisted that Clen come along, although he'd felt odd about crashing their romantic get-away. It had been a slice of heaven, though, and he had needed it—the infinity pool, the endless chilled bottles of Domaines Ott, a certain spicy green-papaya salad delivered right to his umbrella. There had been one night when Mingus retired early and Clen and Elizabeth had drifted from the dinner table to a spot in the sand. They were both quite drunk, Clen able to do little more than gaze at the moon's reflection on the South China Sea. Something had happened, she had said something or he had, and Elizabeth had brought her face very close to his. He had thought *kiss*; it was im-possible not to. That red bikini. But he had backed away, stood up, brushed himself off. She had said, "Was I wrong? I've seen you looking at me."

Was she wrong? No, not wrong. This was before Clen had met Mi Linh, and he was lonely. He *had* been looking at Elizabeth, all week long. But he was not a man to betray his one true friend, and so he had bowed to her, then gone to bed.

* * *

Now, Elizabeth asked him a question, but Clen didn't hear what it was. Something with the word *east*.

"I'm sorry?" he said.

"Do you miss the East?"

"Oh," he said. "I don't know. Sometimes. Certain things. The food in Thailand, the monks in Cambodia, the hotel bars in Vietnam. But not really. Not as much as I thought I would. How about you?"

She cupped her chin. "It was a time in my life that I cherish," she said. "But it's over. I'll never go back. Will you?"

"Only if Singapore calls," Clen said. But then he realized that he was so attached to Dabney that even if a job did materialize in Singapore, he would turn it down. He would not leave her again.

Dinner was served by caterers. Other men might have been impressed, but it just made Clen sad. To be invited over for dinner and then have the meal cooked by other people?

And to make matters worse, it was grilled sirloin. Clen stared at his plate helplessly. He couldn't cut a steak. And this was one of the reasons why he didn't accept invitations out. He lifted his fork and tried a bite of potato gratin, then set his fork down with a *ching*!

"Oh my goodness," Elizabeth said. "I'm so sorry. I didn't... think."

"It's okay," Clen said. "It's fine."

Elizabeth looked around for one of the catering staff, but the three of them were sequestered in the kitchen. Elizabeth stood. "Here, let me cut it for you."

Clen grimaced. It was mortifying for them both, Elizabeth cutting his steak, like he was a child.

Elizabeth said, "I don't think I ever got the lowdown on that."

"On that?" Clen repeated.

"Your arm," she said. "What happened?"

Khmer Rouge, he thought. *Machete. Boring story.*

But to alleviate the humiliation of the moment, he told her the truth. He had been writing a story about girls being bought in the countryside and sold into prostitution in Bangkok. He had a source, a woman all of thirty years old whose thirteen-year-old daughter had disappeared, and was purportedly working on Khao San Road. Clen had gone to all the reputable brothels and re-quested the girl—Bet, her name was. Bet had light skin and freck-les, her grandfather had been an Irishman named O'Brien, and be-cause of her unusual coloring, people remembered her. Clen had been led further and further into the underbelly of the city. Girls, younger and younger, were produced until Clen was offered the services of a girl who couldn't have been more than nine years old. He told Elizabeth it was like his spirit was a dry twig that just snapped in half. He picked the girl up and tried to carry her out of the establishment. She started screaming. She didn't want to go with Clen. She didn't know him, she didn't realize he was trying to save her, and he didn't have the language skills to reassure her. He knew the Thai word for police, *tarwc,* but that served only to ter-rify her further.

Clen didn't make it fifty yards down the alley before the girl was taken from him by the goons of the establishment. The goons were smaller than Clen—every man in Southeast Asia was smaller—but there were four or five of them and they all seemed to be trained in nine martial arts. They beat Clen to a pulp, and they broke his arm in four places, one a compound fracture through the skin, and the only way the doctors at the hospital he eventually landed in knew how to deal with it was by amputation just below the shoulder.

Clen pushed away his plate. It was a story that killed the appetite.

Elizabeth was breathless. "Oh," she said. She reached across the table to take his right hand.

"And is that why you left?"

"That was one reason," Clen said. "I also realized I was never going to get assigned to the Singapore desk." He reclaimed his hand. "I pissed off the wrong person when I was there covering the caning story."

"Who?" Elizabeth said.

"Jack Elitsky."

"I knew Jack," Elizabeth said. "Mingus helped him out once, with a thing, can't remember what now, it's like it all evaporated once I came back."

"Jack is fine," Clen said. "I was a pompous ass. I've always had a problem with authority."

"Rebellious," Elizabeth said.

"Something like that," Clen said.

There was an awkward moment at the door when they said goodbye. Clen had hurried the evening along to this point, refusing dessert and port and another scotch, wanting only to get home and text Dabney. He hadn't heard from her since the Fourth, when he had summarily ignored her after the scuffle with the economist. But now Clen ached for her.

Quick peck on the cheek, he thought. *Thank you for dinner.*

Elizabeth leaned against the closed front door, blocking his way. She gazed up at him through her cinnamon bangs, a siren's look; it must have worked with other men.

She said, "At my party on the Fourth…when you were in the living room with the Beeches…? What was going on? Was there a fight? I didn't even realize you *knew* the Beeches."

"I don't," he said. Then he self-edited. "Well, I don't know the professor. Dabney and I dated in high school."

"*Did* you?" Elizabeth said. "That's interesting."

"I don't know how interesting it is," Clen said quickly. The last thing he needed was Elizabeth believing that anything between him and Dabney was "interesting." "It was aeons ago. Ancient history."

"I saw her a few days ago at our Chamber board meeting," Elizabeth said. "I don't think she looks well. Her skin is quite sallow, and she's so thin. It looks like a case of hep C to me, though I'm no doctor."

Dabney had told Clen that she'd almost fainted. She had said that the room was a hundred degrees and she'd been so anxious about the meeting that she'd skipped lunch. But, with Elizabeth's words, Clen realized that Dabney *did* look sallow—her skin had a lemony tinge—and she was quite thin. The other day, he had been able to count the individual knobs of her spine. He doubted that she had anything close to as serious as hepatitis C, but he would gently suggest that she go see a doctor.

He cleared his throat. "Thank you for dinner." He bent in for Elizabeth's cheek, but she reached up with both hands and met him full on the lips.

Clen pulled back. Elizabeth's expression was one of instant mortification, reminiscent of that other, long-ago night on the South China Sea. *Oh shit,* he thought. Had he led her to believe this was what he wanted? Had she assumed he would be receptive now that Mingus was dead?

"Elizabeth," he said.

She opened the door. "Thank you for coming," she said, recovering. Ever the proper hostess. "It was a lovely evening."

"Lovely," he said, and he all but ran across the moonlit grass.

DABNEY

Miranda Gilbert and her fiancé, Dr. Christian Bartelby, were due to visit for the weekend, as they had the past three summers. But a few days before their arrival, Miranda called to say that Christian couldn't make it. He had to work at the hospital.

"And I'm sure you don't want just me by myself," Miranda said.

"Of course we do," Dabney said. She said this just to be polite. In reality, having Miranda cancel would be for the best. Dabney needed to tell Box about Clendenin and she could hardly do so while they had a house guest.

"Wonderful!" Miranda said. "I was facing the rather dreary prospect of going to the cinema alone, or spending too much money on Newbury Street. I'll keep my flight, then."

When Dabney hung up, she was filled with surprising relief. She was off the hook.

She didn't want to tell Box about Clendenin. It would be too awful.

The lives we lead.

Miranda arrived on Friday afternoon, only a few minutes before Box flew in from Washington, so they all piled into Dabney's Impala and headed to the house together. Dabney hadn't informed Box that Dr. Bartelby was a no-show, and she could tell that he was thrown off by Miranda's appearing alone. Miranda picked up on this, and the whole way home she thanked Dabney profusely for allowing her to come anyway. Boston was a cauldron this time of year, she said, as Box well knew.

Box said, "Mmmmm, yes."

Once at the house, Miranda gushed to Dabney about how lovely the guest room was. Finer than the Four Seasons, she said. Miranda was a tall woman with strawberry-blond hair and porcelain skin and green eyes, her nose perhaps a bit sharp for true beauty. She wore a pale pink cotton sundress and a pair of flat sandals with complicated straps. Her hair was frizzy from the humidity, and her personality was warmer and far looser than Dabney remembered from previous summers. She seemed almost *silly*—but was that possible? Then Dabney realized that not only was Miranda's sundress pink, her aura was as well. She emitted a color like that of New Dawn climbing roses on their finest day.

Miranda was pink.

Box?

Miranda Gilbert and Box, a perfect match? Dabney had always been a tiny bit jealous of Miranda, but she had never thought... there had never been any indication during Miranda's previous visits... but of course Dr. Christian Bartelby had always been with her before... he had caused interference... Dabney hadn't seen it.

Okay, Dabney thought. *Wow.*

"I'll let you settle in," Dabney said. "Can I bring you a drink? A glass of Shiraz? A gin and tonic?"

"Oh, a gin and tonic would be lovely!" Miranda said. She flopped back onto the bed. "I have to say, Dabney, this is a slice of heaven. I look forward to this weekend every year. But Christian... well, he's quite wrapped up with his patients. He just wasn't able to get the time off."

Dabney nodded. "I'll be right back with your cocktail."

Dinner was rib-eye steaks and marinated farm vegetables on the grill, a large green salad, some good rolls, and a lot of Shiraz. Dabney set the table outside and encouraged Box and Miranda to sit and talk while Dabney got everything ready.

"Do you need any help?" Miranda asked.

"I'm a bit of a control freak," Dabney said.

Box let a beat of silence pass. "Confirmed," he said.

Laughter.

Dabney lingered in the kitchen. She kept peering out the kitchen window. Pink? Miranda pink, Box emitting nothing, nada. If he had an aura, it was the color of air. Because Dabney was there, causing interference.

She excused herself right after the last bite of sabayon with fresh, wild strawberries. She had not hurried per se—how could she *hurry* through homemade sabayon and tiny, delectable wild strawberries? However, as soon as she was finished, Dabney stood and cleared, saying to Miranda, who was about to protest, "You stay and enjoy. I *am* a control freak."

Dabney then carried the dessert dishes to the kitchen and popped out to the patio one more time to replenish their Shiraz. Box and Miranda were deep in conversation about Milton Friedman, a particularly favorite topic, as the famous economist was the subject of Miranda's thesis. Dabney didn't think either of them had noticed her. Their glasses might have been magically filled by fairies.

This was a good thing, she thought. This was, very possibly, the solution to all her problems.

And yet, of course, it was perturbing. Was Dabney really just going to *pass off* her husband of twenty-four years? Miranda was emitting a glow like a peony in full bloom—pinker than pink: she was in love with Box, *besotted,* and Dabney felt that he deserved this. Dabney had adored Box and respected him and even desired him, but had she ever been besotted?

Dabney watched them from the kitchen window as she rinsed dishes and felt a pang—not of jealousy over Box, per se, though it was a feeling that could not be ignored. She had been having a lot of these lately—urges, she supposed. Lovesick.

She texted Clen. *Now?*

By the time she had the dishes in the rack, there was a response. *Yes, please get here five minutes ago.*

Dabney exhaled. Could she leave the house undetected? She thought she could. She would say she was going up to bed. Box and Miranda might stay awake for another hour or two talking about Friedman, then Tobin, then Larry Summers. Once they got to talking about Larry Summers, there would be no stopping them. Dabney would go see Clen for five minutes and scoot right home.

She poked her head out the back door. "I'm going up. Do you need anything else?"

Box emptied the contents of the bottle of wine into Miranda's glass and held it up for Dabney. "Do we have another?"

"We do!" she said brightly. Box's cheeks were florid the way they tended to get after a couple of glasses of wine, but he was not emitting an aura. Probably because Dabney was there. Of course! She had to leave them alone. A wave of dizziness overcame her and she steadied herself against the counter. She was not only engaging in awful, illicit behavior, she was hoping that other people would engage in it as well, so that she might feel less guilty.

Dabney hurried to open another bottle of the Shiraz.

Her escape was almost too easy. She slipped out the front door and into the Impala.

*　　*　　*

As Dabney headed around the rotary, she spotted Agnes's Prius a quarter circle away. Had Agnes seen *her?* The damn Impala was impossible to miss. Agnes had been so suspicious lately, Dabney could imagine her zipping around the rotary in hot pursuit of her mother. She would have to abort her mission.

But Agnes must have been daydreaming, or on the phone with CJ, because she exited the rotary and headed toward home. Dabney stepped on it.

"I had a date with Elizabeth Jennings," Clen said.

Dabney felt a stabbing pain in her gut. Her internal organs felt like they were being sliced up by sharp, shining knives.

"A date?"

"She asked me for dinner. I assumed there would be other people, but it was just the two of us."

Dabney and Clen were lying on top of his expensive sheets, naked. The long kiss Dabney had come for had gotten away from them both, even though Dabney had told Clen she didn't have much time.

Had Agnes seen her? Dabney wondered. Would Agnes barge in on Box and Miranda at an inopportune moment and say, *I just saw Mom driving around the rotary. Where was she going?*

This worry was diminished by the thought of Clen and Elizabeth Jennings alone at dinner.

"So how was it?" Dabney croaked.

"She served me a steak," Clen said. "And I couldn't cut it."

Dabney winced. "Ouch," she said. "How was the conversation?"

"There was some reminiscing about the good old days of fish sauce and Asian toilets. She asked about my arm."

"Did you tell her the truth?"

"Yes."

Dabney exhaled through her nose. The pain in her gut was enough to make her cry out. She pictured ten Japanese hibachi chefs fileting her.

"That's pretty intimate," Dabney said. "Did it get any more intimate than that?"

"She tried to kiss me," Clen said.

Oh, God, no. Dabney emitted a moan and curled up in the fetal position, which served only to intensify her pain. She started to cry. She was going to lose everybody and everything. She recalled thirty years earlier, seeing Clen with Jocelyn at the Yale-Harvard tailgate, Jocelyn's hands buried deep in Clen's thick hair.

Clen wrapped his arm around her. "Don't cry, Cupe. I didn't kiss her back. I was very rude, pushed her away and left." He nuzzled the back of Dabney's neck. "I have to live with the thought of you sleeping next to the economist every night, you know."

"I know," Dabney bleated.

"But there isn't another woman in the world for me," Clen said. "There just isn't. I only see you."

The house was dark when Dabney pulled up, and she was filled with relief. She hadn't wanted to leave Clen, especially after hearing about the date with Elizabeth Jennings. *Anyone* but *Elizabeth Jennings,* Dabney thought. She wasn't sure why the aversion; Elizabeth was silly and harmless—but then Dabney admitted that Elizabeth was neither silly nor harmless. She was strong-willed and opinionated at the Chamber meetings; of all the board members, Elizabeth was the only one Dabney felt she had to impress. It was her money, maybe, or her pedigree. And Elizabeth and Clen shared memories of a different world, one Dabney couldn't even begin to imagine. Elizabeth would lasso Clen, move him to Washington, introduce him to people. He would end up writing for the *Post*. He would escort Elizabeth to the Kennedy Center and inaugural balls; he would teach a class at Georgetown and drink at the National Press Club. He would be changed.

Dabney had stayed much longer at Clen's house than she'd meant to, allowing him to reassure her, waiting for the knife pain in her gut to diminish so that she could get to her feet.

Before she left, Clen had said, "You seem to be dropping a lot of weight, Cupe. Have you thought of seeing a doctor?"

Dabney gasped involuntarily. "A doctor?"

"You're very thin," he said. "Damn near skeletal. And your skin is turning a funny color. And you said you nearly fainted in the boardroom. I'm just worried about you."

Dabney pasted a smile on her face, which felt like a picture hung crookedly. "Lovesick," she said.

"I hear you saying that. But, Cupe—"

Dabney kissed him goodbye and scurried to her car.

At home, Dabney eased open the front door, which wasn't a door anyone in the house ever used. When she stepped in, she cried out in surprise.

Box was standing before her, blocking the stairs.

"Where have you been?" he said.

"What?"

"The truth, Dabney."

"I went for a drive with the top down," she said. "I needed air."

"A drive?"

"Yes."

"You didn't stop anywhere?" he asked. "You didn't see anyone?"

She had sort of been telling the truth up until that moment.

She said, "I have horrible pain, Box. I'm still not feeling well."

He narrowed his eyes at her. "You're not answering my question. Did you stop anywhere? Did you see anyone?"

Dabney couldn't tell him the truth, but neither could she lie. She said, "I can't believe you're asking me this. I can't believe you *care*. You haven't paid attention to me in *years*, Box. And now all of a sudden you care where I've *been*, if I *stopped*, if I *saw* anyone?"

"You're my wife," he said.

"Yes," she said. "I am."

"Tell me the truth!"

Tell him the truth, she thought. He was asking for it. He deserved it.

"I was driving," she said. "Driving around the island. Driving makes me feel better."

"That is a load of crap!" he shouted. "Something is going on and I want to know what it is!" He slammed the door shut and the whole house shuddered. And yet Dabney was relieved that the front door was now shut because, from the corner of her eye, she had just seen a light go on across the street at the Roseman house. What on earth would York and Dolly Roseman make of the screaming coming from the Beech household, where two of the most civilized people they knew lived? Would they even believe it? No, they would think there was something horribly wrong. They would call the police.

"I don't feel well," Dabney said. "The antibiotics didn't help, and I thought it was a wheat allergy, but—"

"You need to go to the doctor," Box said.

"Yes," she whispered.

"A real doctor," Box said. "In Boston."

"Okay." Dabney hoped that if she agreed to this, he would let her off the hook.

"And another thing," Box said. "When I was talking to that philistine Hughes at Elizabeth's party, he said the two of you had bumped into each other on Main Street. You had a conversation with the man and didn't tell me. But that isn't the worst thing. The worst thing is that you told him I was in Washington consulting with the president!"

Oh dear God, she thought. Now was the time. She just had to say it. "I'm sorry," she said.

"He's a journalist, and by all accounts, a bloodthirsty, ruthless wolf. I don't want my involvement with the administration reported to the *Times* or the *Journal,* or anywhere else!"

"Of course not, darling," Dabney said. "Clen would never—"

"We don't know *what* he would never do."

"He would never turn anything I told him into a *news story,*" Dabney said. "That I can assure you."

"I didn't realize you had forgiven him so wholeheartedly," Box said. "I didn't realize you two were on such chummy terms."

"We aren't on 'chummy terms,'" Dabney said.

"Don't lie to me!" Box screamed. He had spittle on his lower lip and his glasses had slipped to the edge of his nose; they looked in danger of dropping to the floor. He had officially become someone else.

"Please," Dabney said. "Please stop yelling. You'll wake Miranda."

"I don't care about Miranda!"

"I think she has feelings for you," Dabney said. "She's been rosy ever since she got here."

"I don't give a rat's ass if Miranda is rosy or not!" Box said. "And I am most certain the answer is 'not.' She's engaged to be married, Dabney."

"But she loves you," Dabney said. "I can see it."

"You can see it! You can *see* it!" Box said. "I don't give a good goddamn if you can see it! I have heard enough about rosy auras and perfect matches to last me the rest of my life! I don't believe in it, Dabney. I don't believe in it at all!"

"I've never been wrong," Dabney said.

"You are wrong about me and Miranda! That much *I* can assure *you!*"

At that very moment, Dabney saw Miranda's form at the top of the stairs.

"I'll leave in the morning," Miranda said. "I didn't realize... I...I didn't realize things were...so difficult for you."

"No!" Dabney protested. "Please stay! We're having a picnic at the beach tomorrow. And we have dinner reservations at the Boarding House."

Miranda swayed on her feet. Even in the shadowy dark, Dabney could see her rosy aura.

"Let Miranda go," Box said. "She wants to go."

"I don't *want* to go," Miranda said. "But I feel I should."

"She doesn't want to go!" Dabney said.

Box squared his shoulders, then turned to address Miranda properly. "With apologies, Miranda, I think it would be best if you left tomorrow. I need some time alone with my wife."

AGNES

In all her growing up, Agnes had never heard her parents so much as quarrel. On a rare occasion, they disagreed—Box was a Republican, Dabney a Democrat, so there was an endless debate about politics. And every so often Box would want to go to the

Boarding House for dinner while Dabney would want to branch out and go to Cru or Ventuno. Agnes knew that her parents had their deeper issues—Dabney's matchmaking, Box's slavish devotion to work—but those issues were never, ever aired within Agnes's earshot.

So the screaming match at midnight was startling. Agnes heard every word, Box yelling and Dabney screaming. Miranda's voice eventually breaking in. She was a brave woman, braver than Agnes, who was cowering in bed like a child. Agnes was upset enough to reach for her phone and call CJ, but CJ would offer little in the way of support. CJ would take Box's side.

The person Agnes really wanted to call was Riley. Agnes had been out earlier with Riley and Celerie at the bar at the Summer House, listening to the piano player, drinking champagne cocktails, having what Celerie called an "adult evening." Celerie had trailed Agnes to the ladies' room, and in one of those confidences that could take place only in a cramped bathroom after three champagne cocktails, Celerie had said, "Riley likes you, not me." She had said this in a resigned, nonconfrontational way; she was merely stating a fact. It sounded like she was also giving Agnes permission to like Riley back.

Agnes knew that Riley liked her and not Celerie. It was obvious in his body language and in every word that came out of his mouth.

Agnes said, "I'm engaged."

Celerie had shrugged. "Yeah, but you can't deny that he's a great guy, and he likes you. That has to feel good."

Riley was a great guy, a warm, companionable presence, he was funny and smart and charming, he was a gentleman, and Agnes loved to listen as he sang along with the piano player and tapped out the rhythms on the bar. It did feel good to know that Riley liked her, and as Agnes listened to her parents below, she knew she could call him and explain the situation and he would have something soothing to say. He understood Dabney and appreciated her and valued her idiosyncrasies the way few people but Agnes did.

But as soon as Agnes decided that she would call Riley, the fighting stopped. It was over. Agnes heard footsteps on the stairs and bedroom doors closing.

Did you stop anywhere? Did you see anyone?

Box was only now asking the questions Agnes had been asking for weeks.

DABNEY

Forbearance: In the morning, she went for her power walk, waving to the same people, petting the same dogs. When she got home, the rest of the house was still asleep, so she set about squeezing oranges for juice, frying bacon, and making blueberry pancakes.

She was at the stove when Miranda came downstairs with her suitcase packed.

"I'd really like you to stay," Dabney said. She hoped that the smells of the kitchen would indicate a return to normalcy. "Emotions were running high last night and we'd all had a lot of wine. I know Box wants you to stay."

A shadow crossed Miranda's face. It looked for a second like she might cry, and Dabney thought, *I will then be in a position to comfort the woman about her unrequited love for my husband.* She thought, *How do I get myself into these predicaments?* She thought, *My matchmaking is going haywire. Agnes is still going to marry CJ, Clen went on a date with Elizabeth Jennings, and I have managed to make a grand debacle of Box and Miranda.*

"Please stay," Dabney said.

Miranda sighed. "I can't," she said. "I just can't."

AGNES

Monday after work, Agnes bade her campers goodbye and drove out the Polpis Road toward number 436. Her heart was banging in her chest. She was petrified to discover her mother's secret, and yet she had to know.

Again, she wanted to call Riley. It was he who had done the legwork. He should rightly be her sidekick, the Watson to her Sherlock Holmes.

She found the mailbox for 436 and turned into the driveway. She was buzzing with nerves. What was she going to find?

She eased down the long shell driveway, the Prius's tires crunching along until she came to a clearing, a huge summer home not unlike other showstopping summer homes on the island—it was a fantasy of decks and balconies, gray cedar shingles and impeccable white trim, with a half-moon window over the front door. The house looked unoccupied; all the windows were shut and there was no sign of humanity. Agnes felt an easing in her chest, but also a letdown. This was the address Riley had given her, but it was nothing.

Then Agnes noticed that the driveway diverted behind the house and she followed it. She passed a beautiful rectangular pool shielded by privet. Agnes saw a table and chairs, a red canvas umbrella, a gas grill. And then she saw a smaller dwelling, the guest house, she supposed.

And a man, sitting in a rocking chair on the porch, smoking a cigarette. He was eyeing her warily, and Agnes panicked. She was trespassing, no doubt about it, but she could just say that she'd turned down the wrong driveway; she was lost. She was looking for her mother, Dabney Kimball Beech. Would she be brave enough to say that?

The man dropped his cigarette into a jar of water. He stood up and moved out of the shade of the porch, into the late-afternoon sun. The man, Agnes saw, had only one arm. There was something about him. She had never met him before, she thought, but she knew him somehow.

She put down her window so that they could speak, although the man was huge and bearded and scary-looking and might easily have been dangerous. The man peered into the car at Agnes and his face opened in surprise, and she thought, *He recognizes me.* And the thought that tumbled right on top of that was *Oh my God.*

It was her father.

Couple #14: Shannon Wright and David Kimball, married sixteen years.
Couple #29: Shannon Wright Kimball and Hal Green, together four years.

Shannon: I am the only person Dabney has set up twice. The first time, of course, was with her father.

I started working with David Kimball at the police department in 1973. My father had been on the job in Brockton, and so even though I came to Nantucket in the summer of 1972 intending to wait tables and get a good tan, it was no surprise that I ended up as the dispatcher at the Nantucket Police Department.

I met David the year before his wife disappeared. My first impression was: solid guy, Vietnam guy, maybe a bit angry, with the bitter edge of any vet. He was patriotic, serious, dedicated to his job in law enforcement. He was a fourth-generation islander, he had inherited some pretty nice real estate, and I'd heard he'd married a fancy summer girl, a Sankaty Beach Club member and all that. He had a young daughter named Dabney; he kept a picture of her on his desk, but I never saw the wife or the daughter in person that first year. They didn't stop by and say hello like some of the other families.

Then, in December of 1974, the wife, Patty Benson, pulled an unbelievable stunt. She took the daughter to see *The Nutcracker* in Boston. David talked about their impending trip more than he talked about other things—the orchestra seats, the suite at the Park Plaza Hotel downtown, the black velvet coat for Dabney. "Patty knows how to do things right that way," David said.

Patty really knew how to do things right. She left the child in the hotel room and vanished—with twenty bucks to the concierge and a phone call to David saying, *Come to Boston and get our daughter.*

He never heard from her again, and I thought, *Isn't curiosity, at the very least, killing him?* Then, one night late at the station, he admitted to me that he had hired a private investigator who had found Patty in Midland, Texas, working as a flight attendant on a private jet.

"Are you going to see her?" I asked. "Or call her? Write a letter?"

"What for?" he said. "She doesn't want me."

David was, in the years that followed, a sad, resigned man. He lived for his daughter—but a man raising a daughter alone was a delicate thing. He had his mother, Agnes Bernadette, to help, but the original Agnes Bernadette was something of a battle-ax, with fiery red hair even at age seventy, and a thick Irish accent. So I helped out behind the scenes with raising Dabney. I went to Nantucket Pharmacy and bought her sanitary pads when she got her period. I advised David about the stumbling blocks of training bras and curfew and a frank discussion about sex.

Here, please let the record show that I did advise on birth control. But Agnes Bernadette was an old-school Catholic, and David was afraid to defy her. No information about birth control was provided for Dabney—and look what happened.

Was I interested in David in a romantic way all those years? I would say that, most of the time, our relationship was professional and platonic. David had moods, the most common of which was serious and focused with an edge of gruffness; he wasn't one to joke or flirt. But there had been times when we were working nights and David had returned from a particularly unpleasant call—a drunken domestic, say, where a man had shattered his wife's nose—when David would relay the whole grisly story and then he would look at me in a certain way and I knew he felt something. I had been married once upon a time to a scalloper named Benjamin Copper, who had left the island for Alaska. Ben was long gone, and although I occasionally enjoyed a one-night stand when I was off-island, I had never had any inclination to replace him.

One night, late in the empty, quiet station, David nearly kissed me. But he stopped himself, for reasons I have never figured out.

And then, Dabney got involved. It was her senior year in high school; she was newly accepted to Harvard. Agnes Bernadette was very sick and didn't have much time left. Dabney was, perhaps, concerned about leaving her father alone. When Easter rolled around that year, Dabney called the station and invited me to dinner. I accepted right away. For a woman who lived alone, Easter was hard to celebrate. In years past, I had gone to Mass, and by way of celebration, I watched *The Wizard of Oz* on TV and nibbled a chocolate bunny.

Once I accepted, I had second thoughts. "Wait a minute," I said. "Does your father know you're inviting me?"

Dabney said, "Not exactly. But he'll be happy, Shannon. Trust me."

I showed up at the Kimball house with tulips in a pot, trying not to feel like an interloper. By that point, I had been working along-side David for ten years, but I had never been invited to his house. He greeted me at the door wearing a shirt and tie. It was clear he had made an effort to look nice, and he smelled good. I was wear-ing a dress that I had bought for my niece's confirmation; it was flouncy and flowery, maybe a bit too springlike for the cold, gray, early April day, but I felt attractive in it. I never wore anything like it at work.

"Wow," David said. "Look at you, Shannon."

I didn't know what to say or do; we had never greeted each other socially before. But it was Easter and I was excited to be there, so I leaned in and kissed the side of his mouth. He looked shocked for a second, then he blushed and took the tulips.

Even at seventeen, Dabney was a magnificent cook. She had made hot cheese puffs and a crab dip to start, then at the table we had beef tenderloin with a horseradish crust and creamed spinach and roasted potatoes. Dabney and Agnes Bernadette were drinking water, but David and I shared a bottle of red wine. The wine had been Dabney's idea; she brought it up from the basement, a good bottle that a grateful citizen had given David, and which he'd been saving for a special occasion.

"This is a special occasion, right?" Dabney said. "It's Easter and Shannon is here."

"Our Savior reigns," Agnes Bernadette warbled.

The meal was delicious and conversation eased a bit with the wine. David and I fell into reminiscing about the more memorable 911 calls we'd received over the years: the woman who claimed her husband made her drink Windex, the portly father who got stuck in the chimney on Christmas Eve in his Santa suit. Dabney listened and asked encouraging questions while Agnes Bernadette inserted non sequiturs.

Dessert was lemon meringue pie, made entirely from scratch, and then Dabney presented me with a small Easter basket filled with buttercream eggs and jelly beans. It was one of the nicest Easters I could remember.

Dabney stood up from the table. "I'm going to take Grammie home, and then I'm going over to Clendenin's. I'll be home at ten."

David nodded his assent, although I knew, because he had confided in me, that he didn't like Clendenin Hughes. David felt there was something not trustworthy about the kid, he was smug, and too smart for his own good.

I laid my crumpled napkin on the table. "I should go," I said.

"No!" Dabney said. "Stay! Please stay!"

I looked at David. "Stay," he said. "We can watch *The Wizard of Oz*."

David and I started dating shortly thereafter. We kept it under wraps for the most part, appearing out in public only as "friends," but I don't think we were fooling anybody. Agnes Bernadette died in January, and David proposed to me the following Easter Sunday, in front of Dabney, over the dinner she had once again prepared.

Dabney said, "You two are a perfect match. I can see it."

But the fact of the matter was, David couldn't actually marry me because he was still married to Patty Benson. He had never hunted her down and asked for a divorce. It was when he finally used the information that he had gotten from the private investigator to track Patty down in Texas that he learned she had overdosed on Valium the year before. She was dead.

David had been afraid to tell Dabney. He believed that Dabney had spent her whole life waiting for her mother to come back. Dabney had been in therapy for years, dealing with her fear of leaving the island, which both David and Dabney's therapist, Dr. Donegal, believed was connected to her abandonment. But Dabney took the news in stride.

"Oh," she said. She shrugged. "Maybe I should feel sad? But I hardly remember her."

Dabney was not so levelheaded in her relationship with Clendenin. The romance endured, despite the fact that she was at Harvard and Clen at Yale. There was the disastrous weekend of the Yale-Harvard game in New Haven during Dabney's sophomore year. Both David and I thought that would be the end, but Dabney refused to let go.

And then, Dabney found herself unexpectedly pregnant at twenty-two. Clen was already in Bangkok; he sent her a plane ticket, but Dabney refused to leave the island. She would raise the baby herself, she said.

There was one time during the pregnancy when David was working a double and I heard Dabney crying in her room. I knocked lightly and opened the door. Dabney raised her face from the pillow and said, "I hate love, Shannon! Love is the worst thing in the world!"

I sat with her awhile and rubbed her back. I almost felt like a mother. I asked her if she missed Clendenin and she said yes, she missed him with every cell of her being. I asked her if she was angry at Clen for not coming back to Nantucket. She told me that she had asked him to please let her be. Not to call her or write to her or contact her in any way ever again. This was news to me, and I was pretty sure it would be news to David.

Dabney said, "His dream is over there. I couldn't ask him to stay on Nantucket, Shannon. He would hate me and hate this baby . . . just the way . . ." She trailed off.

Gently, I said, "Just the way, what, Dabney?"

"Just the way my mother did," she said.

"Your mother didn't hate you," I said. But with those words, I was way out of my comfort zone. Who was I to explain why Patty Benson had done what she'd done?

Dabney started crying again. "I thought Clen and I were a perfect match. I have been right about everyone else. Why was I wrong about myself? It isn't fair!"

I agreed. It wasn't fair.

David died of a heart attack in his sleep when Dabney was thirty-four, Agnes nearly twelve. It was a sad time for us all, although Box was around to help us manage things.

I stayed on at the police department until I had my thirty years and could properly retire. Then I decided to leave Nantucket. It was too lonely a prospect to stay, a woman nearly sixty-five, alone on this island. I had cousins in Virginia, and I liked the idea of moving south, someplace milder.

But then Dabney got involved. She asked me, did I know Hal Green, he had been a summer resident for years with a house in Eel Point, and only now had moved to the island year-round. He'd lost his wife a few years earlier to breast cancer, and he was a terrific guy; Dabney knew him because he entered his Model A Ford in the Daffodil Parade each year.

I said, "No, Dabney, I do not know Hal Green."

Dabney said, "That's good, that means he hasn't had any run-ins with the law."

I did not crack a smile. I knew what Dabney was up to.

She said, "I think you should meet Hal Green. I think you would like him."

I said, "Oh, do you?"

Dabney said, "Come for dinner on Saturday. I'll invite him."

"Dabney."

"Please," she said. "Just come."

Hal and I have been married for four years.

CLENDENIN

She was like Dabney twenty years earlier, Dabney as she had been standing on Steamship Wharf just before he left. But there was something else in this woman that grabbed at him: the hazel eyes, and a certain facial expression he had only ever seen in the mirror.

He clenched his right fist and felt his phantom left fist clench in unison; he felt his whole left arm in a way he hadn't in months, except in dreams.

He couldn't believe it.

"Agnes?" he said, his voice no more than a whisper.

"Yes," she said.

It took some convincing to get her inside. He understood the urge to flee. It was scary and confusing, this reunion, unplanned, unexpected—but for him, not unhoped for.

He said, "Can I offer you a cup of coffee? Or some tea?"

She blinked at him.

He said, "I don't bite."

She barely moved her head, whether to indicate yes or no, he wasn't sure.

He said, "I have bourbon."

She turned off her car, a hybrid, more a toy than a car. Clen wondered what Eight-Cylinder Dabney thought about the Prius.

He poured two Gentleman Jacks, neat, and Agnes threw hers back without flinching. His daughter.

She said, "My mother comes here."

He couldn't tell if it was a question or not. "Yes," he said. "We're friends."

"Friends," Agnes said.

Clen downed his bourbon, then poured two more. He didn't know how to proceed; he didn't know what Dabney had told the girl.

He said, "How did you know to come here?"

She said, "That I can't tell you."

He laughed, not because she was funny but because she was so much like him. He felt like he was being born. His daughter, his child, his progeny, his DNA, his his his. How had he missed out on this until now? Tears stung his eyes. It was too much, it was overwhelming. He stared at the grain of the oak table. Agnes held her silence. Any other girl her age might have been shrill or hysterical, angry or dramatic.

Oh, Dabney, he thought. *Forgive me, please.*

He hadn't realized what he had given up—not really—until now.

He said, "Does your mother know you're here?"

"She does not."

"Are you going to tell her you met me?"

"I haven't decided yet."

Clen said, "I answered your letter, years ago. I never heard back. Did you get my letter?"

"I did," she said. "Thank you. It helped me to read it. It was enough."

"It wasn't close to *enough,*" Clen said. "You deserved much more."

"Let's not have that conversation right now," Agnes said. "Okay?"

"Okay," he said, relieved.

"I want to talk about you and my mother," Agnes said.

The relief evaporated. "I think you should probably ask your mother."

"I *have* asked my mother," Agnes said. "She has been disappearing all summer long—leaving work for three- and four-hour stretches. She tells Nina she's 'running errands.' A few weeks ago, I saw her by chance about a half mile from here, and when I asked her about it, she said she was going to have lunch at Sankaty."

Clen nodded. Nobody who knew Dabney would believe Sankaty.

Agnes said, "That was bullshit, of course."

Clen drank his second bourbon. He itched for a cigarette.

Agnes said, "She comes here to see you. She comes every day?"

"Not every day."

"The two of you are...lovers?"

"Agnes..."

"The two of you are lovers, yes or no?" There was no anger in her voice, but her tone was uncompromising. She was demanding an answer. Was Clen supposed to tell her the truth, tell his daughter that yes, in fact, he and her mother were lovers?

"Yes," he said.

Agnes said, "How long?"

Clen poured another bourbon even though the first two shots were making his head swim in one direction and his stomach swim in another. Another man might be able to have this conversation without alcohol, but he wasn't that man.

"I moved back here at the end of April. It started a couple of weeks after that."

"Oooooohweeeeahhh!" Agnes said. Whether this utterance was one of surprise or horror or disapproval, Clen couldn't tell.

He said, "Dabney and I are in love, Agnes. Deeply, truly, passionately in love. This was true for years before you were born, and continues to be true now. More so now that we have each lived lives that had nothing to do with each other. Dabney Kimball is my reason and my answer." Here, his voice failed him, much to his shame. "I can't let her go again."

AGNES

When she pulled out of the driveway of 436 Polpis Road, she was a different person.

Her mother's secret revealed: Clendenin Hughes, her father.

Agnes had to tell someone. She couldn't bear this revelation alone. When she emerged from Clendenin's cottage, she found four voice mails from CJ on her phone. The first message was curious ("Where is my best girl?"); the second message terse ("Um...hello?" *Click.*) The third message, annoyed ("Jesus Christ, Agnes, answer the goddamned phone, would you, please?"). It was the fourth message that took Agnes's breath away. CJ screamed with unbridled fury, *"Where the fuck are you?"*

She thought of Manny Partida: *I couldn't live with myself if I didn't tell you...hair pulling, arm twisting, some not-so-nice stuff...just please, Agnes, be careful.* She recalled CJ's facial expression as he watched Agnes's hair being cut. He had been smug with his power over her.

Agnes deleted all the messages except for the last one. She couldn't talk to CJ about meeting Clendenin. She couldn't talk to CJ about anything, she realized, except for CJ.

She figured she was expected home for dinner—she hadn't told Dabney otherwise—but she couldn't sit at a table with Box and Dabney and eat and make chitchat.

Clendenin had asked Agnes not to say anything. He had begged her, even while realizing that he had no place to ask and even less reason for her to agree.

He said, "This is adult stuff."

She stiffened. "I am an adult."

"It's between your mom and me. And it's between your mother and the professor. You *are* an adult, and so I'm asking you to give your mother the time and space to figure her situation out."

"Do you think she will?" Agnes asked.

"I do," he said.

She had not expected the summer to be like this. There were secrets everywhere she looked.

Agnes called Riley and got his voice mail; she felt a wave of irrational anger overtake her. She needed Riley! There was no one else she could talk to! Except, possibly, Nina Mobley. Should Agnes call Nina Mobley? As Agnes was considering this, her phone rang. It was Riley.

"Hey," he said. "Sorry, I just got done surfing."

"Where are you?" Agnes asked.

"Antenna Beach," he said.

"Stay there," she said. "I'm going to grab a couple of sand-wiches. I'll be there in twenty minutes."

"I'm supposed to meet Celerie at the movies," he said. "It's Diablo Cody week at the Dreamland and they're showing *Juno* tonight. Celerie said it's her favorite movie. She's been calling me 'Bleek' for the past three days."

"Is there any way you can cancel her?" Agnes said. She felt like a big jerk for asking, but this was an emergency like none Agnes could have dreamed of. "I really need to talk."

"I'll cancel her," Riley said.

Less than an hour later, Agnes and Riley were drinking beer, eating lobster rolls, and watching the sun go down. They were sitting in the open air of Riley's Jeep on the lip of the beach. Riley was still in his wet suit, although he had peeled off the top half, so Agnes had a fine view of his shoulders, chest, and abs. She felt ashamed for even looking. There were two new voice mails from CJ on Agnes's phone, but she hadn't listened to them yet.

"Was Celerie upset you canceled?" Agnes asked.

"Devastated," Riley said. "But she didn't cry. She said she would make her roommate go. She said she hoped the friend I needed to talk to knew how lucky she was."

"You didn't tell her it was me, did you?"

"I did not tell her it was you," Riley said. "But who else would it be?"

Agnes sighed. She couldn't have Celerie getting wind of this sit-uation. No no no.

Riley said, "So what's up?"

Agnes said, "I followed your tip and went to 436 Polpis Road."

Riley said, "And what did you find?"

Agnes said, "My father. My biological father, whom I've never met. Until today."

Riley sipped his beer and stared out at the wild, churning ocean. "What did I tell you the first time I met you? What was my exact phrase, Agnes? *Tip of the iceberg.*"

"Yes," Agnes said. "You were right about that." And then she explained: Clendenin Hughes, whom Agnes had never met, who had led a life on the other side of the world, who had won a Pulitzer Prize, who had lost his left arm in pursuit of a story, who had returned to Nantucket three months earlier, was Dabney's secret. He was her lover.

"So," Riley said. "What is he like?"

What was Clendenin Hughes *like*? Agnes hadn't spent enough time with him to know, really. The word that first came to mind was *complex*. She had looked at him and seen a funnel of swirling thoughts and emotions. Clendenin had not come back to the United States and lived a life as Dabney's husband and Agnes's father. *Your mother didn't want that,* he said. *She wanted to go it alone.* But he knew that, deep down, Dabney had wanted him. A stronger man, a better man, would have done the right thing and come home. Clendenin could claim no honor. He had been consumed with shame and regret, he'd told her, and for days and months and years, that shame had been the most powerful thing in his life. He'd made it clear that he was *not* in a position to ask for Agnes's forgiveness. But Clendenin also said that the only reason he had come back to Nantucket was because Dabney was there.

I realized something when I lost my arm, he had said. *And that was, my arm wasn't the only thing I was missing. I was missing my heart. It lies with your mother. Always has.*

Returning to the island had been his only option. It felt like it was written somewhere; it felt like he had been moved to do so by the hand of God.

Do you believe in God? Agnes had asked him.

I believe in something bigger, higher, and more important than ourselves that it is beyond human beings to comprehend, Clendenin said. *Yes, I do.*

Agnes grabbed Riley's arm. "I can't believe this happened. I met my father today. Half my blood, half my genes, half my biology."

"It's big," Riley said. "It's huge. Are you going to tell her?"

"Maybe," Agnes said. "But not yet."

"Are you going to see him again?"

"Thursday," Agnes said. "Thursday after work. He wants to know about me, he said."

"How does this make you feel about your other father?" Riley asked. "The professor?"

"Box," Agnes said. "He's my real father. Clendenin is...well, I don't know what he is to me other than my DNA. But I want to find out. The question is, in finding out am I betraying Box?" She drank some more of her beer. "I don't know. I'm so confused."

"My two cents?" Riley said.

"Please."

"Your mother is an extraordinary woman who has two men in her life. Probably, she loves them both."

"Probably she does," Agnes said.

"I bet it happens more than we think," Riley said. "Although I am strictly a one-woman-at-a-time guy. But my parents always told me to be open to what they called the 'wide spectrum of human experience.' They were in the Peace Corps in Malawi before I was born, so they embrace tolerance, kindness, acceptance." Riley put his hand on top of Agnes's hand, which was still holding his arm, "I think it's okay if you love them both, too, Agnes."

Agnes looked at his arm, her hand, his hand, and then she started to cry. "I don't know what's wrong with me," she said. "You're being so understanding and you canceled Celerie for me and it is so easy to confide in you, and this situation is so screwed up and yet you're making me feel like it's *not* screwed up, you're making me feel like I'm on a reasonable part of the spectrum of human experience and everything might end up okay."

"And that's why you're crying?" he said. He pulled a box of tissues out of his center console and plucked one for Agnes.

What she didn't say was that she knew that CJ, the man she was engaged to marry, *wouldn't* have been this understanding. Because it was Dabney, he would have judged. He would have judged not only Dabney but Agnes as well. Her mother was a liar and a cheater and a slut—and therefore, so was Agnes. Agnes pictured CJ pulling Annabelle Pippin's hair, twisting her arm. If CJ could see her now, sitting in Riley's Jeep, he might hurt her. He just might. Agnes knew that the bad green gunk Dabney saw floating in the air around her and CJ wasn't made up. CJ ridiculed Dabney's matchmaking, but her mother was never wrong. And, Agnes feared, Manny Partida wasn't wrong either. *I couldn't live with myself if I didn't tell you.*

Agnes also didn't say that she was jealous of Riley's future dental patients, all of whom would think he was the greatest dentist in the world. Riley would glide through his office like he was on roller skates. He would look at a recalcitrant seven-year-old patient and say, "Kissing girls yet, Sam?" And when that didn't get Sam to open his mouth, he would say, "Hey, guess what I got for Christmas? Snowman poop!" And Sam would laugh and Riley would deftly move in with his instruments to count Sam's teeth.

Agnes was also jealous of the young women in the audiences who would hear Riley play the guitar and sing Jack Johnson so beautifully that Jack Johnson himself would want Riley to serve as his best man or be godfather to his children. And Agnes was *most* jealous of the woman who would someday be Riley's wife, the woman who would get to wake up next to him every morning and be the consistent recipient of his generous spirit.

Agnes didn't say any of this, however. She carefully removed her hand from his arm, dabbed the tissue at her eyes, and took a deep, cleansing breath. The sky was streaked with the hot pink of the setting sun and Agnes wondered if *this* was the color Dabney saw when two people were a perfect match.

When Agnes got home, she listened to the fourth voice mail CJ had left on her phone. *Where the fuck are you?* And then, fearfully, she listened to the two later voice mails, which had no words, just the sound of CJ's breathing. These, somehow, were even scarier. Agnes picked up the velvet box from her dresser and gazed at her engagement ring.

Tomorrow, she would send it back.

DABNEY

The day Miranda left, Box announced that he realized that for the past three or four (read: eight or nine) years, he had bungled his spousal duties. He had not paid Dabney the kind of attention she deserved, he had not loved or appreciated her ardently enough. But now, all that was going to change.

He didn't leave Dabney alone for a minute.

When she awoke, he was downstairs in the kitchen fixing her coffee. He let the *Wall Street Journal* lay on the table, untouched, and instead engaged Dabney in conversation. How had she slept? What had she dreamed about?

"What did I *dream* about?" Dabney said. "Who can remember?"

She said this to cover for the fact that she had dreamed about Clen; she dreamed about Clen all the time now. Last night, she and Clen had been naked, holding hands, circling. They were models for Matisse's *La Danse*.

Next, Box asked what was going on at the Chamber. How were the information assistants working out, had a love affair started between the two of them? How was Nina Mobley, her kids must be nearly grown by now. Were any of them applying to college? And what of George Mobley? Did he still have a gambling problem?

Dabney stared at Box, nonplussed. It was possible that three or four or eight or nine years ago she had yearned for Box to take an interest in the daily minutiae of her life this way. For years, decades even, she had rattled on about this and that with only half, or a quarter, of his attention. It was as though he had stored up every detail she had ever told him in some mental vault that he had only now magnanimously decided to unlock. She wished he would pick up the *Journal* and let her drink her coffee in peace. Was it horrible of her to think this way?

Box wondered about the date and location of the next Business After Hours. He wanted to go with Dabney; there were people he hadn't seen in years whom he wanted to catch up with. And what about trying a new restaurant this week? What about Lola Burger, or The Proprietors? Should he include Agnes, or would it be more romantic just the two of them?

Romantic? Dabney thought.

She said, "I'm going for my walk now."

"Dabney," Box said.

She stopped at the door and turned around.

"You have to make a doctor's appointment," he said.

"Yes," she said. "I realize this."

"If you don't have time to call," Box said, "then I'll call for you."

"I'll call," Dabney said.

"How's your pain?" he asked.

"You have no idea," she said.

Thank heavens for work. At work she was free, Nina knew all, so Dabney didn't have to lie or pretend. She spent all morning planning the next Business After Hours, which would be held at Grey Lady Real Estate and catered by Met on Main. Dabney chuckled as she thought about how quickly Box would renege once he found out the locale. He detested all Realtors. In the spirit of Holden Caulfield, he believed them all to be phonies, and horrible gossips on top of it. And he had never wanted to go to Met on Main because there was a branch on Newbury Street in Boston that was supposed to be far superior. No, when push came to shove, he would pass on Business After Hours.

In the back office, both Celerie and Riley were on the phone; the rush leading up to August was upon them.

At noon, Dabney said, "I'm going to run some errands."

Nina nodded her assent, and Dabney signed out on the log.

On top of the filing cabinet behind Nina's desk were the wilting remains of the lilies Nina had received the week before from Dr. Marcus Cobb. Nina and Marcus Cobb were falling in love, and they were doing so without any help from Dabney. If Dabney interfered at this point, she would only mess things up. Her matchmaking ability seemed to be stuck in reverse.

Dabney turned to go, but at that moment they both heard the door downstairs open and then slam shut, and they heard footsteps on the stairs. Dabney worried that it was Vaughan Oglethorpe, and that at any second the office would be suffused with the smell of embalming fluid. Dabney would have to deal with Vaughan, and then light her green-apple-scented candles. She wanted to get to Clen; it had been four days since she'd seen him, and, like Nina's flowers, she was starting to wilt.

"Hello, ladies!" The person walking into the office was...Box.

Nina gasped and Dabney felt so startled at the sight of him that she grabbed the edge of Nina's desk.

"Darling!" Dabney said. "What are you doing here?"

"I was at home working when I had a revelation," Box said. "I remembered how much you love that poem by William Carlos Williams, and so I brought you a cold plum."

Dabney gaped at him. *That poem by William Carlos Williams?* "This Is Just to Say"—yes, Dabney had always loved that poem. In the years of Agnes's growing up, a copy of the poem had been taped to the refrigerator door. It was an apology poem—*forgive me, they were delicious, so sweet and so cold.* Box was holding out the plum and a bottle of chilled Perrier with a silly grin on his face.

Celerie picked that moment to pop out of the back office for her lunch break. "What is *this?*" she said. She eyed the white-haired man holding the water and the plum. "You aren't by any chance *Professor Beech?*"

He gave a little bow. "I am."

"Your husband!" Celerie said, as though introducing him to Dabney. "And he brought you fruit and water. How lovely!"

Dabney was stymied. What was going *on* here? She took the plum and the Perrier, and, at a loss for the words to make both

Box and Celerie disappear, she bit into the plum. It was succulent, and juice dripped down her chin. From his pocket, Box produced a napkin. He had thought of everything.

"You must be Celerie," Box said, offering his hand. "I'm John Beech, but please call me Box."

"My roommate is going to *die* when I tell her I met you," Celerie said. "She was an econ major at Penn. She *used your textbook!*"

Box was used to this kind of godlike status among the collegiate and newly graduated. "I hope she doesn't actually die."

Celerie clapped her hands together at her chest, as if prepping for the next cheer. Dabney *had* to get out of there, but how? She made eyes at Nina, who was nervously sucking on her gold cross.

Nina said, "Dabney, you should go. You'll be late."

"Go?" Box said. "Go where? Where do you have to go?"

Nina said, "Dabney has a meeting with a potential Chamber member."

Dabney had never loved Nina Mobley as much as she did at that very moment. On her way home from seeing Clen, she was going to call and order Nina a fresh bouquet of flowers.

"Really?" Box said. "Who's the potential member?"

Nina laughed. Dabney thought, *Who* is *the potential member?* Nina said, "Oh, who can remember? The phone has been ringing all day."

"It sure has!" Celerie said, her blond head bobbing.

Box said to Dabney, "Surely you must know whom you're meeting with."

"Yes," Dabney said. She took another bite of the plum, then wiped her lips. "Internet start-up."

"An Internet start-up is joining the Chamber?"

"Nantucket based," Dabney said. She threw the plum pit and the napkin into the trash. "I have to go."

"Cancel your meeting," Box said. "I'm taking you to lunch at the Yacht Club."

"Awwww…" Celerie said. "Sweet!"

"I can't just *cancel* my meeting," Dabney said. "I was supposed to leave five minutes ago."

"Cancel," Box said. "I'm not asking you." His voice was stern. This was suddenly a showdown, and Dabney reared up. She didn't like Box telling her what to do. She didn't want to cancel her imaginary meeting; she wanted to be with Clen.

Celerie suddenly seemed to realize she was in the middle of something. She signed out on the log, then headed for the stairs. "Toodaloo!"

"Nice meeting you!" Box called out after her. Box checked the log. "You wrote 'errands' on the log," he said. "I thought you had a meeting."

"I do," Dabney said weakly. "I was going to run errands after my meeting."

To Nina, Box said, "Nina, please cancel Dabney's 'meeting.' I'm taking my wife to lunch."

Dabney wasn't able to text Clen until nearly ninety minutes later, after she had suffered through lunch at the Yacht Club. In reality, lunch at the Yacht Club was lovely—a table outside overlooking the harbor while Diane played standards on the piano, a blue crab and avocado salad, iced tea for Dabney and a glass of white Bordeaux for Box, children wearing life preservers headed out for their sailing lessons, couples in white coming off the tennis courts sweaty and chuckling. Dabney wished she could relax and enjoy it, but it was all she could do to keep her toe from impatiently tapping. She wanted to text Clen at the very least to tell him she couldn't make it; she hated to think of him sitting on the porch in the granny rocker, waiting in vain. He had probably made sandwiches and possibly margaritas; Dabney had tucked her bathing suit into her bag, anticipating a swim in the pool.

Every man and woman over the age of eighty who was eating lunch at the Yacht Club wanted to stop and talk to Box and Dabney. All of them wore hearing aids, hence much of each conversation had to be repeated two or three times. These were friends of her father's and the parents of her old summer friends and some were acquaintances of Box's who wanted to know why their investments were doing so poorly. Box was an economist! Dabney wanted to scream. He dealt in theory! If people wondered about their investments, they should call their stockbrokers!

"Dessert?" Box asked.

"God, no," Dabney said. "I have to get back to work."

She texted Clen: *Sorry, Beast, I got ensnared in a situation I couldn't get out of. Can I come see you at five o'clock?*

Clen texted back: *I have plans at five o'clock.*

CLENDENIN

He was like a starving man standing at a groaning board. He had to keep from stuffing his face like a glutton. He wanted to know everything about Agnes. When had she learned to ride a bike? Who had taught her piano lessons? What book had changed her life? Had his name ever been mentioned around the house? What kind of movies did she like? Why Dartmouth and not Harvard, where the economist taught and Dabney had gone? What size shoe did she wear? Did she sneeze in sets of three like he did?

"Yes," she said to this last question. "Actually, I do."

And they laughed.

She wanted to know about Vietnam and Cambodia and Thailand, his life there. Twenty years, and yet his lasting memories were few, and they were general rather than specific—the oppressive heat, the air so thick it was like agar or jelly, you could practically chew it. The stink of diesel fuel and cigarette smoke. The trash, the traffic, the seemingly endless streams of people, so many people, how did one distinguish himself?

Babies on motorbikes, young girls in brothels, the same question repeating on ticker tape through Clen's mind: *Who is in charge here?*

Clen said, "Tell me about your fiancé."

AGNES

She wasn't sure what to tell Clen about her fiancé, who was technically no longer her fiancé. Agnes had sent the ring back by Federal Express with a note that said, "I'm not sure what I want. Please don't call or text me. I need time to think. I will call you when I return to New York on the first of September." She had tracked the package; it had arrived the afternoon before, and there had, surprisingly, been no phone calls to either her cell phone or the house. He was respecting her wishes. Training camp for his NFL players was less than a week away; CJ was probably busy trying to finalize a deal for Bantam Killjoy. There might not be room for hurt feelings about Agnes. He might look at the ring and think that Agnes clearly didn't know a good thing when she saw one, that she was being influenced by her evil witch of a mother; he would take the ring and give it to the next woman he dated, after he wooed her with presents and flowers and his special table at Nougatine.

To Clen, Agnes said, "Can you keep a secret?"

"Are you seriously asking me that?" Clen said.

Right. Clen was a good, neutral person to talk to about this.

"Has my mother told you anything about CJ?"

"Not really," Clen said. "Only that she doesn't approve. No rosy aura or whatever. Not a perfect match."

"She doesn't approve," Agnes said. "But that's not why I did what I did. Or not the whole reason, anyway."

"What did you do?"

"Sent the ring back," Agnes said. "I've been away from CJ for three weeks and two days, and I feel great. I'm my own person again."

Clen raised his eyebrows.

"CJ is very confident," Agnes said. "Very Master-of-the-Universe. He snaps his fingers and things happen. Front-row seats to the Knicks, and to Broadway shows, backstage passes to Madison Square Garden. A car service all the time with a bottle of Veuve Clicquot on ice because he knows it's my favorite champagne. Flowers at work, love notes on my pillow. Victor Cruz, who plays for the New York Giants, showed up in Morningside Heights to sign autographs for my kids. *Really* sweet stuff. And he's smart…and he's funny…" Agnes blinked. What had she *done?* Had she made the world's biggest mistake? "He's a lot older than me, eighteen years older, and he expects certain behavior from me. I've spent the past year wanting to be his good girl. Maybe I was looking for a father figure." She looked at Clen and laughed unhappily.

He said, "Well. That's not impossible."

"But since I've been at home, I realized that my relationship with CJ isn't healthy. He's very controlling. I'm like a marionette. I can't disagree with him, I can't make my own decisions. He hated my friends, so I don't see them anymore. The relationship looks good to most people—Box loves CJ, they're best buddies—but it's bad. Really bad. My mother was right."

"She usually is," Clen said.

"She always is," Agnes said. "It's weird."

They sat in silence for a minute. Then Clen brought two glasses out of the cabinet.

"Bourbon?" he said.

"Please."

"You haven't told your mother you sent back the ring?"

"No," Agnes said. "I don't want her to know yet. I don't want her to know about CJ, and I don't want her to know about you."

"I feel sorry for the guy," Clen said. "Losing out on a future with you."

"He'll find someone else in two minutes," Agnes said. She threw back the bourbon. "I kind of like this guy who works for Mom. His name is Riley, and he's studying to be a dentist."

"I've heard her talk about the dentist," Clen said. "He surfs and plays the guitar. I thought maybe your mother kind of liked him."

"She has too many men as it is."

"Agreed," Clen said.

As Agnes pulled out of Clendenin's driveway that evening, a blond woman driving a Mercedes pulled in. They nearly collided, but the Prius was small and handled well, and Agnes scooted out of the way, giving the woman a little wave. The woman looked at Agnes with great interest, then finally offered half of an uncertain smile.

It wasn't until Agnes was out on the Polpis Road that she wondered who the woman was. The owners of the big house didn't arrive on island until August, Clen said. It might have been the cleaning lady, but what kind of cleaning lady drove a Mercedes?

A friend of Clen's? A woman he was dating? Of all the surprising emotions Agnes had felt this summer, here was one more: Agnes felt jealous on her mother's behalf.

DABNEY

Box was relentless. He went with her everywhere now. She was never alone. They went to dinner together, they read together, they went to bed together. There were still no sexual overtures from him, which was a blessing.

During her walk, she called Clen.

He said, "Jesus, woman, when am I going to see you?"

She said, "I was free yesterday at five, but you had plans. What plans?"

He said, "That I can't tell you."

She said, "Elizabeth Jennings?"

He said, "I hate to tell you this, Cupe, but you sound jealous."

"I am jealous," she said. "What were the plans?"

"I can't tell you," he said. "But it wasn't Elizabeth. She did, however, drop off a homemade blueberry pie on my porch with a little note."

"Homemade pie? Elizabeth?" Dabney said. "Her chef probably made it."

"Jealous *and* catty!" Clen said. He sounded delighted.

"I can come today at five, " Dabney said. "Or do you have plans again?"

"No plans," he said. "Except to devour you."

*   *   *

Dabney went to see Clen at five, but she had to do so under the auspices of going to the salon to get her hair cut. She figured this bought her an hour and a half, which she and Clen desperately needed. She listened to his voice in her ear, she tasted his skin, she felt him squeeze her—it hurt! But squeeze harder!—and it was just like she had never been apart from him. He was hers, she was his, they were one.

But then the countdown began. They had fifteen minutes left, then ten, then five.

"Will you miss me?" she asked.

"I miss you already," he said.

As Dabney gathered her car keys, she watched the storm cloud cross his face, which exactly matched the shadow over her heart. She hated to leave him.

"I have to tell Box," she said. "I want to be with you all the time."

"So tell Box," he said.

She nodded. "I will." And then she thought, *I can't.*

She had asked Clen again what his plans had been the day before at five o'clock and he had again declined to say, calling her a nosey parker. Her gut told her it was Elizabeth Jennings and Clen just didn't want to admit it, but they had such a good time together that Dabney didn't want to spoil it in a tug-of-war of accusation and denial.

He deserved his privacy, she thought. Though she didn't believe this.

When she arrived home, Box studied her hair with narrowed eyes. "It looks the same," he said.

"My hair always looks the same," Dabney said. "It's looked exactly the same since the fourth grade, when my grandmother bought me my first headband. Pink grosgrain ribbon with navy-blue whales, purchased at Murray's Toggery." Dabney narrowed her eyes right back at him. "God, I remember that day so vividly. Why do you think that is? Because of the headband? My grandmother didn't spend money on pretty things, but she bought me that headband to keep the hair out of my eyes and I was thrilled with it."

Box moved in closer, then lifted a lock of her hair and sniffed it. "It doesn't smell like it usually does when you get back from the salon."

Dabney swatted him away. "What are you *talking* about?"

"Your hair doesn't have the salon smell and it looks the same as when you left."

Dabney couldn't believe this. Box had never before noticed the "salon smell" of her hair.

He said, "Dabney, did you go to the salon?"

"Yes!" she said. There was exasperation in her voice that was exasperation about having to lie. "Call the salon yourself if you don't believe me!"

For a second, she thought he might do exactly that. She tried to imagine how compromised Box's dignity would be if he stooped to calling the salon to confirm that Dabney had actually been in for an appointment. And then when Lindsey, the receptionist, said that no, they hadn't seen Dabney that afternoon, Dabney's appointment was for Saturday afternoon (so that her hair would look nice and smell pretty for the Levinsons' annual Backyard BBQ on Abrams Point), what would Box say?

Thankfully, she didn't have to worry, because Box let the issue go, and Dabney was able to breathe. That night, they went to the

Proprietors with Agnes—who seemed preoccupied and strangely quiet—and a certain normalcy was restored.

But as she and Box brushed their teeth and climbed into bed that night, she thought, *I don't want normalcy.*

She wanted Clendenin.

BOX

He received the news of Miranda Gilbert's resignation not over the phone, as he would have expected, but by a letter mailed to the Nantucket house. The letter was written on heavy, creamy stock; initially, Box thought it might be a thank-you note for the ill-conceived and aborted weekend on Nantucket. But when he read it, he realized it was something else entirely.

Dearest Box,

I am writing to thank you for four of the finest and most stimulating years an economist could ask for. What a joy and a blessing it has been working with you.

A collusion of circumstance has made it necessary for me to leave Harvard. I have broken my engagement to Christian, for reasons that I dare not explain in this letter, and at nearly the same time, I was approached by Dr. Wilma Dresdalay at Columbia University about a research opportunity. For both personal and professional reasons, it feels like a move from Harvard and Cambridge to Columbia and Manhattan is the right one. New York is the epicenter of economic thought, as you know, and I can hardly pass up this chance.

I will miss you terribly—your intelligence, your patience,

your kindness, and your wit. I'll send along a new e-mail and
physical address as soon as I can so that we might stay in touch.

Fondly and with inexpressible gratitude,
Miranda

Box set the letter down on his blotter, then let out a long, frustrated stream of air.

"Goddammit!" he bellowed.

He was losing Miranda. She had been with him a long time, longer than any other postdoc research assistant; their compatibility had been remarkable. He would never find anyone like her, not anyone close.

"Goddammit!"

Dabney was somewhere in the house. No doubt she heard him yelling, but she wouldn't knock. She found the closed door to his study intimidating.

He read the letter again. Certain things about it nagged at him, starting with the first word, *Dearest*. "Dearest Box."

Was he, in fact, her dearest? Was all this related to the nonsense Dabney had conjured up? Was Miranda Gilbert *in love* with Box, as Dabney had claimed?

There was the use of the word *stimulating*.

There was news of the broken engagement, the details of which she dared not mention. A broken engagement today, when a week or so earlier, everything had been hunky-dory? Box had asked after the good doctor, and Miranda had told Box that Christian was utterly absorbed with work, but that this was as per usual. *For reasons that I dare not mention in this letter.* What did *that* mean? To Box, it felt like Miranda must have gone directly home from Nantucket and ended the relationship.

What had Dabney *said* to her?

Then the zinger that Miranda was moving to New York, to Columbia, to work with Wilma Dresdalay. Wilma's name had been mentioned casually, as though Miranda were *unaware* that Wilma was the only living economist whose work Box consistently admired and even envied. There was only one person Miranda would be wise to leave Box for, and that was Wilma. He couldn't fault her one bit.

Then the line *I will miss you terribly.* This was the line that Box fixated on. She would miss him terribly. It sounded heartfelt, nearly romantic. Well, yes, Box would miss her terribly as well. She was singular and extraordinary. He tried not to think of how her smile lit up the offices, or how he enjoyed her accent the way one enjoyed music, or how on the occasions when they went to the movies together, she grabbed his arm in excitement or fear. When they went to dinner with colleagues, she presented beautifully, with her strawberry hair in a loose bun, and her clothes soft and feminine; she wore a lot of ivory and peach, which flattered her complexion. Her knowledge of wine was comprehensive; she liked trying new varietals and vineyards and she always chose wines that she knew would excite and please Box.

He admitted to himself that he would miss Miranda Gilbert terribly as well, and not only as a colleague. The thought of her leaving caused his heart to sputter like a dying engine. She had been, perhaps more than anything else, his friend.

Fondly and with inexpressible gratitude—those words were appropriate, and mutual.

"Goddammit!"

The third time brought Dabney to the door.

"Box?" she said, knocking lightly. "Are you all right?"

He opened the door and thrust the letter into Dabney's hands, but he didn't wait for her to read it.

"Miranda has resigned, she's going to Columbia to work with Wilma." He cleared his throat. "Seems she's broken off the engagement with Christian."

"Oh," Dabney said. "Wow!"

AGNES

Five days of silence from CJ. It was now a standoff. He was waiting for her to break down and change her mind. The silence was also eerie; she hadn't believed him capable of it.

She started joining Riley for trips to the beach after work. She swam while he surfed, then they lay around on his cherry-red beach blanket like a couple of seals and enjoyed the golden hour—the hour when the sun was sublime and mellow. Despite the turmoil of the summer, Agnes relaxed with Riley.

One night, she let Clendenin cook her dinner. Fried rice with authentic spices that he had ordered on the Internet—the fragrant rice was a deep yellow and was studded with delicious tidbits—golden raisins, lacquered pork, rock shrimp—that looked like tiny gems. That night, Clen talked about what Dabney had been like in high school—how popular and confident she had been, her elaborate matchmaking schemes, even among the faculty, her love of Nantucket. Dabney had been salutatorian of their class, and Clen the valedictorian; Dabney had been bitter about that, Clen said. He had her by three-tenths of a percentage point in GPA and forty points verbal and ten points math in the SAT—but she had gotten into Harvard and he hadn't. Back then, it had been easier to get into Harvard as a girl, or so Clen had told himself at the time. Dabney used to keep a notebook, he said, of her favorite streets on the island. Charter Street, in the fish lots, was her very favorite. She wanted to live on Charter Street when she grew up, and if not Charter, then Quince, or Lily.

After dinner, Clen poured them each a bourbon and he smoked a cigarette on the front porch while Agnes did the dishes. Then she joined him on the porch and they looked at the stars in the sky, and at the large, empty, illuminated house that it was Clen's job to care-take.

Agnes said, "Will you stay here on Nantucket?"

"I don't see ever leaving again," Clendenin said. "Unless something happens to your mother. For me, this island is home, but it's home because of Dabney. I moved here when I was fourteen. I lived here only three weeks before she befriended me, and as soon as she did, I never wanted to leave. She gives this island its meaning. Dabney, Nantucket. Nantucket, Dabney." He exhaled. "And long as she stays, I stay."

Agnes wanted to ask him what he thought was going to happen. Did he think Dabney would leave Box? And...marry him? At that moment, Agnes understood that she had gotten way too involved in the love triangle. Her mother, her father, her other father.

She gathered up the keys to the Prius. "I'd better go," she said.

DABNEY

She was at the farm, selecting ears of corn for dinner. She felt so weak and so sick, she could barely stand. She should have called the doctor weeks ago—but as soon as she resolved to do it, she felt better, or life got in the way. That morning, Dr. Marcus Cobb, Nina Mobley's beau, had gone fishing and caught five striped bass.

When he came into the office to take Nina out to lunch, he gave Dabney a heavy bag of fresh filets.

Dabney had been thrilled with the fish; she instantly planned dinner: grilled striped bass, corn on the cob, farm greens lightly dressed. It had sounded like the perfect meal at noon, but now, at five, Dabney was in so much pain that she wanted to take a pill and sleep until morning.

Forbearance. She would choose the corn. The fish was already marinating on her kitchen counter. With a few simple instructions, Agnes could pull dinner together.

Suddenly, there was a woman at the corn crib, trying to get Dabney's attention. It was Elizabeth Jennings.

"Elizabeth!" Dabney said. "Hello!" She was in too much pain to talk to Elizabeth. The pain was like a black marble, and Dabney was suspended inside.

"Dabney!" Elizabeth said. "I'm so happy I bumped into you. I have the most interesting piece of news to share."

Dabney was wary of "interesting pieces of news," because they were usually rumors or gossip, and yet people came to her with "interesting pieces of news" all the time. Dabney did *not* want to hear any "interesting pieces of news" from Elizabeth Jennings, that was for darn sure.

"I'm in a terrible hurry," Dabney said. She indiscriminately stuck two final ears of corn into her recyclable shopping bag.

But Elizabeth either didn't hear Dabney or she chose to ignore her. She said, "You're friends with Clendenin Hughes, right?"

Dabney froze. Her insides contorted. Lovesick.

Elizabeth said, "When we had dinner a few weeks ago, he told me the two of you have known each other since high school. So sweet!" Elizabeth smiled, showing off her capped teeth. She was wearing a turquoise-and-white dress with matching turquoise sandals, and her toenails, Dabney noticed, were painted the same shade of turquoise. Was it possible that Elizabeth Jennings had her pedicure done each day to match her outfit? It wasn't impossible. What else did Elizabeth Jennings have to do all day except gossip and chase after Clendenin? She wasn't even at the corn crib to pick out *corn,* Dabney realized. She had come only to torment Dabney!

"I have to go," Dabney said. She turned to her cart and loaded in her ears.

"I went to Clen's house to drop off a pie I made," Elizabeth said.

Involuntarily, Dabney shook her head. There was *no way* Elizabeth had made a pie.

"And there was a young woman pulling out of his driveway as I was pulling in. A very beautiful young woman. I think Clendenin has a girlfriend!"

Dabney barely made it to the Impala before the pain became unbearable. Elizabeth Jennings had been jealous, spiteful even, and possibly suspicious of Dabney's relationship with Clen. Either she had wanted Dabney to tell her who this young mystery woman was or she wanted Dabney to commiserate. Men always chose younger women. Life was unfair in many aspects, but this, perhaps, was the most unfair.

At the very least, Dabney knew that Elizabeth Jennings hadn't been the guest at five o'clock. Someone else had been.

Dabney called Clen from the parking lot.

She said, "Who were your plans with the other day? When I wanted to come over at five o'clock and you said you were busy?"

He sighed. "I'm sorry, Cupe. I can't tell you."

"Clen!" she shouted. She was in *so much pain,* and now this. "A young woman? A beautiful young woman?"

"Dabney," he said. "I can't tell you."

*   *   *

The sharp, shining knives piercing her gut....She moaned. Her insides were being gnawed on by millions of tiny razor teeth.

I think Clendenin has a girlfriend!

I'm sorry, Cupe. I can't tell you.

Lovesick.

No, she thought.

In the morning, she called Genevieve at Dr. Field's office. "I need to talk to Ted," she said. "Please, I think it's an emergency."

"Like, an emergency-room emergency?" Genevieve said.

"Please, Genevieve," Dabney said. "I need to talk to Ted. Can you make that happen?"

"For you, I can make anything happen."

Ted Field set it all up. He sent Dabney's blood work to the correct person at Mass General, and they scheduled a CT scan for Thursday morning.

"You do realize," Ted Field said, "that you have to go to Boston."

"Yes," Dabney said. It had long been her mantra that she would leave the island only if her life depended on it. Now, she was suddenly certain, her life depended on it.

She told Box first.

"I spoke to Ted Field," she said. "I'm going to Boston for a CT scan."

"That sounds serious," he said. "I'll go with you."

"No," Dabney said. "I'm going alone."

"It's my city and it's been aeons since you've been there, or anywhere else, by yourself. Let me go with you. We can end the day with dinner at Harvest, spend the night in my apartment, and come back in the morning."

"That sounds like your idea of a lovely time," Dabney said. "I want to go and come back, and I am going alone."

"You have *got* to be kidding me," Box said.

"First flight to Boston on Thursday," she said. "Last flight back Thursday."

"You can't possibly expect me to believe that you're going alone," he said.

"I'm going alone," she said.

She told Clen next.

"Boston on Thursday," she said. "I have to have some tests."

"I don't like the way that sounds," he said. "Let me go with you."

"You can't," she said.

"Wanna bet?"

"Clen."

He frowned. "Is the economist going with you?"

"No," she said. "I'm going alone."

She told Agnes, and then Nina. Boston on Thursday for tests. Before either of them could open her mouth, she said, "I'm going alone."

At the airline counter, she accepted her boarding pass and thought, *Am I really doing this?* It would have been far easier with Box or Clen or Agnes or Nina there to prop her up. But she felt it was important that she go alone, self-motivated, powered by her own two feet.

At the very moment the airplane lifted off the ground, something fell back down to earth. Her spirit, her soul, her self. She was nothing but a shell.

Taxi, Ted Williams Tunnel, Cambridge Street, Mass General. She had seen the Prudential Building and the Hancock Tower as she flew in. Skyscrapers, the wider world. It was just Boston, she reminded herself, only ninety miles from home. She had gone to college across the river, she had made it through four years of higher education; she would make it through today.

Blood pressure, temperature, needles, hundreds of medical questions, culminating with the CT scan, which was like something out of science fiction.

Then, a rather lengthy wait, while a doctor read the scan. Everyone at the hospital was being solicitous. Rosemary, the nurse-practitioner in Imaging, treated Dabney like she was a minor celebrity.

She said, "This is all being expedited. We know you want to get home."

Dabney supposed that Dr. Field had some influence here, or maybe Box did, via Dr. Christian Bartelby.

She ate a tuna fish sandwich in the cafeteria. She looked around at all the other people—some sick, some healthy, some hospital employees. There were so many people in the world, people she didn't know and who didn't know her. That was, perhaps, the scariest thing of all.

Dr. Chand Rohatgi was a handsome Indian man with kind eyes.

"There's someone here with you?" he said.

"No," she said. "I came alone."

He nodded. His face was pained.

"Just tell me," she whispered. "Please."

"Not a great prognosis," he said.

*   *   *

Cancer of the pancreas, which had metastasized, already, to her liver. The lungs would likely be next. It wasn't resectable, and considering her level of pain, she wouldn't be strong enough for chemotherapy, and there was no guarantee that chemo would do anything other than make her sicker. At this point, Dr. Rohatgi said, there was little they could do but hope the progression was slow. He could help her manage the pain.

She said, "How long...?"

"Difficult to say."

"Will I live to see the lights on Main Street at Christmas Stroll? It's my busiest weekend of the year."

He looked puzzled. He wasn't familiar with Christmas Stroll, he said, but if it was in December, there was a chance, maybe. Again, difficult to say.

A chance, maybe? she thought. Christmas Stroll was only four months away. Was he telling her then that she didn't even have *four months?* She felt blindsided. Someone else should not be able to tell you you're dying.

No wonder she felt like a shell. Her insides were being consumed by disease.

She said, "I've always been an intuitive person. I thought it was something else. I thought I was... lovesick."

He said, "Yes, I can understand that. The symptoms are probably similar."

Or perhaps Dr. Rohatgi didn't say *the symptoms are probably similar,* perhaps he didn't say *a chance, maybe,* perhaps he didn't say *metastasized, already, to the liver.* Dabney walked out of the hospital in a state of extreme confusion, and the most confusing thing was this: she wasn't thinking about Agnes, or Clen, or Box. She was thinking about her mother.

Dr. Donegal had asked her time and again, during the eight or nine years that she had gone to see him, to describe what had happened the night Dabney's mother left. Time and again, Dabney had stared mutely at Dr. Donegal because she couldn't remember.

Why, then, all these years later, with the onset of this…news… was the scene so crisp in Dabney's mind? The suite at the Park Plaza, a ceramic vase holding ostrich feathers, the chandelier in the lobby that was as big and bright as a bonfire, the king-size bed that Dabney had been allowed to jump on for as long as it took her mother to put on her makeup, the front-row-center orchestra seats at *The Nutcracker,* her mother tapping out the rhythm of the music on Dabney's hand during the "Dance of the Sugar Plum Fairy," and Dabney agape at the beauty of the ballerina, her ability to float, twirl, fly. At the hotel afterward there were cheeseburgers from room service and, for Dabney, a hot fudge sundae. Her mother had been drinking red wine, which was what she drank at home, and it always turned her teeth blue, which Dabney found funny. *Why blue and not red, Mama?* It was quite late, Dabney remembered, pitch-black outside, and it had started to snow, and Dabney's mother lifted her up to the window so she could see. Dabney was wearing her white flannel nightgown, she had spilled chocolate sauce down the front, which upset her, she grew weepy, she was tired. She brushed her teeth and climbed into the big bed and her mother sat on the edge of the bed and smoothed her hair from her face. Her mother was engulfed in green smoke, she might have been a bit drunk, her words were slurred, she said some things about Dabney's father that Dabney didn't understand, how he had come back from the war and vowed, *Nantucket, always Nantucket,* and her mother couldn't do it anymore but her father wouldn't live anywhere else. *I'll always love you, Dabney, you will always be my little girl, this is hard for me, so hard.* Her mother's perfume had smelled like a sugar plum, or so Dabney had thought that night. Her mother's pearls had glowed even in the darkened room. She was right there on the edge of the bed, and then when Dabney woke up she was gone. May, the Irish chambermaid, was there.

Mama! Where's my mama?

Your father is coming for you, my sweet.

Bye bye, Miss American Pie.

Mama!

Dabney climbed into a taxi. She was just able to tell the driver, "Logan Terminal C, please," before the tears squeezed out from the corners of her eyes. They were not tears about the news, because the news was incomprehensible. She cried all the way to the airport because her mother had left, and still, to this very day, Dabney missed her.

There was no rhyme or reason to her thoughts. It just wasn't possible, it was too terrifying to comprehend. She was very sick. She would die. She would die? It was a door she would step through without knowing what was on the other side. Her grandmother, Agnes Bernadette, had believed in Heaven, fluffy clouds, angels, harps, peace, and that was what Dabney had grown up believing. But now that she was faced with the concrete reality, she thought, *Angels? Harps?*

Then she thought, *Everyone dies, absolutely everyone, there is no escaping it,* so the only reasonable option was to focus on the time she had left.

Dr. Rohatgi had urged her not to look too far ahead. *Take things a moment at a time,* he'd said. He had given her some literature, which she stuffed into her purse, and a prescription to ease her pain. She thought of Clen, Box, Agnes, Nina Mobley, Riley, Celerie, Vaughan Oglethorpe, Diana at the pharmacy who made her coffee, people she cherished, the people who made her who she was. She would tell no one. But was that feasible? She was holding in so many secrets now. How long would it be until she burst, like a dam?

Dabney's life had been safe with her mother, and then not safe. Then safe again, and then when Clendenin left, not safe. Then safe for a long time, but now, not safe. Everyone's life had moments of both. She liked to believe she was special because of what she'd survived, but this last thing she would not survive. Incomprehensible. The literature in her purse was supposed to help her grapple with being terminally ill, but who wrote such literature? And how did they know the best strategies for grappling? Nobody knew what happened next.

She was relieved when Nantucket came into view—historically preserved homes and lighthouses, ponds and moors, the blue-and-white ribbon where the ocean endlessly hit the shore. The only thing Dabney had wanted, all day long, was to be back home.

In the car driving home, she decided that she would wait until Monday to tell everyone the news. She thought of Dr. Rohatgi saying, *Take things a moment at a time.* She wanted to go to the Levinsons' Backyard BBQ on Saturday night, she wanted to dance, she wanted to drink wine and laugh and have fun.

She wanted to have one last perfect summer weekend.

Box asked first, and then Agnes, then Nina, then Clen: *How did it go at the hospital?*

Dabney said, "I had a lot of tests. One thing I know for sure is that I do not have a wheat allergy."

*   *   *

Dabney would someday be too sick to go to a party, but she wasn't too sick yet, and so on Friday morning she signed out of the log, writing *errands*—but instead of going to see Clen, she went to Hepburn to buy a new dress. She selected a white Dolce Vita sundress with a racerback and fringe around the waist that would swing when she danced. Despite her fear and confusion, she decided that she would dance. This, after all, might be her last chance. She bought new white sandals to match the dress—flats, nothing fancy. Dabney loved the new sundress and the new sandals and she hung the dress on the door of the closet, where she could look at it. When she woke up in the middle of the night, she saw the dress glowing white; it looked like a ghost.

Would she haunt this house after she was gone?

She supposed anything was possible.

Box brought a glass of wine up to the bedroom as Dabney was getting ready for the party.

"Here you go, darling." Box set the wineglass on her bureau. "A dressing drink."

Dabney moved into an embrace with her husband and clung to him in a way that probably qualified as histrionics, but what did it matter now? Surprisingly, Box reciprocated. He said, "It's nice just to hold you."

Dabney squeezed her eyes shut. There was no pink with Box, there had never been pink with Box, but he was a good man.

He led her over to the bed, and she worried for a second that he had intentions, possibly he wanted to try to make love to her, an endeavor that would surely embarrass them both. But Box sat on the bed next to Dabney, with her hand in both of his.

He said, "I have a confession to make."

"You do?" she said.

He said, "I have been dreadfully jealous of Clendenin Hughes. Since the minute I learned of his existence, really. But even more so now that he's back on Nantucket."

Dabney stared into her lap.

Box said, "I know your past relationship with him is complicated, possibly beyond my limited understanding. I'm sure you still have still some residual feelings for him, and although I don't know what form those feelings take, I want to apologize, because there have been some anomalies in my behavior this summer that have to do with my jealousy of him."

"You don't have to apologize," Dabney said.

"I just want you to know that I am not as hard-hearted as you may think. Nor am I unreasonable. You should work out your feelings for Hughes, and when you come to a resolution and sense of peace regarding your relationship with him, do let me know so I can finally put the green-eyed monster to rest." Box patted Dabney's hand. "I'm sure it's difficult to have him back on the island."

"Well, yes," she said. It was a relief to finally speak a few true words about Clen. "It is, actually."

"Thought so," Box said. He stood up. "Let's go have fun tonight, shall we?"

At the party, there was valet parking; a pretty blond girl from the catering company was stationed at the entrance next to a table of deep-orange cocktails. Dabney was so entranced by the color of the drinks that it took her a second to realize the pretty blond girl was Celerie.

"Dabney!" Celerie shouted.

Dabney startled, then tried to recover quickly as Celerie gave her a power squeeze.

Dabney said, "You're working for...?"

"Nantucket Catering Company!" Celerie said, her hands forming a V in the air. "And Riley is here, too! He's playing the guitar in the garden!"

"Oh," Dabney said. "How did you...?"

"My roommate works for NCC and they needed extra hands tonight, so I said I'd help out, the money is great, and I hooked Riley up." Celerie beamed. "When the Levinsons found out we both worked at the Chamber, they were *so excited!* They love you! They said you *matched them!*"

Celerie was using what Dabney thought of as her stadium voice, and Dabney was a bit embarrassed.

"Yes, well," Dabney said. "That's what I do."

Box wisely sidestepped Celerie and the bright orange drinks—tangerine cosmos, Celerie announced—and entered the party ahead of Dabney. When she stepped through the trellised archway, she found Box shaking hands with Larry Levinson. Marguerite Levinson was on Dabney immediately, taking both of Dabney's hands in hers.

"Dabney," she said. "How are you *doing?*"

Dabney had adored Marguerite Levinson since they'd met a dozen years earlier up at Tupancy Links with their dogs. Dabney's chocolate Lab, Henry, had still been alive, and Marguerite's golden retriever, Uncle Frank, had been little more than a puppy. Larry had frequented Tupancy with *his* golden retriever at the time, Arthur Fielder. Dabney had introduced her brand-new friend Marguerite to her more established friend, Larry, and there had been pink auras before a Frisbee had even been thrown.

How *was* she doing?

I'm dying, she thought. *And my soul aches for Clen.* Box had made such a kind and thoughtful speech in the bedroom, he had proved himself to be an evolved person, he had been trying to tell Dabney that whatever her feelings were for Clendenin, he would understand. She had had her chance...but she had blown it.

Forbearance. To Marguerite, she said, "What a beautiful night! This is my favorite party of the year, you know. I can't *wait* to dance!" Dabney shook her hips, and the fringe on her white dress shimmied.

Marguerite whooped and said, "Great! Let's have us some fun!"

Dabney finished her tangerine cosmo. It was surprisingly good, and she might have gone for another one but she thought it best to keep her forward momentum and not go back and distract Celerie from the other guests. Dabney stood in line at the bar to get a glass of wine for herself and one for Box. It was a crystal-clear, bug-free, blue-skied stunner of an evening and the Levinsons' property at Abrams Point faced south over the harbor. There was enough breeze to keep the flag lazily waving and to carry Riley Alsopp's voice over the lawn.

Take things a moment at a time. There were few moments of her life that had been as aesthetically pleasing as this one.

Wine in hand, Dabney found Box and together they headed to the raw bar to attack some oysters.

There were people to talk to, endless people. Dabney knew everyone, although certain people she knew only because she saw them at this party every year—Donald and Irene from Newport Beach, California, and Marguerite's unmarried brother, Charles Baldwin. Charles had a stick up his ass and a bad case of lockjaw; he was a private-equity guy with a house in Potomac, Maryland. But he was lonely, Marguerite had confided, and Marguerite was perennially hoping that Dabney would set him up with someone wonderful. Charles had used every Internet dating service known to man—eHarmony, Match.com, It's Just Lunch—but none of them had worked. Dabney had promised Marguerite that she would keep Charles in mind. Years ago, she had nearly set him up on a blind date with Nina Mobley, but then she'd thought better of it. Dabney had to admit, she probably didn't have an arrow in her quiver meant for Charles Baldwin.

Take things a moment at a time. She enjoyed her conversation with Charles, or rather, she enjoyed listening to Charles and Box converse (Box excelled with the stuffy) while Riley sang James Taylor, and she tasted all the hors d'oeuvres—the coconut shrimp with mango-curry aioli, the pork satay, the phyllo cups of lobster and corn salad—and she enjoyed the mellow sunshine on her face.

At the end of the James Taylor song, there was a smattering of applause and Riley caught Dabney's eye. She floated over to him.

"Look at you!" she said.

He stood up and moved away from the microphone. "I hope you don't mind that I'm moonlighting," he said. "I realize I probably should have asked your permission."

Dabney laughed. Had anyone used the term *moonlighting* since 1989?

She said, "I'm thrilled you get to show off your talent and make a little extra money in the process."

He said, "Yeah, what they're paying me is ridiculous."

Dabney's mind wandered away like a puppy left off a leash. She thought, *Please, Riley, do not leave the Chamber.* Riley had a chocolate Lab named Sadie, a fact that had captured Dabney's heart because she missed Henry, missed him so profoundly that she had never gotten another dog. She wished she could go back to the days of Tupancy Links with Henry and Uncle Frank and Arthur Fielder—rolling green hills overlooking the Sound, half-a-dozen Frisbees in the air at once, red and purple and yellow disks against the blue sky. Agnes had still been in high school then, and Clen was living in a place so far away that it seemed imaginary. Riley Riley Riley—he would be perfect for Agnes. How much easier it would be for Dabney to leave this world if she knew that Agnes had Riley Alsopp in her future. Agnes would inherit the house on Charter Street. She and Riley could bring their children to Nantucket for the summers, Dabney's grandchildren, the grandchildren she would never meet. Dabney thought that she would like to be a ghost in that house; that way, she could set eyes on her grandchildren and kiss them as they slept.

Riley, it seemed, was asking her something.

"I'm sorry?" Dabney said.

He said, "Where's Agnes tonight?"

Dabney blinked. Where *was* Agnes? Dabney and Box had left before Agnes got home from work. Dabney had written a note saying there was chicken salad in the fridge and homemade cheddar scones if Agnes wanted supper. Agnes had been out on her own a lot lately, it seemed, and the one time Dabney had asked her about it, Agnes said she had stayed late at work. Dabney wondered if Agnes was interested in Dave Patterson, her boss. That would be good. They weren't a perfect match, but any relationship that took Agnes away from CJ was welcome. Anyone but CJ! As Dabney thought about it, she realized that she hadn't heard Agnes talk about CJ in a while, a week or ten days at least, and neither had Dabney heard Agnes on the phone with CJ in her bedroom. And of course CJ hadn't shown his face here on Nantucket. Dabney wondered now if maybe she should have pried a little deeper into what was going on with Agnes—but Agnes was twenty-six years old, an adult, and the last thing she wanted was to explain her every move to her mother. If Agnes wanted to talk, she would come to Dabney.

However, Dabney had been self-absorbed. To say the least.

"I don't know where she is," Dabney said.

AGNES

As she was leaving work, a call came to her cell phone from an unfamiliar number. Agnes was afraid to answer it, so she let it go to voice mail. She didn't listen to the message until she had pulled into her driveway. It was Rocky DeMotta, one of CJ's partners at work. Agnes had met Rocky at the U.S. Open the preceding September. Rocky was calling, he said, because CJ was...missing. AWOL. The ink had just dried on Bantam Killjoy's contract with the Chiefs, and training camp had started the day before, and CJ was supposed to *be* in Kansas City *with* Bantam, but he had never shown up for his flight. Nor had he come to work, or called in, or even checked his e-mail. He wasn't answering his calls or texts.

Rocky said, "We're all a little worried about him. Worried enough that I grabbed your number off the office records, sorry about that, but would you *please* call us if he's there with you, or if you've heard from him."

Agnes sucked in her breath and thought, *He's dead, he's dead, he's dead, I killed him.*

She listened to the message again. Rocky sounded panicked, of course he sounded panicked; CJ was never, ever out of touch, he carried a BlackBerry, two iPhones, and a laptop. What reason would he possibly have had to miss his flight to Kansas City? Had he hanged himself in his apartment, leaving a suicide note weighted down with the returned engagement ring?

It was about two hundred degrees in her closed-up Prius, and yet Agnes shivered. She was so, so cold. She headed inside. She needed her mother.

But the house was empty, although there was a note on the kitchen table about the things Dabney had left for Agnes's dinner. The end of the note said, "Daddy and I are at the Levinsons'. Don't wait up—hopefully we'll be home very, very late!"

The Levinsons. Dabney loved the party at the Levinsons'; she had really been looking forward to it. Agnes could not call Dabney or Box at the Levinsons' and ruin their night out just because CJ wasn't answering his phone.

Agnes sat at the kitchen table and bit her nails. She tried to come up with a plausible reason why CJ had missed his flight. If he'd hurt himself or gotten sick, he would have called in to the office. What else could it be? Had he gotten hit by a bus? Had he gone on a weeklong Dirty Goose bender once he received the ring back, and was he now passed out facedown on a bar somewhere? Should Agnes call someone? Both of CJ's parents had passed away; there was a brother somewhere in Upstate New York, but he and CJ no longer spoke. CJ knew a million people, but he wasn't close to anyone, really, except Agnes. And Rocky...he played squash with Rocky. He had gone to high school at Collegiate, on the Upper West Side, and then had a PG year at the Berkshire School before going to the University of Florida. He never talked about anyone from high school or college, except for the Gators, who had later become his clients. Agnes then thought of Annabelle Pippin in her waterfront home in Boca Raton. Should Agnes call Annabelle and ask about CJ...about...Charlie Pippin, her ex-husband? Was it weird that CJ had changed his name after his divorce? Agnes had all but decided that she wasn't going to marry CJ, at least not right away—so why did she care that he was missing?

No answer for this, but she did care. She felt responsible.

What to do?

She called Riley. Riley would be able to calm her.

But her call to Riley went straight to voice mail, which was unusual. Agnes considered driving to Antenna Beach to see if he was surfing. She stared at her phone. She needed more friends. It was CJ's fault that she had no friends.

She tried Riley again—straight to voice mail. Then, she called Celerie. Celerie wouldn't be able to help at all but Agnes craved someone's positive outlook—and, well, Celerie was a cheerleader.

Her call to Celerie also went straight to voice mail, which was even stranger than Riley's call going to voice mail. Celerie lived and died by her cell phone.

Agnes wondered if maybe Riley and Celerie were on a date somewhere. She wondered if they were in bed together. She had to admit, the thought bothered her.

What to do? Call her mother? Drive out to Antenna Beach in search of Riley? Call back Rocky DeMotta?

Almost against her will, she dialed CJ's number, then racked her brain for what she might say in her message. Should she say, *Hey, it's me?* or, *Hey, it's Agnes?* Now that she had returned the ring, she figured she had pretty much given up the right to say, *Hey, it's me.*

"Hello?"

Agnes was so startled, she nearly dropped the phone. CJ had answered.

"Hey," she said. Her voice sounded bright and normal, but her thoughts darted around like a school of frightened fish. What was she going to *say*?

"Hey, Agnes," CJ said. His voice was calm, and a little flat. "Where are you?"

"On Nantucket," she said. "At my parents' house. Where are you?"

Click. CJ had hung up.

DABNEY

It was as Dabney was standing in the buffet line, eyeing the mashed-potato bar and thinking, *bacon, chives, sautéed mushrooms, caramelized onions, cheddar, a dollop of sour cream,* that she saw Clendenin walk into the tent with Elizabeth Jennings.

Not possible.

But there they were. Together, indisputably together. Clen was…what, then? Dating her? Lying to Dabney?

The thick white china plate wobbled in Dabney's hand and her vision started to splotch. She couldn't help herself to the mashed-potato bar or the grilled lobster tail or the beef tenderloin or the luscious-looking tomatoes with burrata cheese. She couldn't eat a thing right now; she felt like she might never eat again. But she also couldn't move through the buffet line with an empty plate. Box was right behind her, and she knew *everyone* at this party. She took a scoop of potatoes, a lobster tail, a few spears of grilled asparagus, and a lone tomato, then she cast about for a place to sit. There were two empty seats at the Levinsons' table, but in her present state of mind, Dabney didn't want to eat with the host and hostess.

Someone touched her back. Dabney turned around. Clen and Elizabeth.

"Hey there, Dabney!" Elizabeth said. She looked like the cat that ate the canary.

"Hey there," Dabney said. It hurt to make herself smile, but she did it. "Look at you two."

Clen was wearing a crisp blue-and-white-gingham shirt with the cuff turned smartly back on his right wrist, and he had trimmed his beard. His expression, however, was one of sheer misery. He looked the way Dabney would have looked if she weren't trying so hard to conceal how she felt.

"Dabney," Clen said. He bent down to kiss the side of her mouth. It was like a stranger kissing her.

Elizabeth said, "Where is that naughty husband of yours? I'm still angry at him for leaving my party without saying goodbye."

Dabney hunted around for Box; he had been right behind her in the buffet line. He hadn't been more than three feet away from her all night long. But now, Dabney saw, he was sitting down with the Levinsons. He must have noticed Clen and peeled off. From across the tent, he beckoned to Dabney.

Dabney waved at him. "He's over there," she said to Elizabeth. "Go say hi."

"I will," Elizabeth said. To Clen she said, "Be right back."

Dabney waited until Elizabeth was safely at Box's side before she raised her eyes to Clen.

"Let's get out of here," he said.

"What?" she said.

He took the plate of food from her hands and set it on an empty waiter's tray. "Come out to the lawn with me so I can talk to you."

"Are you crazy?" Dabney said. "Everyone is watching us."

"I don't care," Clen said.

"Well, I do," Dabney said. She heard the trill of Elizabeth's laugh, but Dabney knew that no matter how witty Box was being, he also had one eye glued on his wife.

"Come out onto the lawn," Clen said. "So I can talk to you."

He cut a path through two tables and headed for the opening in the side of the tent and the purpling night outside.

This was, Dabney saw, a defining moment. *We all make choices.*

Dabney followed him out.

*   *   *

You've been lying to me. You're seeing Elizabeth Jennings.

We didn't come together. We met at the entrance and she latched on to me. It was an awful coincidence.

You expect me to believe that.

I rode my bicycle. She came in Mingus's old Mercedes, is my guess.

You didn't plan to meet here?

Did not plan.

Who is the beautiful young woman Elizabeth is talking about?

Dabney.

Tell me! This, practically, loud enough to silence the tent—but no, it was only in Dabney's imagination. In reality, the tent hummed with voices and laughter and the band tuning up.

My new cleaning lady, Clen said. I've been taking some time to get to know her.

Dabney furrowed her brow. Weeks earlier, she had sent Clen a new cleaning lady from Brazil named Opaline.

You mean Opaline?

Opaline, yes.

This didn't sound right to Dabney. Opaline was in her late thirties and had five sons back in Rio; she wasn't someone Dabney would consider young or pretty. She had dyed orange hair and a hard-line mouth.

Elizabeth is after you. You said she tried to kiss you.

She did try, yes. However, kissing requires two interested parties.

Why can't you stay away from her? Tell her to go away. What are you doing? Are you trying to torture me?

No, Cupe, I'm not trying to torture you.

Well, you are! She started to cry.

How do you think I feel, knowing that you're still living with the economist? Sharing a bed with him? You've been telling me you're going to leave, but you know what, Dabney?

His use of her real name frightened her.

What?

You're never going to leave him. I want you to be truly only mine, but you never will be. Ever.

Dabney stepped forward into Clendenin's arms.

You jerk. You stupid, stubborn, difficult man. I have always been truly only yours.

He squeezed her so tightly that her insides screamed out in pain, and then he kissed her until her vision went black and she saw stars. She was going to faint from love, die right here of it.

"Dabney!"

Dabney didn't bother turning around to look at Box, nor did she pull away from Clendenin. At that moment, she didn't see the point.

AGNES

She called CJ back three times, but there was no answer. Agnes supposed she should feel relieved. She had nothing to say to CJ anyway. She was merely glad he was alive. If he didn't want to show up for his client, he didn't want to show up for his client. It wasn't Agnes's concern.

She wished Riley would answer his phone or listen to his messages and call her back. Or Celerie. She wished her parents would come home. She had never once felt scared or uncomfortable in this house, but she felt scared now. She turned on the TV for the voices, and helped herself to her mother's chicken salad and a cheddar scone, which she heated up and slathered with butter, but she was too agitated to eat. She could go out by herself, she supposed—to the Straight Wharf bar or down to Cru—and get a glass of champagne and some oysters. She had a wallet full of cash—Box pressed twenties and fifties and hundreds into her hand every time she left the house. She might meet someone nice, someone new—man or woman. She was pathetically low on friends.

She thought she heard a noise outside; there was a rustling like someone poking around in her mother's hydrangea bushes. Agnes was afraid to check out the windows, then she chastised herself. Nantucket was one of the safest places in the world. Half their neighbors didn't even lock their houses; Dabney and Box only did so because of their art.

Agnes's apartment door in New York had four dead bolts.

Agnes scooped up her car keys. She couldn't stay in the house alone.

She found herself involuntarily driving out the Polpis Road toward Clendenin's cottage. He would be at home; he was a self-described hermit, and Dabney was at the Levinsons' with Box, so there would be no danger of disrupting a rendezvous. Agnes found Clen easy to talk to. He listened in a way that so few men listened, even Box. Box heard every third word you said—only when he was talking economics was he present. Agnes understood how seductive it would be for Dabney to know that her words were being cherished and appreciated.

Agnes would talk to Clendenin.

She pulled into the driveway, but the cottage was dark, and

Agnes's heart sank. Where *was* everyone tonight? It felt like the whole world had abandoned her. The big house was lit with the usual lights, which were on timers. Clendenin had told Agnes that the family who owned it, the Joneses, weren't coming to Nantucket at all this summer; they were going to the south of France instead.

Agnes sat in the driveway outside Clen's cottage and rested her forehead against the steering wheel of the Prius.

Headlights swung into the driveway, which meant that Clen was home, thank God. He used the Joneses' Volvo only when he had to get groceries or had another errand for which his bicycle wasn't suitable.

The headlights pointed right into Agnes's windshield, blinding her, and she realized it wasn't Clen in the Volvo. She thought to panic—it was a lot quieter out in Polpis, there weren't any neighbors nearby to hear her yell for help—but then Agnes assumed that the car belonged to someone who was lost and had turned into the wrong driveway. Agnes got out of her car, thinking she would help this lost soul, then leave Clen a note and head into town for a drink.

A man got out of the other car and started walking toward her.

Agnes blinked.

It was CJ.

DABNEY

Box didn't speak, and Dabney hoped that he would believe she was working out her feelings for Clendenin Hughes, trying to find a resolution and a sense of peace, and that he would sensibly walk back into the tent.

The problem was that Elizabeth Jennings had followed Box out.

Dabney casually extracted herself from Clendenin's arms, then she faced Box and Elizabeth head-on and said, "Everything is okay, everything's fine. I just wasn't feeling well is all."

Box glared at Clendenin, and Dabney thought there might be another fistfight. She wanted to vaporize. Her mind was racing with the scandal of it all. Tomorrow, everyone would be talking about Dabney Kimball Beech; the island's most beloved citizen, and its fiercest champion, would be revealed as a liar and a cheat.

And yet, she realized that *this* was her chance; all the other chances had been practice, trial runs. She wasn't sure if she believed in Fate, but she was pretty sure that Clendenin Hughes had lost his arm and returned to Nantucket for a reason. He had been meant to reconcile with Dabney before it was too late. *Take things a moment at a time.*

Dabney cleared her throat and aimed her words at her impossibly dignified husband. She didn't care one bit about Elizabeth. "You told me today that you thought I might have residual feelings for Clendenin, but that you didn't know what those feelings were. The answer is that…I'm in love with him." She paused, wondering if she'd really just said those words. "I've been in love with him my whole life. I'm so sorry."

Box nodded, but it looked like the lightbulb was slow to come on. Was there a way that Dabney could have been clearer, or kinder? Finally, he said, "Thank you. Thank you for telling me. I thought I was going crazy. It's nice to know that my instincts were correct and that my sanity, at least, is intact." With that, Dabney watched him go, her brilliant and esteemed professor, the man who had saved her, the man who had loved her and allowed her to be herself, the man who had raised Agnes as his own, a good, principled man. Dabney decided to do him the favor of not chasing after him and exhibiting more histrionics.

Elizabeth made a noise—a sniff or a soft cry—then said, "I had no idea."

Clen said, "Really, Elizabeth, this is none of your business."

"I knew something was going on, too," Elizabeth said. "On the Fourth of July I knew." She shook her head as if to clear it, and then gave Dabney a wobbly smile. "You've got yourself a regular love triangle."

Dabney thought, *Was there ever anything* regular *about a love triangle?* Maybe there was. Maybe years ago, while "overseas," Elizabeth herself had been involved in a love triangle with Clen, or had wanted to be. What did Dabney know? Regret overwhelmed her at that moment. She had made a spectacular mess of things. As she gazed at the tent, its pearly, incandescent walls containing light and music and food and conversation, she realized that among her regrets was that she wouldn't dance tonight.

Elizabeth said, "I'm going back in. See you two later, I guess."

Clen said, "Have a good night."

Elizabeth strolled back into the party with purpose, and Dabney shuddered. Her good name was about to be destroyed.

Clen said, "Well."

Dabney said, "Well, what?"

Clen said, "You'll have to ride home on my handlebars."

AGNES

There was a bottle of Grey Goose dangling from CJ's left hand, two-thirds gone. Agnes noticed this, then his rumpled suit, which looked like he'd slept in it three days straight. His hair was standing on end, and he bared his glinting teeth. He was absolutely terrifying.

He said, "Hey, baby."

"Hey," she said. Her emotions surged at the sound of his voice, and at the raw physicality of him. He was here—he had skipped out on precious Bantam Killjoy and come to Nantucket to see her. There was something desperate and romantic about that, and she felt herself rethinking her decision.

He handed the bottle of vodka to Agnes and said, "You want?"

She accepted the bottle; it was icy cold. She brought it to her lips and threw back a little more than a shot, grateful for the cold burn down her throat and into her chest. Deep breath. She set the bottle down on the hood of the Prius.

What to say?

She wasn't sure. She waited.

CJ took her face in his hands and kissed her hard, his teeth tearing at her lips. He grabbed her by the hair—it had grown past the nape of her neck over the summer—and yanked her head back like she was a doll he intended to decapitate.

"You sent back the ring," he said.

"I..." She couldn't talk; her neck was so stretched that the skin was taut, he was hurting her, and she was having a hard time getting air. "Let...go," she said.

He lunged at her with his mouth, biting and sucking on her clavicle, chewing on her like a rabid dog. He was *hurting* her.

"Get off me!" she said.

CJ held her by the back of the head and grabbed her left wrist, right below her Cartier love bracelet. His grip was ironclad, a different kind of bracelet, a bracelet of fury. He shoved her up against the side of the Prius. She felt him hard against her leg, but she didn't find it arousing. She wasn't about to have sex with CJ here in Clendenin's driveway.

She tried to push him away, but he only tightened his grip on her wrist.

Bruises, she thought. *He's going to leave bruises.*

"Let go of me," she said. He had a fistful of her hair. "You're hurting me, CJ."

"Hurting you?" he said. "*Hurting you?*" he screamed. "Let's talk about who's hurting who here. You sent back my ring! After all I've done for you!"

"Yes," Agnes said, trying to placate him. "You have done a lot for me—"

"You don't know the half of it!" he shouted. "Your little favorites, the ones you worry so much about? Quincy and…?"

"Dahlia," Agnes bleated.

"I bought their mother an apartment!" CJ screamed. "A fucking apartment, so that they would have a home. I wanted to surprise you."

"Oh my God," Agnes said. CJ had bought Quincy and Dahlia's mother an apartment? Agnes couldn't believe it. And yet, it was exactly the kind of thing CJ did. He was insanely generous with material things, because there was some kind of deficiency in his heart.

"Thank you," Agnes said. "That was very kind…"

"*Kind?* You think I did it to be *kind?* I did it because *I love you!*"

"Let go of my hair, CJ," she said. "And let go of my arm." She heard Manny Partida, clear as day: *I couldn't live with myself if I didn't tell you.*

"I sent the ring back because," Agnes said. "Because—"

"Because why?" he demanded.

"Because I don't want to marry you, CJ."

CJ brought her head forward, nearly to his chest, and then he slammed her head back against the Prius. Agnes gasped. In the morning there would be a lump, she thought. An egg.

"Stop," she said. "Please, CJ."

"Please, Charlie," he said. "Please Charlie please Charlie please Charlie please Charlie." He slammed her head against the car again, and then again. Agnes was confused about what was happening; she felt something warm and wet in her hair. Was she bleeding?

"You bitch!" he screamed. "After all I've done for you! You came up here and started screwing somebody else!"

"No," she said. "I did not! I swear I did not!"

He slammed her head again and this time the pain made Agnes's knees buckle. CJ lifted her up by one arm; he was going to rip it out of its socket. *Hair pulling, arm twisting, some not-so-nice stuff.* She was going to faint. *Is your fiancé a nice guy?* There was a sticky trickle down the back of her neck, and Agnes vomited into the shells of the driveway.

"What the hell is going on here?" Another voice, growling and bearlike. And then a high-pitched cry that Agnes knew belonged to her mother.

Darling!

CJ let Agnes go and she collapsed in a heap. She touched her head. Blood. Her left arm was numb.

She heard a struggle, heavy breathing, fists against flesh. CJ was fighting with Clendenin. Clen, who had only one arm.

Dabney cried out, "Clen, stop, you're going to get hurt."

Hurt, Agnes thought. *Hurthurthurthurthurt.*

The blood running down her neck was half Clendenin's blood.

Agnes opened her eyes in time to see Dabney climbing the porch stairs and Agnes thought, *Call the police, Mom! Go inside and call the police!* She couldn't say the words. CJ was punching Clen the way she used to see him go after the bag at the gym. Relentlessly. And yet Clen was still on his feet, still swinging his right arm.

Agnes thought back to the moment when CJ Pippin was introduced to her, in the Waldorf ballroom, with a full orchestra playing in the background and canapés being served on silver trays. Their gala benefit had been the polar opposite of the cause they were raising money for. Agnes remembered being discomfited by this, even as she knew that throwing glamorous events was how one kept the doors open. CJ had asked Agnes to dance, and afterward he had brought her a glass of champagne. Then, during the Ask, he had raised his hand and donated a hundred thousand dollars. Agnes had gushed at his generosity. He had seemed like such a hero then.

"Leave him alone, you monster!" Dabney said. She was standing on the top step of the porch and she was holding a gun.

Gun? Agnes thought. *My mother?*

It was Clendenin's BB gun, she realized then. But in the dark, the gun looked formidable, or at least it must have to CJ because he immediately backed off Clendenin and held his hands up in the air.

"You're crazy," CJ said to Dabney. "Crazy insane psycho nuts. You know that?"

"Yes," Dabney said, walking toward CJ with the BB gun and pointing the muzzle straight into his face. "I'm well aware."

Agnes closed her eyes. She was suddenly very, very tired. She thought, *My mother is pointing a gun at CJ.* She thought, *My mother is crazy. But I love her. I love her so much.*

BOX

He packed a bag, nothing unusual in that; his entire life with Dabney he had packed a bag each Monday and unpacked it on Friday, his entire life with Dabney had been two lives, his life here on Nantucket with her, and his life in Cambridge—or Washington, New York, London—without her.

Had that been the problem?

Which had been his "real" life? He had never had occasion to ask himself this question, although in the early days of their marriage, Dabney used to badger him. Did he love Harvard more than he loved her? Did he love economics more than he loved her?

You are my wife, he always answered. *I love you in a way that one cannot love a university or a field of study.*

She had asked—fifteen or twenty years ago—because she loved something else more than him, someone else, the boy who had left. She had never lied to him about that. The day Box proposed, she said, *I will marry you but you must know that I will never recover from my feelings for Clendenin Hughes. He didn't only break my heart, he stole it.*

She had warned him.

Another man might have backed away. After all, who wanted to be number two? But the truth was, the specter of Clendenin Hughes had never bothered Box. Clendenin Hughes lived on the other side of the world. He would never return, but if he did, he would be faced with the ruins of what he'd left behind. He would certainly not be in any position to reclaim Dabney or Agnes.

That was what Box had thought.

Maybe if Box had been a more attentive husband, Dabney would have been able to withstand the temptation of Hughes's return. Box was guilty of being busy and distant, of taking Dabney for granted, of leaving enough space in their marriage for Dabney to slip back and forth undetected. In better, closer marriages, he knew, there were no such spaces. Or maybe Dabney's feelings for Hughes had grown stronger and deeper only because she had given him up. Box had never been good at understanding the complexities of other people, or even, sadly, of himself, but he did realize that unattainability was a powerful aphrodisiac, nearly impossible to battle against. It was, he thought with no small amount of irony, the simple law of supply and demand at work. We always want what we can't have.

Box packed a bag, two bags, three bags. He was taking everything of consequence, even things he had duplicates of in Cambridge. Childishly, perhaps, he wanted Dabney to walk into this room tonight and feel his absence.

I'm in love with Clendenin. I've been in love with him my whole life. I'm so sorry.

Sorry, Box thought. *Sorry?*

He could reason all he wanted, but the truth was, he was in crisis, his bank had defaulted, his personal economy had crumbled. He would leave this house. He would leave the finest woman he had ever known, indeed, the finest human being he had ever known—and yes, he still believed that. He was John Boxmiller Beech, the Harvard professor, the textbook author, the economic consultant to the President of the United States, but none of that mattered without Dabney.

CLENDENIN

He went down to the police station with CJ and the arresting officer while Dabney took Agnes to the emergency room. It ended up being a very long night. CJ was charged with aggravated assault, and Agnes received thirty-five stitches in her scalp and was held at the hospital overnight for observation.

When Clen and Dabney finally met back at Clen's cottage

around quarter of four in the morning, Clen poured a shot of Gentleman Jack for himself and a glass of wine for Dabney and they sat at his big oak table in the dark. Clen threw back his shot; he wasn't feeling that great himself. CJ had bloodied his lip, bruised his cheek, and given him a nasty black eye. On her way home from the hospital, Dabney had stopped at the grocery store for a bag of frozen peas and a porterhouse steak.

"For your face," she said.

He said, "And maybe tomorrow night, it will be dinner."

Dabney sipped her wine. "The beautiful young woman you've been seeing? It's Agnes?"

Clen poured himself another shot, but let it sit in front of him. He slowly spun the glass.

Yes," he said. "She came out to the house looking for you, and she found me."

Dabney's eyes were shining with tears. Happy ones, he hoped, although he wasn't sure. "And how has it been...between you and her?"

Clen knew that his answer was important; this had been an emotional steamroller of a night. There was no road to take but the true, straight one.

"Things between us have been lovely," he said. He threw back the shot. "You have raised an intelligent, thoughtful, kind human being. She is your daughter, Dabney. I have absolutely no claim to her."

"Box is an excellent father," Dabney said. "I couldn't have asked for better. But there are things about Agnes that are purely you."

"I've seen those things," Clen said. "Even in the short time I've known her."

"Well, now that you've found her, don't let her go."

There were no words he could offer in response to that, so Clen took Dabney's hand and led her to bed.

AGNES

When Agnes woke up in the hospital, Dabney was sitting in a chair by the bed. She was wearing her headband and pearls, but she looked exhausted.

Agnes said, "Have you been here all night?"

Dabney said, "No, I went back to Clendenin's for a little while, took a shower and a nap, but I wanted to be here when you woke up."

Agnes noted the phrase *went back to Clendenin's* but she didn't know what to do with it.

She said, "Where's Daddy?"

Dabney said, "He's in Cambridge. He caught the late ferry last night. He...had to go back."

"Does he know what happened?"

"I called and left him a message," Dabney said. "I'm sure he'll call you, or come see you. He loves you very, very much."

"I know," Agnes said. She leaned back into her pillows. Her head hurt and she was thirsty. "You were right, Mommy. CJ wasn't my perfect match."

Dabney squeezed her hand. "There *is* going to be a perfect match for you somewhere down the road, darling," she said. "That I can promise."

CJ's arrest got two inches in the sports section of the *New York Post,* and a call came to Agnes's cell phone from a producer at ESPN who wanted to do a segment about "Charlie Pippin's Fall from Grace." Annabelle Pippin had already agreed to talk, the producer said.

Agnes did not return the call. Let Annabelle talk to the media about Charlie Pippin's fall from grace. Agnes wanted to forget the man had ever existed.

He had been charged with aggravated assault, but he would plead down. There would be jail time, twelve to eighteen months; there would be anger-management classes and hours of community service. He had been fired from his firm. Bantam Killjoy was now being represented by Tom Condon.

It was his own fault. Agnes had broken the engagement and his heart, but there were other ways of dealing with this than bashing Agnes's head in. CJ needed help. He would do it again to the next woman if he didn't get help.

In the next few days, voice mails piled up on Agnes's phone: Wilder from work called, as well as Manny Partida; Dave Patterson from Island Adventures called; Jane Meyer, Agnes's roommate from Dartmouth, called (she had seen the *Post*); Rocky DeMotta called, saying how sorry he and the rest of the firm were; Celerie called, as did Riley.

Really, the only message Agnes cared about was the one from Riley. He said, "Hey, Agnes, I heard what happened. I'm going to give you your space, but when you're ready, I'm here to talk. We can walk the beach and throw the ball to Sadie."

Agnes would miss a week of work. She was taking Percocet; her head had to heal. There was lots of time to lie in bed and think.

Her mother delivered trays of food, her meds, ice water with thin slices of lemon; she brought DVDs and novels. Agnes wasn't hungry, and she couldn't focus to watch TV or read. The ice water and the meds were all she wanted, and the dark room and the soft pillows and the knowledge that Dabney was there. She had a repeated vision of herself and Riley walking along Ladies Beach with the sky pinkening as a tennis ball flew through the air. *Go get it, Sadie! Run!*

Her mother came in and sat on the bed. She patted Agnes's leg.

"Do you feel any better today?" Dabney said.

"Yes," Agnes said. "Actually, I do." Her vision was clear, her head felt lighter, the pain was lifting. She was ready to get up, to get on with it.

But her mother had something to say. "You may have noticed Box hasn't been here."

"He's called me every day," Agnes said. "He wanted to come back, but I told him not to worry. I feel better."

Dabney took a breath. "Box left, honey. He left me, he's gone. He found out about Clendenin…he found out that Clen and I are friends again. That we're in love."

"Oh," Agnes said.

"I've made a royal mess of things," Dabney said. "A fine royal mess." Dabney started to cry into her hands and Agnes felt well enough to reach out and hug her mother. She had not been blessed with any supernatural powers or special vision, but she was able to understand that her mother loved two men at once. Agnes would forgive her for that because she knew Dabney couldn't help it.

DABNEY

By Friday, Agnes was healed enough to stay home by herself, and Dabney could return to the Chamber. She had received numerous messages from Nina Mobley, asking Dabney to please call her — at the office or at home, no matter the time of day — but Dabney had been focused on Agnes. She had called Box daily with updates and was consistently treated to his voice mail. Aside from Clen, Dabney hadn't talked to anyone.

At ten minutes to nine, Dabney found Nina Mobley sitting on the bench outside the Chamber office holding two cups of coffee.

Nina's eyes filled with tears. "Thank God," she said. "I've bought two coffees every day this week, hoping you would show up, and every day I had to drink them both myself. The caffeine has been hell on my nerves."

Dabney took one of the coffees. It had been perfectly made by Diana across the street at the pharmacy, with cream and six sugars. Dabney sat on the bench next to Nina and gazed at the front of the Chamber building, which was so familiar to her that it was like looking into a mirror.

Nina said, "I don't know how to tell you this."

"Tell me," Dabney said.

Nina said, "Vaughan Oglethorpe is upstairs waiting for you."

Dabney sipped her coffee. She wasn't sure why she felt surprised at this news. Vaughan had come to fire her. And why not? She was a tart and a floozy and an embarrassment.

"I guess I'd better go upstairs, then," Dabney said. "He knows everything?"

"I wish you had called me back," Nina said. "I nearly came to your house, but I thought you and Agnes deserved privacy."

"Thank you," Dabney said.

"Vaughan has the log," Nina said. "I told you not to sign out. I told you I would cover for you."

"I didn't want you to have to lie," Dabney said. More coffee. The coffee was the only thing that was keeping her from screaming. "You've got your ear to the ground. What are people saying?"

"It could be worse," Nina said. "But you know how people on this island are."

Yes, Dabney did know how people on this island were—they gossiped mercilessly, they tore people's reputations apart like sharks with a bleeding seal. Her eyes fluttered closed as she remembered how brutal people had been to Tammy Block when the news about her and Flynn Sheehan hit. Dabney shuddered. She had been *responsible* for that, or partially. She alone had seen the pink aura around them.

"What have you heard exactly?" Dabney asked.

"That you admitted to being in love with Clendenin. That you've been seeing him secretly since he got back to the island. That you've been secretly communicating with him for the past twenty-seven years. That you've been sending him money in Asia."

"*Not* for twenty-seven years!" Dabney said. "*Not* sending him money in Asia!" But even as she said this, she realized that where gossip was concerned, you didn't get to make a distinction between what was true and what wasn't.

"There's also a rumor that you and Box have an 'arrangement' because Box is gay and is having a sexual relationship with the Federal Reserve chairman."

"You must be kidding me!" Dabney said. "Someone actually said those words? Sexual relationship with the Federal Reserve chairman?"

"Yes," Nina said. "Theater of the absurd. I don't know where people come up with this stuff." She stared into her coffee cup like it was a deep well. "Even weirder—someone heard that you have terminal cancer and you wanted to be back with Clen before you died."

Oh, God, Dabney thought. She felt dizzy then, dizzy like she might faint, and she focused on her penny loafers, side by side, as steady as the horizon.

"I wish you had called me back," Nina said. "I would have suggested that you call Vaughan and head it off at the pass. He adores you, Dabney. He's hard on you, yes, but like a favorite teacher. You could have explained."

"What is there to explain?" Dabney asked. "The man has known me my entire life. He can hardly have been surprised."

"I would have burned the log, or dropped it off Old North Wharf," Nina said. "I might not even have had to do that. Vaughan might have forgiven you the missing hours. After all, the Chamber runs like clockwork, and our coffers are at an all-time high, thanks to you." Nina put her gold cross into her mouth, then took it out and slid the cross along its chain. "But there was one board member, there's always one, who wanted your head on a platter."

"Elizabeth Jennings," Dabney said.

Nina nodded morosely.

Dabney said, "Well, I'd better go up."

Vaughan Oglethorpe was sitting in Dabney's chair with his feet up on Dabney's desk, which she found offensive. It was her father's old *Dragnet* desk, a desk Dabney loved more than any piece of furniture or objet d'art in her home. Vaughan had the log open in his lap; he was paging through it, making notes on a legal pad. When he saw Dabney, he got to his feet.

He was seventy-eight years old, the same age Dabney's mother would have been. Vaughan and Patty Benson had gone steady one summer; it was all gin and tonics and dinner dances at the Sankaty Beach Club and rides down the Milestone Road in Vaughan's convertible MG, which was what he drove when he wasn't driving the hearse for his father. He was the only person Dabney still had contact with who had known her mother well. But Patty had dumped Vaughan, and Dabney suspected he had always hated Dabney a little bit for this reason, despite his outward displays of avuncular affection.

The room smelled of embalming fluid.

She would be cremated, she decided.

"Dabney," he said. His voice was as heavy and somber as a thundercloud. He had never been replaced as board president, she guessed, because people were afraid of him the way they were afraid of the Grim Reaper.

"Vaughan," she said. Bright smile. Fresh-faced in her headband and pearls, although she had slept a total of ten hours all week and she was down below a hundred pounds. Maybe he wouldn't fire her. Maybe just a warning.

"It's come to my attention that you've had personal issues that have kept you from doing your job." He held up the log. "Since Daffodil Weekend, you've missed fourteen full days, and the days you have been present, you've been out of the office a total of a hundred and ninety-two hours."

Could that be *right?* All those stolen lunches, entire afternoons at the beach with Clen. Days she was legitimately sick in bed. The past four days taking care of Agnes. The stupid lunch at the Yacht Club with Box. Clen Clen Clen. A hundred and ninety-two hours she had missed. She was appalled. She would have fired herself.

"The board isn't pleased," Vaughan said. "One member in particular. She feels your personal life has gotten in the way of your work performance."

She wants Clen, Dabney thought. *Hell hath no fury.* What was Elizabeth doing on the board anyway? She didn't own or work for a Nantucket business. But she had money and influence; she was a summer person who "cared" about Nantucket. She had used her charms with Vaughan Oglethorpe, batted her eyelashes, flashed her pretty manicure, and maybe promised him a back scratch.

Still, Dabney said nothing. Was he going to drop the hammer?

He said, "The board took a vote and it was decided that it's time to ask you to step down."

At that instant, Dabney realized that both Riley and Celerie were at their desks, quiet as church mice, staring right into the front office, listening to every word.

"Step down?" Dabney said.

"I'm asking for your resignation, Dabney," Vaughan said.

Asking for her resignation? Asking her to step down? She, Dabney Kimball Beech, *was* the Nantucket Chamber of Commerce. She had, with Nina's help, turned Nantucket into the thriving business community it now was. In 1992, the Chamber had 340 members, a budget of $175,000, and there were thirty thousand visitors annually. Twenty-two years later, under Dabney's leadership, there were 620 members, a budget of $1.2 million, and seventy-five thousand visitors annually.

Should she quote these statistics? Surely he already knew them. But it didn't matter, because she, Dabney Kimball Beech, had done what so many great people before her had done. She had proved to be human.

"Okay," Dabney said. "I'll just collect my things." She looked around the office, wondering where to start. The desks were hers, the oriental rugs, the original Abigail Pease photographs, which every single visitor to the office commented on, the green-apple-candle smell. How could she pack up that smell?

"I'm asking Nina Mobley to take over as executive director," Vaughan said. "I assume you approve of that choice?"

"Yes," Dabney bleated. She couldn't imagine that Vaughan Oglethorpe or anyone else on the board cared what she thought now. She was being discarded like a piece of trash.

Suddenly, Nina was at the top of the stairs. She said, "If you're asking for Dabney's resignation then you might as well ask for mine as well, because I will not work here without her."

"Nina," Dabney said. But Nina was already collecting things from her desk. She took down the calendar from Nantucket Auto Body, which they had each consulted a hundred times a day. Dabney realized that what Nina had said was true. She would never have been able to work in this office without her.

Vaughan clasped his hands together in front of him; the false sympathy required of a funeral director rose to the surface. "I'm very sorry to hear that, Nina. Let me encourage you to reconsider."

"I quit, too," Celerie said, standing in the doorway of the back office. "Dabney Beech is my idol! She is my hero! I have never known anyone like her! She inspired my love for this island! She made me appreciate its uniqueness and she made me want to serve as its advocate! She made me think of it as home, and I grew up far, far away from here! I am devoted to Nantucket, but more than that, I am devoted to Dabney Kimball Beech!"

"I'm leaving, too," Riley said. He was holding his guitar case and a copy of *The Grapes of Wrath* and the framed photo he kept on his desk of Sadie, his chocolate Lab.

"Wait," Vaughan said. "Everyone please just wait a minute. You can't all leave."

Just then, the phone rang, and this seemed to give Riley great joy. He smiled widely, showing off his perfect teeth.

"With all due respect, sir," he said to Vaughan, "you'd better answer that."

BOX

He loved Cambridge in the fall, winter, and spring, but he did not love it in the summer. He wouldn't have liked it under the best of circumstances, but now he found it unbearable—air-conditioning instead of open windows, the campus inundated with foreign visitors. Even the Charles was a disappointment; it looked like spoiled chocolate milk and smelled even worse.

Box ate every meal out, most of the time venturing across the river into Boston proper to do so, because it stretched out his night. He walked for the same reason. Now, there was nothing more depressing than his apartment after dark. If left to his own devices, he would sit in a chair facing the window and drink an entire bottle of wine by himself while listening to Mozart's Requiem.

What had he done wrong?

His thoughts skipped like a broken record: he had put work first, he had taken Dabney for granted, he had become complacent with their arrangement, he had not always returned her passionate advances and especially not in years of late, he had settled into contentment, he had assumed she would create her own happiness and excitement—and guess what? She had!

He couldn't pretend to be surprised.

If he had known twenty-five years earlier that it would end this way—Dabney would return to Clendenin—would he have married her anyway?

Yes. The answer was yes.

*　　*　　*

Coming out of Grill 23 one night, Box bumped into a fellow he recognized. It was...he couldn't quite grasp it at first. He had drunk a lot of wine. It was...

The man stuck his hand out. "Box?" he said. "Christian Bartelby."

"Oh!" Box said. "Hello!" And then once his brain processed who exactly *Christian Bartelby* was, he summoned some enthusiasm. "Yes! Hello, Christian Bartelby! The good doctor!" Box was swaying on his feet. He had eaten at the bar and the comely bar maiden had enticed him into ending his evening with a glass of vintage port. Box had gazed upon the bar maiden and had wondered why it was that no other woman in the world could maintain his interest, no matter how beautiful or charming she was.

Christian held on to Box's hand for an extra beat. "I assume you've heard that Miranda has gone off to New York."

"Yes," Box said. "She's left us both, it seems."

Christian Bartelby let go of Box's hand and ran a hand through his hair. He was wearing a navy T-shirt under a navy blazer and a pair of khakis and loafers with no socks. Box wondered if Christian Bartelby was going into the restaurant to meet a date. Was everyone moving on but him?

"And your wife?" Christian Bartelby said. "How is she?"

"Ah," Box said. "She has left me as well."

"Left you?" Dr. Bartelby said.

"It seems so," Box said, but he couldn't bring himself to say any more, so he saluted the good doctor and sidled away.

Every few days, a call came from Agnes, "checking in."

"Daddy?" she said. "Are you working?"

"Yes."

"Eating?"

"Yes."

"What?"

"What what?"

"What are you eating?"

"Out, mostly. The usual places. Freddy at the Russell House is sick of me." Box cleared his throat. "How is your mother?"

"She…lost her job," Agnes said.

"What?" Box said.

"Vaughan Oglethorpe and the board asked for her resignation."

"For what *reason*?" Box said. "Certainly not over the business with Hughes. That's hardly legal. Her personal life is private and separate."

There was a long pause. "She missed a lot of work this summer, Daddy," Agnes said. "It was all documented. And Elizabeth Jennings sits on that board, and Mom felt like maybe it was a personal vendetta."

Now it was Box's turn to be quiet. *She missed a lot of work this summer.* Because she was with Clendenin, because Box was around and Agnes was home and thus Dabney had to conduct her rendezvouses during the workday.

Oh, Dabney, what have you done? Your life is falling apart. It didn't have to be this way. Was he worth it? Was he?

And still, Box felt indignation on Dabney's behalf. Vaughan Oglethorpe was a pompous, self-important ass, and Elizabeth Jennings was petty and jealous. They had done an unconscionable thing in asking Dabney to resign. It didn't matter how much time Dabney had missed. Box and everyone else in the world knew that Dabney could run the Chamber of Commerce in her sleep, or from an outpost on the surface of Mars.

Leave my wife alone! he thought.

"Is she there?" Box asked impulsively. Dabney had called every day with updates about the healing of Agnes's head wound, but he hadn't answered once, because even her voice on the message made him too upset for words. But it seemed impossible to him that Dabney would have been *fired from the Chamber* (the very phrase was inconceivable), and she hadn't called him to tell him. But that, he supposed, was what their new arrangement meant. Separated.

"Um…" Agnes said. "No, she's not home."

Not home, he thought. *Of course not.*

DABNEY

There was only one more secret she was keeping, and it was time for that to come out as well.

Clen took the news silently, as Dabney had known he would. She waited until after they made love because their lovemaking was precious to her and she wasn't sure how much more of it there would be. It would be one of the things she missed the most—Clen thrusting into her, his hungry mouth on her breasts, his animal moans of joy and gratitude. He was so tender that he brought her to tears every time.

She lay spent and sweating, with her head on his chest. It was astonishing the way he could encircle her with one arm, how he could make her feel safer and more protected than any man with two. She thought back to when she had believed that her symptoms—the ache in her gut, the constant exhaustion, the breathlessness, the lack of appetite—were the result of the impossible position she had put herself in. Loving two men at once.

She would give up everything—her home, her morning coffee,

the sunrise and sunset, the field of flowers at Bartlett Farm, the bluebird sky, the crimson moors in fall, the bump and rumble of the Impala's tires over the cobblestones; she would give up good books and champagne and ribbon sandwiches and lobster dipped in melted butter and the rainbow fleet sailing around Brant Point Lighthouse and her dirty tennis serve and her pearls and her penny loafers and she would give up the chance of ever holding her grandchild. She would give it all up to Death, *but please,* she thought, *please do not take away Clendenin.*

"I'm sick," she said. The dusk was gathering, but Dabney still heard birds and bumblebees outside the screened windows of Clen's cottage. "I have pancreatic cancer, it's terminal, a matter of months. A few more good months."

Clen squeezed her until she thought she would break. It genuinely hurt; her organs, already so compromised, were being crushed like soft, overripe fruit. And yet it felt good. She knew what he was doing, what he was thinking; he wanted her so close that she became him. *Come live inside me, we will be one, I will keep you safe, and you will not have to die alone.*

Telling Agnes, of course, was even worse. It was one thing to leave a husband or a lover behind, and another thing entirely to leave a child.

Dabney told Agnes over breakfast—French toast with fresh peaches, crispy bacon, and home fries with herbs cut from the garden. It didn't matter how beautiful the food was; as soon as Dabney opened her mouth, neither of them would be able to eat a bite. And yet it was Dabney's nature to feed people. She couldn't stop now.

"Darling," Dabney said. "I'm sick."

Agnes suspended a perfect slice of golden-pink peach over her plate. "What?" she said. "What kind of sick?"

"Darling," Dabney said.

Agnes dissolved into tears. They were the tears of Little Girl Agnes—Agnes when she cut her knee on the sharp stones of the jetty, Agnes when she had a bad dream—and the heartbreak of it was almost too much for Dabney to bear.

Some days were still okay. Some days Dabney made it out for her walk and said hello to the same people and petted the same dogs. She then drove out to see Clendenin, and they swam in the pool of the big house and Clendenin made sandwiches, and Dabney ate them slowly, never wanting to arrive at the last bite. Dabney napped in the afternoon, she had to nap, she was so tired now, and in pain nearly all the time. She slept in Clendenin's large, white, luxuriously sheeted bed while Clen read his newspapers at the oak table.

Some nights Dabney stayed at his cottage and cooked for him, and some nights she went home to see Agnes. Agnes was spending a lot of time with Riley. She met him at the beach after work, and they went out for oysters at Cru, or they grabbed fish tacos at the Easy Street Cantina.

The rosy aura around Agnes and Riley was so bright that Dabney could have seen it in the dark. Dabney wanted to ask what was going on between them, but she had learned, after forty-two couples, when to push and when to leave well enough alone. After all that had happened that summer, Agnes needed a friend, not a boyfriend.

But still, Dabney could hope.

Dabney called Nina and asked to meet her on the bench in front of the Chamber. Dabney brought two coffees from the pharmacy, with a cup of ice for Nina, and a wad of napkins in case Nina spilled her coffee upon hearing the news.

But when Dabney told her, she set her coffee down neatly between her feet, then dropped her face to her hands and cried. Dabney gave her the napkins, so she could wipe her face and blow her nose.

Dabney didn't know what to do, think, or feel about Box.

He'd left a pair of readers by the sink in the bathroom. Everyone else Dabney knew bought their readers at the drugstore, but Box's one vanity was specially made readers, the square black frames that defined him. Dabney couldn't look at Box's readers without thinking of Box's eyes, the startling blue, the blue of glaciers—cold, she'd always thought. Frosty, indifferent, superior, when she was ill-disposed toward him.

His eyes had been so hurt that night at Elizabeth Jennings's and then again at the Levinsons'. She had never before seen Box *hurt,* she realized. And she was the one who had done it to him.

She wanted to talk to him, tell him she was sick—but she couldn't bring herself to do it just yet. He might think she was fabricating a story in order to gain his sympathy; he might think she was using her illness as some kind of excuse for her actions. He might think it was the ultimate in histrionics—and wasn't it? *I'm dying, Box, please forgive me!* She didn't call him because she had no right to ask him for mercy, no matter what her circumstances.

Agnes said, "Does Daddy know you're sick?"

"No," Dabney said.

"Do you want me to tell him?" Agnes asked.

"No. Please don't. It's not your responsibility. It's mine."

"You need to tell him, Mommy. I might slip."

"Yes," Dabney said. "I realize this." Hiding things from Box hadn't gone well.

Dabney called him, and as ever, was shuttled to his voice mail.

"Box," she said. "Please, *please* call me back." She swallowed. "Please."

Dabney missed her job. It was nearly wedding season, and time for the fall festivals. Who would judge the best cranberry chutney, who would pin the ribbon on the biggest pumpkin, if not Dabney? She thought about the Chamber all the time, night and day. She worried about it, as she might have about a child who had been removed from her care and placed in a foster home.

Dabney couldn't believe that no one had called her for help or advice. The fall audit would soon be upon them, and their grant proposal for the tourist council would be due. Nobody could deal with those things but Dabney. What was *happening* up there?

Nina Mobley was immediately hired as the PR director at Nantucket Cottage Hospital. It was a great job with better benefits and a large jump in salary. Dabney actually felt guilty. Had she been keeping Nina from an opportunity like this all along?

"My job at the Chamber was never about the job," Nina said, when Dabney first went to visit her at the hospital. Nina had a corner office that overlooked the Old Mill. "It was only ever about working with you. It was about being the pulsing heart of the island. It was about strawberry frappes and you chewing your pearls and making fun of Vaughan Oglethorpe and watching to see who was driving up Main Street and Diana's perfect cup of coffee, and the cadence of our days, which became weeks, which became months, and then years. Together." Nina blinked and tears fell. "Eighteen and a half years I worked with my best friend. I know I should feel blessed."

"Nina," Dabney said. "Stop, please. I'm still here."

"I know," Nina said. "There is no way I can deal with this, other than to tell myself that we're both going to live forever."

Riley took a job playing guitar at the Brotherhood of Thieves three nights a week. One night, Dabney and Clen and Agnes went to see him. Dabney felt like a spectacle—she was out in public with her lover! But she hadn't announced the desires of her heart to the world just so the two of them could remain sequestered at home. And her bravery paid off: they ended up having a marvelous time. They ordered a cheese board for Agnes, a favorite from her child-hood, and they got thick sandwiches and chowder and curly fries, and they drank frosted mugs of beer and listened to Riley play.

He sang "Brown Eyed Girl," by Van Morrison. Dabney had se-cretly requested this, and when Riley strummed the first chord, she grabbed Clen by his hand and they danced together in the small space in front of the tables. They were a broken couple—Clen with one arm, Dabney with cancer—but they could still spin like they had in high school and college, or almost, and the crowd cheered them on.

Making love in the green grass, behind the stadium with you...

She might never dance again, she realized, as she sat down, breathless, her pearls in a twist. She didn't care. That had felt so good—wild, free, precious, lawless, the way dancing was supposed to feel.

The Brotherhood was packed with familiar faces—Julia from the office-supply store, Genevieve from Dr. Field's office, Diana from the pharmacy lunch counter—and they all came up to Dab-ney, saying how sorry they were that she had retired from the Chamber and how Nantucket would never be the same.

*   *   *

It was Agnes who let Dabney know that Celerie wasn't doing well. She had been devastated by the news of Dabney's illness, and she had had her heart set on making a career at the Chamber, which wouldn't happen now. Agnes said that Celerie had taken to her bed, and could not be persuaded to leave her house.

"Took to her bed?" Dabney said. She had a hard time imagining Celerie lying down at all; the girl was always on the move. "Really?"

"She's like your...groupie...your disciple," Agnes said. "I mean, look at her, Mom. The headband? The pearls? Come on."

Celerie was working the occasional catering job, but she had no long-term plan beyond volunteering as the cheerleading coach at the Boys & Girls Club. She was considering moving back to Minnesota.

Dabney decided to call Vaughan Oglethorpe. Clen was in the room when she did it.

Clen said, "I can't believe you're calling that grotesque zombie bastard."

Dabney said, "It's the right thing to do."

And as it turned out, Vaughan was happy to hear from Dabney. He sounded as he had always sounded, prior to showing up in the office to fire Dabney—like an uncle hearing from his favorite, long-lost niece.

"Dabney!" he said. "Your voice is music to my ears."

Dabney heard actual music—the heavy, doomed chords of Bach's Toccata and Fugue—in the background. Funeral-parlor music. Anyone's voice would be an improvement over that.

"I have a matter I'd like to discuss," Dabney said.

"I hope you're calling to tell me that you want your job back," Vaughan said. "Because ever since I asked for your resignation, I've been itching to retract my words. The Chamber is nothing without you, Dabney. The second you walked out of there, it started falling apart. I had to hire a temp, and Elizabeth Jennings agreed to handle the phones, but only during hours that are convenient for her. I'm at a loss. I need you to come back. I can even offer you a pay raise."

Dabney stifled a laugh. What Vaughan didn't understand was that Dabney would have done her job all those years for half, or a quarter, of her salary. Hell, she would have done it for free.

"I'm not coming back, Vaughan," she said. "I do have a suggestion for a new director, however."

True, Celerie was young. But she had energy and enthusiasm and a fresh outlook. She was bright and she learned quickly. She had the fire. She also would have a direct line to Dabney. Dabney would consult with her until...

"Well," Dabney said. "Until I'm not able to consult anymore."

Vaughan made some phlegmy, throat-clearing noise that Dabney knew was meant to conceal his relief.

"Okay," he said. "Have Celerie e-mail me her résumé. Pronto."

Next, it was out to Celerie's house—a sad little rental on Hooper Farm Road. As soon as Dabney pulled into the driveway, she realized that this was the house that her friends Moe and Curly used to rent. Moe and Curly had surfed at Madequecham Beach back when Dabney and Clen were in high school and college. Dabney had come to parties at this house; she had thrown up in the backyard after too many vodkas with grape soda.

Dabney chuckled as she walked up to the front door. She was Dabney now and she had been Dabney then, but they were two different people.

Sometimes life seemed very long.

And other times, not.

Dabney knocked, and Celerie opened the door right away. She was holding a paperback copy of *Emma,* by Jane Austen. She was wearing a short blue terry-cloth robe. And pearls. And the navy headband with the white stars.

Dabney knew she had been right to come.

Celerie's mouth formed a tiny O of surprise, the way other girls her age might react to a visit from Justin Beiber, or the way Dabney's grandmother, Agnes Bernadette, would have reacted to a visit from the Holy Father, Pope John Paul II.

"That's my favorite book, you know," Dabney said.

"Yes," Celerie said, and her eyes brimmed with tears. "I know."

"Can I come in and talk to you for a minute?" Dabney asked.

"Of course." Celerie indicated the room before her, featuring a gray, tweedy-looking sofa, a large square rag rug, a boxy TV with rabbit-ear antennae, and a rotary phone. "We call this room the museum because nothing actually works."

Dabney laughed. She could just barely smell the marijuana smoke of thirty years earlier, and see the hazy silhouettes of Moe and Curly and a girl they all called Meg the Drunk Slut, crowded around a red glass bong.

Celerie wiped at her eyes. "I just made a batch of watermelon lemonade. Can I offer you a glass?"

"Yes," Dabney said. "I would love a glass of watermelon lemonade."

Celerie vanished into the kitchen, which Dabney could see was outfitted with the same linoleum and Formica of three decades before. That refrigerator used to be filled with Miller beer and the dreaded vodka and Welch's grape soda. Moe and Curly used to brag that they spent ten dollars a week on groceries, leaving the rest of their disposable income for booze, weed, and Sex Wax.

She was the only person she knew who salvaged such details.

Dabney sat on one end of the sofa; at the other end was a feather pillow that held the soft indentation of Celerie's head.

Celerie returned with a pink frosty glass.

Dabney tasted the drink. "Delicious perfection!" she said, and Celerie actually smiled. She sat next to Dabney.

Dabney said, "First of all, I owe you an apology."

"No," Celerie said. "You don't. I get it."

"Well," Dabney said, "you shouldn't. You should be madder than hell at me. I skipped out on a lot of hours of work this summer. I cheated not only my husband, but I cheated Nantucket. I cheated you and Riley and I cheated poor Nina, leaving her to hold the office together."

"You held the office together," Celerie said. "Because it was like you were there even when you weren't there."

"Thank you for saying that," Dabney said. "But I didn't come here so you could compliment me. I came here so *I* could compliment *you*. You did an incredible job this summer, once again. I couldn't have dreamed up a better information assistant. Now, that being said, I have a question for you."

"A question?" Celerie said. "What is it?"

"Would you—please—submit your résumé to Vaughan Oglethorpe? Today, if possible? I want you to apply to be the new executive director of the Nantucket Chamber of Commerce. I will guide and advise you for as long as I'm able."

Celerie stood very still, and then she broke out in a war whoop and raised her hands in a V over her head.

"Yes!" she said.

BOX

There was no reason to continue putting off the inevitable, so he scheduled a dinner at Abe & Louie's with Michael Ohner, the divorce attorney. Ohner talked all night about depositions, subpoenaing credit cards, tax returns, financial statements, shared assets, and alimony.

Ohner said, "Do you see giving Dabney the Nantucket house in exchange for a lesser payout? Because as unjust as it seems in this case, you are going to have to pay Dabney."

Box waved his hand. "She can have whatever she wants."

"I'm not going to let you give away the farm," Ohner said. "Do you see naming this fellow Hughes as a third party?"

A third party? Box thought. There was a time, decades earlier, when Box would have considered himself a third party.

The next day, Box called Dabney to warn her that legal action was pending. He had a pile of messages from her in his voice mail inbox, including one desperate-sounding message from a week or so earlier. Possibly she'd had a few glasses of wine and was feeling guilty for the way she had publicly embarrassed him. Or she had woken up and realized that Clendenin Hughes wasn't worthy of her in any respect. Her so-called love for him was little more than a leftover teenage romantic fantasy.

She answered immediately. "Hello?" she said. "Box? Is it you?"

Something in her voice caught his attention. For possibly the first time in twenty-four years, he had a gut feeling where his wife was concerned.

He said, "Dabney? Are you all right?"

"No," she said. "I'm not."

When he hung up the phone, he was shaking. He had only just begun to come to terms with the idea of living his life without Dabney by his side. But the news that she was dying, that he would, in a matter of *months,* be living in a Dabney-less world, pierced his heart like a long, sharp needle and drew out whatever lifeblood had been pumping through it.

He quickly wrote Michael Ohner an e-mail, saying that he would not need his services after all.

PART 3

THE FALL

AGNES

She was staying on Nantucket through the fall and maybe the winter.

She was staying on Nantucket until...

She called Manny Partida and asked for a leave of absence from the Morningside Heights Boys & Girls Club. It was decided that Wilder would take over at the helm while Agnes was gone. Agnes could work at the Island Adventures after-school program twenty hours a week. Dave Patterson was thrilled to have her.

CJ and his attorney pleaded down, as Agnes had known they would. He was sentenced to ninety days in jail and eighteen months' probation. There was a restraining order in place. CJ wasn't allowed within a hundred yards of Agnes for the next five years.

What would Agnes's life be like in five years?

A week after Labor Day, Riley had to head back to dental school at Penn. Agnes drove him and Sadie to the airport. She couldn't believe how sad she felt. The night she had spent with Riley eating cheeseburgers in his Jeep and then going on a wild-goose chase in search of Dabney seemed like aeons ago, and yet she hadn't gotten enough of him somehow.

They stood in the crowded airport terminal. Everyone was leaving—heading back to Manhattan or Washington, D.C., or Los Angeles, heading back to work or school, sweaters and real shoes, football games and Broadway openings. Summer was over. It happened every year, but this year it was hitting Agnes the hardest because the one thing about a Nantucket summer was that no one ever wanted it to end.

She was afraid she might cry.

"You saved my summer," Agnes said. "Thank you for being my friend. Thank you for helping me find Clen. Thank you for loving my mother. Thank you for . . . being you."

"Hey," Riley said. He grabbed Agnes's chin and she felt her heart spin in its socket. "You're welcome." He bent over and kissed her. They kissed and they kissed and they kissed—it felt like an entire summer's worth of kissing—until his flight was called and he had to leave Agnes to board his plane, with Sadie barking in protest.

CLENDENIN

As soon as the night air got a chill, she started to careen away from him.

Careen away from him. The phrase came unbidden, borrowed from their ancient history together, one of their first dates—sledding, during an unexpected snowstorm in December 1980.

Clen and Dabney hadn't so much as held hands in December 1980, but this was not to say that they didn't have a relationship.

Dabney had pursued Clen with an enthusiasm that he suspected was based in pity. He was the new kid, too much smarter than anyone else to have made any friends. Dabney approached him one day after English class and asked him if he'd ever read Cheever.

Was she teasing him?

Of course, he'd said. He had gobbled the red volume of stories the year before, on recommendation from the young, vivacious librarian, Eleanor, back in Attleboro. He now knew all about commuter trains, gin and tonics, and adultery.

Dabney had taken to engaging him in conversations about books—she liked Jane Austen, he preferred Chekhov and Kafka—and from there she probed a bit into his personal history. What was his affinity with the depressing Russians? Had he moved to Nantucket from a gulag? Clen was hesitant to talk about himself, but he let certain details escape: He lived with his mother, he said. He was an only child. His mother waited tables at the Lobster Trap. They lived in a cottage out behind the restaurant.

That must be fun! Dabney said. *Do you ever get to eat free lobster?*

Clen nodded. His mother brought home lobster for dinner every night, along with dried-out crab cakes and small potatoes coated with congealed butter that looked like beeswax. He was sick of lobster, although he did not say this.

Dabney took to sitting next to him in the cafeteria, and at study hall, where she doodled in the margins of his loose-leaf paper. The doodles became notes. The notes said things like, *I am an only child, too.* And, *I have no mother.*

He raised his eyebrows at that one. Wrote below, *Is she dead?*

I don't know, Dabney wrote back. *Probably not.*

Clen wrote, *My father died drinking.*

To which she drew a face frowning, with two fat tears.

Clen had wanted her to know that he didn't cry over his father's death. He hadn't felt sad, only relieved, because his father had been a very large man with an even larger drinking problem, and...well. Clen had been surprised when his mother cried, but not surprised when she said they were moving.

We need the ocean, she'd said.

Clen had wanted the city, Boston; he'd wanted a shot at going to Boston Latin or Buckingham Browne & Nichols, where he could really get an *education,* but his vote didn't matter. Nantucket it was.

Do you hate it here? Dabney wrote.

He looked at her. On that particular afternoon, they were swaddled in the hush of the high school library and Dabney was wearing her headband, and a strand of pearls that he assumed were fake—or maybe not, because something about Dabney announced *money,* even though he knew her father was a policeman. She had a freckled nose and those big brown eyes, which seemed to shine a warm light on him.

No, he wrote back.

When the surprise early snow came, they were not boyfriend and girlfriend, but they were not nothing. The snow piled up outside and Dabney wrote in the margin of his paper, *Dead Horse Valley, 4pm. Dress warmly. I'll bring my toboggan.*

Clen had done his fair share of sledding and other winter sports in Attleboro, but he hadn't enjoyed them. He was big and heavy, clumsy on skates and skis. If it was snowing, he preferred to stay inside and read.

Okay, he said.

The after-school scene at Dead Horse Valley during the first snowfall of the year was frenetic, but most of the kids were younger. The other high school kids, Clen surmised, were probably hunkered down in someone's den, drinking beer and smoking pot. Dabney was waiting right on the road, wearing navy snow pants and a bright pink parka and a pink hat with a white pom-pom on top. She held up the most beautiful toboggan Clen had ever seen. It was made of polished walnut and had a graceful bullnose at the front; secured to the base was a green quilted pad.

"It looks too nice to ride," he said.

"My father and I have been using this toboggan since I was little," she said. "We take good care of it."

Clen nodded, and again thought, *Money*. There wasn't a single piece of furniture in his rental cottage as nice as that toboggan.

Dabney manned the front and held the reins. "This is great," she said. "You can push. We are going to *fly!*"

Clen wasn't afraid of the speed, although the hill looked steep and bumpy and he wondered how the hell there could be a hill this steep on an island where the highest elevation was 108 feet. The other kids—the ten-year-olds and twelve-year-olds—were shooting down with high-pitched screams, some of them spilling halfway, some of them catching air off a bump and landing with a thud, then picking up even more speed. What frightened Clen was the athletic feat that was expected of him—to push the toboggan while running behind it and then to launch himself neatly onto the toboggan, tucking his legs on either side of Dabney. He didn't think he could do it.

But for her, he would try.

He bent over and placed his gloved hands flat on the toboggan, and with his head down, he started running, pushing with all his might. Dabney whooped. Clen felt the momentum of the hill pulling him down. Inertia was real. He could not stop his legs from running. He would never be able to fling his legs up and get on behind her. Never.

No wonder the horse was dead, he thought.

He sent the toboggan down the hill while he stumbled behind it for a few steps before doing a spectacular face-plant into the snow. He raised his head to see Dabney flying indeed; the fancy toboggan might have been a magic carpet. She careened down the hill away from him, getting smaller and farther away, until she disappeared behind a stand of fir trees. He had lost her.

He had thought, *When she gets back up to the top of this hill, I am going to kiss her. I am going to make her mine.*

Thirty-some-odd years had passed, but there was an eerie similarity in Dabney's tobogganing down the hill at Dead Horse Valley and the slide for the worse in her health, which had started in late September. Clen felt as helpless and inept and incapable as he had then. She was going. He could not go with her.

For days, she was bedridden. The pain, the pain! Agnes called Dr. Rohatgi. There was nothing he could do; this was how the disease progressed.

She was being eaten from the inside. That was how it felt, she said. Like thousands of tiny razor teeth. Her healthy cells were being attacked and colonized by the mutant, deformed, cancerous cells. There was pain medication, but many times Dabney cried out in the night. She cried for him, mostly, but also for Agnes, and for her mother.

Mama!

Clen tensed, believing he had misheard her. But then she said it again, in a voice that was much younger than her adult Dabney voice.

Mama!

There had been times in their growing up—high school and college—when they had talked about Dabney's mother, Patty Benson, and what she had done. Dabney had consistently spoken with what Clen would have called "resigned indifference." *She wasn't cut out to be a parent. Whatever. Lots of people aren't. She didn't smother me with a pillow or drown me in the bathtub, she walked away. She left me in capable hands. I am grateful for that. I'm sure she has her regrets, wherever she is.*

Clen had puzzled over her attitude. He knew that Dabney had spent years in therapy with Dr. Donegal in order to achieve such insouciance. But really, wasn't she angry? Clen himself was furious at his father, the empty bottles of Wild Turkey on the coffee table, the long hours at the bar after work and all weekend long when he should have been teaching Clen how to throw a spiral pass, or how to run skillfully behind a toboggan and then jump onto it. He had cared only about drinking, drinking, drinking until it killed him.

The ugly truth was a punch to the gut: Clen was no better than his father or Dabney's mother. He was no better.

Mama!

Clen wiped Dabney's forehead with a cool washcloth and watched her eyelids flutter closed.

There were still good days, days when Dabney got out of bed smiling and went for her walk, although slower, and then slower still. One day, Dabney came home and said, "Mr. Lawson asked if he could drive me home. I said no, and still he slowed all the way down and trailed me for the last quarter mile. Do I really look that bad?"

Clen kissed the tip of her nose. "No," he said. "You look beautiful."

He could feel sand running through the hourglass. There wasn't enough time to tell her how beautiful she was—how much he loved her or how sorry, how hideously, awfully *sorry,* he was that he hadn't come right home from Bangkok. He should have *come right home!*

He had wasted twenty-seven years!

Twenty-seven years, it seemed impossible. Where had they gone? It had taken him seven years to learn the country of Vietnam, to learn how to live with people who looked at him in fear and distrust. His language skills were poor; he had gotten by with French and broken English. The country was as hot as soup; the only place he had truly loved had been Dalat, in the hills. The *Times* had gotten him a room at the Dalat Palace and every morning he opened the wooden shutters and gazed out over the lake. Every night he drank a dozen bottles of ice-cold 333 and shot billiards in the stone-grotto bar. Best billiards table in Southeast Asia, he could attest. People would come and go—French, Australians, soldiers, doctors, entrepreneurs who said that communism wouldn't hold. It was human nature for man to want to make his own money, it didn't matter if he lived in Dalat or Detroit.

Clen could have been with Dabney all that time. He had smoked so many cigarettes, and eaten so many bowls of pho and so many banh mi prepared on the side of the road by a woman wearing a triangle hat, squatting by the grill, turning the meat, layering the meat on a freshly sliced baguette with carrots, mint, cilantro, cucumber, and the sauce of the gods.

He could have been with Dabney.

He'd spent five years with Mi Linh, but she wouldn't come with him to Bangkok. Bangkok was a hole, she said. He was lucky to have gotten out of there after his first year. Why go back? She had been right, it was a hole, far worse the second time. And then, he'd lost his arm.

He did not rue the loss of his arm the way he rued all those years without Dabney.

While Dabney slept, he worked on a surprise for her. It was taking him hours and hours to interview and transcribe—and still it would be incomplete. He just didn't have the resources. Agnes helped him where she could. Agnes assured him that what he was doing was awesome in the truest sense of the word. *It is the best thing,* she kept saying. *It is the very best thing.*

Dabney was well enough to go to the Cranberry Festival. She donned her cranberry cable-knit sweater and her matching kilt and she and Agnes and Clen drove out to the bogs in the Impala with the top down. The weather was spectacular—a sky so blue it was painful to look at, and mellow sunshine, a gift in mid-October.

"Days do not get any more beautiful than this one," Dabney said. She had, for the first time, allowed Clen to drive the Impala. She hadn't come out and said so, but she was too weak to drive—and she leaned her head back with her face in the sun.

She was asleep by the time they arrived at the bogs.

"What should we do?" Clen asked, once they had parked in the space reserved for them. EVENT JUDGE, the sign said, because Dabney was to judge the chutney and the muffins.

"Wake her up," Agnes said. She climbed out of the backseat. "Here, I'll do it." She jostled Dabney's shoulder. "Mommy! Mommy, we're here."

Dabney's eyes flew open and she sat straight up, adjusting her sunglasses. "Okay!" she said. "I'm ready!"

The bogs were crowded with visitors. Dabney was thrilled to see so many people in attendance—parents and children and older, year-round residents, all of whom knew her by name. There were free balloons and face painting and half-a-dozen food booths— chutney, cookies, sauce, juice, muffins—all made from the fruit harvested a few hundred feet away. Clen tried samples of everything, even though he didn't much care for cranberries.

Suddenly, Celerie appeared, her hair in one long braid down her back, her cheeks as red as apples. She was wearing a cranberry-colored wool dress and black tights. Headband and pearls. She was a younger, fair-haired version of Dabney. Clen had been warned about this, but still he chuckled when he saw her.

"The guest of honor!" Celerie said. She hugged Dabney so hard that Clen saw her wince. Dabney was fragile, everything hurt, brushing her teeth hurt, she'd told him, and folding a napkin hurt, and he was tempted to tell Celerie to take it easy, but Dabney just smiled with relief when Celerie let her go and said, "You've done a brilliant job!"

Celerie beamed. She turned to Clen. "It's an honor to meet you, Mr. Hughes."

Clen bowed and said, "The honor is mine, Miss Truman."

At the same time, they said, "Dabney has told me so much about you."

Dabney sat at the judging table alongside Nina Mobley and Dr. Ted Field and Jordan Randolph, publisher of the *Nantucket Standard*. Tastes of this and that were placed before the judges, and Dabney made notes on her clipboard. Clen took a few steps back so that he could observe her in her element. He knew she wanted to give every participant a blue ribbon.

At one point, she raised her face and scanned the crowd. She was looking for *him,* he realized. He raised his arm and waved.

I'm here, Cupe. I'm right here.

After the festival, Clen, Dabney, and Agnes drove out to the airport to pick up Riley. He was staying for two nights to enjoy Nantucket in the fall; he had wanted to come earlier but he'd had a practical exam that morning.

Agnes was buzzing with excitement. When Clen pulled up in

front of the airport, she jumped out of the backseat and said, "I'll run in and get him."

Dabney watched her as she hurried for the entrance.

"She's rosy," Dabney said. "Rosy like I've never seen."

That night, Dabney cooked the four of them dinner in the gourmet kitchen of the Joneses' big house. Clen lit logs in the enormous stone fireplace and they all hunkered down on the deep, soft sofa and chairs while Dabney ferried in platter after platter of delicacies—dates stuffed with blue cheese wrapped in bacon, Nantucket bay scallop ceviche, rosemary cashews. It was a feast already, and those were just the appetizers. Riley acted as bartender, pouring champagne for Agnes, filling Clen's scotch, and making himself a series of increasingly stronger Dark and Stormys, which they all sampled, even Dabney. Riley talked about the rigors of dental school and Agnes told stories about the kids in her after-school program and Dabney checked to make sure everyone was eating and that everything was delicious.

She stopped on her way back into the kitchen and kissed Clen.

"You're beautiful," he whispered.

There wasn't enough time.

Dabney decided it was so nice by the fire that they should simply eat dinner there, like a picnic, rather than at the table. Dinner was beef Wellington with homemade mushroom duxelles, real foie gras, and homemade pastry, and a cheesy potato gratin and pan-roasted asparagus with toasted pine nuts and mustard-cream drizzle, and a salad with pears and dried cranberries and pumpernickel croutons.

"Mommy," Agnes said. It was always "Mommy" now, Clen noticed, or maybe it had always been that way. What did Clen know? "You've outdone yourself."

"I can barely move," Riley said. He fell back into the cushions of the armchair. His plate was clean; he had gone back for seconds of everything, which had made Dabney fuss over him more, if that was even possible. "It was so delicious, boss."

"I first made beef Wellington back in the spring of 1982," Dabney said. "Before Clen and I went to the junior prom."

"This one was even better," Clen said.

Dabney tucked herself under Clen's right arm, and he felt her smile against his chest. She had eaten next to nothing, but neither Clen nor Agnes had nudged her about it because it did no good. Dabney ate when she was hungry, which was about once every three days. That she had outdone herself was right. Clen knew that this was the last meal she would ever cook.

There was, no doubt, an elaborate and scrumptious dessert waiting somewhere within the confines of the Joneses' enormous SubZero refrigerator, but none of them would partake in it tonight. Dabney fell fast asleep against Clen's chest. Agnes and Riley rose to silently do the dishes while Clen sat and enjoyed the dying embers of the fire before carrying the ninety-six pounds of Dabney Kimball back to his cottage to bed.

Stop time, he prayed. *Now. Stop it now.*

DABNEY

There was something she wanted, but she couldn't bring herself to ask for it.

AGNES

By the end of October, her mother was in a wheelchair. She slept all the time now, and, at her request, she was staying at Clen's cottage. Dabney weighed almost nothing. She was so thin, it was as though a part of her had been erased.

Agnes didn't know what to do. She talked to Riley every night on the phone. Her mother was going to die. Christmas Stroll didn't seem like a realistic goal. Agnes was going to have to call hospice, and soon.

CLENDENIN

November 6 was Dabney's birthday. She was forty-nine.

He asked her what she wanted to do to celebrate, and she said that she wanted to order Cuban sandwiches from Foods for Here and There, and she wanted to watch *Love Story* with Clen and Agnes.

"No cake?" he said. Dabney liked proper pomp and circumstance when it came to birthdays: cake, candles, cards, and presents. That had been true when she was a teenager, and he'd assumed it still was.

Dabney shook her head. Just the sandwiches and the movie, she said.

He said, "Don't you think *Love Story* might be too...maudlin?"

"It's my favorite movie," she said. "I'd like to see it one more time."

*   *   *

Agnes arrived at his cottage, looking very, very sad. She and Clen had decided that afternoon to call hospice. They would let Dabney enjoy her birthday, and then hospice would come every day for as long as they were needed.

Dabney would not live to see fifty.

Before the sandwiches and the movie, Clen decided to give Dabney her surprise. She held it in her lap and turned it over, admiring the plaid wrapping paper in navy blue, Nantucket red, and Kelly green.

"I love this wrapping paper," she said. "I wish every present I'd ever gotten had been wrapped in this paper."

A good start, he thought. Agnes had picked out the paper.

Dabney touched the present some more, fingering its edges. Taking her time with the last present she would likely ever open.

"I think it's a book!" she said.

"Open it, Mommy," Agnes said.

Dabney opened it. The cover of the book was pink, a dusty-rose blush. And in black letters on the front it said, THE MATCHMAKER: DABNEY KIMBALL BEECH.

"Oh," Dabney said.

She turned to the first page. Couple #1: Ginger (née O'Brien) and Phil Bruschelli, Married twenty-nine years. Ginger: *It would have been presumptuous of me to call myself Dabney's best friend, because even in 1981, freshman year, Dabney was the most popular girl in the school.*

And so on and so on—through Tammy Block and Flynn Sheehan, and Dr. Donegal, and the Levinsons, and Genevieve and Brian Lefebvre, and the failed story of Nina Mobley. Clen had managed to collect nineteen of the forty-two stories. He had done the interviews, and had edited each story to make it readable.

Dabney paged through the book, laughing and cooing, and saying, *Yes, yes, I remember that!* When she looked up at Clen, her eyes were shining with tears.

"I can't believe you did this," she said. "This is the most wonderful thing anyone has ever given me."

"You have brought so much love into the world, Mommy," Agnes said.

Clen said, "I thought it was important. Agnes will keep it. Her children will read it. And their children. They will know you through those stories."

Dabney blinked. Tears dropped onto the pages. "Thank you," she whispered.

DABNEY

There was something she wanted. She was afraid to ask for it. *Forbearance,* she thought. She was running out of time.

It was the middle of the night, three or four in the morning, her birthday officially over. The present of the book had overwhelmed her. It was a living history, her life story really, that her grandchildren and great-grandchildren would read. They might think of her the way she thought about Dabney Margaret Wright and Winford Dabney Wright and all the other women who had preceded her. She was merely taking her place in line.

The Cuban sandwich had been delicious, and *Love Story* had been okay until the scene where Oliver tells his father that Jenny has died.

"Turn it off," Dabney had said.

"Are you sure?" Clen said.

"Yes." Dabney knew what was coming, and she couldn't handle the sight of Oliver sitting alone in the snow.

Dying wasn't sad, she thought. Leaving people behind was sad.

There was something she wanted. It was exactly 3:44 in the morning. Dabney slept much of the day away, but in the very late hours, so late they were early, sleep often eluded her. *Forbearance.* Her great-grandmother, Winford Dabney Wright, had stood on the corner of Main and Federal Streets eight hours a day for six weeks petitioning for a woman's right to vote, talking and arguing with anyone who would listen. Dabney's beloved grandmother, Agnes Bernadette, had changed sheets and scrubbed toilets six and a half days a week her first five years on the island. She had taken off Sunday mornings to attend Mass.

Dabney poked Clen in the ribs until he stirred.

"What?" he said. He always snapped out of sleeping sounding cogent, but Dabney knew he might not remember this conversation in the morning. She had to make sure he was really awake. She sat up and turned on the light. This took effort. Her insides were now jelly.

Clen sat up beside her, blinking. He checked the clock, and drank from his glass of water. "Dabney?" he said. "Do you need a pill?"

"No," she said.

"Do you want to talk?" he asked. "Are you afraid?"

She shook her head. They had had some frankly terrifying conversations about what came next. What would happen when Dabney died? What would it be like? Dabney appreciated Clen's candidness—*We don't know, Cupe. Nobody knows.* And so, Dabney had decided to focus only on her time alive for right now. The death door was closed.

Her time alive.

She said, "I want to see Box."

Clen was silent, as she figured he might be. She reached out and touched the stump of his left arm.

"I want you to call him and tell him to come."

"Me?" Clen said. "Why me? You should call him. Or Agnes."

"No," Dabney said. "I've given it a lot of thought. I want you to call." Dabney reached for her ice water; her hand was barely strong enough to lift the glass. She took a pill. Clen would be the easiest person for Box to say no to, and so if he came, Dabney would know it was because he really wanted to. "I'd like you to call in the morning."

Clen sighed, as she figured he might. But she had also thought he might refuse.

"All right," he said.

BOX

There wasn't a free minute in any of his days. The semester was in full swing and he was teaching three classes—two seminars and the Macro class. Normally he let Miranda or one of the department TAs handle the bulk of the Macro class, but this year he did it himself. Busy, busy, busy. The braver or more compassionate of his colleagues sometimes asked how he was "doing." They knew Miranda had migrated, and they had heard Dabney was sick, perhaps, but they didn't know the rest, or at least he hoped they didn't.

He didn't teach on Fridays, so that was the day he hopped the Delta shuttle to Washington.

He was in the West Wing when the phone call came. His cell phone was silenced, but he felt incessant vibrations and checked once discreetly—an unfamiliar number. He would deal with it later.

But less than an hour later, an aide entered the room with a message slip for Box.

"Sorry," she said. "It's urgent, apparently."

Box saw the name *Clendenin Hughes* and bile rose in his throat—not only because he despised the man but because he assumed the call could mean only one thing.

Dead? Box thought. The day before had been Dabney's birthday, and he had sent a dozen long-stemmed roses to the house. Pink roses, whereas usually on her birthday and their anniversary and Valentine's Day, he sent red. But he couldn't do red roses, the *I love you* rose, although he did, of course, love her; he loved her enough to move mountains. He ordered pink to make a small point. Things had changed. Dabney would notice. She was all about details.

He had texted Agnes to see if the roses had arrived and she'd responded that yes, they had, and although Dabney wasn't home just then, she would tell Dabney the roses had come.

Agnes's final text on the topic said, *You are such a good man, Daddy.*

Box was stuck back on *wasn't home just then.* Not home to receive the roses and notice the change in color, making him wish he hadn't sent the roses at all!

He had assumed Dabney was spending her birthday with the philistine boor—but now, as he eyed the message, he worried that what Agnes wasn't telling him was that Dabney was in the hospital.

He nearly knocked his chair over as he stood up, thinking, *She's dead. My wife is dead.* The Treasury secretary and his deputies snapped to attention.

"Professor?" the secretary said. "Is something wrong?"

Box said, "Please excuse me."

An aide found him a quiet, empty cube of an office from which to make the call. Hughes picked up on the first ring.

He said, "She's still alive. She insisted I call you. She wants to see you."

Box was consumed with something beyond anger, beyond fury. But, also, relief. She was alive. *Breathe, breathe.* She was alive.

"How is she?" Box said. "Tell me the truth. How much time does she have?"

"Nobody knows for sure," Hughes said. "Weeks, maybe a month? Maybe longer, maybe not. Agnes called hospice. They're coming on Monday. We want to make sure she's comfortable."

"We," Box said, involuntarily.

Hughes cleared his throat. "She wants to see you. She's asking for you."

"Yes," Box said. "I hear you saying that."

"She insisted I call you," Hughes said. "Believe me, I didn't dream this up."

"No," Box said. "I imagine not."

She wanted to see him. Fury trumped relief, and hurt appeared out of nowhere. She wanted to see him *now,* after she had lied to him, *cheated* on him, such an awful word, such an incomprehensible concept. Dabney Kimball, a liar and a cheat. What had he done to deserve such ruthless public humiliation? She had lied to him again and again and again and again! She wanted to see him *now,* but there had been any number of times when she had wanted to see only Hughes.

He knew she hadn't been to the salon! And yet it had been beneath him to question her.

She had made a fool of him! She had made a laughingstock of John Boxmiller Beech.

And why did she have Hughes call? Why not call herself? Why make Hughes do it? Agnes could have called. Why Hughes?

Box wasn't good with interpersonal drama or motivations of the heart; he despised murky emotion, most of all in himself. He preferred to keep above it. But even so, a part of him understood what Dabney was doing. She was trying to bring him and Hughes together. It was matchmaking of the most twisted kind. This time, she would not have her way.

Box decided: he would not go to her.

Hospice, weeks, months, a lifetime going forward without Dabney. The bite of strawberry pie, the icy cold root beer, she wanted to want him but her heart was elsewhere, he had seen it even at their wedding reception in the backyard of her grandmother's house on North Liberty Street, but he had ignored the shadow in her eyes because he was just so happy that she was Mrs. Dabney Kimball Beech.

It would be better if she never saw him again. She could remember him as he had been: dignified to the end, at least he could say that. If there were to be another meeting of the two of them, who knew what he would say or do. How could he hide his pain, his sorrow, his incredulity, and this other emotion, the one beyond anger and fury. He would never be able to hide his broken heart from her, that was certain, and he didn't want her to die holding herself responsible for it.

He would not go.

CLEN

She told him she wanted to spend her final time at home, and by home she meant the house on Charter Street.

I love you, she had said. *And I have valued and treasured the time I've had with you in this cottage, but this cottage isn't my home.* She swallowed. *I want to go home and if you want to be with me, which I hope you do, then I'll have to ask you, humbly, to come with me to Charter Street.*

Clen bristled. Now, at the end, she was asking difficult things of him. She expected him to spend time in the house she had bought and lived in for twenty-four years with the economist. He would, what? Sleep there? In the guest quarters?

And yet he understood that this cottage wasn't her home, it wasn't even his home, and it was too small for nurses and hospice workers to move around in comfortably. She had to go back.

"I don't want to let you go," he said. He felt dangerously close to tears, but he had promised her he wouldn't cry, and so he poured a bourbon instead, and then he called Agnes and told her they were coming.

AGNES

So many people wanted to visit that Agnes had to draw up a schedule: two people a day for ten minutes apiece. Dabney was propped up in bed, pearls on, headband in place. She could sometimes hold together a conversation, sometimes not.

Morphine. She said it made her feel like a dragonfly on the surface of a pond.

"I took you to Jewel Pond a dozen times the summer you were three," Dabney said. "It was hard to get to, and more than once I got the Nova stuck in the sand, but you liked to throw rocks there, and we used to look for turtles. In the sun, it did look like a jewel. Like an emerald some days, a sapphire others. Do you remember it?"

Agnes said that she did, but she didn't. She liked the picture Dabney painted: Agnes and Dabney alone at a secluded pond, Agnes wading in to her ankles to throw rocks while Dabney watched from her towel under the red-and-white-striped umbrella. Agnes taking a nap facedown on the towel while Dabney rubbed her back and read a Jane Austen novel.

Agnes and her mother, suspended alone in a happy, peaceful bubble. If Agnes had been three, then Box had been in the picture. He had been her "father," he had adopted her in the months after he and Dabney were married. But he had been working, traveling, speaking, teaching, writing.

Agnes had held only one grudge against her mother, a ten-year-old grudge that was really the grudge of a lifetime: Dabney had waited sixteen years to tell Agnes who her real father was. Sixteen years. It had always seemed an egregious misstep on Dabney's part. Agnes should have known much earlier; she should have *grown up knowing.* She remembered a comment made by Mrs. Annapale, her Sunday-school teacher, who had owned the bed-and-breakfast where Box had stayed while he was courting Dabney. Mrs. Annapale had said of Box, "He stayed with me every weekend until your mother agreed to marry him. Your mother used to bring you sometimes, too. Such a sweet baby you were!"

And Agnes had thought, *Huh?*

When Agnes recounted this conversation to her mother, her mother had looked *very worried* for an instant, then she mentioned that Mrs. Annapale was getting older and might soon be mixing up Mary Magdalene with the Virgin Mary.

That had been a lie, or almost a lie. Not telling Agnes about Clendenin had been a lie of omission, a willful deception of the very worst kind.

Or so Agnes had believed until now—today, this past summer, since Agnes had met Clendenin. Now, her feelings had changed. She understood now, in a way she hadn't before, just how *gone* Clendenin had been for Dabney. He had been on the other side of the world. The only way Dabney had survived was to pretend that he no longer existed. Agnes also understood how profoundly Dabney loved the man, and had continued to love him over all that time. The combination of the love and the hurt was powerful enough to keep Dabney from telling Agnes the truth. Plus, Box had been there to step in, a real father in every aspect but blood. *What,* Dabney had asked—calmly in the face of Agnes's near hysteria at the age of sixteen—*does it matter?* Clendenin Hughes was just a name; his parentage was a matter solely of biology. He had never been Agnes's father, Dabney had said ten years earlier, and he never would be.

But he was something now. Agnes wasn't sure exactly what. At the very least he was someone else who loved her mother. In this he was a comrade, a teammate, possibly even a friend.

One evening as the light was fading—darkness came early in the fall—Agnes sat watching Dabney breathe as she slept and she said, "I forgive you, Mommy."

Tammy Block came to visit, and Marguerite Levinson came with her golden retriever, Uncle Frank. Genevieve Lefebvre came, and

Vaughan Oglethorpe came, smelling of embalming fluid. And every third or fourth day, Celerie came to discuss strategies for the future of the Chamber.

Nina Mobley came, announcing the news of her engagement to Dr. Marcus Cobb! Dabney asked Agnes to open champagne, although she herself could not drink any.

The woman Agnes had once seen pulling into Clen's driveway showed up, identifying herself as Elizabeth Jennings, but when Agnes went up to announce this visitor to her mother, Dabney groaned and said, "Tell her I'm sleeping."

When Agnes reported back to Elizabeth Jennings that Dabney was sleeping, Elizabeth nodded once sharply and said, "I knew she wouldn't want to see me. Please tell her I'm sorry and give her this." Elizabeth thrust forth a tarte tatin. "I'd like to say I made it myself but really, it was my cook."

"Oh," Agnes said. The tarte was dazzling with its glazed golden orbs of apple and caramelized sugar, but Dabney hadn't eaten solid food in over a week. "Okay, thank you."

Dabney's former therapist, Dr. Donegal, came and stayed past the ten-minute limit. He was upstairs with Dabney for nearly an hour, and when he came back downstairs he was wiping his eyes.

And then the most surprising visitor of all. Or maybe not. Agnes had, after all, been wondering, hoping, praying, but she had been afraid to ask.

When she heard footsteps in the hall, she had thought it was Clen. Clen was staying at the house on Charter Street most nights, sitting with Dabney until she fell asleep, and then sleeping in the awful, tiny bedroom in the attic. *Like a scullery maid,* he had joked. He wouldn't take the regular guest room because he felt he didn't belong there. The attic room had only one twin bed. Agnes didn't know how Clen got any sleep, but he wouldn't switch rooms no matter how she implored him.

But the footsteps in the hallway did not belong to Clen. When Agnes looked up, the person she saw standing in the doorway of the kitchen was her father.

Box.

And only then did Agnes break down and cry.

DABNEY

She had everything she needed. Except...

The hospice workers were white angels with wings and soft voices. They wiped Dabney's brow, smoothed her hair, rubbed her feet. They gave her morphine. Morphine eradicated the need for forbearance. Forbearance was, now, left to the healthy, the living. The hospice workers read aloud stories from the book Clen had made for Dabney. Or Agnes came in and read them.

Ah, Dabney thought. Ginger O'Brien and Phil Bruschelli, ninth grade, the smell of the gym when basketball was being played in the winter, the squeal of sneakers and the thunk of the ball against the polished floor, the rustle and cheering and chatter of kids in the bleachers. Dabney used to stop in the gym for a few minutes after she was finished with Yearbook. Dabney used to mock up pages of the yearbook using rubber cement, and jellied squiggles of it would be stuck to her hands. She had worn her pearls and an oxford shirt and her Levi's perfectly faded and broken in, washed only on Sundays and ironed while she watched *Sixty Minutes* on TV. Her penny loafers, perfectly scuffed, replaced at Murray's Toggery the first of every August so that she could wear them around the house for a month before school started, breaking them in.

Could she go back to those days when she was happy and safe?

She said to Clen, "You had both your arms in ninth grade."

"Yes," he said. "I did."

Clen was by her side. He gave the hospice workers a break or they gave her and Clen privacy, Dabney wasn't sure which way it worked. Clen fed Dabney ice chips and put balm on her lips with the tip of his finger, and a few tears fell because Clen's other hand, his left hand, had been strong and beautiful, too, but now it was gone. Turned to dust, Dabney supposed, somewhere on a distant continent.

She said to him, "You'll know when to call the priest?"

Clen nodded, his lips pressed together until they turned white. He didn't want to call the priest because he didn't believe in Catholicism, maybe. Or he didn't want to call the priest because it signaled the end. The priest meant something to Dabney, she wanted to confess her sins, she wanted Extreme Unction, she wanted permission to pass on to whatever came next. Her grandmother Agnes Bernadette had received last rites, and her facial expression had immediately settled into one of peace and acceptance, like a marble Madonna.

Clen had promised to call the priest.

But not yet. Not yet.

Ice chips, angels, hands soothing her aching feet, Clen's voice, his mighty voice. How had she lived twenty-seven years without it? How had she lived without the green glen and weak tea of his eyes?

She said to Clen, "You have to find someone else. I meant to help you, but…"

"Hush," he said.

"I couldn't bear it," Dabney said. "I was selfish, I wanted you all to myself. But, Clen, you can't be alone."

"Cupe," he said. "Please."

"Promise me you'll try."

"No," he said. "I will not try."

Clen, Agnes, the hospice workers—and then, finally, the priest. Not Father Healey, who had seen Dabney from Baptism to First Communion to Confirmation, but a new priest, a young man, a man too handsome for the cloth, if you asked Dabney. Father Carlos, he had a Spanish accent and soft brown eyes. He sat at Dabney's bedside, took her hand, and said, "Pray with me."

She had everything she needed except... And it was time to stop longing for that. *In the name of the Father, and of the Son, and of the Holy Spirit, Amen.* She had confessed her sins and said her penance, but her real penance was that she would go without the one thing she needed.

Her journey was coming to an end. Forty-nine years. She had hoped for ninety-nine, didn't everyone, but Dabney couldn't complain. She hadn't sunbathed on the golden shores of Saint-Tropez, she hadn't visited the Taj Mahal, she had never seen the Hollywood sign or Mount Rushmore or the pyramids. She hadn't shopped in Moroccan souks or eaten in a greasy spoon on Route 66.

But, Dabney knew, she had Nantucket. She had been born and raised here, she had worked twenty-two years in service to this island, and she would die here. She had been faithful to Nantucket. Oh, Nantucket, more of a mother than her own mother.

Everything she needed. Except.

And then, she heard his voice, or she thought she did. It was too soft at first to tell.

"Darling?"

She couldn't believe it. She was dreaming, or in a morphine

delirium. She had a hard time now discerning what was real and what was visiting her from another time. Agnes at three years old, throwing rocks to disturb the placid, emerald surface of Jewel Pond, was as vivid as Agnes yesterday reading to Dabney from the last pages of *Emma*.

Darling.

Dabney opened her eyes, and there he was. Box. If she had had the ability to cry or cry out or smile or laugh, she would have.

She tried a word. *Here!* She meant, *You're here! You came! You did not forsake me even though I so gravely forsook you. Darling? Am I darling? You have found it in your heart to come back to our home and call me darling.*

Box understood *here* to mean, *Sit here.* He sat next to her. He held her hand.

He said, "Oh, Dabney."

His tone of voice was not one she'd ever heard before. It was full of pain, sadness, regret, love. She couldn't bear for him to say another word. What else could he possibly say?

"I love you," he said. "I will always, always, always love you, Dabney Kimball Beech."

She was able to blink at him. Her eyes were all she had left, but not for long, she didn't think.

She tried again. "Please."

He nodded. "Sshhh. It's okay."

"Please," she said, or tried to say. The effort of it was too much. She was so tired. She closed her eyes.

She heard voices and felt things, she did not know what. She heard the voice of May, the Irish chambermaid, singing "American Pie."

Where is my mother?

Your father is on his way, love.

Mama!

Dabney had taken an entire Saturday of her life to learn how to make beef Wellington so she could prepare it for Clendenin before the prom. The key to the puff pastry—which had to be made by hand, Pepperidge Farm wouldn't do—was *very cold butter.* The chef at the Club Car, an old man when Dabney was in high school, had repeated this several times: *very cold butter.*

Albert Maku had found Dabney crying on the steps of Grays Hall. Everyone else was thrilled about starting Harvard—everyone but Dabney and Albert. He had spoken to her in Zulu and she had cried, because the world was so foreign and strange without Clen by her side. Clen was 140 miles away, in New Haven.

A blizzard on Daffodil Weekend—that had seemed such a travesty! Nina Mobley had nearly chewed the cross off her chain as she and Dabney looked out the office windows at the snow piling up on Main Street.

Oysters—Island Creeks and Kumamotos. She could have eaten ten times as many, and still it wouldn't have been enough.

A 1963 Corvette Stingray split-window in Bermuda blue with matching numbers. That would have been nice, too, although where in the world would she have driven it? The point of that car had been in the wanting.

Matisse, *La Danse.* Maybe that was heaven. Blues and greens, naked, dancing, dancing in a never-ending circle, each time around as thrilling as the first.

She had been ambivalent about the pregnancy. For the eight months after Clen left, she stayed at home, cooking and cleaning for her father, playing solitaire, and reading novels of shame—*Tess of the d'Urbervilles* and *Vanity Fair*—as her belly grew rounder and harder and more embarrassing each day. The friends she'd had in high school and college had been stunned into silence. They stayed away. She was as lonely as she'd ever been.

In the delivery room it had just been Dabney, a nurse named Mary Beth, and Dr. Benton. The birth, in Dabney's memory, had been painless, probably because she didn't care if the baby lived or died, or if she herself lived or died. What did it matter without Clendenin?

But then, of course, they placed the baby in Dabney's arms, and the loneliness melted away. A mother first, a mother forever.

Agnes!

Dabney had jumped on the bed while her mother applied mascara at the dressing table.

Dabney said, *Look how high I'm going!* She was in her red Christmas dress and white tights. Her mother had instructed her to remove her Mary Janes.

I am looking, darling, her mother said. Her eyes flashed in the mirror. *That's very high indeed. Be careful now. You don't want to fall and break yourself.*

"Mommy."

Dabney's eyes opened—yes, they opened still. Agnes stood at the foot of the bed with Riley; they were holding hands and they were engulfed in pink clouds, fluffy as cotton candy.

Agnes at the carnival in the sticky heat of summer, cotton candy all over her face and in her hair, begging Dabney to go on the Scrambler.

I'm afraid! Dabney had said.

But you're a grown-up, Agnes said. *Grown-ups aren't supposed to be afraid.*

Agnes and Riley, all that pink. Dabney knew it. She knew it!

Clendenin was on her left, holding her hand, and Box was on her right, holding her hand. They were both there. Dabney felt that she did not deserve this, but she was grateful. She had everything she needed. Her heart was a kite, tethered to the earth by two strings, but it was time for them to let go so she could float away.

She was a dragonfly, skimming. Heaven was a Corvette Stingray in the sky, maybe.

Heaven was that they were all right there with her.

Clen squeezed. "Cupe," he said.

Box said, "She's going, I'm afraid."

It was okay. In the end, after all, it was sweet, like freedom.

"Mommy!" Agnes said.

When Dabney closed her eyes, everything was pink. So pink.

Couple #43: Agnes Bernadette Beech and Riley Alsopp, together six months

Agnes: We buried my mother's ashes on the Friday of Daffodil Weekend in the family plot where her father and her grandmother and great-grandparents and great-great-grandfather and great-great-great-grandmother, the original Dabney, were laid to rest. My mother used to say that she hated to leave Nantucket because she was afraid she would die and never return, so it was a relief for me—and for Box and Clen, too, I think—once she was safely in the ground. We kept the burial private, just the three of us, Riley, and Nina Mobley, but at the tailgate picnic following the Antique Car Parade the next day, people surrounded the Impala to pay their respects—laugh, cry, and share Dabney stories. Celerie had made a huge platter of ribbon sandwiches in my mother's honor, and this year they all got eaten, and all I could think of was how happy this would have made my mother.

A year earlier, I had agreed to marry CJ.

Riley liked to say that he fell in love with me before he even met me, on the day he saw my photograph on my mother's desk at the Chamber office. He said he saw the picture and stopped dead in his tracks and thought, *That is the woman I am going to marry.* He said that his heart had never been broken before but the closest he'd ever come was when he found out I was engaged.

My feelings for Riley developed more gradually, which he understood. My emotional plate was full—with CJ, with my mother, with Clendenin. I know that I love him, I know he is the kindest, most delightful, most handsome, most talented surfing dentist on earth and that I would be nuts to let him go—but I'm not ready to talk about marriage. Especially not this weekend. We have agreed to see what the summer brings—we will be together on Nantucket—and maybe, maybe, I'll move to Philadelphia with him in the fall.

My mother would be ecstatic about that.

After the tailgate picnic was broken down and all the antique cars headed back out the Milestone Road toward town, I waved goodbye to Box. He was going to the Boarding House with the Levisons. In the morning, we would have coffee together and then I would drive him to the airport—the way my mother always had—so he could head back to Cambridge.

Clen had ridden out to the Daffodil festivities on his bicycle, and he was getting ready to ride home. I was worried about Clen in a way that I was not worried about Box. I left Riley to pack up our picnic and help Celerie with the last of her tasks, and I walked over to talk to Clen just as he was climbing onto his bicycle.

I said, "What are you up to tonight?"

He said, "Bourbon. Fried rice if I feel ambitious. Sox game on the radio, maybe."

"Riley and I are breaking out the grill," I said. "Ribs. Will you join us?"

He shook his head. "You're sweet to ask, but I'm fine."

"Are you fine?" I asked. There had been a couple of nights when I had gone to Clen's cottage and we'd both drunk bourbon and one or the other of us had broken down crying because we just *missed her so much.* Where had she gone? She had been here, so alive, the most alive person either of us had ever known, and now she was gone. Snap of the fingers: poof, like that.

When it was Clen who broke down crying—great big heaving sobs that sounded like the call of some enormous animal, a moose, or a whale—I had thought, *That is my father, crying over my mother.* It was true, but it was so weird that I had to say it multiple times to make it sink in. What would our lives have been like if he had stayed on Nantucket and raised me? Or if my mother had been brave enough to go to Thailand?

"Agnes," Clen said. And I knew something was coming.

"What?"

"I've been offered a job," he said. "Running the Singapore desk for the *Washington Post*. It's an assignment I've wanted my entire career. The job comes with a two-bedroom flat, just off the Orchard Road." He must have noticed the look on my face, because he started talking more quickly. "Elizabeth Jennings mentioned my name to someone who owed her husband, Mingus, a favor or three. She feels guilty, I think, about the way she treated your mother."

"You're accepting favors from Elizabeth Jennings?" I said.

"It's the job I've always wanted," Clen said. "I'll grow old drinking Singapore Slings in the Long Bar at the Raffles Hotel." He smiled weakly. "Agnes, I can't stay here without her. Every day is excruciating. I can't stay here without her, and I have nowhere else to go."

Leaving me, I thought, when we had just found each other. That part of the world would swallow Clen up for another twenty-seven years, and I would never see him again.

He said, "I agreed to the job on the condition that I be allowed to come back to Nantucket for the month of August every year. It's monsoon there; most of the country takes a vacation. So you'll get me thirty-one days a year, when I'll be at your disposal, I promise."

I felt my face soften. Every August together was a good compromise.

He said, "And you and Riley can come visit. You can come to Singapore on your honeymoon!"

At that moment, Riley swooped up behind me and hugged me with such gusto, he picked me right up off the ground. "Did somebody say 'honeymoon'?" he said.

Couple #44: John Boxmiller Beech and Miranda Gilbert. Together.

Box: There was always work. Harvard, my textbook, the secretary of the Treasury, who was now bandying my name around for Federal Reserve chairman, as the current chairman had been caught in a scandal and would most likely end up resigning. I would teach my seminar at the London School of Economics in June, and I was to be the keynote speaker at the annual Macro conference, this year held in Atlanta.

It was on a whim that I found myself in New York City. I had a former student named Edward Jin who had abandoned graduate work in economics in order to train as a chef. Apparently he was quite talented and successful; he had secured enough backing to open his own restaurant, called The Dividend, on the Bowery, and he invited me to the soft opening. It just so happened that I had nothing scheduled the weekend of this invitation, and I was partial to Manhattan in the springtime. I called Edward Jin and told him I would attend, and I booked a junior suite at the St. Regis.

The soft opening at The Dividend was an intimate affair—thirty or so friends and family and investors of Edward Jin's gathered in the bar area, which featured wood floors salvaged from an Amish farm in Lancaster, Pennsylvania, a chandelier made from an old wagon wheel, and a lot of copper pots and candlelight and hand-muddled cocktails made from ingredients like kale and fresh ginger. This was the way with many restaurants now—farm-to-table, organic, produce and meats assiduously researched and hand-sourced. It was good and fine and noble, but I missed Dabney's cooking.

I knew no one except Edward Jin and he was, naturally, too busy for anything but a warm hello and a single introduction—to his married sister who was a stay-at-home mother in Brooklyn. I mentioned that I had taught Edward at Harvard; she responded that the family had all been stunned when Edward was admitted to Harvard since he'd been rejected from Brown, Duke, and Dartmouth, and I laughed and said that yes, college admissions were arbitrary and capricious.

After that, we had pretty much exhausted our conversational possibilities. I panicked and wished fervently for Dabney, who used to be able to carry on a conversation with an ox or a doorstop.

I was saved, however, because at that moment, Miranda Gilbert walked in.

If I say that my heart stopped or my breath caught I would

sound like the heroine in one of the English novels Dabney so loved to read. Leaping heart, snagged breath, I wasn't sure how to describe it but something happened when I saw Miranda.

What was she doing here?

Then of course I realized that she had been Edward Jin's TA for more than one of my courses, and I remembered that they had hit it off rather well and used to meet for beers at the Rathskeller, which I did not approve of since she was, after all, responsible for giving Edward Jin his grades.

I was initially consumed with jealousy. Were Miranda and Edward now seeing each other?

Miranda gasped when she saw me and came over right away. The lighting was low in the restaurant but I thought she looked flushed.

"Box," she said. "My God, I had no idea you would be here."

"Nor I you," I said. I kissed her cheek while holding both her hands. She smelled like Miranda always smelled, like an apricot rose, or something as delicate and lovely.

She said, "I was so sorry to hear about Dabney. You got my card?"

"Yes," I said. "Thank you." I had gotten many, many cards; most of them, including Miranda's, I had left unopened because it was too difficult to read them. I put them in a larger envelope and forwarded them to Agnes.

"She was a special woman," Miranda said. "She had a gift for love, the way other people have an eye for color."

This was so true, it made my eyes burn, and I blinked rapidly.

"Yes," I said. "She did. She was always right about love. It was uncanny."

Miranda and I switched place cards at the long harvest table so that we could sit next to each other, and we spent the evening in a bubble of great food and better wine and esoteric conversation that left everyone else at the table out.

I said, "Have you seen much of Edward, since you've been in New York?"

"Edward?" she said, as if she didn't know whom I was talking about.

"Our host," I said. "The chef."

Miranda laughed. "No," she said. "I haven't seen him at all before tonight. I didn't even know he was in the city. He tracked me down on Facebook."

I felt happy to hear this. Miranda and Edward were not together! But this didn't mean she was available.

"Are you...dating anyone?" I asked. "Has anyone replaced the good doctor?"

She sipped her wine and nudged her glasses up her nose in a way I found bewitching.

"No," she said.

Dabney had said Miranda Gilbert, but I hadn't listened.

I hadn't listened, Dabney, because I was married to you. You you you.

But I heard Dabney's words now: *Miranda Gilbert. She loves you, Box.*

Dabney was never wrong. She had the gift of love, the way some people have an eye for color.

At the end of the evening, I helped Miranda on with her coat.

I said, "Another drink?"

"I'm sorry to say I'm tuckered out, Box. And I have an early meeting tomorrow. I'm afraid I must head home."

"No!" I cried out. Showing my hand dreadfully, I knew.

She smiled in a way that thrilled me. "Take me to dinner tomorrow night, will you? Someplace just the two of us?"

I said that I would.

And I did.

And somewhere in the atmosphere, or dare I say the heavens, the spirit of another woman was sighing in bliss at being right, once again.

CLENDENIN

The late spring night was mild, so Clendenin stood out on the deck of the ferry, where he could watch the lights of Nantucket recede.

He would spend the night in Boston, then fly the following day to London, and then on to Singapore. He had packed one trunk, which would precede him, and he traveled now with a large rolling suitcase, easily manipulated with one hand.

Singapore. He couldn't believe it. He had waited so long, to no avail, it had always been just out of reach, and now it was like a golden apple that had dropped into his hand.

He had called Elizabeth Jennings to thank her, and she had said, "I had nothing to do with it. I only mentioned to Jack that I knew you. He took the ball and ran with it. You can hardly be surprised, Clen. You have a Pulitzer. Any foreign desk in the world would be lucky to have you."

Gracious of her to say. He doubted it was true, but he wasn't going to argue.

Singapore was his perfect match.

He recalled a similar ferry ride, over a quarter century earlier. A young man, twenty-three years old, with two healthy, strong arms, a sense of adventure, and a big dream, was heading out to conquer the world.

He had waved madly at Dabney and had called out *I love you*s.

Dabney had told him, again and again, *We are a perfect match. No matter what happens, we are going to end up together.*

End up together. Yes, he supposed they had.

The foghorn sounded its long, lonely note. Dabney was gone. He would forever dwell in the prison of her absence.

But he had been so lucky. She had granted him a second chance: six months of the purest happiness he'd ever known. He pictured Dabney pulling into his driveway in the Impala and climbing the three steps to the porch of his cottage. Her hands on the sides of his face. Her smile.

In his jacket pocket, Clen fingered Dabney's pearls. She had given them to him in her final days. When he first held them, they were still warm from her neck.

Keep these, she said. *And think of me.*

As if anything else were possible.

ACKNOWLEDGMENTS

Reagan Arthur: I wish there were words complex and fabulous enough to describe my gratitude that an intellect and a sensibility such as yours exists in this world. Thank you!

Michelle Aielli: To paraphrase Allison Pearson, *I Don't Know How You Do It.* You are my publicist, my keeper, and my friend. Thank you!

Michael Carlisle and David Forrer: My favorite quote of 2013 was "Now *that's* good agenting!" You are both indescribably dear to me. Thank you!

To PJ Martin, the actual director of the Nantucket Chamber of Commerce, who is NOT Dabney Kimball Beech, THANK YOU for meeting with me and THANK YOU for keeping Nantucket the special and unique place it is for those of us who live here, and for those of us who visit.

To Chand Rohtagi, an actual oncologist in the Lehigh Valley (PA) and also the oncologist character in this novel: THANK YOU for the background on the symptoms and physical manifestations of pancreatic cancer. Yours is noble work.

To Sarah Cutler: You faced the three-ring circus that is the Cunningham family with a winning combination of excellent driving, careful lifeguarding, a sense of fun, and serenity and grace. Thank you!

In memoriam: Clarissa Porter. It was at Clarissa's memorial service that I heard (and then later borrowed) the line, "She had a gift for love, the way one has an eye for color." Clarissa did have a gift for love. The special quality of friendship she brought to my life I will always fondly remember, and always profoundly miss.

To my three children, Maxwell, Dawson, and Shelby: I have been accused of giving you everything you want, but in fact, the opposite is true. You have given me everything I want—you are strong, smart, independent, adventurous, and pure of heart. You are my sun, moon, and stars, and every word I write, I write for you. xo

ELIN HILDERBRAND

The Rumour

A friendship is tested in this irresistible page-turner from
New York Times bestselling author Elin Hilderbrand.

Nantucket writer Madeline King couldn't have picked a
worse time to have writer's block. Her deadline is looming,
her bills are piling up, and inspiration is in short supply.

Madeline's best friend Grace, is hard at work
transforming her garden into the envy of the island with
the help of a ruggedly handsome landscape architect.
Before she realizes it, Grace is on the verge of a decision
that will irrevocably change her life. Could Grace's crisis
be Madeline's salvation?

As the gossip escalates, and the summer's explosive
events come to a head, Grace and Madeline try desperately
to set the record straight – but the truth might be
even worse than rumour has it.

Out now

HODDER